The Y Factor

By Darrell Bain and Stephanie Osborn

D0879594

Twilight Times Books
Kingsport Tennessee

The Y Factor

A Cresperian novel

This is a work of fiction. All concepts, characters and events portrayed in this book are used fictitiously and any resemblance to real people or events is purely coincidental.

Paladin Timeless Books, an imprint of
Twilight Times Books
P O Box 3340
Kingsport, TN 37664
www.twilighttimesbooks.com/

First paperback printing, November 2009

Library of Congress Cataloging-in-Publication Data

Bain, Darrell, 1939-
  The y factor / by Darrell Bain and Stephanie Osborn.
    p. cm.
  "A Cresperian novel."
  ISBN-13: 978-1-60619-089-0 (trade pbk. : alk. paper)
  ISBN-10: 1-60619-089-X (trade pbk. : alk. paper)
  1. Human-alien encounters--Fiction. I. Osborn, Stephanie. II. Title.
  PS3602.A559Y4 2010
  813'.6--dc22
                                        2009046070

Cover art by Darrell Osborn

Printed in the United States of America

Once again, for my wife Betty.

And for my husband and staunchest supporter, Darrell O.

CHAPTER ONE

"WHO ARE YOU, and how in the hell did you get in here?"

I stared at the man who had somehow talked his way past Carol, my administrative assistant. He was youngish-looking, with a lazy smile.

He stopped in front of my desk, waiting for me to say something. Which, I might note, I just had, and I didn't want to repeat myself.

Carol Genoa is a *very* hard person to fool. She can change the expression on her normally pretty face to an icy formality capable of stopping a tank in its tracks if need be. He must have known in advance I wasn't seeing visitors and walked right past her without checking. Still, why hadn't Carol alerted me?

Barging in without an appointment isn't the way to start on the right foot with me, either: I hate being interrupted at work. This man had walked into my laboratory office on Tuesday afternoon, just when I was sitting at my desk in the middle of a creative haze.

I was mapping out the design of a new ultra microscope I hoped to one day use to study specific genes in the very act of assembling organic protein catalysts, from transcription to translation to assembly, all without disturbing the living cells, nuclei, chromosomes or genes.

One of its key elements would involve highly sped-up data observation and transfer, using a computer program I had partially designed to manage the process. The programmers were already working with it, chasing bugs and inconsistencies.

If it all fell into place, I thought that maybe in another decade or so I could start getting a handle on the specifics of how gene expression is affected so greatly by the environment. All we know at present is that the environment affects them, not how it does. Not much about how, anyway.

"I didn't say who I'm with, Miss Trung, but I represent an agency of the United States government. My name is Gene Smith." He smiled but didn't offer his hand, probably knowing I'd refuse it. He also pronounced the "Miss" so there was no mistaking it with the more generic Ms.

I doubted his name was Smith. He had the same air of secrecy about him as the security agents I'd been forced to deal with during that one period of temporary insanity I'd spent doing research for the National Health Administration.

"It's Ms. Trung," I said coldly, just to throw him off balance. If he already knew I'd rather be referred to as Miss, he knew too much about me already. "And I don't believe I have anything to say to the government."

"Oh? I think I can convince you otherwise. And I would have sworn you preferred to be addressed as *Miss* Trung so long as we're being formal." He smiled again, as if he didn't have a care in the world, but I sensed some steel beneath that handsome exterior.

How much background did he have on me, anyway?

Not that it mattered. I was perfectly satisfied working for the Havel brothers, Lester and Chester, the founders and still majority stockholders of Havel Genecrafters, Inc. I liked the area, too. Near enough to Houston for the things a big city can supply, but far enough from the bustle of commuters not to be bothered by them.

"The exit is that way, Mr. Smith." I pointed. "Please use it. And make an appointment next time you want to see me."

Not that I would grant it, but I wanted to emphasize my point. I didn't want to work for the government again. Too much paperwork, not enough real work.

He stood fast, making me wonder if I'd have to call security to get rid of him. But the next thing he said made me hesitate.

"Miss Trung, suppose I offered you a job doing research at a level I know you and only a very few others are qualified for. At a much higher salary, I might add. You could do whatever research you please. We'll order any instruments you think you might need or have someone design and engineer them for you if they don't exist. We'll pay whatever you like and take care of all the moving for you. If there's anything else you want, all you have to do is ask and we can probably arrange it."

"No thanks." I admitted to myself I was interested but was careful not to let it show. Whatever agency he represented was obviously well funded and desperate for personnel in my specialties, evolutionary and environmental genetics and molecular microbiochemistry. And maybe someone like me who also grokked computers.

Still, he was talking about a government job. "Not unless you tell me more than you have so far and it would be very doubtful even then," I added.

He noticed I hadn't asked him to leave again, though. Smart man. He reached into his pocket and pulled out a little black rectangular object about two inches long and a half inch in the other dimensions. He turned away from me and mumbled something while holding it close to his mouth. When he turned back to me, it was cupped loosely in his hand at about waist-level.

"Xenobiology," he said, one word and nothing else.

While I was staring at him, Carol came in, looking flustered and very embarrassed. She brushed a strand of fine blonde hair from her forehead.

"I'm sorry, Miss Trung," she said. "I don't know how he got in here. He must have walked right by me when I had my back to the door looking for a file."

"It's all right, Carol. Something to drink, Mr. Smith?"

"Some coffee would be nice. It's been a long day. Black, please."

"Bring me a cup, too, Carol, please. Then close the door and don't let anyone else inside."

"Yes, ma'am." She was being very formal, the way she always is when others are around. In private, we use first names. She looked speculatively at Mr. Smith, then hurried off. She was back in a minute, carrying the coffee on a tray.

Once she was gone, I leaned back in my chair and took a sip of the rich Columbian, brewed as only Carol can make it. She won't let me near the coffee pot. She says I must have learned how to brew coffee at an all-night burger joint.

"You have one of those aliens," I stated.

"Right you are, Miss Trung. More than one, actually. And let me start off by apologizing. Someone dropped the ball by not contacting you as soon as we began assembling our first team. You should have already been aboard."

How long had they been working with the aliens?

Their presence on Earth had been widely-accepted fact ever since the body of one had been recovered in Mexico a number of months earlier, but no government was admitting they knew much about them, including ours. There was no denying the way developments in space had suddenly sped up, though.

I had wondered about it and thought maybe we had recovered the ship the Mexico alien arrived on. And I seriously doubted that huge explosion that ripped up China's spaceport had been caused by them playing with firecrackers. But a live alien? Goddamn it, I would have given both tits any day of my life to see what the gene structure of a completely alien species looked like—or didn't look like. They might not even use genes.

My mind was whirling with so many possibilities that he had to repeat himself. I hadn't heard him the first time.

"I said, 'How soon can you leave?'"

"Oh. Sorry." I thought for a moment. There was no question of me not taking the job, even as little as I knew about it, but there were other factors involved. "I'll have to give notice. I can't leave Les and Ches without some preparation for my replacement."

He waved a dismissive hand. "We'll take care of that. They both hold reserve commissions. If necessary we'll call them back to active duty and have them work for us."

"I don't like that approach. They deserve better."

"You misconstrue, Miss Trung. I believe they would be glad to come under any conditions, or release you from further obligation once they know why you're leaving." He pulled another gadget out of his coat pocket, this time an ordinary PDA, and spoke into it. "Anything else?"

The man did appear to be the type who got things done in a hurry, an unusual trait for a government employee. Which reminded me.

"Yes. May I bring Carol, my administrative assistant, with me?"

He winced first, then eyed me speculatively. My mixed Vietnamese and American ancestry left me with dark brown hair and a slight tilt to my eyes, the bare remnant of an epicanthic fold. I'm no beauty, but I know I'm not bad to look at, and I do have more on top than most Oriental women.

"Did we miss something? I thought…" His voice trailed off, leaving him at a loss for words for the first time.

"No, you didn't miss anything, Mr. Smith." I had to laugh, knowing what he was thinking. "It's nothing like that. Carol Genoa is simply the most efficient person I've ever worked with. I'd have a hard time getting along without her."

He had the grace to blush. I could see him relax, but not completely. "Call me Gene. You'll be seeing a lot of me. I'm the guy you'll go to when you have an administrative problem that's hampering your work. About Carol—I wasn't expecting that, so she'll have to be vetted, and it would be much better if her disappearing from sight didn't leave any loose ends.

Never mind, though. We'll manage, one way or another. It's my job to see that the scientists get what they want and paper-shufflers don't bother them."

That made me feel better.

Carol would love working with an alien, too. We had first met at a science fiction convention in Amarillo where my parents lived before they were killed in the Goldenrod Mall Massacre by home-grown Islamic Jihadists, the worst kind because they're so hard to identify. Carol had impressed me by the way she organized the convention that year – I'd never been to one that went off so smoothly, from hotel room service to the Con Room and everything in between.

We kept in touch, and two years later she came to Havel Genecrafters with me. Our relationship is as much friend to friend as supervisor to subordinate.

I smiled to myself, thinking of the look I'd see on Carol's face when I told her we'd be changing jobs and meeting an alien.

"That's fine, then. We can leave as soon as you've cleared it with the Havel brothers. Most of my friends call me Mai, or sometimes Cherry."

"I wondered about that so I looked it up. Mai Li Trung. I take it the Cherry comes from cherry blossom. Is that right?"

"Yes. Mai means 'Cherry Blossom' when it's pronounced correctly. Vietnamese is a tonal language."

"So I've heard. It's a pretty name either way, but I'll call you Mai if I may."

"Certainly. Just don't read anything into my middle name. I don't know why my parents stuck Li in there and I never bothered to ask. Enough about names. What comes next?" I don't like wasting time on idle chatter, not at work.

"Let's get Carol in here so I can get some background on her."

"I can tell you a little about her myself if you'll tell me how you sneaked by her."

"I used an invisibility cloak," he said without cracking a smile. "Okay. Shoot."

CHAPTER TWO

IT TOOK A MOMENT or two to gather my thoughts after the invisibility remark. I didn't question him about it; it might have been true. That was about the only way he could have gotten past Carol.

I started to remember some of the things she'd told me while we were corresponding. I've found that many of us tend to be more open with mail than in person – certainly it had been that way for us.

"She's probably free to move without upsetting anyone," I informed him. "Her parents are still living but she's not close to either of them. They practically disowned her while she was still a child. She was shuttled back and forth between them and spent a lot of time in boarding schools. She's been divorced for five years and doesn't have any children. She's seeing a couple of men right now, but nothing serious with either of them."

I saw the way Gene was looking at me, wondering how I knew so much about my administrative assistant. "She's as good a friend as she is an employee. We go out together occasionally when I want to get my mind off work for a few hours. She's a lot of fun to be with."

"I see. I'm going to have to have words with the agent who did your background check. She missed that."

"It's not something you'd ordinarily look for these days," I pointed out. "Most people keep their distance from subordinates for fear of being charged with harassment."

"True. Okay, the investigator gets a pass there. Anything else you'd like to tell me about her?"

"That's enough from me. I just wanted to let you know there probably wouldn't be a problem with her suddenly leaving town. Other than gossip, of course, but you'll have that anyway when both of us disappear suddenly."

"So we would, but cover stories are easy to contrive. Okay, let's see what she thinks about going into hiding, but I need to have you both sign a secrecy oath before I go any further."

"Paper shuffling?"

"Some of it can't be avoided." He shrugged, not embarrassed in the least. "This is a case in point. I shouldn't have said anything about an alien even to you, but that seemed to be the only way to get you to talk to me."

"It was." I punched the intercom button.

"Yes, Miss Trung?"

"Carol, turn on the closed sign and come on in. Please bring some more coffee, along with your cup."

One minute later she was inside with us, bearing a pot of freshly-brewed coffee. Efficiency. I love it. Why can't more people anticipate? It's not rocket science.

Once Carol was seated with all our cups full, I broke the news to her.

"Carol, this is Gene Smith. Call him Gene. He's with the government. They have some of the aliens we've been hearing about and want me to go to work for them. You're invited if you want to come, too."

"Did you use an alien invisibility cloak to get by me? Never mind, when do we leave?"

Gene laughed. "It's not a cloak, just a little gadget that absorbs or scatters light, I forget which. Here are the forms." He handed me one of the secrecy oaths, already filled out.

I read it while he got Carol's full name and social security number, then unfolded his keyboard and told his PDA to print a form for her too. I read the penalties for disclosure, which began with exile for life and ended with death by firing squad. I signed it anyway and Carol did the same with hers a moment later.

Gene stuffed the forms into his inside coat pocket, then leaned back and crossed his legs. He took a sip of his coffee and nodded his head toward Carol as a gesture of appreciation. Then he told us about the aliens.

"There was a disaster in space aboard a giant exploration ship the aliens were on. A number of lifeboats made it to Earth but most didn't. That happened about six months ago. We were lucky that at least two of them landed in the United States. Unfortunately, the alien from one of them fell into the hands of some nefarious elements of our own government. Fortunately, however, another landed almost on the doorstep of a man who was almost a perfect tutor for her—it. After it converted its body to human form—" he waved for me not to interrupt, so I didn't. "—He and the alien had a rather hard time of it. But they were instrumental in helping us rescue one of the others, and…"

He stopped suddenly, as if worried about telling us too much, too soon.

"The explosion in China? That's never been satisfactorily explained. Something went wrong, obviously. But back to the alien in human form—"

He held up a hand, palm outward, making me pause, already knowing I would have a jillion questions. "I know what you're thinking, given your specialty. How could an alien convert itself into a human woman. Right?"

"Are you telling me that it went from an alien form to a human, both externally *and* internally? Why, that's im—"

I started to say it was impossible. Realized how stupid that would be. Arthur C. Clarke's maxim popped into my mind: *Any sufficiently advanced technology is indistinguishable from magic.*

He nodded. "Absolutely human, impossible as it sounds. A very pretty and congenial woman as well as an extremely intelligent one. As a matter of fact, she married the man who rescued her from her wrecked lifeboat. The other one we're working with has become a man, by the way."

I thought I detected an undertone that the male alien might not be as congenial as the female, but let it go. My thoughts were that knowing how they became human would advance our knowledge of genetics a couple of centuries in one leap, at least, assuming they could explain it to us mere mortals.

And microchemistry. Computer science. How far had they advanced in those fields—or had they gone beyond them? Nanotechnology, and...

My mind reeled from thinking of all the possibilities.

Faster than light space travel. Gene had implied, probably without realizing it, that they almost had to have a form of that. And to change their form so completely that they could marry a human? That was almost beyond my comprehension, and I've never been accused of thinking small!

"Close your mouth, Cherry, and come back to Earth." Carol was grinning at me. She called me Cherry every time she saw me get excited.

I grinned back at her, knowing how foolish I must look but unable to help myself. Gene had said the man married one of the aliens. I wondered what he was like. At the very least, he must have an open mind.

"What did they look like originally?" I had to ask. Just knowing would give me a good idea of how the guy thought. I was assuming I'd be working with him.

"BEMs. Bug-Eyed Monsters."

"Seriously?"

"Yup. Four arms, pyramidal head, all the stuff out of science fiction novels. They're called Cresperians, by the way. Crispies for short."

"And they can change to human form? Damn. What they must know about genetics!"

"That's not the half of it. I can't go into all the details right now but I can tell you that we desperately need your expertise. The aliens have the knowledge but we need a lot of very bright scientists to help convert it into terms we can understand. Once we get you to where we're working, you'll learn a lot more of the details of what's going on."

"We can guess some of it," Carol said.

"Uh-huh," I added. "We've talked about it, just between the two of us. The recent urgency about developing better manned space travel. A couple of new gadgets on the market. Reports of conflicts inside our borders attributed to terrorism that didn't ring true. That horrendous explosion in China right on top of its primary rocket launching and research facilities. But most of all, the negative information gives it away."

"Negative information?"

I nodded. "The government admits aliens have visited the Earth but won't admit to being excited about it. That body the Mexicans displayed was authentic but I've been unable to get any data on the studies they allowed our team of scientists to conduct. They keep saying a report is 'in progress' and putting off inquiries. And most of all, the way our senior politicians talk around the subject and the way China and the Islamic Confederation have clammed up on talk about aliens. And how stridently Russia is demanding that information be released so that everyone can share in it. It all adds up to the fact that two and possibly three governments have aliens in custody and that they're working on something big. Several somethings, if I had to guess."

He was appalled. "I hope to hell you've kept your speculations to yourselves."

"We have, but Gene... we're not the only intelligent Americans in the country. Why does the government insist on treating its citizens like grade school children, as if we're not old enough to be told the facts of life?"

"Take it up with the President when you meet him. You probably will eventually." He shrugged as if that were no big thing. "Look, I'd like to get the two of you under wraps as soon as possible. How about you go to your homes and start packing? Get everything you'll need for the next six months together. Don't worry too much about dressy clothes. It's a pretty casual group. In fact, that's what we've been calling it, 'The Group.'"

"You mean start now?" Carol asked.

I felt a little rushed myself.

"Now. I'll have a clean-up crew come behind you and take care of the rest of your household goods. There will also be a security team watching you, but you'll probably never notice them."

"Why so soon?"

"China, India and the Islamic Confederation have a hell of a lot more sleeper agents in our country than is generally known or that we ever thought possible before the aliens came. Many of those sleeper agents have been alerted to watch for just such activities as the recruitment of top-notch scientists. Where you're going is absolutely top secret and we want it to stay that way. Maintaining that secrecy is our number one priority – over and above *everything* else."

"As bad as that?"

"Bad enough that if the location were known, I'd give about 50-50 odds of a suitcase nuke going off on top of it eventually. The only reason I've said as much as I have is because of the little gadget I activated right before mentioning xenobiology; it keeps sound waves from traveling more than ten feet. And because I've already put you under surveillance."

CHAPTER THREE

WHEN A MAN TELLS A WOMAN not to bother packing many dressy items, I usually disregard the remark and pick clothes that can fit just about any occasion, from a ballroom to a beach party. Especially if I'm going somewhere with little chance of shopping for more.

It's not that I really care that much for formal dress. I'm much more comfortable in jeans and pullovers, or blouses that fit close enough and are designed well enough to keep the jiggling to a minimum so I can discard the bras.

That meant a basic black cocktail dress, a couple of dress suits with both skirt and pants and a lot of casual outfits that can be worn just about anywhere. I love the informality of modern styles, compared to what my grandmother must have had to put up with when she was young.

Fortunately, most of my clothes were clean; I'd washed several loads that weekend.

I left the housekeeper a note with a recommendation, and a check with a respectable bonus to carry her until she could find work somewhere else, and trusted the "cleanup crew" to see that she got it. That wouldn't make much of a dent in my savings; the Havel brothers paid well and I don't live extravagantly.

Books were the big items. I had most of my fiction and part of my professional library stored on portable drives, but there were a number of new reference works with formulas and data I might have a hard time finding online.

For that matter, I didn't know how much net access I'd even be allowed. The hell with it. If Gene's crew was that good, they could pack the books themselves.

He'd given me a number to call if I ran into difficulties, so I used it. He told me not to worry; whatever I left behind would eventually find its way to me, although the less-important stuff might take a while.

Carol rang the doorbell just about the time I was winding it up. I had gotten a shower and changed into slacks and a blouse, with a light windbreaker handy just in case. I still had no idea where we were going.

"Finished already?" I asked as I let her in.

"Yup. A van picked up the suitcases and dropped me by here. Said they'd be back in an hour or so for you and whatever you're taking." She looked around and saw my three closed suitcases, and the one I still had open for last minute items. All of them were medium-sized. "You're traveling light if that's all you have."

"Just my carry-on. I assume we're flying."

"Me, too. They'd better pay the extra baggage charges if we go commercial!"

I laughed and offered Carol some coffee before I rinsed the basket and turned the pot off. After that, I finished stuffing my remaining gear in the last suitcase, including my large .45 caliber Glock automatic pistol.

I had very carefully asked Gene about taking my personal weapons with me. He'd given permission to bring them – they wouldn't be needed, he'd said, but "bring them along if they make you feel more comfortable."

They did. There was my big .45, and the little S&W .40 I kept in my purse. It's a smaller version of the big Glock but made by S&W. I still didn't know our mode of transportation, but at the last minute I decided to let the little automatic go ahead and live in my purse where it normally resided. If someone wanted to confiscate it now… well, Gene had said I wasn't to be bothered by the small stuff, so I'd just refer the matter to him.

Carol is one of the few people who knows I have a license to carry a concealed weapon. She had planned on getting a permit and her own gun, but Gene had arrived first. As far as I'm concerned, more of us ought to go armed. If my parents had felt the same way, they might be alive today. And as it was, a lot of lives had been saved because of a few people at the mall who *had* been carrying.

Damn crazy terrorist bastards, I thought. I hate them. I hated them even before they killed Mom and Dad and 300 other innocent Christmas shoppers at the mall.

Right on time, the van showed up. We left ten minutes later.

ജ്ഞ

Carol and I were the only passengers. There were also the driver and another man in the front passenger seat. Neither was talkative, but I finally did worm some information out of the one riding shotgun. He said we'd be traveling by jet from a private airport. Mostly they kept their eyes on the road and the rear-view mirrors. I had the impression we were being accompanied by chase cars in front and behind, but didn't ask.

When the driver said "private," he really meant it. The ride ended well over an hour later, at a tiny private airfield somewhere in the Eastex Piney Woods.

"Y'all ladies wait here in the van while I see if your plane is ready," the driver told us. His shotgun left, too. I gave them a couple of minutes then rolled the tinted back window down so we could see what was going on. On my side, there was nothing but pine trees.

Carol tapped me on the shoulder. "That's our luggage being loaded."

I looked over. The only building I could see was a shack that looked like something from a hillbilly movie. Nearby was a small jet that looked as if it had seen its best days twenty years ago. Our luggage was being thrown aboard with little regard to what might be in it.

I found myself wondering if I'd left a round in the chamber of the .45, in one of the suitcases. If I had, the way they were throwing our bags probably gave the gun at least a fifty percent chance of going off. I was starting to wonder if we'd gotten into in the right van when Gene appeared and opened the side door.

He had a half-grin on his face, as if the rest of the world amused him no end. That seemed to be his usual expression until he started talking, and it didn't always vanish then.

"Okay, all out. We're ready, and sorry for the wait."

He held a hand out to help each of us step down. It was unnecessary, but I like a man who shows those little courtesies. It tells me he'll probably treat women with dignity and respect.

Gene hadn't said so, but I already suspected the reason I'd been passed over initially was because of my sex. Being a woman wasn't supposed to mean anything special either way in the workplace nowadays, but there's still a lot of hidden prejudice, especially in academia.

That's one reason I've always loved science fiction. The best authors in the field, even during the days of pulp fiction, wrote women into their stories as if their equality was an established fact, even in military science fiction. Perhaps even more so in that sub-branch. Women fought beside men and commanded men and were spaceship captains long before the present-day military began opening up, and women are still barred from some ground combat. As if an enemy soldier gives a damn who's shooting at him.

For that matter I'd bet our own infantrymen wouldn't care who was guarding their flank so long as he or she was competent. I served one hitch in the army but left because there was still too much sexual prejudice for me, although I'll admit things are getting better.

I slung my purse and gave my handbag to the man with Gene when he reached for it. He introduced himself as Baggert and told us to call him Bag. It turned out that he was our pilot.

When we got close to the jet, I noticed it wasn't nearly as bad as I first thought. What I took for dirt and dents were *painted* on! Talk about security; these people really took it seriously. I was anxious to get to wherever in hell we were going so I could find out the reason for it all. I don't mind some secrecy when it's called for, but sometimes our leaders take it to ridiculous lengths. The bad part is that once something is classified it's like removing epoxy glue from composites to ever get the stamp taken off.

Inside the plane were eight comfortable seats arranged in two aisles, spaced so they could swivel half around. Nice arrangement for conversation. You don't have to talk to your neighbor over a backrest or wind up with a stiff neck from twisting around in the seat.

The baggage was out of sight in the rear and the pilot and co-pilot were concealed behind a folding door in the cockpit. Just before Bag pulled it closed, I noticed a heavy rifle and automatic pistol secured on racks. Security for sure.

"Can you tell us where we're going now?" I asked as the jet began rolling down the dirt and gravel runway. From what I'd seen earlier, it looked more like a country road than something an aircraft would use to land or take off on.

Gene shook his head. "Not yet. There's always the chance we could get shot down or have engine failure. Whatever. No sense in taking chances."

"You're not seriously saying we could get shot down in our own country, are you?" Carol asked.

Gene raised a cynical brow. "I thought you'd been paying attention to the news."

"I have, but… Oh. The airliner carrying all those scientists from their convention."

"Yes, that one. Despite the statement the FAA put out, that was no accident. Other countries have aliens, too. They don't want us getting ahead of them—and we don't want them coming up with a weapon or a device we can't counter."

Carol didn't say anything else for a while and neither did I, but I suspected her mind was working as busily as my own. I was going back over the last six months or so and trying to sort out serious news stories from tabloid speculation. And remembering incidents that should have gotten more coverage but hadn't.

Gene didn't have to tell me. There was a clandestine war going on. I wondered how much effort was going into restraining the media in the interests of security. A great deal, I'd bet. We're a free country, but most citizens with power - such as the media moguls - will cooperate if it's put to them in the right terms. If the matter's serious enough, they'll do it even if they disagree with the government's activities. And obviously they considered this to be serious enough.

It was the extent of the underground war that bothered me. Just how far would either side go? I guessed right away that most countries wouldn't start something with us they couldn't finish decisively; the exception was the Islamic Confedaracy, run by a gang of crazy left-wing nut theologists.

No telling what they might do. I hoped like hell they didn't have an alien, especially one that was cooperating with them.

We were still climbing, and I was still musing over what amounted to an undeclared war inside our own borders, when we got caught in a piece of that war.

I was gazing out the side window when I saw a jet fighter streak past us at a steep angle, with a roar you could hear even inside our pressurized compartment.

Bag sent our little plane into such a violent maneuver that the seat belt practically cut me in half. A second later I was thrown into the back rest just as hard. A clatter of small bits of debris hitting the plane came to me through the roar of the engine as Bag leveled out and poured on more speed.

I couldn't hear an explosion, but I knew something had been blown to pieces.

Chapter Four

"What—?" I started to ask Gene what had happened but I stopped when I saw he had his phone to one ear and a pull-down earpiece attached to the other.

He nodded his head, and a moment later he fed the earpiece back into its alcove and snapped his phone shut. His perennial, congenial little grin had vanished completely. He looked at Carol and me from across the aisle where the other row of four seats ran.

"The jet fighter you saw go past us just took a missile. Now you know how serious things are."

"Was... was he killed? The pilot of the fighter?" Carol asked hesitantly, anxious.

"No, don't worry about it. What happened was planned, sort of. The terrorists wasted a missile, I believe."

I don't like to think what the expression on my face must have looked like. No wonder Gene had said the situation was serious! I wanted to know more.

"How in hell are those bastards getting *missiles* into the country? I thought our borders were a lot more secure now."

"Any nation or group that's determined enough and has fanatics who'll give their lives to the cause will get them in eventually. We might get 99% of the ordnance but all it takes is one—as you just saw. What's bothersome is how those motherfuckers knew where we were. I thought our security was as tight as my asshole got when I saw that missile contrail."

He spit out the curses without showing any embarrassment. I don't think he was really all there, in a sense. He must have been worrying about getting us the rest of the way to our destination now that the original schedule had been compromised.

There was a little dinging noise. Gene looked up and pulled down the earpiece again. It seemed to be a direct connection to the cockpit. He listened for a moment and turned back to us.

"That was Bag. We're going to land in a half-hour or so and take part of the trip by ground. Maybe all of it, depending on security. Damn. I wish I dared make some phone calls from here, but I guess it better wait. They might be traced." His half grin finally came back into place. "I suppose you weren't planning on quite so exciting a voyage, huh?"

"Not quite," I admitted, "but damned if I won't be glad to get to wherever you're taking us so I can find out more than I know now."

"You can include me in that, too," Carol said. "Is there anything to drink? I could use one."

"I guess we all can. But only one. I'd rather us stay sharp, just in case."

I didn't particularly like the sound of that. Instinctively, I reached down under the seat and brought my purse up onto the empty space beside me. I made sure the little S&W was in its easy-draw side pocket, that it hadn't been jarred loose during Bag's violent maneuver. It was fine. There wasn't enough space under the seat for it to have moved far. Maybe I was being silly, but I left my purse where it was, within easy reach.

Gene's grin turned a little lopsided. "I think your instincts were sounder than mine when you insisted on bringing your personal weapons with you."

I shrugged. "Carrying a gun always has made me feel safer, especially after what happened to my parents."

"Yeah. I lost a friend in that mess myself. The FBI was on their tail; they were just too late to stop them until the damage had been done." He was talking over his shoulder as he filled three plastic glasses with ice from the jet's tiny galley.

"Sorry, the cupboard's about bare," he said, bringing them back with some tiny bottles. "Whisky or rum?"

We all took whisky.

"Are you with the FBI?" I asked as I uncapped the little bottle and poured Jack Daniels Black Label over the ice.

"Me? Hell, no! I hate bureaucracy and the FBI is steeped in it. They're just now finally catching up with the rest of the world in digital data handling. It was the damned paper shufflers that put them in such a sorry state to begin with when the terrorists and Jihadists and those crazy sons of bitches in the IC became active."

IC is the acronym for Islamic Confederation. It is already in such common usage that the last dictionary updates added it to their lexicon. Iran is the leader of the pack, with Syria, Jordan and Egypt in their orbit after the financial crash and its repercussions had toppled their original governments.

22

We still had a tenuous toehold in the Middle East on the rim of the IC, but Congress and a new president had finally gotten their act together on a sensible energy policy. There always had been alternatives to Middle Eastern and South American oil, but environmental pressure groups combined with a craven Congress and weak presidents kept us dependent on outside energy sources for two whole generations after the first oil crisis. Now, though, it wouldn't be long until we could tell the rest of the world to go climb a tree so far as energy was concerned. It was working so well that other manufacturing was beginning to come back to the country as well.

"Who do you work for, then?" Carol asked.

"Leave it be," I told her. "He'll tell us soon enough."

"That I will," Gene assured us. "Even if we have to drive the rest of the way, we'll be there tomorrow. Late maybe, but tomorrow."

I finished my drink but took Gene's advice and didn't ask for more. Whisky is my flavor of ethanol when I have a choice but normally I don't drink a lot. I would have then, though.

₧℃₹

We did drive. Or more accurately, we were driven, in a succession of different vehicles. Once we rode in an old van where there was room to stretch out on the carpet on blankets and get a little sleep, but there was no stopping for anything else except bathroom breaks. I never asked why the frequent switch in cars. I just assumed it was a form of security precaution.

By the time we were in the mountains of what I thought was western Virginia, I was feeling grubby and ill-used. I hadn't been able to brush my teeth more than once, or change my underwear at all. Only the thought of working with a real, live alien kept my spirits up.

On the last leg we didn't even have Gene to amuse us with the wild stories he had begun to tell of his travels. Another appointment, he said. Our drivers were laconic and much more interested in making certain we weren't being followed than in talking. I doubt they would have said much anyway.

I began paying attention to our surroundings as the country became less populated. Then we changed vehicles again and this time the driver blanked our windows. A darkened divider rolled down between the front seats and the back, shutting us into a claustrophobic, dimly-lit compartment.

For the next hour and a half we rode on twisting, bumpy roads that became progressively worse. It was like a carnival funhouse ride—except it wasn't at all fun.

Carol became nauseated from motion sickness. She stretched out on the seat and put her head in my lap. I was only marginally better off. The nightmare finally ended at the point where I was seriously debating how and where to use my little automatic—either on the driver or the car windows.

We bumped to a stop and waited. A long five minutes later the car began moving again and suddenly, like the universe being recreated, there was light. The windows were transparent again. The driver and his companion reappeared as the divider rolled up.

I squinted against the sudden light and realized we were about to enter a tunnel. Carol sat up and looked out too.

"Where are we?" I asked, but not really expecting to be answered.

Surprisingly, the man in the front passenger seat turned around and not only spoke, but grinned at us. "Welcome to the Brider Enclave, home of the Cresperian Research and Studies Group. CRS for short and also known as SFREC for Space Force Research Center, but we old timers just call it 'The Group.'"

"Cresperian?" I asked, pretending not to have heard the term before to see if he'd open up even more. He did, not even glancing at a supervisor for approval.

"That's what we call the aliens. It's the nearest we can come to pronouncing their name for themselves. Crispies will do for them. They don't mind."

"It sounds like you've been here a while."

"Yup. It was nice to get out for a change. Doesn't happen very often these days. Most folks fly in and take the main entrance, but I understand y'all ran into a little trouble on the way."

"If you call someone firing a missile at us a little trouble, yes. Yes, we did."

"Something else new. Goddamn Chinks. Ought to hit them again to teach the fuckers some manners."

That was a surprise statement, coming from someone obviously Oriental speaking to a woman who looked like me. That made him either Vietnamese or Japanese. No other Oriental nationals hated the Chinese more than those two if you don't count some of our own village idiots.

"Vietnamese?" I guessed.

"Yeah. You?"

"My father. Mom was Caucasian."

"My name's Nguyen, but it doesn't matter much. You probably won't see me again unless you leave here." He held out a pack of chewing gum. "If pressure changes bother you, better take some. We've got a big elevator drop coming up."

I didn't hesitate. I hate flying for that very reason and my ears still hadn't recovered from the brief ride in the jet the day before.

Nguyen wasn't kidding. The sedan drove right into the elevator. The doors closed behind us, and a moment later we were dropping into the depths of the earth as fast as a commercial airliner gains altitude when leaving the ground. My ears popped and popped again. I chewed furiously, yawning and swallowing at the same time. Damn, I hate that sensation. It makes my whole head feel like it's stuffed with cotton and sometimes it takes days to go away.

The elevator slowed abruptly, forcing my body into the seat cushion. I barely noticed it for the pain in my ears. It made me wonder how far under the earth we were. I also made a mental note to ask to go out the other way when I left. Which might be quicker than they thought, if I didn't find a hot shower, a soft bed and something to eat besides sausage biscuits and hamburgers. I imagine Carol was feeling much the same way.

This trip hadn't gone at all the way I'd expected, not from the moment I saw that jet fighter streaking by the window and heard the bad guys taking a potshot at us. I wasn't very happy when the elevator doors opened and we came into another tunnel, so dimly-lit that the car needed to use its headlights.

And then we passed through an arched opening into a fairyland of bright lights and busy people. My eyes opened wide. I could practically feel the rush of my body and mind regaining their usual energy and enthusiasm.

CHAPTER FIVE

WE HAD BEEN RIDING SO LONG that just getting out of the blasted car and standing on my feet would have been worth a magnum of good champagne and a big filet. And that's exactly what I wanted, as soon as possible. I'd never been so glad to get anywhere.

Nguyen stopped the car at the edge of another archway. He turned around in his seat.

"This is where I'll be leaving you ladies for now. Perhaps we'll see each other again one day." He shook both our hands. "Sorry about the rough ride." He got back into the vehicle and drove away.

A man and woman had been waiting to greet us. The woman was wearing jeans and a blouse as casually as if they were a uniform. They looked good on her, but every woman that young looks good if they're not overfed. The man was dressed in unpowered army cammie fatigues, making them look a silvery color.

On one collar was a Chief Warrant Officer pip. On the other was an emblem I didn't recognize; it looked like a rocket ship. They were the ones who each extended a hand to help us out of the back seat, as if thoroughly understanding how tired and enervated we must be. After the car was out of the way, the male introduced them both.

"Hi. I'm Kyle Leverson," he said,"and this is my wife, Jeri. You're Mai from the description, and you must be Carol." They each took the time to shake hands with firm grips and bright smiles. "We're glad to have you with us, really glad. And General Shelton sends you an apology for the rough trip. We hadn't been expecting trouble from that source."

"That seems pretty obvious." I forced myself to smile. "I've never been fired at with anti-aircraft missiles. Or ridden for almost 36 hours with nothing but bathroom breaks. And speaking of…"

"Come on. We'll take you to your rooms right now," Jeri said with a sympathetic grin.

As we walked along a pathway, I was torn between wanting to get acquainted with the couple and wanting to see all the activity. We were in a giant cavern, supported here and there by wide, solid columns that flared at top and bottom for extra support. Where columns broke up the expanse there were usually people doing something with machinery or instruments, but the noise level wasn't as high as I'd expected for an enclosed space.

And it was certainly brightly lit, almost like daylight. In fact, the light seemed strange. I couldn't tell where it was coming from. As we passed through this cavern I saw a number of large entrances leading to other areas. Jeri and Kyle were alternating explanations of the activities as we walked. Kyle waved a hand, taking in all of the huge area.

"Ordinarily, you wouldn't have met us yet, nor seen much of this until later but you came in through an emergency entrance. Beyond those other archways are some alcoves where different kinds of research and development are taking place. Some are closed off but others are pretty well open so long as the people working aren't disturbed. We haven't had time to section everything off for privacy yet. Just the real scary stuff. Here's where we turn off." He led us into a hallway.

We walked about 30 yards, passing walls painted with murals; mostly science-fiction and military art predominated. After that we passed a series of doors on each side of the hallway. Most of them had nameplates attached. Some were single names, others were couples. Some had the same last names while others didn't but almost all the double nameplates had a man and a woman's name. We passed one door bearing two male names and another with two females. There was a third where two males and one female name were attached. Many of them were preceded by rank designations, ranging from Army to Marine to Navy. I didn't see any Air Force or Coast Guard.

It was evident we were in the living quarters and even more evident that over half the residents were either married or cohabiting. It made sense to bring families along when outside contact was restricted but I hoped there were at least a few acceptable single men around the place. Too bad Kyle was not only married but obviously deeply in love with his wife. Jeri reciprocated the attitude. I don't think I've ever seen a couple so obviously taken with each other but still capable of acting casual about it in the company of others.

It made me envious. Every man I've been involved with has turned out to have major flaws. The most common has been their inability to associate romantically with a woman more intelligent than them, but I'll be damned if I'm going to play the 'dumb little me' routine for anyone, not with two Ph.Ds on my resume. Most men just can't stand it, though. They wind up ignoring your work and bragging about their own accomplishments, no matter how minor. You'd think I would have met a lot of brilliant men in my line of work, and I have. But the interesting ones are usually married or such obnoxious nerds that I couldn't stand to be around them socially.

As we walked, Jeri and Kyle made heroic efforts to put us at ease after the horrendous journey. I liked them both, right from the start.

Kyle was about six feet tall and well built. He wasn't that good looking but had a strong young face with a hint of Amerindian ancestry showing in his cheekbones.

Jeri was just short of beautiful, with auburn hair that tumbled in what looked like natural waves past her shoulders. It practically glowed with a healthy sheen and showed little evidence of the mistreatment so many women subject their hair to. She had a good figure as well. Her breasts jounced just a bit beneath the opaque blouse as she walked, evidence of not wearing a bra—and having little need of one.

They both seemed to have the kind of strong personalities that practically radiated intelligence and self-confidence. They gave off a feeling of cheerful interest in their friends and fellow workers.

Jeri was the more talkative of the two. I later found out that Kyle was actually shy when around people he didn't know well; it took me by surprise. You'd never know it unless you caught him having to deal with strangers when his wife wasn't present. With Jeri around, he talked and interacted much more effusively. I found out after starting my job that their attitude set the tone for the whole enclave. Even with the strict security it ended up being a great place to work. It made me wish I had been there at the beginning.

At the time, I felt a slow burn begin to build towards whoever it was that had passed me over when the team was being assembled for this huge underground complex—then sternly told myself to forget it. Besides, I suspected the person responsible had probably been disciplined already. The corners of Jeri's lips tilted slightly, as if smiling to herself over my self-admonishment, but that did seem to be just her natural expression.

"Here's your rooms," she announced. She showed us the touch plates that would serve as a lock once they had been activated for us. "I knew you were both going to be whupped from that trip so I took the liberty of arranging some snacks and drinks for you. If you could stand a little company while you freshen up, I'll go get them."

I loved her accent. It was a mixture of Texas and another region of the south I couldn't place but even with the twang it sounded sweet and girlish coming from her elfin, almost beautiful face. It made me wonder where she was from.

"You bet," Carol and I chimed together in response to her offer of food and drink, almost like mind readers. I was badly in need of a drink for the second time in two days and even more in need of water and a toothbrush. After a shower, I'd feel a lot more confident standing upwind of them.

"Here comes your luggage," Kyle said.

I watched and tried not to look as stunned as I felt as a cart skimmed along a few inches above the floor. It stopped by Carol's entrance first and used its robotic arms to neatly deposit her bags, then moved on to leave mine by the doorway. It made a U-turn and went back the way it had come. I made a note to ask how it managed that levitation trick later, but right now but there were too many other new things to worry about.

"How about if Jeri helps Carol with her luggage then finds the snacks, while I show y'all how to operate the doors from inside and where things are located. Both your rooms are identical and it'll save time." Kyle spoke with a pure Texas twang.

We accepted the offer. After keying the touch plates and showing us a few things inside, I asked Kyle to give us twenty minutes to shower and change and suggested we all meet in my room afterward. Carol went off to her room with Jeri while Kyle helped bring in my luggage. He grinned, gave a casual wave and suddenly I was alone for the first time in two days.

ಌಗ

For an underground refuge, which is what I took the Brider Enclave to have been originally, the individual suites were much roomier than I would have thought. I had a regular bedroom, a smaller one for guests, a kitchenette already stocked with some of my favorite snack foods, an office already equipped with a computer and notebook, and what I suppose you'd call a den. It had a large couch, a smaller one like a love seat and several comfortable, well padded chairs with ottomans or extensions. End tables and coffee tables and a few other pieces of furniture completed the picture.

I took all of it in without wasting much time on exploring. What I wanted was a shower and fresh clothing. I didn't know it then but the little suite was the type reserved for senior scientists.

ตงดง

Fifteen minutes later, I felt like a new woman with a clean body and garments to match. I still had my hair wrapped in a towel but I'd changed into a pair of soft old jeans and a pullover that was thick enough not to show a shadow of my nipples but thin enough to make the lack of a bra obvious. If Jeri could get away with it then so could I, even though she did look to be ten years younger than my 29. Kyle seemed to be in his late twenties. There was something about both their personalities that suggested wisdom beyond their years but I couldn't pin it down. Whatever it was, Jeri sure didn't act like a 19-year-old. Anyway, I was supposedly in my own digs so I could dress like I pleased.

The door chimed pleasantly, an old tune I recognized but - like the age factor with Kyle and Jeri - I couldn't place. I told the door to open and it did, recognizing my voice pattern just like it had been taught 20 minutes beforehand.

All three of them were there. Jeri and Carol were holding plates of sandwiches and finger food while Kyle had his arms full of a six-pack of beer and a bottle each of rum, whisky and vodka. As he set his load on the kitchen counter I saw he had brought all good brands, Jack Daniels in particular. I wondered where the scotch was but I wouldn't miss it if no one else did. Like I said earlier, I reserved most of my alcohol intake for special occasions.

As I helped Carol and Jeri set out the food I began salivating and had to sample a bit here and there. Whoever had made the sandwiches did a good job. I said so.

Jeri grinned. "Kyle is still better in the kitchen than me, but I'm trying to catch up."

Well, she was young. Time enough to learn and Kyle didn't seem to mind. Regardless of all the progress in sexual equality for women, we are still expected to do most of the cooking. I like to cook, so it doesn't bother me - unless I see the man *expecting* me to do it all the time regardless of how busy I might be with work and other activities. That's usually the end of an affair for me. It was why I'd kicked Ken out, two weeks after he'd moved in with me. Well, that and a few other traits I didn't discover until too late.

We were all seated and I immediately discovered that someone who knows furniture had selected the couches and chairs in the den. It was crowded but cozy and the gremlins that furnish hotel rooms had obviously been banned from this place. Or maybe they couldn't get past the security.

I tried them all over the next day or two and they were unbelievably comfortable, but right then I enjoyed sitting in one of the easy chairs and satisfying my appetite with a sandwich and my thirst with a pickup drink.

Kyle and Jeri were good company, although Jeri did most of the talking. They alternated between telling how the enclave was organized and what the group did, and asking about Carol and me. Kyle seemed surprised that Carol had a bachelor's degree in biology as well as a master's in Business O&E. That's Organization and Efficiency to the uninitiated, a relatively new specialty that I hadn't heard of until meeting Carol. I remembered it when I asked her to come to work at Havel's and it proved to be a godsend.

"Well, we weren't expecting you, Carol, but it sounds like we hit the jackpot. As fast as we're moving on some projects, it takes a genius in organization to keep us from getting tangled in our own feet. We've managed *that* all too often."

"Carol is a genius, all right," I stated emphatically. "I had three different research projects going at the same time at Havel's and she kept them all running as smooth as a pup's belly."

They laughed but, the mention of research reminded me what I was here for. Even tired as I was I couldn't stand not knowing any longer.

"Okay," I said. "We're here. Now what I want to know is when I'm going to meet the aliens. I won't be able to sleep tonight until I do."

Kyle and Jeri roared with laughter. I couldn't see what was so funny about what I'd just said. As the laughter continued, I began to get irritated. I guess they noticed because they quieted down.

"Do you mean no one has told you?" Kyle said, disbelief obvious in his voice.

"Told me *what?* Would you mind letting me and Carol in on the joke?"

He pointed to Jeri. "You've been talking to an alien ever since Jeri was introduced to you. She's a Crispy. Or was, I should say."

CHAPTER SIX

"NO ONE TOLD ME," I said rather plaintively. I was staring at Jeri but I couldn't help it. Neither could I picture her as ever having been an alien. Kyle was being very quiet and that didn't make much sense, either.

"I'm very sorry," Jeri said. "As soon as I realized you didn't know who Kyle and I were, I thought it would be a good joke to withhold the fact for a little while. I can see now that it wasn't very funny to you two. I apologize. I'm still learning how to act like a human, you see, even after all this time."

Now I stared at Kyle. "Jeri included you in that statement. Don't tell me you're an alien, too!"

"No, I'm just her husband. And the man who rescued her from her lifeboat after it crashed."

"Oh. Oh! Gene told me about you two, but he never mentioned your names!" That happy-faced scoundrel! He'd probably done it on purpose.

"And that's more than I heard," Carol said. "He must have already told Mai the story before they called me in to ask me along to the circus."

That got a chuckle from all of us. I was beginning to relax again but for the life of me, I couldn't keep my eyes off Jeri. I guess she was used to it because she met my stare and answered my questions with good humor.

"Could... I mean would it be okay if I saw what you looked like before you... transformed? Converted? Whatever you call it when you change your form from Cresperian to human."

"Certainly. And it's perfectly all right to use the short form of the term. Crispy. Cresperian is used only in formal reports and the like. Here, I'll show you how I used to look."

She wore a wide gold band on each of her upper arms that shone like polished brass. It struck me as an odd type of jewelry when I first spotted it but it did look rather attractive on her. And as it turned out, it had a use. She touched one of the bands with two fingers and held them there for a moment.

A holograph—or what I took for one—of her former image appeared in the middle of the den. Her head was pyramid-shaped, with two large bisected eyes in a lumpy face, and set squarely on an upper body. No neck. The torso was about the same size as a human's, but held four arms instead of two. Each ended in two opposable thumbs and six limber fingers. The long lower appendages were much like our legs and feet, except for a backward facing toe-like extension as well as several in front. I could see no visible genitals.

She was covered in a pale lime-colored pelt so fine that at first I mistook it for reptilian scales. When I peered closer, it looked as if it would be sleek and soft to the touch. The being wore bands like the ones Jeri did on her arms, also a lime green color but darker.

I kept glancing back and forth from Jeri to the image and trying to reconcile the two. Frankly, I couldn't do it. I'm a geneticist and a damn good one but how in hell could something like that creature convert itself to a human female? And not just the form but the complete genome, or so I was told.

I shook my head. "It's hard to believe."

"Try thinking in terms of a species that's been civilized so long it's forgotten its own history," Kyle said. "One where manipulation of genes and changing of bodily form and function are as natural to them as eating a slice of apple pie is to us. A species that's learned to tap into the quantum foam to help it do these things. And, finally, one with a perceptive sense that goes down to the molecular and atomic level. Does that make it easier?"

"Intellectually, I suppose." I sighed. "Practically? It's something I'm going to have to get used to. Gene Smith told me it could be done but I only half believed him. Maybe not even that much."

Kyle reached to the small pitcher of alcoholic punch he had stirred up in place of whisky and refilled his glass. He raised his brows in my direction.

"One more, then I have to get some sleep, come the revolution and the rapture in one fell swoop."

"Same here," Carol said. "In fact, my eyes are closing. I'm going to have to call it a day." She stood up, thanked Kyle and Jeri for their hospitality, and headed out.

After the door closed behind her, Kyle became serious.

"Mai, I hope you're anxious to get to work because we're going to be rushing you. Don't feel like we're singling you out; we're all rushed, here. Jeri and I took part of the day off to welcome you personally after the rough time you had, but we all have projects going that are little short of urgent. You'll be in the same position because we won't be around much longer and part of Jeri's work is going to fall into your hands."

I started to comment then bit my tongue. *Me,* pick up on an alien's work, one of a species that's been around so long they've learned to use the quantum foam to manipulate genomes as easily as kids playing with marbles?

I know I'm smart, but *that* seemed like a stretch. However, I told myself they knew what they were doing and let it slide for the moment.

"Rest easy," Jeri said. She reached over and patted me on the knee. "I'll leave you plenty of notes and show you how to use the instruments we've devised."

"What am I supposed to do with them?"

"Nothing real hard," Kyle said with a smile. "Just figure out how to lengthen the human lifespan indefinitely without a Crispy to assist during the process. And how to help humans develop a perceptive sense. Or if you'd rather leave part of that research to others you can take the SF combat course that's been set up and maybe go out with one of the spaceships. Starships, I should say."

I made a sudden leap of intuition while I was wondering whether he was joking about the spaceships or not.

"Neither one of you is as young as you look," I said.

"See?" Jeri remarked as they exchanged glances. "I knew she was the one just as soon as I ran across her bio." To me she said, "Sorry, Mai. I didn't intend to talk past you. As my sweetie here said, we're kind of rushed. The man who passed you over when we were assembling this madhouse is still around, but he's being... er, re-educated. Right now I believe he's studying the life histories of a hundred or so female scientists and other notables of the gentler sex, as he so unfairly put it, like Madame Curie, Maria Mayer, Sonya Kovalesky, Grace Hopper and others of equal merit. After that he'll get into Israeli and Russian military exploits by females and follow it up with women in the United States armed forces and scientific fields. The course will end with a week of hand-to-hand combat training conducted by female marines who've been through infantry combat training and are experts in martial arts. I believe he'll be a better man after completing his studies, don't you?"

I laughed at the image of a doofus male macho smartass who thought men were so high and mighty having to study superior females until his brain was stuffed full of their exploits and then having his ass kicked up between his shoulder blades by women half his size for a couple of weeks. If that didn't change his attitude, nothing would. But...

"When did the military relent on allowing females into infantry combat specialties? And were you kidding about going on a starship?"

"I believe it was General Shelton who put it over for our little group but it was Kyle's idea, not mine," Jeri said. "He's also responsible for dreaming up the re-education course for males who were downplaying women's role in the planned expeditions beyond the solar system. I think it's so good I want to combine that course with another of the opposite extreme, women who think their gender is superior. I just wish we had more time, but after we get into space we'll be able to get a lot of training done during travel. And no, I wasn't kidding. The spaceships are being built and we are going to go exploring."

"Where to?" The remark about beyond the solar system had just sunk in. I was flabbergasted.

"Cresperia, my home planet—if we can find it. All our navigators were killed when the ship broke up. Ishmael and I—he's another Crispy and you'll meet him later—have convinced General Shelton to send the first two craft in the general direction of our home just in hopes of finding it, but there'll be lots of exploring along the way."

It was all moving too fast for me, especially the way my vision was beginning to blur. The food and that third drink had just about done me in. Kyle must have noticed.

"Sweetheart, I think we'd better take the rest of this up tomorrow. Carol's already gone to bed and if we keep Mai up much longer she's going to collapse right there on her couch."

"You're right, hon," Jeri agreed. She and Kyle stood up. "We'll see you tomorrow when you pass through our stations, but someone else will handle your orientation. That shouldn't take more than a day. Then we'll find you some space in my office, and you can get to work."

I yawned as I was telling them good night, and I think I was asleep within five minutes after the door closed behind them. I dreamed of flying that night, flying on a giant spaceship out among countless stars, just as I'd daydreamed of since I was a little girl.

CHAPTER SEVEN

THE BED WAS SO COMFORTABLE I didn't want to get up the next morning. There's nothing like a good top of the line memory foam mattress about four inches thick laid over a firm foundation to make a person sleep well. I threw the sheets back, yawning and stretching and wondering what time it was. My bedside clock seemed to have disappeared. And why hadn't the room started its gradual brightening routine when I told it to? Then I suddenly remembered where I was—or hoped I was! I was going to be awfully disappointed if this was all a dream.

I sat up in bed, heart pounding. *Had* it all been no more than an extraordinarily vivid dream? Or was it really true? I looked around. I wasn't at home; that was certain. There was no one in bed with me, so I surely hadn't overindulged and gone home with a strange man. *By God, it was true!* I had really and truly met an alien, a being who had traveled distances unimaginable to the human mind, only to wind up as one of the few survivors from a wrecked spaceship.

I hadn't bothered looking for a nightie before crawling into bed the night before. I swung my legs over the side and stood up. The bathroom was... that way. The door was partially open with a thin shaft of light coming from it into the room, just like I remembered leaving it when I couldn't locate a night light.

I found a pot and coffee and got it going first thing so it would be ready by the time I finished my usual morning ablutions. By my standards, I was already running late. I like a light compact breakfast and an early start.

Apparently the organizers here knew it, too. The phone rang just as I finished eating the cereal and banana that had been left for me.

"Are you dressed?" It was Gene and the phone's viewscreen showed he was back to his usual cheerful self.

"Sure. What—oh. Sorry. The phone was set for receive only." I punched the transmit selector and a second later Gene's image grinned.

"Ah, much better. Now I can see your smiling face. Are you about ready for your orientation?"

"I've been ready."

"Okay, I'll come for you in ten minutes."

೮೦೦೮

Carol was with him, along with several other people. One was a slim but well built man in his thirties, with blond hair and bronzed skin from outdoor activity. He wore army cammies with shirt sleeves rolled up above the elbows. It was the same shiny silvery color as the military's new powered camouflage wear; the silvery color meant it didn't have its power on. Same as I had seen Kyle wearing the day before.

When the cammies were powered, the fabric would take on the colors and tints of its surroundings. The double bars of a captain's insignia were attached to the collar of his shirt. He held out his hand, displaying a tanned, well-muscled forearm.

"Roy Jenkins. I'll be around for a couple of weeks before I leave for the SF Marine training."

"SF—Space Force?"

"Yep. Ain't it grand?"

I nodded. Space Force. It sounded good to me. And the way he was dressed—was that going to be the uniform or had he come here from some other military unit? I knew NASA had been picked up by the scruffs of their necks and told to get their ass in gear with development of long range manned spaceships, but a military contingent in space told me volumes about how far they'd come in the short time since aliens arrived on Earth.

Or was this place part of NASA? It had more of the aspects of a military venture than NASA. And the secrecy. I began to get an inkling of wheels within wheels going on here. I kept that observation to myself, figuring I'd be told what I needed to know soon enough.

Gene drove the group around in a big bastardized golf cart without wheels that seated six people, and it was full. It moved like the baggage cart, a few inches above ground level. I asked about it.

"It's an adaptation from the survival packs that came with the lifeboats. Really pretty simple once Jeri explained how they work. It's not anti-gravity, in case that's what you're thinking. It's more like surface magnetism without ferrous metals being necessary or so I was told when I asked, but I'm sure there's more to it than that. I'm not a physicist. The repulsion force works on the inverse square law, so there's a limit to how far from a surface a unit can get."

I nodded, suspecting I was going to run across a good number of developments that hadn't gotten out to the public yet.

The first part of the orientation concerned the place we were at now. The Brider Enclave was built originally back in the last century when the

Cold War was our main concern and at its height. Many citizens of that era built backyard shelters in case of nuclear warfare, which at the time seemed inevitable if not imminent. Survivalists bought acreage in wild parts of the country and stocked up on food and ammunition. Remnants of them are still active here and there but now they worry what the IC is up to with terrorism or biological warfare.

Back in those days a tycoon by the name of Brider decided to construct a shelter that would keep a few dozen people safe from a giant nuclear exchange, the worst imaginable, for a number of years. He built it deep and big and made it to last. He worked on it for years and was still improving it when he died. After his heirs split up his fortune it was sold to a mining company and then passed through several other hands. Eventually it wound up being controlled by Army Intelligence, acquired by a smart general in military procurement for pennies on the dollar. After its location was removed from the state and county tax rolls, its existence was kept secret and gradually it had faded from everyone's memory.

The Army Intelligence service was using only a small section of the giant underground enclave when Kyle rescued Jeri from her smashed lifeboat. After several run-ins with nefarious characters who wanted Jeri's knowledge and cared little about how they obtained it, Kyle contacted an old friend from the days when he served in Army Intelligence himself, William Shelton, since promoted to general.

The general had put together enough help to rescue Kyle and Jeri but not without several really hairy escapades that just hearing about made my skin prickle with goose bumps. That last bit was skimmed over and I didn't learn until a little later what a desperate time Kyle and Jeri had had their first few months together. It sure hadn't been a typical honeymoon!

That was the historical part of the orientation. Then came the present.

The Brider Enclave was a joint forces intelligence, research, development and acquisition command at the time the aliens landed. After Jeri and Kyle were rescued it was simply incorporated into the newly formed Space Force Research and Exploration Command, SFREC, pronounced Sefwreck, with an Army three-star, Bill, now in charge of it. It worked out fine. NASA was maintained simply as window dressing but jacked-up in order to keep this place secret.

This was where all the research and development for the space forces took place, while the testing and construction of the actual space ships being built was disguised as private enterprise. When they left it would be from spaceports leased from a couple of the private firms, one in deep West Texas and one in New Mexico. No one expected to keep that part secret for long, but the Brider Enclave, "The Group," was where the aliens lived. It had to be under deep cover and was. Activity above ground was disguised as a new coal mining operation now that clean coal technology was coming on line and part of the topside was also designated as an army training command. Both served to disguise what took place beneath them.

After a break for lunch we were taken on a tour of the facility, or at least some of it. We passed several shops where electronics work of various sorts was being done. Some of it I recognized, but in a couple of places I didn't even know what the instruments were for or if what I was looking at was even built to measure or manipulate electrons.

I'm not an electrical engineer, of course, but anyone doing research in the hard science specialties has to know something about electronics. Frequently you have to design your own instruments before you can do the research—and just as frequently the instruments you design become *part* of the research.

Gene gestured. "Here they're working with Ishmael on devices humans can use to stimulate their minds into paths that can contact the quantum aspects of reality in the same manner they use their minds alone to do so. Or trying to construct them, I should say." He nodded in my direction. "You may have more success by going at it from a biological angle."

Biological manipulation of quantum reality? They weren't expecting much from me, were they? And why couldn't Jeri or Ishmael just show us how to do it? They had the perceptive sense, as they called it; they were bound to know scads more about it than me. If Jeri didn't introduce me to the job really well I was going to feel about as lost as a northbound goose in the middle of January. In a blizzard, no less.

We didn't stay there long. A couple of workmen delivered some folding partitions carried by one of the ubiquitous floating carts. We got out of the way and moved on. I looked back and saw the partitions already being erected.

"As you've probably noticed, we're rushing," Gene said. "We're trying different solutions to problems with parallel experiments. There's no time to do it one way then possibly—probably—fail and have to start from scratch again."

"Expensive," Carol noted.

"Yup, but we've got the funding and there's no problem with finding the personnel, other than having to vet them all and then losing so many of them from being family types who don't want to be separated. We can accommodate only so many dependents. We have to rush because other nations have Crispies working for them, too."

I made a note to myself to ask about that one later.

I was awed at the vast expanse of the enclave. Old man Brider must have spent a veritable fortune, and that was before the government had started pouring money into it.

We walked on past a few more small shops, then entered another huge cavern. A large boxy shape, rounded on both ends, sat in the center of the enclosure. It was at least twice as high as the dozen or so workmen around it, but was raised off the floor so it appeared even bigger. There were a number of projections like thick antennas at both ends. What looked suspiciously like torpedo tubes were visible beneath and back from one end, and some different kinds of openings at the other. There was room beneath it for easy access, where several men and women in white coveralls were busy.

"Now there's our real beauty," Gene announced. "It's a scaled down but fully functional version of the FTL spacecraft we built. This is where we do the designing and such testing as we can without going into space, although we trundled the model out one of our hidden tunnels and actually took it into space."

He grinned. "It worked perfectly, but this is a two-person test craft. We've gone about as far as we can with the small version although as you can see, we're still making modifications and improvements. The first really big one is being built on site at the New Mexico spaceport where there are plenty of materials and supplies. It's been a killer job constructing it and keeping its location more or less secret but it's almost finished now. As soon as it's ready for flight, Jeri and Kyle Leverson will be leaving—as well as a rather large complement of crew, scientists and marines. There's another one about halfway done. It's the one you folks will be on if you decide to go into space rather than stay here and do research."

The rest of the tour was kind of a blur. Just the thought of being able to go into space had my mind reeling.

And not just to space, but to the stars!

CHAPTER EIGHT

THE TOUR ENDED back at the dining room. I was told we could have drinks and snack-food in our apartments but no major cooking. That suited me. I figured I'd be too busy most of the time once I got started. When I was back in my suite I saw the message light flashing on the console at the little work station that each place came equipped with. It was an invitation from Kyle and Jeri for an informal get-together at their place. I noted the time and decided on a quick shower beforehand. We'd done a lot of walking and some of the places we'd been to were dusty.

ഇ൪ര

Jeri was hosting, wearing casual jeans and top and looking great in them. I decided she was one of those women who can look good in just about anything, damn her beautiful eyes. It must be nice to be able to sculpt your body to whatever dimension you like. Or was that how she'd done it? I reminded myself I really didn't know yet.

"Hi Mai. Come on in." She gave me a brief womanly hug, just as if she'd been doing it all her life.

"Thanks." I held up the little purse I'd brought just in case.

"In there." She pointed.

I deposited it and went over to the bar where Kyle was dispensing drinks.

"Hi, Mai." He grinned. "Good to see you. And just in case you think this is a regular affair, it's the first occasion Jeri and I have had to relax and have some folks over in weeks. We used it for an excuse to introduce you to some of the people you'll be seeing here and there."

"Who all will be here?"

"Oh, you, Colonel—I mean General—Haley and his fiancé, Carolyn; Major Seabrook; a few of the guys I've been on operations with. Not many. Ishmael may come if he can get away from all the women chasing him. What do you want to drink?"

"Ishmael? That's the other alien?" I asked, and pointed at the whisky.

"Yeah. Him, and now there's Sira, one we rescued from the IC. I think she'll be around but maybe not." I thought I caught a hint of an undercurrent in his voice but decided not to pursue it.

I took my drink and thanked him then moved off. Their place had lots more space than mine. This room was larger than my entire suite. I wondered if Jeri being an alien had anything to do with it; probably. We'd be treating them extra nice.

꙰

People came and went throughout the evening, but there were never many there at one time. General Haley proved to be a big man of the kind who practically exudes command presence.

Somehow or other Roy Jenkins and I got to talking with Jeri about the Crispies landing on Earth and how they were in different countries, which I still didn't understand.

"How did it happen?" he asked her. Apparently he didn't have the full story either.

"There were maybe two dozen lifeboats that made it clear of our spacecraft when it was wrecked, and only eight, or possibly nine or ten— we're not real certain—of those made it safely to Earth," she told us in a calm but rather somber voice. "The others all perished. Those of us who arrived with little or no harm still landed in a widely dispersed pattern, everywhere from America to Mexico to England to India and China."

"It's a good thing the IC didn't get one," Roy Jenkins commented.

"They did," Kyle corrected him. "She just didn't mention it. The IC also had some agents in our country who found where Ishmael was being held by some renegades of our own people. A group from Army Intelligence got there just about the same time the IC tried to grab him for them- selves, probably planning on spiriting him out of the country. Fortunately the FBI was on the scene, too, because we were outgunned."

"Sounds like it was one big clusterfuck," Jenkins said.

"It was. And Ishmael—that's the name he took—still hasn't fully re- covered from the treatment he received. He's converted to a male human now but he's… well, you'll meet him later so I'll let him speak for him- self. He's involved with spaceship design, too, but only part of the time. Jeri and Ishmael sort of combine their knowledge since neither of them were specialists in FTL propulsion. They each have other projects going too."

FTL. Faster than light! *Whee!* I wanted to go!

"I guess I'm making it all sound easier than it was," Kyle continued, glancing at Jeri.

"You are," his wife agreed. "I knew little of human affairs at the time. While learning about humans through the internet I managed to contact Ishmael, who had been captured and was being very rudely treated, so I was wary of falling into government hands at first. Kyle got us out of several scrapes before he convinced me to let him contact General Shelton. It's a good thing he did, too. I doubt we would have stayed free much longer without his help."

"Don't let her underplay her own role," Kyle said. "If it hadn't been for her survival kit and perceptive sense we'd probably be stuck working for the Russian Mafia or some other outfit just as bad." He shivered theatrically then grinned when Jeri punched him on the arm.

General Shelton caught my eye and winked. I got the impression that an odyssey of adversity, anxiety and frightening encounters with very nasty characters had just been passed over with those few words. I hoped I would get more of the story from Jeri after starting on my job, whatever it turned out to be.

"Are you going on the first flight?" I asked Roy. I could feel a sense of jealousy building toward anyone lucky enough to be on that first trip but I did my best to suppress it.

"Me? No, I'm just starting my training. I'll be on the crew of the next ship, I hope. At least that's what I've been told."

"You'll be able to go eventually if you want to," Jeri said to me. She was smiling as though she knew how much I'd love to be on a starship… and she was dead on. I wouldn't give a rat's ass where it was going or when it was coming back so long as I was on it. *Why me, though?* I wanted to ask.

"But…"

Kyle laughed at my expression. "I told you things were moving fast. We've got several ships in various stages of construction. If ours doesn't blow up and we come back from our first little jaunt, then the rest of them will head out, too."

"But I thought—oh. You're talking about the big ship, not the model."

"Right. We, or rather one of our test pilots, flew it out to the Oort cloud and back so we know we're on the right track. Sometimes unexpected problems occur when scaling up though, which is why the other ships will wait until we come back. Or six months if we don't."

CHAPTER NINE

ROY WAS GOING TO BE SENT OFF to the Space Marine incoming troop section for processing the next morning; too bad. He was interesting, even if a little younger than me. He told us he had already undergone an extremely rigorous physical and mental evaluation before being accepted; he'd had the evaluation without knowing what it was even for!

"I was scared silly," he said, laughing. "I was bored with training duty and when the notice came down it read, *Adventure Minded Marines needed for special missions. Must be physically fit, prepared for combat and long separation from family if accepted.* I thought, 'what the hell.' I wasn't married and the folks are used to me being gone on long deployments anyway so why not?" He laughed again.

"Besides, I was curious as a mouse trying to get into a cheese factory. I really thought the 'combat' part meant a Special Forces deployment inside the IC and I was already qualified there. To top it off I hate those bastards, but I guess they can wait."

"Maybe not," Kyle said, his tone as serious as any I'd heard from him so far. "We know the Islamic Confederation got that one lifeboat with Sira in it but Jeri thinks there's some Crispies who probably made it to Earth that are still unaccounted for. We've got plenty of intel types searching for where they might be held, but you can bet getting others out won't be as easy as bringing Sira back here was."

"Easy?!" Jeri looked at her husband as if he was crazy. He just grinned. "Easy compared to China."

"Oh. Well, yes. What I think, Roy, is that rescuing a Crispy being held by force might take priority over an immediate trip into space. If they want to be rescued, that is."

"Well, I guess I'll find out, won't I?" Roy said. "Nice meeting you all. I have to leave early in the morning so I'd better go." He told us all good night and left.

I was confused and didn't mind saying so. I asked Jeri a leading question, hoping I wasn't putting my foot in my mouth.

"Why are you Crispies so different from each other? And... well, I hate to put it like this but any of you working willingly for the IC has to be a little off specs. Sorry, but that's the best way I know of expressing it."

"It's hard to explain, Mai," Jeri said, then was silent for a moment before continuing and that only confused me more because I thought I'd offended her and she was going to clam up. But she didn't.

"Cresperians are a very, a *very* old culture," she explained. "We're slow to change even though we are heirs to a staggering amount of data accumulated through the ages. Somewhere long ago we lost most of our adventurous spirit. We only began exploring outside our own solar system a few hundred years ago, and that in a limited fashion. Up until the malfunction of our spaceship we had never run across anything even remotely like you humans. You have such an extreme range of emotions and attitudes that when we change our form and become human we necessarily take on some of the attitudes of the humans we're with.

"This is particularly true if we're limited in the amount of data we're allowed access to, which I believe was the case with Sira and the one who was working for the Chinese hegemony. We think now that a second lifeboat landed in China, and there are at least one and possibly two of us still there. Intelligence reports tell us that they weren't near the explosion that temporarily crippled their space launch capabilities. And Ishmael... by the time we rescued him—and he was the first one rescued—his thinking was somewhat warped. He's still recovering."

She paused and moved closer to Kyle. He put his arm around her and drew her close and she went on. "Until I experienced what it's like to be human, I could never have imagined the depths of emotion your species is capable of or how much your thinking is influenced by your hormones, your sexual drives and especially the way your genome is governed so heavily in its expression by the particular environment you're subjected to." She looked up at Kyle in a manner that practically shouted her love. "I was extremely fortunate to have landed almost on Kyle's doorstep and had him to guide me through the process of becoming human. He never tried to persuade me to accept a particular philosophy or belief and that allowed me to discover, that for all your faults, America is still the best place to be."

I frowned, but not because I didn't understand her explanation. It was something else. "Jeri, I guess I can accept all that, but why... I mean, what made you and the other Crispies want to become human in the first place? If you didn't know what it was going to be like in advance, weren't you taking a terrible risk of stumbling into something you didn't like? Or even detested?"

"Certainly, there was that chance, but there was a compelling factor that made most of us choose to become human. At the time none of us imagined there would be such brilliant scientists on Earth, not at first glance at your technology. And at the very first we also had no idea you had attained a technical society such a short time ago or that you were such an innovative species. Bearing all that in mind, we thought we were stranded here forever. You saw what we look like. Can you imagine us functioning in human society other than as prisoners of your governments? Or at the very most, as curiosities?"

"I guess not. But one more question, if you don't mind?"

"I don't mind, but I already know what it is. Why not change back now that we know we might be able to get home, assuming we can find it again? Isn't that it?"

"Yes," I admitted. She nailed me.

Jeri leaned into Kyle as she spoke. "I would never *want* to be a Cresperian again. Not after being human, with all that implies." She snuggled even closer to her husband.

Oh. I could easily guess why sex was part of the attraction of the Crispies to the human form, especially if their species used it only for reproduction rather than recreation like we do. Procreation comes second to enjoyment for the enlightened women of our planet. Mostly, anyway. And it's always been secondary with men.

The doorbell rang. Kyle answered it and came back with a big blond hunk who was as handsome as Adonis was said to have been. He wore a short-sleeved shirt that showed his muscular arms to advantage. Kyle led him over to me.

"Mai, this is Ishmael, one of the other Crispies working with us. Ish, Mai Li Trung. She just arrived and will be working with Jeri for a while, at least until we leave."

His grip was just firm enough. The gaze from his blue eyes was disconcerting. I felt as if I were being undressed even though he kept his eyes on my face. It was... not unpleasant, but I felt a shiver of emotion run through my body as if in preparation for a confrontation. "Hello, Ishmael. I'm glad to meet you," I said.

"Thank you. The feeling is mutual. And please call me Ish. You're very pretty—and very learned, so I hear."

"And you're very complimentary."

He smiled disarmingly. "I believe in honesty rather than flattery, much more so than most humans seem to. I was only telling the truth. I read your paper on environmental influences on the enzymatic suppression of adjacent genes. Very well thought out."

"Are you a geneticist? No, that was a silly question, wasn't it? Anyone who can alter their own bodies to the extent you and Jeri have are already far past us in genetics."

"Ah, but we do much of it instinctively rather than with true knowledge. In order for us to help the masses of your population I believe we're going to have to re-learn some of the science that goes with the art. You'll certainly be valuable in that respect if for no other reason than to point us in some directions we might not otherwise go."

"Y'all can talk shop later, Ish," Kyle said. "Is Sira going to put in an appearance?"

For some reason the last remark took most of the smile away from Ishmael's features.

"I don't know," he said, rather bluntly.

Kyle nodded and didn't carry the conversation any further. Ishmael touched his forehead with a finger, rather like a salute, and smiled at me before moving on into the room.

Jeri came up and put an arm around Kyle and nudged his shoulder with her cheek. He turned and kissed her fondly. I looked around for someone else to talk to and saw Carol ensconced in a conversation with General Shelton, the commander of The Group. He had originally said he was staying only a short time but when someone mentioned Carol, he headed straight for her. I wondered what they were talking about but didn't get a chance to ask, as he left a few minutes later and took her with him.

Kyle and Jeri embraced and kissed again right after the general and Carol left, completely unembarrassed. Kyle saw me looking their way and, perhaps by prearrangement, left Jeri and headed for another part of the room. She immediately came over to talk with me.

"I know, most couples aren't so blatantly public with their affection. We're trying to start a new trend," she said.

I laughed. "That's fine with me. Damned if I wouldn't love to have a man like Kyle. You were right when you said you were lucky. From what I've seen so far you have a real winner."

"Uh-huh. I take it you're not involved with anyone at present? No one is coming later to be with you?"

"No," I said. "The last one turned out to be traveling under false colors. Nice enough until he moved in then all of a sudden I was expected to be his personal servant. Compensation for being smarter than him, I think. He resented it."

"I'm sorry."

I shrugged. "Not your fault. I shouldn't have gotten in a hurry."

"Yes, but... well, I believe I'm more intelligent than Kyle, but he doesn't resent it. In fact, he seems... grateful? No, that's not the word. He admires my intellect and finds uses for it but manages to forget it most of the time and always when we're intimate. It makes life wonderful." She hugged herself. "I love him so much. I still don't really understand why so many couples aren't happier but I'll admit most humans are still puzzling to me."

"Join the crowd. We are a crazy, ornery species. There's usually some good even in the worst of us and some bad in the best, and all of us have our quirks."

"Yes. Each of you is so different from the rest. I believe that's part of what gives the human species so much potential. What makes you so dynamic. Once your lives are extended and the race has existed another hundred thousand years or so, you'll have the greatness of humanity spread galaxy-wide. My own opinion, I admit."

Well, she sure didn't think small!

"Tell you what, grab another drink and I'll show you our shop, as I call it. It's near here. Right now it's just me, Ishmael on a part-time basis, a microbiochemist, a physicist, plus a couple of wizard technicians. We're still missing a neurologist but so far Gene hasn't found one that's suitable."

ഇറ

Jeri's "shop" consisted of a number of rooms or bays. Some were devoted to research. There was a main computer room whose individual units were networked but, for security reasons, not connected to the internet. There was also her office, another office divided into cubicles, and a small kitchenette where individuals could get a bite to eat or something to drink at odd times during the day.

She took me to her office first. She went to the coffeepot and started it going. "The most important instrument in the shop. Stimulants like this drink I'm holding were something new to me. As Crispies, we never used them, but as a human, I think all of us will probably like coffee as much as Ishmael and I do. In fact, I believe your psychologists have missed a factor in the evolution of civilization that's obvious to me."

"Are you talking about coffee?"

"Yup. It energizes the body and stimulates original thought. Look back to the time when coffee use became widespread and cheap enough for the masses to afford in some areas, then look and see how much faster inventions and innovation occurred there. The exception is the Islamic culture. Their religion stifles originality."

I thought about it and decided Jeri had hit on a not-very-obvious truth. So little recognized, in fact, that no one ever noticed the connection between caffeine consumption and the ever-faster advance of technology. It made me wonder how many other observations that members of a different species might make about us—and vice versa. If we ever found them, that is.

There was a bit of small talk as she gave me the tour while the coffee was brewing. I was introduced to the husband and wife team of Eugene and Margie Preconder. Her doctorate was in quantum physics and Eugene was the microbiochemist, a specialty similar to one of my degrees, molecular microbiochemistry, but with subtle differences only apparent to ones who know the fields well. They were cheerful but both looked like they had been working 20-hour days for weeks on end—and later I found that that wasn't far from the truth. Jeri told me the others were off consulting with related specialists.

Back in her office, Jeri ignored the executive chair behind her desk and seated us opposite each other on the same kind of ultra-comfortable chairs I had found in my suite. She leaned back and crossed her legs while sniffing appreciatively then sipping at the rich Columbian brew. There was nothing at all wrong with her legs. If fact, if I had to bet, I thought that undressed, I wouldn't be able to find a single flaw in her body.

As if sensing my thoughts Jeri told me the story behind her appearance, making us both laugh at intervals. "Kyle had some collector issues of Playboy he had fallen heir to. When I asked him what kind of woman I should look like he told me to suit myself, but did suggest that so long as I was going to become a human woman I might as well make myself into an attractive one. With big boobs, naturally. Well, big enough."

We giggled. They certainly weren't undersized, but she was built so that she didn't appear top heavy or so large as to be freakish. Men tend to say they like large breasts, but I've noticed it's mostly talk. They really prefer well endowed but proportionally-sized women, ones like Jeri or myself.

"Anyway, that's where my body came from—straight out of the pages of an old Playboy magazine and sort of like one of Kyle's favorites. The hair color, height and weight in particular. He didn't mention my fanny so I built it to suit myself. The conversion wasn't exactly easy."

Another giggle then she became more serious. "The human genome is simpler in some ways than a Crispy's, but the genes are much more subject to environmental influences in expression, and most genes also influence expression of others. You know all that of course, but once we get you down to the quantum level you're going to be amazed at how it all ties together." She frowned. "If we can manage to do so, that is. It's a big problem. We're born with the ability as Crispies and even in human form we retain our perceptive sense. I've been able to manipulate Kyle's genome simply by being with him almost all the time, but it's still a delicate process and isn't something that can be applied generally. For instance, Kyle is much older than he looks. I've gotten his aging factors under control. He could look as young as me, but he told me to keep his appearance at the late twenties in order to avoid complications."

"You better know it!" I exclaimed. I was both enthralled and concerned. "God, Jeri, if the public ever becomes aware you can control the aging process, even individually, the whole world will turn upside down! Everyone over 50 would be after you, and I *don't* mean just to talk. They'd do damn near anything for the secret, even if you told them there wasn't one."

"So Kyle told me. Even here, hardly anyone knows about it. I'm telling you only because that's going to be one of your main projects, doing research on how to apply it generally rather than specifically as I've done with Kyle."

I didn't know what to say to that. Research into the aging process was well-funded by the big pharmaceutical companies, but their results so far were more propaganda than solid data. And a lot of the so-called anti-aging developments were purely cosmetic, designed to appeal to women. The National Science Foundation had rather heavier going. Funding was held back by a few fundamentalist religious groups touting the Bible's "four score and ten" as the ordained age for all of us. I would be willing to bet that most women would forget their religious teaching in a heartbeat should they have a method of halting or reversing the aging process. The way our species has evolved, physical appearance, particularly for women, means much more than brains in the genetic competition.

Jeri misinterpreted my befuddled expression. "Don't look so confounded, Mai. I believe it's possible to achieve but there are limits to the time we've been able to devote to it what with getting the ship and crew ready to go. That's always been the top priority. I don't want to even think of what might happen should the Chinese or ICs find our home before we do."

I didn't want to think about that, either. A load of Americans descending on Cresperia would cause upset enough, but if China or the IC made it there first… it would be the mother of all cultural conflicts.

Jeri showed me a few other things around the shop then we wandered back to the party. It was still in full swing. I wound up talking to Ishmael some more. He was polite but I could see the interest in his eyes. I couldn't help but wonder what it would be like to make love with him. I didn't know whether I would be able to put the image of what he'd looked like before converting to human out of my mind or not. It was probably academic though. There was something about him that put me off stride and I had no intention of becoming anything more than friends with him until I discovered what it was.

General Haley had Kyle cornered in a little alcove but when he saw Ishmael leave me to go talk to a tall brunette I hadn't met yet, he motioned me over. I hadn't really talked to the general. In fact, I didn't know what his position was.

"Mai, I think I'm a bad host," Kyle said. "I never did formally introduce you to General Sam Haley. And Sam, you know Mai will be working at Jeri's place, don't you?"

"I do now. Sometimes I think people quit telling me things officially once they put that star on my shoulder. I have to find out what's going on through gossip or at parties. Not that we've had much time for that."

"I'm glad you took time, General," I said. "It's been fun meeting all these people, although I haven't gotten everyone sorted out yet as to what they do. You, for instance. How come two generals in such a small place?"

"Right to the point, huh? Well, I won't be around much longer. As soon as the Crispies and engineers tell us the big ship is safe, we're gone. In the meantime, I haven't much to do except shuffle papers and talk to new recruits." He grinned wryly. "It's pretty hard to plan what you're going to be doing on other planets until you arrive and see what's waiting for you. Other than the Cresperian home planet, of course. We have a couple of diplomats along in case we get lucky enough to find it."

"Sam will be vice captain of the ship on its first expedition," Kyle told me with a wink. "He's all the time dragging me along on crazy missions."

"Actually just the opposite, Mai. Kyle got me into this mess to begin with."

"You two go back a ways, I take it?" I could see the easy familiarity between the two, and Kyle had called him 'Sam.' They would almost have to be old friends, a general and a warrant officer being that close.

"We certainly do. I had a nice peaceful job doing next to nothing, then one day I get this call from my buddy here and it's been nothing but trouble ever since."

"You wouldn't have missed it for anything, you old fake," Kyle said, grinning.

He laughed easily. "You're right, but I'm ready for something new. Two generals in a place this small is one too many."

"I wish I were going with you," I said wistfully.

"Patience. Most of the people we're recruiting are ones who we hope will eventually man our ships."

"I'd like that," I said simply. "Now, I want to ask you a question and hope security won't prevent you from answering it."

"You can always ask."

"Why was the plane I was in shot at? Surely I'm not that important to terrorists."

"I wondered when you'd bring that up. Some bright paper shuffler near the top of the Intel heap got the idea to provide a leak that the plane you were on was carrying a Crispy. They were hoping that once we took out the bad guys that shot at us they'd think they killed Ishmael, especially since we provided a plane that actually did go down. I would have stopped it had I known, or tried to anyway. It was a harebrained idea to begin with and you're damn lucky you weren't shot down. Thing is, the group that popped that missile turned out to be a cell we didn't even know about and the intentional leak told them someone on the plane was important, maybe even a Crispy. You can see from that how serious this underground war is, though. And now that it's over and you're safe, I'll have to admit the bad guys might have been thrown off course and we picked up some bad guys we otherwise wouldn't have known about."

I didn't comment, but the general had just told me we were fighting a war. Undeclared, but a war all the same.

೫)೦೪

As time passed, I learned just how vicious and dangerous the fight to control Crispies and their technology was. Neither of them told me but I found out later from sources here and there that Kyle and Jeri had flown the first test model FTL ship from desperation rather than choice. And it was from China, not one of our spaceports, and it crashed coming back to Earth in America, damn near killing them both.

That happened when a team including them had infiltrated into China in an attempt to bring out a Crispy by any means possible whether it wanted to come or not. It didn't, or rather he didn't because the Crispy had converted to a human male by the time they arrived and he had gone way around the bend. He called himself Lau and was intending to pilot himself back to Cresperia while leaving the Chinese with plans for more starships.

Just to prove he was nuts, he'd made a gross error in both ships. The one Kyle and Jeri stole malfunctioned in orbit and they had to get back in a reentry capsule that wasn't well designed, causing them to crash. The other caused a giant explosion that wiped out the Chinese space launch facility and everything around it when it was tested.

They also didn't mention how close they both came to buying the farm while making another rescue attempt in Iran, successfully that time. Nice introduction to the human species, huh?

CHAPTER TEN

WORKING WITH JERI was an education in itself. For one thing, she didn't always think or act like a woman. Having been human for less than a year she was still learning the nuances, the little intricacies of interpersonal relationships that make social interactions work. Even wearing her wedding ring, she got propositioned occasionally by newcomers to the enclave, men who thought they just had to try to seduce any good-looking woman they met. She still had problems coping with approaches like that.

I learned that her perceptive sense allowed her to gauge other people's attitudes. She had to be careful about when to use it, or she would have soon been accused of mind reading, something normal humans simply wouldn't stand for—not unless everyone could do it, and even then I had my doubts about its value.

I watched her a few days later as I was leaving the cafeteria. I was lagging behind her after stopping to answer a question from someone I'd met earlier. While she was waiting for me to catch up, she was approached by a man I hadn't seen before. He came over to her and began talking. I saw her flash her ring, but it didn't even slow him down. Then she leaned close to his ear and whispered something that caused him to blush a violent red. He stuttered and left, walking quickly.

"What did you tell him?" I asked when we resumed walking together. I was curious over what could have caused such a peculiar reaction.

"I told him men who talk too much are usually compensating for a small dick."

I practically choked while trying to keep from laughing. When I could speak, I asked, "Was he?"

"Was he what?"

"Small." She had implied she could see beyond our clothes when telling me of how she had stopped the aging process in Kyle.

"Small enough that I doubt he'll bother me again," she said with a chuckle, "but I shouldn't have looked. Now I'll have to ask Gene to make sure our paths don't cross often. Damn. I never know how to handle those kinds of advances."

"Who was he? Do you know?"

"A new technician in the propulsion section. I think someone goofed when they recruited him but we can't throw the errors back because of security concerns."

I could see the problem. What did they do with employees who became dissatisfied? They certainly couldn't be returned to the general population with what they knew. I decided not to ask. If you don't want to know the answer sometimes that's the best idea.

⁋Cγ

Carol was waiting on us when we returned to the office. I hadn't seen her since the party and that was days ago. Neither had she been in her room the several times I'd checked. But here she was now, all smiles. We hugged briefly then she told us what she'd been doing.

"Cherry, I'm really sorry but I'm not going to be working for you any longer. Gene told me I was needed more in headquarters than here. After I spent a day or two observing operations there I had to agree with him." She twisted her lips in a caricature of a smile and shook her head disparagingly. "They've been so devoted to recruiting scientists and putting them to work while maintaining the tightest security since the Manhattan Project that no one was paying much attention to organizational efficiency. After I pointed out a few obvious bottlenecks to the manager he took me straight in to see General Shelton and he grabbed me."

"Wow. The girl moves in high circles already. Can I touch you?"

General Shelton had the type of leadership quality that made him a presence everywhere, whether he was there in person or not. I had already learned a lot about the man from listening to others talk about him. So far I hadn't heard a single word of dissent concerning the way he ran the place, even when the rapid buildup of personnel caused the inevitable bumps and log jams in procurement, personnel and most importantly the R&D on the FTL ships. Problems were compounded by the fact that the ships were being built in separate spots and far away from the enclave.

"Sure. Touch me now, because you probably won't be seeing much of me." She laughed merrily. "I even had to move my quarters so I'd be close to the general. That's why you haven't seen me in my room."

Things did move fast here, bottlenecks or not. I had been looking forward to having Carol with me but for the time being I probably wouldn't miss her—I probably wouldn't have time to miss her. Almost all of my work at first consisted of reading and studying the notes Jeri was going to leave behind for me and listening to her explain some of the more difficult parts. Except it was all difficult.

Carol and I reminisced for a few minutes, then she said, "I've got to scoot. The general will have my hide if I'm late. Oh, guess what? Roy asked to see me when he gets back if we ever have any time off together!" She waved and was gone.

I wished her luck. At first sight, Roy Jenkins had impressed me, too. However, it seemed that the man preferred blondes. Drat. I wondered idly what sort of women appealed to Ishmael. He was a hunk, no doubt about that; but a little too... self-confident? Something.

After she left I went back to my studies while Jeri worked on a contraption she thought might help humans tap into the quantum foam the way Crispies did. It couldn't ever be exactly the same way, because Jeri and the other Crispies retained a core of their previous identity and genome that allowed them to use their perceptive powers even in a human body. Or as a human, I should say. Whatever.

On an x-ray it would look like a very dense tumor about the size of an orange, nestled in the mid portion of their bodies back near the spine. It tapped into the spinal cord and thus the entire nervous system. Jeri was attempting to design an inorganic replica of the part of their organic core dealing with the perceptive sense that could be implanted into humans to give them at least some of the same powers.

She had no idea so far whether such a long shot would work or not and time was running out. She and Kyle would be leaving soon. In any case, Jeri said she doubted the non-organic gadget would ever allow humans to achieve a perceptive sense anywhere near as functional as the ones the Crispies had designed into their bodies untold ages ago, so far in their past they had forgotten how it happened. And simply duplicating their core and sticking it in a human wouldn't work, because it also contained parts of their very personality that were so inextricably entangled that they couldn't be separated from it. Trying to would cause the whole thing to malfunction in unpredictable and probably lethal ways.

It's a good thing I had taken some extra courses in electronics. I could read an ultra-fine circuit diagram in three dimensions if I had to, especially the parts dealing with quantum factors.

But when I first looked at the spaghetti tangle Jeri was playing with, I almost quit. It was the most complicated maze I'd ever seen outside of a high-end physics research lab. If it turned out the way she hoped, she told me, it could be redesigned as a solid circuit interactive chip and mass produced, but first it had to be proven and she was a long way from that stage.

After skimming over her notes and all her previous work, I backed up and started from the beginning again and went through it much more slowly. There was a whale of a lot of it and I kept running into a problem with some of her assumptions and equations dealing with the genetic transformation of Crispies to humans. I spent a solid month reviewing and studying and going back over it before admitting I needed more help from Jeri.

At first I had thought the problem was that they were so far ahead of us technologically that I wasn't grasping it, but I think I've made it plain that I'm no moron myself. I finally decided that wasn't what was wrong. I hadn't seen Jeri lately but assumed she was getting ready for her trip. I rang her apartment but got no answer there either, so I went back to the drawing board.

Two weeks later I was still bogged down and still hadn't seen Jeri despite repeated calls, all answered the same way: Jeri was "temporarily unavailable." Nevertheless, I needed her help to sort out my problem before I went any further. In fact, I didn't want to talk to anyone else *but* Jeri because if I was wrong I'd look as stupid as one of Santa's elves showing up in July. But if I was right… then we had other problems. Big ones.

I sent word to headquarters that I needed to talk to Jeri whenever she could break loose and put an urgent tag to the request. Carol called me back.

I brightened when I saw her face. I hadn't seen a lot of her, either. She had told me when I met her once for a hurried lunch that Roy had returned and she thought she was in love.

"Hi girlfriend," I said. "How goes it working for the general? And how's your marine?"

"Torrid. Sorry I haven't had a chance to talk lately, but with the ship getting ready for launch I haven't had time to turn around and neither has General Shelton."

"How about Jeri? Can I borrow her for a day?"

"Problems?"

"Big ones. Maybe."

"Anything I can do?"

"Sorry, Carol but I better talk to her first."

I heard her sigh. "No can do. This isn't for publication, but she and Kyle are together in New Mexico, troubleshooting a problem with the FTL ship. The general won't allow any communication unless it directly involves the space ship and the timetable for launch."

Now it was my turn to sigh. What to do? The problem didn't involve the ship, per se, but… damn. I needed to think before I upset a bunch of apple carts.

"Okay. Tell you what, would you call me the instant Jeri's back in the enclave? I don't care what time it is, just call."

"That much I can do if I can keep my head on straight. I told you Roy was back from training and such time as I've had to spare… well, you know how that goes."

Indeed I did, and only wished I'd met someone as compatible as Carol apparently was with the big marine. So far the men I'd run across were mostly married. The others, for one reason or another, were all lacking that certain something. I could always tell. If I felt a little tingle from my nipples I was willing to explore the possibility of a relationship. Otherwise, nothing doing. Call me picky, but I like to at least start with what appears to be a compatible man. Given my luck so far though, I was about ready to turn my romantic endeavors over to a matchmaker and be done with it. However, I doubted there was one of those in The Group.

Amoebas have it lucky. No males, no females, just split in two when they feel like reproducing.

"Okay, I guess that'll have to do," I told Carol. "Just be sure and call soon as she's back."

"Will do. Hey, did you hear? They named the first ship!"

"Oh yeah? What's it called?"

"How about USSS *Zeng Wu?*"

"USS… S?"

"United States Space Ship."

"Oh. Hmm. It fits, I guess." I'd heard how both those men died while helping Jeri and Kyle escape from China in that experimental space ship, which we'd based our own designs on. "Thanks. Later."

I killed the connection, then stood there in the little alcove I was calling an office where I did my searches, formulated algorithms and also carried out my preliminary design work on a computer before running experiments. Most of the time I had to run simulations for lack of equipment that hadn't arrived yet or hadn't been assembled—or more often hadn't even been designed.

"Damn!" I said out loud, an idle oath directed at nothing and no one in particular.

"Is there a difficulty?"

I recognized the voice even before turning around. It was Ishmael, speaking in his pleasantly deep bass, purposely selected to sound commanding, I thought.

"Hello, Ish. Yes, I have a problem, but it's not one that you can help with."

"Are you certain? Since Jeri isn't here, perhaps I could be of assistance if it's anything related to Cresperian modalities."

Huh? Modalities? Such big words he used. "Um, no, I don't think this is anything you can help me with, Ish. Thanks anyway."

"All right then. Perhaps you're in need of some relaxation. Frequently getting away from a problem for a little while allows a person to see it in a new light."

He could be right at that. At least rumor had him doing a lot of relaxing of the horizontal nature—but not sleeping, if you get the drift. I gazed at his movie star-handsome face and well toned body, just muscular enough to be attractive but not overdone. Maybe that was the problem I found with him. He appeared to have done everything in the book to make himself as perfect as possible. Not just good, perfect.

On the other hand, there was my research that indicated he might be… the hell with it. I was tired of analyzing every item in the universe.

"Maybe I do need to get away. Let's go have a drink. I've been here twelve hours today and haven't accomplished a thing."

"Good."

I swung by the front office slash lounge for my section to tell whoever was there that I was going, and found that Eugene and Margie Preconder had already left for the day, too. In fact, everyone had. I picked up my purse from my desk drawer and we headed back toward family quarters. There was a dayroom of sorts where you could get drinks and sit and talk or play computer or board games right near the quarters. However, I steered him toward my apartment and at the same time wondered why I was doing it.

From the gossip Jeri and Carol had passed on to me before they both became so preoccupied, it wasn't at all unusual for him to visit single females in their rooms or vice versa. Not that there was anything wrong with it, but I wasn't looking for a casual fling. I just needed a little company, preferably male, and he was handy. So far as anyone knew he hadn't formed any permanent attachments so I wasn't twisting anyone else's panties by going with him.

Oh hell, let's admit it. I was horny and had begun thinking about him in the sense of getting laid, although I certainly didn't intend to that day, especially when my research was indicating there might be problems. Besides, I wanted to get to know the newly minted man a little better before allowing anything like that to happen. If I did at all.

After we were seated, I asked a leading question. "Ish, have you applied to go out on the next ship?"

"No." He shrugged disarmingly and smiled. "I have no desire to be cooped up in a space that small for months on end."

"I take it the Crispy ship was very large then?"

"Oh yes, a small city in essence. Exploration ventures were designed to be gone from the home planet for years, decades. There had to be room for everyone to continue studies in their specialties and room to interact without overly intruding into perceptive groups not your own."

"Groups?"

"One of our social—sociological I could say—methods of integrating memories into modular archives each of us could access. It was one of many methods used to keep individuals from becoming overloaded with data. Without possessing a perceptive sense it's rather hard to explain."

"I should think so," I mused, sipping at my whisky and water. "It must be wonderful."

"It's as natural to us as breathing, so I can't judge it in that sense. I understand Jeri is attempting to devise an instrument to give humans at least a touch of the perceptive ability."

"Yes, but she's not making much progress. How goes your work?"

"I've about finished what the humans brought me here for, helping with the design of FTL ships. The model captured from the Chinese was all that was needed to complete it, or I should say Jeri's memory of it. The ship itself was destroyed and they came home in a reentry capsule."

I picked up on the odd way he'd referred to us. "Ish, you said, 'the humans,' as if you're removed from them. But *you're* a human now, in case you haven't noticed."

"Oh, yes I am," he said and shrugged negligently. "I wouldn't go back to being a Crispy, but I still feel as if that's my species. Unlike Jeri, who seems to have gone further in identifying with humans than I have. Perhaps in time I'll feel differently."

"Hmm. I haven't heard Jeri talk like that."

"We're individuals, just as you are."

"I guess so. Another drink?"

"Not just now." He slipped an arm around my shoulders.

Oh, well. Test the waters, I thought. I tilted my head back and our lips touched. I have to admit he did it well. I could feel my body responding but I wasn't sure whether it was because of him or because it had been so long.

Suddenly I found myself with my blouse unbuttoned. His hand was inside it and he was caressing my breasts. Curiously, I had no thoughts of anything leading up to that point. The last I remembered we were kissing—and still were—but I had no memory of anything in between.

Suddenly I found myself with my blouse completely gone and he was moving his hand down toward my thighs while he was kissing me but curiously, I had no remembrance of how it had happened so fast.

Jeri! I remembered her telling me how she had removed short-term memories a couple of times while she and Kyle were on the run. I twisted my body and broke from his embrace.

"Get out!" I said forcefully, feeling my gorge rise. I grabbed for my blouse which he had discarded and held it in front of me.

And suddenly I was alone again, wondering what had happened. Where was Ish? The last I remembered he was kissing me. And why was my blouse off?

Jeri! I remembered her telling me how she had removed short-term memories of people a couple of times while she and Kyle were on the run. God damn him, he must have done it to me! The son of a bitch! No wonder his seductions had been so successful!

CHAPTER ELEVEN

JERI HAD ALSO TOLD ME she thought that if a person realized a short-term memory had been diffused, and if they concentrated hard enough soon enough, they could recover the memory, but that most people would never notice it. I wouldn't have if I hadn't talked to Jeri.

I did my best, screwing up my face in concentration, probably making me look like I was in pain even while I felt sick at my stomach over what Ishmael had done. Must have done, damn him. And Jeri was right. Sure enough, a few minutes of intense thought and the whole sequence gradually began coming back; me saying "no" repeatedly, him wiping the memory and proceeding a bit further and doing it all over again.

Damn him! I wasn't going to stand for this, Crispy or no Crispy. I didn't give a shit how important to our space flight efforts he might be. I wanted him drawn and quartered, but first someone needed to know the kind of shit he was pulling, right away. I couldn't think of a better person than the commander of the whole shebang, General Shelton.

I called Carol at headquarters but she was already gone, which meant the general was, too. She wouldn't have left before him. Well, it could wait for morning, I thought. I had a couple more stiff drinks while I ran the scenario over and over again in my mind. It took me a long time to calm down but finally a bite to eat and a long shower did it. I had a hard time getting to sleep that night even though I locked my door for the first time since arriving at the Brider Enclave.

While I was lying awake I began going over my research in my mind. What Ish had tried to do certainly helped confirm the problem I thought I'd discovered.

৪৩০৪

"Let me get this straight. You're accusing Ishmael of using his perceptive powers on you by removing your short-term memory in an attempt to seduce you?"

General Shelton's face was grim but troubled, as if he didn't want to believe me. I knew what his problem must be. Any Crispy was so highly valued for its knowledge that it would be hard to crack down on one. Some commanders probably wouldn't have, but Shelton didn't strike me as that type.

"That's not all, sir. My research is indicating that we may have problems with any Cresperian who converts to male rather than female. It has to do with the Y chromosome and will tend to make them unstable unless positive environmental influences are provided early and often, during and after the conversion process. And even then, the possibility will remain. That's if I'm right, of course. You can't make a call like that on the basis of one example like Ishmael."

"*Lau!*" He practically shouted the word as his expression suddenly became animated with an epiphany I didn't understand.

"Sir?"

"Lau," he repeated. He shook his head, as if in disgust. "That was the name the Crispy in China who became a male took. He turned out to be a fanatic in some sort of philosophy he got hold of and… never mind. Are you certain of your research?"

I was honest. "No, sir, I'm not absolutely certain, but I've been going over and over it and can't find any flaws. I've been trying to contact Jeri Leverson for weeks so I could get her to look at it. I had intended to make an appointment with you if Jeri didn't return soon, though. I think it's important."

"You'll play hell seeing her now," he said with an ironic laugh. "Her and some others' absences have been disguised by security as troubleshooting on the FTL ship but it was actually their final prep for the voyage. The *Zeng Wu* left the solar system yesterday and probably won't be back for six months at least, and possibly as long as two years. That's how long we've given them to find the Cresperian system, or come back if they haven't. They'll have to find some compatible foodstuff to stay gone two years, though." He thought for a moment. "Damn. Carol, is there another geneticist in The Group who can confirm Mai's work?"

Carol had been sitting in on the conference at my request although she might have been there anyway. I wasn't familiar with how she and the general worked together.

"Not of her caliber, sir, and I don't say that just because we've worked together before. Mai is in a class all by herself."

General Shelton's face firmed. "All right, but we still need to get to the bottom of this. Carol, see if you can find Ishmael and have him report here immediately. We'll see what he has to say about his misbehavior and Mai's theory at the same time. And…" he debated something internally then made up his mind. "Let's record the conversation just in case he tries to wipe *our* memories. Can you do that without him knowing, Carol?"

"Yes, sir, as long as he's not aware of it."

"Do it, then."

But it was too late. Ishmael had already flown the coop during the night, using his ability to remove short-term memory to get past the guards and his perceptive ability to disable part of the security system and steal an automobile. It could have been set up to stymie even a Crispy's abilities but no one had thought one of them might want to leave. Besides, the security system had been designed to keep bad guys out, not good guys in. Until I upset the buggy, Ishmael had been considered a good guy.

I waited in the general's office until we were sure he was gone, then I decided I had done all the damage I wanted to for one day. I asked if I could go. General Shelton nodded absentmindedly and I left him sitting there, undoubtedly running over different options in his mind before acting.

Or so I thought. Later that day I was called back to his office. Carol smiled when she saw me.

"Go on in, Mai. He's expecting you."

"Thanks." I tapped on the door to the office then pushed it open. I was surprised to see our other Crispy, Sira, in with him. She was the one who'd been in the hands of the Islamic Confederation, been snatched from their grasp and brought back here. Jeri told me she'd been reluctant to convert to human form after her experiences with the Muslims, but had changed her mind after talking to Jeri. Apparently she had adapted well.

I'd met her a few times but our work didn't coincide that much so we weren't well acquainted. From what I knew of her she was smart but not nearly as open and outgoing as Jeri. In fact she seemed rather lost the few times I'd talked with her. That tied in with another part of my theories, too, that I hadn't mentioned to anyone yet. I had wanted to run it by Jeri first. Too late now.

"Hello Sira. It's good to see you again." I gave her my best smile.

"Thank you, Mai. Jeri always spoke well of you whenever we talked."

"That's always nice to hear." I smiled again and then saw that General Shelton was impatient. I turned to look at him.

"Sira said she'd be glad to go over your work with you if you'd like." It was put that way as a suggestion but his tone told me it was more of a command. "We need to have it either proven or disproven as rapidly as possible. Do you think she could help?"

"I believe she might, sir."

Why not? It was the notion of them being able to tap into the quantum foam with their perceptive sense that was giving me trouble. I couldn't do it, and without one of them to verify some of my equations, I wasn't able to tell if I was right or way off base.

"How long?"

Hell, I didn't know. That depended entirely on Sira.

"I don't know, General Shelton. I'll work as fast as possible consistent with avoiding errors and that's all anyone can do. Is there a reason for the great rush now that the barn door is already open, so to speak?"

"Damn right there is!" His strong countenance appeared worried for the first time since I'd met him. "Look, we've sent a FTL ship out to look for the Cresperian home planet and now it turns out that we may have gotten it off under false assumptions. God only knows what harm another mad hatter like Lau could cause on their home planet. There are other factors involved that you haven't heard about or shouldn't have. India is building a ship too, and is close to launching it if our intelligence is correct. We haven't been able to find out whether their Crispy—or Crispies—have converted to male or female but they'll sooner or later run into the same situation as us if you're right. We have plans for working with other Crispies as quickly as we can locate them, if we can, or convince the U.K. to send their Crispy here. I want to be damn sure we know what we're doing next time, especially if Intel knows what it's talking about and there are others at large."

"Well, certainly, sir, but—"

He cut me off. "You need to have Sira verify your work, and even if she can't, you're going to have to turn it over to her and another genetics team in the near future anyway."

"Why is that, sir?"

"Isn't it obvious? Well, no, I guess it wouldn't be to you. See, the first ship is not only looking for Cresperia, the planet, they're on a voyage of exploration as well. Their itinerary is pretty well set for the first part of the trip but after that it's just a search in a very large area of space with not much chance of finding the Crispy planet, not so soon. We're working on the location from very little hard data because none of their navigators survived. But just on the chance, we need to try to catch the first ship before it leaves the last star system on its list and have your data passed on to them by a person who thoroughly understands it. It would be a disaster if a lot of Cresperians converted to male humans, then became nutty, like Ishmael or Lau. Of course Ish got off to a bad start but still..."

"I see what you mean, sir. I worked closely with Jeri during the first part of my research. Sh—shucks. She's the one I wish I could talk with."

"Well, you may get your wish if the second ship finds them before they go into the search pattern in the area where we think the Cresperian planet is. You're going to be on the ship that's going to be looking for the one Jeri is on. That is, if you volunteer." He looked at me closely, trying to gauge my expression.

It couldn't have been hard, not with that silly grin on my face. I was going!

৪৩শ্ব

It wasn't all that simple, of course. The first thing I had to do was take a refresher course in small arms and small-unit tactics at one of the isolated training facilities in northern Georgia, one where the SFR had sent the scientists and non-military people who left on the first ship. General Shelton wasn't allowing any civilians to venture into unknown environments unless they had the training to provide backup for the military contingents on each ship. Those who had no former military training had to take four weeks of quickie basic training followed by the two-week course at the same camp I was being sent to.

For me and other ex-military it would just be one week for the small arms refresher course and one week for tactics. But before leaving, I had to work with Sira on my theories to see if she could validate them. After returning, I'd have an estimated departure time only a couple of weeks afterward! The general was pushing hard to have the second ship ready by then.

CHAPTER TWELVE

TWO DAYS BEFORE LEAVING for the refresher courses, I was sitting in my office with Sira, talking about what we'd done together. She didn't exactly confirm my theories of unforeseen trouble with the Y chromosome but she could find nothing to disprove them, either.

As she put it, "I think Jeri is really the person you should be asking, but of course that's impossible. I can't find any flaws in your work, but that doesn't mean there aren't any. You see, I'm not the mathematician she is. That was her specialty and she is extremely intelligent as well. More so than me, I'm afraid. She may not have said anything to you, but the crew of our ship had a great deal of respect for her despite her youth. She was an exceptional person among Cresperians just as she is proving to be as a human. Even with our history of manipulating our genetic structure, we still have a great variety among our people, purposely so, in order to keep our society stable."

"It would seem to me that so much variety would tend to destabilize it over the long term, or am I missing something?"

"Remember, we don't have sexual forces at work as humans do and either we eliminated the territorial aspect of our species or it was never there to begin with. A variety among individuals is all that keeps us from complete stagnation and eventually dying out as a species."

"Hmm. Yeah, I guess I can see that. What bothers me is why Jeri didn't pick up on the sexual aspect of the conversion in relation to the Y chromosome when she changed to become human."

"Now that I can answer, I think," she said confidently. "By the time she began to think about such matters, she was already a human female with the female hormones dominant. She had made a successful conversion and really saw no reason to look into it then, nor even later after meeting Lau. She attributed his failings to the influence of his Chinese handlers. Her attitude of thinking all was well was probably reinforced by Ishmael since on the surface he appeared to have become a normal male despite having undergone torture. She thought perhaps he was a bit too promiscuous sexually but believed he would settle down when he met the right woman."

Uh-huh. Jeri had told me more or less the same thing. She thought he was as normal a human as a Crispy could ever be, given that they kept their previous knowledge and perceptive powers.

"How about that Lau Crispy General Shelton was talking about? Tell me more about him."

"I don't know too much about him. Jeri was devastated by that mission, especially when she had to kill him. She never talked about it much."

"I can vouch for that. She hardly ever mentioned the mission, secrecy aside."

"On the other hand, I do know a little about the other survivor who landed with me. He decided early on to convert to a man after learning how females are treated in the IC."

"Wait a minute. Other one? That's the first I've heard about another Crispy in the lifeboat with you."

"Well... no, I suppose I haven't mentioned it to anyone. We... were rather at odds about our situation and..." Her voice trailed off as she saw me reach for the phone.

"Mai, what's wrong? Did I—?"

I waved a hand at her to wait while I got through to headquarters. "Carol? I have what may be a piece of news the big boys haven't heard of yet. Do you know whether or not the general knows that there was another Crispy in Libya with Sira?"

I waited impatiently while she talked to General Shelton, then when she came back to the phone all she said was, "Get over here quick and bring Sira with you!"

ಜುಗ

I guess by then I was getting a reputation for upsetting apple carts. Sure enough, not a single soul knew of the other Crispy. I could see the general holding back an angry outburst at Sira after we arrived, the last thing he wanted to do. She was already upset over failing to tell us something that might impinge on the safety of the whole Group—or the nation, even. I guess he knew she was feeling very contrite when he saw her expression because he contained his anger and spoke softly.

"Sira, didn't you know or at least suspect that the presence of another Crispy under the control of the IC would be of utmost concern to us, especially considering the lengths we went to in order to pull you out of that situation in Libya?"

"I thought you knew. Otherwise, how did you know how to find me? Besides, events were very confusing at that time, going from a prisoner to a respected guest. And the rescue was kind of... filled with action that happened so fast and furiously I had trouble keeping up with everything that was going on, much less worrying over my companion whom I hadn't seen for weeks. Also, the debriefing from your intelligence section while I was also concentrating on converting to human form wasn't conducive to coherent thought. Remember, my conversion went very fast compared to Ishmael and especially to Jeri. Afterwards no one from Intelligence followed up and I thought no more about it."

It made sense, I guess, but that didn't help matters.

"All right," he said. "It's done and as much our fault as yours. Someone dropped the ball by not talking to you at more length, but I should have picked up on it, so I'll take the blame. However, let's see what we can find out now. Sira, would you mind talking to our intelligence staff again and describe the first part of your, uh, captivity?"

She gave the general a wry smile. "It wasn't a captivity at first, General, as I told your people to begin with. After our lifeboat came down near a military post, soldiers surrounded us quickly and we went freely with them. There wasn't much else to do. And then it wasn't more than a few minutes afterward that our survival packets were taken and we were separated from each other. I thought at first it was simply for transportation purposes but I never saw Frstiminith again. After a while I quit asking. That was after I learned Arabic, of course. Then after staying there a few weeks I was moved in great secrecy but it wasn't secret enough, obviously, since you found me. Sooner or later I would have escaped on my own but I was waiting until I had more knowledge of human affairs and other societies. I didn't care for the Muslims."

"We don't care too much for them these days either, Sira. I still don't see how Intelligence missed knowing you had a companion during the first part of your captivity, though." He shook his head ruefully. I knew some analysts were probably going to be skinned alive before he was through with them. "Be that as it may, sometimes the littlest thing can yield a lot of information of a useful nature. So if you don't mind...?"

"General, please wait a moment."

"What is it, Mai?"

"There's some more of my research that might be important which I haven't told you about yet. I need to talk to Sira some more about it, since

Jeri is already gone. And I'm scheduled to leave for the refresher course in just two more days." I guess my expression gave away the fact that I was on the verge of tipping another apple cart.

"I can tell by looking at you that it's not going to be good news, either. Is it important enough to delay her talking to the intelligence branch?"

Sira interrupted. "I can go without sleep for quite a while, General Shelton."

"Okay. Go with Mai, then report to Intelligence tomorrow morning. They're still housed in the same place. Do you remember where?"

"Of course."

"Right. You don't forget much even as humans, do you? Okay, that'll work. Mai, you come see me before you leave and tell me what else you've found out, hear?" He looked as if he'd like to just forget I'd said anything if that were possible. I couldn't blame him. I had dumped a wagonload or two of apples in his lap already.

"Yes, sir. I will."

As we left, Carol had lost her usual smile, Sira was looking embarrassed, the general looked dour and I wasn't all that happy with matters myself.

ಬಂಡ

Sira and I stopped for a hurried lunch then headed for my office again. Once there, I got some fresh coffee going. We settled into the comfortable chairs and I began discussing the other matter I'd discovered. Or thought I had.

"Sira, I don't think you ought to talk about what I'm going to tell you to anyone else without permission. It's not really a life and death matter but it can have very important repercussions in the future if we do find your planet again."

"That's if the big ships work as well as the model. We won't know until one of them comes back."

"Well, yes. And if we find some more of your comrades here on Earth it could be very important." I glanced over at the pot and saw it was ready. "Coffee?"

"Please."

I poured for both of us and we settled back in our chairs. I gazed at her there, a small pretty young woman with strawberry blonde hair and a hint of dimples. She didn't look a day over 18 in her slim-fit slacks and simple pullover with her hair gathered loosely behind her neck with a wide ribbon. It was hard to picture her as the 200-year-old alien she was.

I had to begin somewhere so I just put it to her bluntly. "Sira, are you happy here?"

She smiled wryly. "You've noticed, have you?"

"Well... maybe it's just the contrast with Jeri. She's such a bright, sweet character and so much in love with Kyle and yet so smart she scares me sometimes. Much smarter than him but it doesn't seem to matter. She's outgoing, too, what we call an extrovert. On the other hand, you're so quiet one would hardly know you're around sometimes. And you don't talk much."

"That's true. And you're right. I can't say I'm really unhappy but... well, take sex. Sure, it's wonderful, something we never imagined as Crispies. But it's so complicated!"

I almost laughed out loud at her expression. It was one just about every woman in the world is prone to on occasion. Somehow I held it in and nodded for her to continue.

"I was with a man after I'd been here several weeks. I really liked him and thought he cared for me but it turned out he just wanted the novelty of going to bed with an alien. The next man was nice at first but then became possessive and tried to dominate me. And the third—I should have learned to be careful by then, but I didn't know he was married, damn him. I was hurt each time and I don't mind admitting it to you. And yet Jeri and Kyle are so happy it's scary, to use your term."

"How about your work? Is it satisfying?"

"Somewhat, but unlike Ish and Jeri, there's nothing I'm doing here that's even remotely like my specialty as a Crispy. It would be hard to even describe it to you since it involved perceptive abilities. I was helping with the FTL research but that's about done for now. I'd really like to travel and learn more about America but I know that's impossible."

Not necessarily, I thought darkly. Ishmael is managing it.

But I didn't say that. "Is there anything I can do?"

"Perhaps." She smiled at me like a small, bashful child. "Your knowledge and research in genetics is fascinating even though we grow up knowing much of our own instinctively. I wouldn't mind doing that, working with you and carrying on your research."

"I'll be leaving."

"I know, but you'll be replaced. If you could leave me all your notes and give me some direction... well, you know how fast we learn, even as humans. I'm not as smart as Jeri, but I could do it. And I could be very helpful to your replacement."

"We'll have to ask the general." I made a note to myself to see if I could remember someone, a single male geneticist who might be willing to leave the outside world for a while. Little old matchmaker me. In the meantime...

"But forget the general for the moment. I'm glad you talked to me so frankly, Sira. Now as I said, I'm going to trust you with something that shouldn't become general knowledge. It would hurt some feelings and cause resentment in others. You said you're not entirely happy and I think I know why. The same parameters I used that pointed me toward the Y chromosome as a potential source of trouble also made me look at some other areas where difficulties might arise in the conversion from Crispy to human and I think I've discovered some. In short, I believe you went too fast in becoming human."

"Converted too quickly?"

"Yes, that's it exactly. Remember, my specialty, or one of them, is environmental genetics, how the environment affects genes and their expression. Jeri took it slow and easy and look at the results she got."

She frowned, thinking deep thoughts, maybe even calling on that core of her Crispy self still buried within her. "Surely that's not all?"

She might not be as smart as Jeri but she hadn't fallen off any hay wagon lately either.

"No, it isn't. I was involved quite a lot with Kyle and Jeri right after I got here. What do you think of him?"

She dimpled. "Would that I'd seen him first!"

I laughed. "Me, too, for that matter, but you just stated indirectly what my research is telling me. I believe Kyle and his attitudes and beliefs and personality and their effect on her are all reasons Jeri turned out so well and that Ish and you..." How to say it without hurting her feelings?

"Didn't," Sira said bluntly.

"Not quite as bad as that, especially in your case. Remember, Ish became a male. You have the double X and aren't influenced by the Y chromosome as he is. Still, I believe any Crispy needs to have a... oh, let's call it a mentor, during the conversion process, someone who's really open-minded and willing to change his or her mind if necessary. Someone who can guide you in the process of becoming totally human, not just the outward form. You don't meet many humans like Kyle, male or female.

"Most humans are opinionated rationalizing beings, thrown this way and that, willy-nilly, by their genes and the environmental influences that determine the way they're expressed or turned off and on or which and how many proteins they code for. And all of that determines how the brain is wired, which in turn determines what kind of personality, attitudes and traits the person exhibits." I paused for breath. "Whew! That was a mouthful, huh? And I didn't even come close to including everything.

"Now, Sira, we're all like that to a certain extent, the way our personalities develop, I mean, but Kyle demonstrates less of it than most people. He is… stable? Not exactly the right word. But to make it short, he's the epitome of what I think of as a perfect man. The only fault I've noticed in him is a tendency toward shyness, but on him it goes well." I grinned at her. "As I said, you're not the only one who wishes she'd met him first!"

Now she laughed out loud but then quickly sobered.

"So you think me being rushed through the conversion and not having an individual mentor like Kyle is the reason I'm not as happy as her or as well adjusted?"

"Yes, I do," I told her bluntly. "Kyle is an extremely well read man. He was a science writer, you know, after being medically retired from the army. He was able to steer her in the right direction and more importantly, kept her on an even keel, pointing out both the good and bad aspects of humanity. He is a very well balanced person, Sira. You'd never know he was a warrior type if someone didn't tell you. Also, he and Jeri had the full internet for her to work with and he helped her sort through it by explaining what was trash and what was worth pursuing. We're limited here in that all our access has to be funneled through so many devious paths that it takes a long time to download data because of the fear of giving our location away. The minute we opened up we'd probably be spotted. Jeri managed to locate Ish through the internet. That perceptive sense, you know."

"We still have a lot of data available."

"Uh-huh, but only because we have couriers doing nothing but bringing some specialized data we need in on hard drives and uploading it into our computers, and others doing nothing but appending all their downloads to disguise what we do on the internet. It's a hell of a way to have to work, with a monitor gauging every single download to be sure we don't reveal how much research we're doing in, well, genetics for instance. Past a certain point and any Crispy monitoring the net might find us, the same way Jeri found Ish. For that matter an AI program could probably do it."

Sira wrinkled her brow. "That shouldn't be necessary."

"Really?" I sat up straighter. "What makes you say that?"

"I'll have to think about it but I believe I can get us into the net without danger by using some of the knowledge I was working on while we were still on the spaceship before the disaster. It involves a specialty Jeri wasn't familiar with and that's probably why she didn't work it out. In the meantime could I see your research notes that led to your discoveries?"

"What I think are discoveries. Sure."

"I'm almost convinced without seeing them, Mai. It would explain a lot."

"That it would," I agreed. "Okay, let's get busy."

She was still there going strong when I finally had to leave to get some sleep. Of course it doesn't take a Crispy long to go through a tremendous amount of data. Jeri, for instance, was practically a page-at-a-glance reader, with an eidetic memory to boot. Sira wasn't quite that good but she was fast. After she went through most of my data stores she began correlating it all in her mind and asking for more data from the net. I could only imagine how impatient she must have gotten sometimes while waiting on her requests to be parsed to disguise our location and the data she was after. So impatient, in fact, that a week later she presented Carol and General Shelton with a method for letting selected computers enter the net without risk and download great stores of data. It sped up a lot of research in vital areas.

CHAPTER THIRTEEN

THE EVENING BEFORE I was to leave for the refresher course, Sira and I thought we had things pretty well sorted out. She was a very fast learner, as I said. Give her access to the net and I had no doubt she could begin working with the geneticists who replaced me before very long. And again, she couldn't find any flaws in my work which dealt with the XY chromosomal aspects of the conversion from Crispy to human. Which didn't necessarily prove there weren't any, since I couldn't get down and "see" molecules and atoms and enzymes working their magic like Crispies could, but it made me confident enough to want to talk to General Shelton one more time before the training course.

"Do you think I could go with you to see him and ask that I be moved to your department now?" Sira asked.

I had been planning on it, but I needed the reminder. Too many things happening all at once. Besides, she looked at me so appealingly that I laughed as I called Carol and told her I wanted Sira with me when I saw the general to confirm some other findings I'd made.

"No problem, Mai. He wanted to see her about that other Crispy before she reports to Intelligence again anyway."

"Good. See you in a bit."

Sira already knew the answer with her hyperacute hearing but she probably would have known from my expression anyway. "Okay, let's go beard the bear in his den."

"I take it that means we're going to see General Shelton." If she'd overheard me, she was politely pretending she hadn't. Little things like that were what had made Jeri so easy to get along with, and Sira was picking up on them.

"Right as rain, but don't ask me where that expression comes from. I don't have a clue."

᪤᪢

"General Shelton, sir, while it's true Sira can't exactly confirm my work, she can't disprove it either. However... well, let her speak for herself."

He shifted his position behind his desk and turned his attention to Sira. I thought I could see a faint smile on his face but wasn't certain.

"Sir, Mai has done some tremendously exacting work. It's especially admirable considering the short time she's been about it. And while I can't prove conclusively that she's right, I feel intuitively that she is."

"A woman's intuition?" His gaze turned skeptical but he was still listening. I didn't think he really believed that was what she was implying, though. He was just yanking her chain a little.

"Not at all. When I said 'intuitively' it was only for lack of a better word. Call it a quantum thought process, of sorts. Or a perceptive sense. Her data has already caused me to change my attitude in respect to what it means to be human. Jeri was worried about Ishmael before she left but wasn't able to figure out what the problem was. Mai did. That should tell you something right there about the accuracy of what she's been doing. And from what I've learned since talking to you last, I think that Lau, the Crispy Jeri killed, was suffering even more from the conversion than Ishmael."

"Tell me more about your attitude change."

"I'm convinced now that I got in too much of a hurry to convert to human. It went too swiftly and I lost something in the process that Jeri acquired by going slowly. Also, Mai's equations tell me that the neural pathways in my brain were 'set,' so to speak, too rigidly from not having a suitable mentor during the process. Jeri was so busy with other work that she hurried me though it, not realizing she should have taken more time or should have turned me over to someone with a personality and attitude similar to her husband, or like Mai, only male.

"If I'm reading it right, the mentor should be of opposite sex in order to get the best results, although I don't think it is absolutely necessary. Last night while Mai was sleeping I very carefully 'reset' some of my neural synapses and pathways in order to change very slightly the way my brain is wired. That involves changing the complex of genes in various ways to alter the number and types of proteins they code for. It would have been much easier if I'd done it right in the first place and it's going to take time to rearrange everything but I can do it. Already it more accurately reflects how some of my genes should have been expressed as related to environmental influences. Please understand that I'm using colloquial language for lack of proper words to describe the process. I don't dare do too much too soon or I might wind up like Ishmael or worse, but Mai's thesis appears to work. I feel much better today despite the lack of sleep."

"This is getting a little deep. I'm an old warrior, not a scientist, but let's see if I understand it. Basically, what you're saying is that when a Crispy converts to human it should be done slowly, with a human mentor constantly present, one who is adaptable, congenial and rational, or as rational as a human can be. And preferably of the opposite sex. That's the kind of man Kyle is and Jeri turned into a human woman we all admire."

"Exactly!" Sira said enthusiastically. "But in the case of a Crispy converting to a human male, there appear to be other problems, as Mai has outlined to you. She doesn't know the answer yet, nor do I; but I can tell you and her, too, that I don't believe it's beyond us to correct. If I could take Mai's place when she leaves and if I could work with a few geneticists with something near her intellect and personality, I believe that in the near future it can be done safely. If taken slowly, that is. And if others of us turn up so we can try it."

"Ah. Now I see. You want her job."

Sira missed the attempt at humor. "I want to change jobs. I haven't been doing anything of importance since the FTL propulsion engineering was completed. Not that I contributed too much to it anyway. Basically, I don't think my talents have been utilized to their fullest extent."

"Carol?"

"I'm going to have to accept some blame myself, sir." This was part of her domain. She brushed a strand of hair from her face. "I thought Sira was happy here and doing useful work. She's been assigned to the weapons development team and they've come a long way."

"They probably would have anyway," Sira said. "Jeri had already pointed them in the right direction and Ishmael helped more than I did."

"I'm wondering now if we can trust his work."

"I'll be glad to go over anything you're uncertain of, sir."

"I'm going to take you up on that. Ishmael has disappeared completely, and given how easily he can change his appearance, I don't think we're going to find him except by accident."

"Can I move over to Mai's department after going over Ishmael's work?"

"You can move there as soon as you're satisfied the ship is safe, to the best of your ability. Just be aware that you'll be on call for weapons evaluation and review and available to answer the usual silly questions from new arrivals."

That got a big laugh, but then the general turned serious again. He rubbed his chin for a moment then looked at me.

"Mai, since Ishmael deserted, Sira is the only Crispy we have immediately available. Just to help confirm your theories, I want you two to stick close together."

"You're speaking of Mai being the mentor I should have had to begin with, I take it?" Sira had sort of an impish expression on her face.

"Exactly. That and learn everything she's done so far. Or wait—should you have a man as mentor?"

"It would have been nice to begin with but as far along as I am now I think she would do fine. If Mai agrees and you're not blaming Jeri for being remiss, certainly. I'd love it, in fact!"

"Mai?"

"Well, sure. She can even move in with me if that would help. It's not like it would interfere with any romantic ventures on my part at the moment," I said with a sour smile. "But I'm supposed to leave for my combat refresher course tomorrow."

"How about if we delay it for two or three weeks? You'll still have a chance to go through it but for the time being I believe keeping Sira happy is going to take priority."

She and I exchanged glances. She gave me a tentative smile, then when she saw me nod it broadened.

"Okay, that's settled. Keep Carol apprised of your progress and make an appointment for a week from today, and let's see how you're getting along."

Chapter Fourteen

It was kind of nice having someone else around after hours to talk to. I had been so immersed in the enormous number of finicky details of my research that I hadn't gotten out much. The only people I'd talked to in depth had been Kyle and Jeri but that had tapered off as they grew increasingly busy with their pre-flight preparations.

Along with the research I did my best to show Sira some of the girl things Jeri had obviously been too busy to teach her and others had apparently supposed she knew already. It was a breakdown in communication but not unusual in a place like this, still growing and harried with requests and demands from the government types who had to be involved and the rush to beat our competitors into interstellar space. Fortunately there were damn few politicians who knew much about The Group, and even fewer who knew where we were located. I had heard rumors of another enclave being built but had no idea if it was true or not.

Anyway, Sira and I got along fine. Even better than that. By the second day we were old friends and a day or two later I began thinking of her almost like a little sister—despite her being almost 200 years old and an alien. After hours I coached her on some of the little ways to tell when a man isn't being truthful or is only interested in sex and stuff like that. Even with my record, I could tell her about some of those things. Or possibly because of it. I'd been fooled enough so I could spot the types she'd be better off without. I told her of the ways some women dissemble in order to attract men, such as disguising their own intelligence, bolstering the fragile male ego, pretending interest in things and so forth.

"It's a common practice and if you want to play it that way few women would think the less of you for it, but personally, I think in the long run it defeats your purpose—if you're looking for a long term relationship, that is."

"Is that what you want, Mai?"

I raised a brow. "Yes, I'd love to find a man I could respect and fall in love with. Unfortunately, I seem to put them off once they learn what my IQ is."

"But why should that be? I would think they'd like being with an intelligent woman rather than one who isn't."

"Remember what I said about the male ego?"

"Oh. Yes, I remember. It's disconcerting."

"Oh, don't give up all that easily, Sira. Hell, maybe it's me. Maybe I'm just too hard to please. Not that men don't like to think they all have balls bigger than Texas grapefruits."

"I doubt it's your fault. Tell me more."

So we had another drink and I did. During that period she dropped the Mai and began calling me Cherry like most people I was close to.

It was on another night, toward the end of the first week when she sprang the surprise that would impact the rest of my life. We had stopped by the day room and lounge after calling it quits at work, but found nothing interesting going on there. No interesting men, I should say, so after two drinks we left.

We had stopped for a sandwich in the cafeteria first so we'd already eaten. I cracked open a bottle of wine when we got back to the apartment and turned on the television to see if there was anything worth watching. Nada. There seldom was, to my notion. I switched over to the news. We sat and sipped our wine and talked when nothing worth listening to was being reported, just gabbing.

Perhaps it was the liquor that made me agree. Or maybe not. Anyway, the news anchor was devoting what little time they allowed for science news that night to a discovery that might eventually contribute to lengthening the human life span. I think Sira noticed how closely I was paying attention to the segment because when it was over she eyed me carefully, then said, "Mai, are you interested in extending your life?"

I shrugged. "Depends. I can't see any purpose if it's simply lengthening the time I'd spend drooling in a wheelchair. They always very carefully leave those things out. If we learn how to extend or slow down the aging process, it simply leaves us open to more debilitating diseases. Or maybe I'm a pessimist. Some approaches involving telomeres and the RAS2, SCH9 and SIR2 genes, along with a few others in various combinations or deletions are promising, but we're a long way off yet. And even if we find the key, we'll need to learn how to reverse the aging process or a lot of people will be very unhappy. Anyway, I've looked into the approach that was just mentioned on the news and don't think there's much to it."

"Suppose you could stay young? Would you like that?"

"Sure. Who wouldn't?" I suddenly realized from her expression that she wasn't just making idle chatter. "Are you getting at something, Sira?

Did you find anything in my notes that might lead to such a thing?"

"No. I could do it for *you*, though. I'm not familiar with the nomenclature yet but I know how aging works in humans."

"What! I mean... you could? You do?"

"Didn't you know Jeri did that for Kyle? Made him younger? And stronger? Healed his old war injuries?"

It was news to me. "How do you know?"

She looked slightly ashamed. "While Kyle was with her once at the time she and Ishmael were helping me with my conversion, I inadvertently examined Kyle with my perceptive sense. I didn't know that much about acceptable mores at the time. Anyway, I couldn't help but notice that she'd worked on him and when I asked her about it later she told me the whole story. She cautioned me not to broadcast it, though. She said humans would become very upset if they knew only special ones were being given extended life spans and superior bodies."

"So why are you telling me, then?"

"She didn't say I couldn't tell anyone, just not to go public with it. It's not something that can be done instantly is why. Even if it could be, can you imagine Jeri and me standing still while the whole human race passed in a march past us in order to extend their lives? We'd die of exhaustion before even making a good start. It took Jeri several weeks of work with Kyle, but she showed me how it could be speeded up now that it's a proven success. Not by *that* much, though."

"And I still have a couple of weeks before I report for my training course? Is that why you brought it up now?"

"Yes."

Lord help me. What to do? Did I want it? Of course! Not much of a decision there. But how about being one of the few? The one-eyed woman in the country of the blind isn't the queen—she's a prize to fight over. But most of all, why me?

"Why me, Sira?"

"Because you deserve it," she said simply. "Just as Kyle did. Just as some others do, which I'm sure Jeri will provide for. As will I, as time and circumstances allow."

I lowered my eyes while thinking about it. And to repeat, perhaps it was the drinks that made me agree, because I was intelligent enough to know it wouldn't be a picnic if anyone ever found out. Finally I looked at

her and nodded. "Go ahead. And thank you, Sira. That's the finest compli-
ment I've ever been paid."

We hugged, both of us shedding tears. And then she got busy.

ഇ൦രു

"I don't feel a bit different," I told Sira a couple of days later. We were
reviewing my equations and models of how the effects of possessing a
number of particular genes of the XX chromosomes during the conversion process from Crispy to human tempered the ill effects of the coding
for microprotein formation of adjacent genes. It is a subtle process and
Sira was working with me on the models, using her perceptive sense to
show where I'd gone slightly wrong in the way I'd oriented one of the
proteins.

"You won't ever feel it but in another ten days or so you'll be a new
person inside and out, much stronger and with an indefinite lifespan," she
said, touching the keyboard and flipping the model 45 degrees so I could
get a better view of it. "There. Can you see it now?"

I bent forward to get a closer look. "Oh, yeah. No wonder I couldn't
make it work the way I thought it should. Sira, that perceptive sense
must be what propelled you guys so far into microbiology that you
learned how to change shapes and genomes without killing yourselves." I
brushed an errant lock of hair from my forehead while thinking how nice
it would be if I could change my hair color at will, the way she could. I
like the dark brown I've always worn but any woman wonders what she
would look like in various other colors and most experiment some time
during their lives.

"Oh, we figured that out long ago but it happened so far in our past
that no one knows how it occurred. Now it's instinctive. That's why we
don't have a real science of genetics like you do and why we work well
together. You provide the theory and I can check it with my perceptive
sense."

Sira didn't start altering my facial features to remove the trace of wrin-
kles and the faint crow's feet from my eyes until two days before I left
the enclave. I had just turned 30 and ordinarily they weren't even notice-
able with makeup. When I looked in the mirror the last morning as I was
getting dressed I realized they were gone completely and that I no longer
looked my age. In fact, I seemed to be not much older than Sira, who
resembled a teenager. We were counting on being gone for two weeks

of training to make people forget my original appearance. And it wasn't as if I had been seen around a lot. I had spent much of my time buried in work.

When I returned I'd claim all that fresh air and exercise contributed to how good I looked. I never felt a thing during the process and it wasn't until after I reported to camp for my training that I realized what a change had taken place in my body.

CHAPTER FIFTEEN

"ALL RIGHT, LISTEN UP, PEOPLE! My name is Staff Sergeant Juan Melandez. I'll be your primary tutor while you're here. We've got one week to run you through this course, so pay attention."

He stood with hands on hips and glowered at us. I wondered what was going through his mind at having to teach an abbreviated course in small unit tactics to a bunch of civilians, some of them already approaching middle age. He must be curious as a pup in a new home even though all of us had either been through basic at one time or had just graduated from the baby basic or refresher course. Whatever he was thinking, his expression indicated that it probably wasn't very complimentary

We'd finished the small arms course, a refresher for me but for others it had been their first contact with army weapons—or even first contact with weapons at all! It must have grated on him, knowing a bunch of barely trained civilians had to be going on some kind of special mission that involved danger, adventure and excitement while he was stuck at the training base somewhere in Georgia.

We had been told that's where we were but the actual location had been very carefully concealed from us. I didn't think it was in Georgia but it might have been.

Someone in the front row had the temerity to complain.

"Sergeant, are we going to be doing much running?"

I guess the guy thought once he'd finished the baby basic training he'd never have to exercise again. It made me wonder about the criteria used to pick prospective starfarers!

"You're goddamned right you'll be running!" Melandez shouted at him, and glared even more fiercely. "You'll also be hiking and walking and crawling in the mud, for that matter. What do you think this is, a Sunday school picnic? You're learning how small groups function in combat situations, and I'll be damned if I've ever seen combat take place on a golf green or slow down to accommodate someone who doesn't like to run."

"Well, there's no need for profanity just because I asked a question."

"Bud, I'll be just as fucking profane as I think I need to be, in order to drum it through your thick civilian heads that combat isn't a game of badminton. It's life and death, not only for you but for your comrades.

And in case you haven't been told, you have to pass this course to go wherever the hell you're headed for. And I'm the son of a bitch who can give you a down check and send you back to wherever you came from. Now let's get started."

I didn't hear very many more questions. The ones I did hear were usually astute and needed to be asked. Sgt. Melandez had very little time to teach the basics of what every space-bound scientist and technician had to know, by order of General Shelton. There was no telling what we might run into that the military contingent couldn't handle by itself.

We spent 12 hours a day for seven days studying tactics, maneuvering as an attacking unit on rescue missions and then retrograde movements while defending a site or bringing out a party that was in trouble. First we studied the tactics then practiced them in scenarios as realistic as possible. Having been through basic training and kept in shape, I was far better off than some of the group. I have to give it to them, though. Almost all of those men and women were in their late thirties and early forties and they all hung in there. I guess the chance to go on an interstellar expedition was a pretty good motivator. I know it was for me!

I had an easier time of it than most of the others for two reasons. First, as I said, I'd already been through basic training, albeit a number of years ago, and had kept in shape. The second reason manifested on a day when John Smackers, a young man in his late twenties, got into trouble. It was his own fault.

Most of the training involved surprises just like you'd run into during combat. I was crawling along the edge of a narrow ravine with him and three others. Our leader for the day was Madeline Graham, a pleasantly pretty astronomer with graying hair I'd met a few times back at SFREC. Everyone called her Maddie. She had already spotted a crossing point a hundred feet up ahead where we could get to the other side and come back in time to set up a defensive position to allow the following squad to jump past and set up the same kind of site for us. Smackers decided to take a short cut instead of obeying orders. He found a spot he thought he could leap across. He backed up a few yards.

"Hey! Get down!" Maddie yelled. "You'll get spotted."

"Here's how to do it the easy way," he yelled. He bent down lower as instructed but went his own way otherwise. He stayed crouched down while he ran toward the edge of the ravine, intending to leap across and show how simple it was. Instead, he tripped and rolled sideways over the edge, saving himself from a nasty and possibly fatal fall by grabbing hold of the trunk of a small bush embedded in cracks on the rocky side slope.

I saw the bush start to pull loose. I was the nearest person to him and without even thinking, I jumped to my feet and ran to him. I reached down and grabbed his wrist just as the bush came loose. By all rights, his weight should have pulled me over the edge. Instead, I gave a hard yank and fell backward, dragging him back up and down on top of me. I shoved him off my body and shouted, "You stupid shit! Never try to be a goddamn showoff. All it'll do is get you killed."

He was still shaking but once he got to his feet he forgot all about how he almost killed himself and me, too. "I could've gotten back up by myself."

"The hell you could." I turned away, seething inside at his stupidity. He was treating the training as a lark, a game.

The others came running up. "It's okay," I said. "Let's finish the problem."

We did, with Smackers keeping his distance from me the rest of the day.

That evening, Sgt. Melandez stopped me while I was on the way to the showers, which consisted of an outdoor drum rigged up to pour enough cold water on top of you to ruin your whole day, not to mention your hair.

"Are you a weight lifter?" he asked. "You really don't look like one." His countenance was much more pleasant than the first morning when he had introduced himself. In fact, he was rather handsome when not glowering at over-aged trainees.

"No." I tried to let it go at that. I'd been thinking about what I'd done and knew damn well I shouldn't have had the strength to pull Smackers back up from the side of the ravine. And I'd noticed how easy the rest of the physical part of the training was for me. It had to be Sira's work but she hadn't told me that what she was doing would turn me into a superwoman. Or had she? Then I remembered her saying something about how I would be stronger. Sure, but...

"You've got to have some kind of muscles under that outfit to do what I saw." He eyed my body in a way that might have been either offensive or pleasant, depending on the situation and the man doing it. In his case I decided it was more pleasant than not.

"He helped with his feet," I said, hoping he didn't question our young would-be hero.

Melandez clearly didn't believe me, but he let it go.

The outfit he was referring to was more or less what we'd be wearing if and when we landed on an alien planet. It was army gear, a tough chameleon material normally a silvery shade but capable of changing colors to match its surroundings when power-activated. It was covered with pockets and places to attach weapons and equipment. It was called a chameleon suit but its functioning was stolen more from the cuttlefish than the little lizards it was named after.

"Wherever you people are going, I sure as hell hope you aren't going to face as much trouble as it appears you are," Melandez said late the third morning after we'd trudged back to the base camp for lunch and lectures. "Where are you going, by the way?"

No one answered.

"Good for you." He grinned slyly. "I was going to flunk anyone who told me. All right, take out your maps and compasses. We'll pretend you don't have a GPS module."

It was doubtful any planet we touched down on would have a magnetic field matching our north and south exactly enough to use standard compasses, but the ones we'd be issued would presumably be capable of setting to a new alignment if a planet had a magnetic field.

An hour later a helicopter took us out a ways and dropped us into a deep forest in pairs. I was with Maddie again but this time I was in charge. They tried to give us all a chance at leadership roles during the training. A good idea, I thought.

"We'll have the drinks waiting on you!" Smackers called to us over the noise of the idling helicopter blades thwacking the air.

I grabbed my hair to keep it from blowing around my face and ran toward the tree line from the narrow clearing we'd landed in. I gathered up my hair, retied the band that had come loose, and waited until the noise had abated.

After the chopper was gone I lined us up with the compass and map coordinates, then double-checked by asking Maddie if she thought I was correct.

"Looks good to me, Cherry. Bet you a dollar John Smackers won't ask his partner's opinion."

"I wouldn't take that bet. He's going to be trouble if he goes on the ship with us."

"Any reason why he wouldn't?"

"Maybe we'll get lucky and he'll flunk. He just barely passed the small arms course and the grades were lowered quite a bit from the army standard."

"That's right, you've been in the army, haven't you?"

"Uh-huh. Been a while though." I glanced up ahead and down at my compass. "To the right a smidgen, I think."

"Ugh! We've got to go through *that*?"

That was a mud bank along a stream, thick and gooey from a recent rain. "Yup, unless you want to go around, and we haven't got all that much time."

Maddie sighed. "At least in space there's no mud."

I laughed. She was going to be one of our astronomer/navigators. The term astrogator hadn't quite caught on yet but I thought it would before long, especially once we were under way. It still seemed unreal to me. Something I'd dreamed and read about in fiction all my life was actually coming true. And it had all happened so suddenly. At this same time one year before, there'd been no inkling of aliens or interstellar travel. Now we were building starships. The prototype model had actually gone out to the Oort Cloud already and the first real one was on its way to the stars!

We did get muddy. And scratched. And bug bitten. However, I was pleased when we were the first team back. John Smackers and his partner were the last ones in and they weren't speaking to each other.

CHAPTER SIXTEEN

I WAS LOOKING FORWARD to our graduation exercises. Everyone had made it, even Smackers, damn it. I just hoped he stayed away from me in the spaceship. I finished the ice cold shower and was back in the barracks, such as they were, with a towel around my hair and dressed in jeans now that the training was finished. I wore a pullover and light jacket, the one I always carried my little S&W in.

Graduation was set for an hour later, giving me time, I thought, to freshen up. Then, at the little party that would follow, I intended to see if I could convince Sgt. Juan Melandez to show me where he slept, since he would no longer be an instructor. He was a real alpha male and I found myself attracted to him. I liked the glint of humor in his eyes, too, even if it hadn't manifested much while he was instructing us in weapons and tactics. Or maybe it was just biological pressure built up over time and demanding to be let loose. Whatever, I was looking forward to the festivities and what I hoped would follow if he proved to be as compatible off duty as I hoped.

Maddie stuck her head in the door. "Cherry! Someone to see you outside!"

I blinked, then remembered I was Cherry. Not many people used that name for me. Damn. Now what could this be? I finished toweling my hair on the way toward the front of the building, slicked it back and tossed the towel away. I stepped outside. General Shelton, commanding officer of the Brider Enclave, was waiting on me.

"Hello, Mai. Come along, no time to waste."

"But... my gear, I have to... my hair..."

"I said we can't waste time. I'll have someone send for your gear and you can use my comb if you're worried about your hair. Let's go. I'll tell you what's happening on the way."

I had heard the thwacking of helicopter blades a little earlier but thought it was just the first arrival of the ones that would take our group back in the morning. It wasn't. I knew that as soon as I saw the star painted on it. It was the general's personal chopper.

"Where are we going?" I asked, hurrying to keep up with his long strides.

"To an airport, then to the Rocky Mountains."

And that's about all I learned right then. Helicopters aren't conducive to conversation. I don't even know where the little airport was located. Probably it was simply presenting a front as a civilian airfield owned by a big corporation and was really run by one of the security agencies. Maybe even Army Intelligence; I never asked. But once we were aboard the private passenger jet I learned plenty. General Shelton himself briefed me.

"Mai, sorry to cause you to miss the graduation, but this is far more important."

"I'll live, sir. What's happening now?" Graduation wasn't all he caused me to miss, damn it, but I nodded affirmatively. I could gauge the seriousness of the mission by the fact that the general himself was wearing a machine-pistol strapped to his chest.

"We've located two other Crispies here in the United States. They landed in the Rockies and have been hiding all this time, gradually accumulating lore on us humans."

"Did they contact us?" Wow. Exciting, and Sira would be glad.

"No, we learned of them after another exhaustive analysis of the radar and atmospheric anomalies we turned up when all their lifeboats fell to Earth. Sira helped, too, with her additional knowledge, once someone thought to ask her. Once we had their location pretty well pinpointed we began searching by satellite. It was difficult but we did it. We got photos of two Crispies yesterday from space."

He shook his head as if disgusted and he probably was, what with us having had the data in hand all this time and not knowing it. Frankly, I couldn't blame him. For a group that started out with Army Intelligence, their performance had been singularly unremarkable.

"And I take it we're going to bring them in. But why me?"

"There are problems. They must have built themselves a pretty good little hidey hole and have been using their cloaking gadget to bring equipment to it and set up a base."

"But what were they intending to do? Just the two of them? And you said they used the cloaking gadget. I guess that means they haven't converted to humans yet, huh?"

"No. I told you we have photos of Crispies! And we want to make sure they don't convert to human before they have a look at all your research on the potential problems. And here's the thing: they obviously don't trust us or they wouldn't still be hiding."

I thought of all the data they might have picked up about us from the net, without a human around to guide them in sifting through it, and shuddered. "If they've tried learning about us without help, it's no wonder."

"Right. And we need you to convince them we're trustworthy. You know more about Crispies than anyone else we have now that Jeri and Kyle have gone."

"Why me? Why not Sira? Seems like she should be the one going to talk to them."

"You know why, Mai. She's the only Crispy we have until the U.K. gets theirs over here, if they ever do. They keep stalling so we can't risk her. In fact, had we known how retentive the Brits were going to be with the ones they control we'd never have allowed Jeri to go on those two missions where she damn near died. As it was, I got reamed out over the mission to China and damn near got relieved of command."

"But... but all my research data is back at SFREC. I can't show them anything without that. I have a good memory, but not that good!"

He grinned. "Give me a little credit. I brought your notebook computer and duplicates of all your files. Sira showed me which ones."

"Oh." I should have known. General Shelton wasn't commander of SFREC because he was a dummy.

ॐ౦ಚ

I spent part of the time during the flight trying to rest up. I spent the rest of it reviewing the data I had accumulated on why Crispies converting to male had problems and why any conversion, whether to male or female, could run into trouble without having good mentors and going slow. Damn, I sure wished I had Sira with me but wishes get no points in heaven. I'd have to make do without her.

There were two other scientists in the plane and the rest of the ten seats were filled with a half dozen well-armed soldiers. I was introduced to them but I had too much on my mind to pay a lot of attention. This was a hell of a thing to throw at me fresh from a week of grueling training.

By the time we landed my eyes were blurring from reading so much in the dry air of the jet but there was no time to rest. We immediately transferred into two separate helicopters and took off again, quieting any more talk. I did have a good view of a snow-covered mountain but I didn't recognize where we were.

The pilots were good. They brought the choppers down in a little clearing where they had to practically whack off the limbs of the surrounding firs and aspens to get them down. Two Humvees with drivers were waiting there. It was a tight fit but they got us all inside. We drove a half hour on little more than a hiking trail and then even that played out. The jeeps came to a stop and we all bailed out.

"Come on, Mai," the general said to me. To the soldiers he said, "Guard detail, trail us but keep your weapons shouldered. We don't want to present ourselves as a threat. You other two, wait here."

The two scientists didn't like being left out but there wasn't much they could do about it. I followed Shelton as he consulted a piece of paper, probably a map, and wondered why bring the guards at all if we didn't want to look threatening? Whatever, I soon quit wondering because I had to save my breath. We began hiking, mostly uphill, then across the steep side of a mountain and gradually worked our way farther up. The exertion didn't seem to bother Shelton. He couldn't be sitting at his desk all the time.

Eventually we came to another clearing, even smaller than the other.

"This is it," he said. He checked to see that a little radio at his belt was working right, then told the guards to stay alert. To me he said, "Let's go, Mai. And remember, they don't know we're coming, so take things slow and easy."

We followed a barely-discernible trail 50 yards into the forest then came to a stop where a giant boulder seemed to be holding up the mountain. There were smaller ones around it and a few stunted firs trying to get a toehold where soil had been blown into crevices in the rocks.

"This should be where they're holed up, according to our contact team's coordinates," Shelton muttered. He never mentioned how they'd gotten the information but obviously he trusted it. He turned in a full circle, looking around. Nothing. I spent that bit of time examining the big boulder. Something about it didn't look right. For a moment I couldn't put my finger on it, then it came to me. It wasn't weathered enough. I took a couple of steps closer to it and began running my hands over the surface. They came away almost completely clean. No rock dust. Hardly any dirt. From there it didn't take long to spot a cleft in the rock above eye-level. It looked too conveniently handy. I reached up and ran my hand into it and felt around.

"Watch for snakes," the general said, just as the rock moved.

I had to hurry to get out of the way as it slid to the side, revealing an entrance into the mountain—and a Crispy in its original form standing there with a little gadget in its hand I recognized.

I was startled silly at first by its unearthly appearance but then my eyes focused on what it was pointing at me with one of its middle arms. Jeri had shown me hers. It was a disintegrator. If the Crispy used it on me, I'd turn to dust and blow away.

"We're peaceful!" I said hurriedly, hoping it had learned to speak English. I sure as hell couldn't speak their language.

"That's debatable. Come inside."

"Thank you," I said, with General Shelton echoing my words.

They had carved out living quarters from solid rock, presumably with their disintegrators, and somehow rigged up a lighting system. The fluorescent bulbs were just like the ones back at the enclave but the power had to originate from their survival packs, proving they'd made an easier landing than some of the others.

We were led along a short hallway to a room that was suspiciously designed for human occupancy.

"Is there a human living here? Or have one of you converted to human form?" I asked.

"It doesn't matter. The question is what are we to do with you?"

I looked at General Shelton. He nodded, telling me to do the negotiating.

I decided to start right off with a bombshell. "I sincerely hope none of you have converted to human form yet, particularly male. We've seen instability result from it."

Silence. Apparently I'd hit them where they weren't expecting it. I decided to go for broke. "We've made friends with two others of you. One we rescued from a foreign country where she was unhappy." I gave them Sira's and Jeri's Cresperian names as closely as I could enunciate them. I had learned both of them just for fun and now I was damned glad I had.

"What of the third?"

So they knew about Ishmael. Again, I went for the throat. "We rescued him from some very bad humans, at great danger to ourselves. Many humans lost their lives getting him away from those people. We brought him back to our place and tried to make friends with him. We also attempted to rescue another of your compatriots from China but it was too late. He'd already gone too far into madness."

Even without having human features, I knew they were bound to be befuddled, so I plowed on. "I worked with both Jeri and Sira, the human names they took. During the course of our work, or research I should say, we learned that any Crispy converting to human should go slowly. And that especially applies to Crispies converting to the form of human males. The sex-determinate chromosomes lead to an unstable personality if not monitored very carefully. I'm sorry to say that Ishmael was hurried because we knew no better at the time. Jeri, one of your own highly re-garded comrades, even helped. Ishmael, the name the male took, turned out to be unstable, as I said. He became obsessed with sex and power. He left our security and we have no idea where he is now."

The two Crispies were apparently having problems assimilating all I'd said so quickly. The general and I were both still standing, since they hadn't asked us to sit. They ignored us and jibber-jabbered in their own language for awhile. Finally one of them spoke to me. I couldn't tell them apart so I don't know which it was.

"I can tell with my perceptive sense that you are speaking the truth. However, human society is so unstable that we'd like to speak to another of our kind. Are either Jeri or Sira available?"

"No, we feel like they are better off staying where they are now, both for our own security and theirs. And to be very frank, Sira is now the only one of your kind we have to work with so we didn't want to risk her away from our enclave."

"I see again that you are truthful, but where is Jeri?"

"She's already left on the first spaceship, looking for your home planet. We're hoping they can find it, but there's a huge problem. They left be-fore I made my discoveries about the dangers of conversion. Now we're getting another ship ready as rapidly as possible in order to try catching the first one before they find your home planet, if they do. It would be horrible if many Crispies began converting to human form without being aware of the dangers, especially the ones converting to male."

"What dangers? There is no danger in converting to a male human."

The voice came from behind me. I recognized the son of a bitch who was speaking, too. It was Ishmael.

CHAPTER SEVENTEEN

"ISH!" I SAID. "Thank goodness we found you! You need to come back to SFREC and let us help you."

"Yes, Ishmael," General Shelton added. "I can only offer our apologies for not exploring the conversion process more thoroughly before you did it. Our only excuse is that it had worked so well with Jeri we thought it would go as well with all of you. Damn it all, the horrors we experienced with Lau should have warned us, Ish. He was verging on crazy by the time we got to him but we thought it was because he'd been subjected to malevolent influences by his Chinese captors."

"No, you're completely wrong!" Ishmael said loudly. "Lau was preparing to lead the Chinese to glory, to their proper place at the head of the human hierarchy. And since Jeri killed him, it falls to me to take over his unfinished duties. *I* will show my friends here how to construct a new ship and take the wealth of human pleasures back to our people."

"Ishmael, please, no," I said. "Look, I brought all the research notes that Jeri, Sira and I have. It will show you where we went wrong, but there's hope. Sira and I believe that with proper guidance you can repair the damage to yourself."

"I have no damage." He turned away and spoke rapidly to his friends. I guess they were friends. He had evidently been living at the place with them. We were probably in his room right then.

I noticed he was becoming angry. Apparently what he'd told these two Crispies and what we'd told them didn't jibe too well and it was already beginning to look as if they were going to believe us rather than Ishmael. Or at the very least, they were willing to listen to us before making a decision.

"You said you had your research notes with you?" a Crispy asked. Of course it knew what I'd said, but I suppose it was being polite or making a peace offering of sorts.

"Yes. Do you have a computer connection here? I brought my notebook with me but I was in such a rush I don't know how much of a charge I have left on it."

"Certainly. It's farther back."

"Don't believe them!" Ishmael yelled in English. I guess his temper got the better of him.

They ignored him. Shelton and I began following the Crispies.

The next thing I knew Ishmael's strong arm was around my neck, choking me, and he was shouting.

"Goddamn you fucking humans!" Then he added something in the Crispy language.

I don't know what he intended but he certainly didn't use his perceptive powers to examine my body or he'd have known I wasn't the same person as the last time we'd met, there in my room. I snapped my elbow back so hard that I heard his ribs crack and twisted in his grasp at the same time, breaking contact and stepping back several paces to put some distance between us. Fortunately, he didn't possess a disintegrator but he did have a gun. He went for it at the same time I drew mine but his broken ribs slowed him down. I was just a little bit ahead of him.

I should have shot to kill but I didn't. I still had hopes of salvaging him. If I'd had any idea what horrible things he'd done a few minutes before arriving in the cave, I would have put a bullet right between his eyes. My shot took him in the left shoulder just before he fired his gun. I know he was aiming to kill *me*, but the wound from my gun threw him off. His slug hit me in my right hip. The force of it twisted me half way around. I started to fall but hit the wall of the tunnel first and managed to stay upright.

He fired one more time. General Shelton took the bullet full in his chest and fell to the floor. He shot again, aiming for me. The only thing that kept me alive was my preternatural reflexes, which he still wasn't allowing for. I managed to get out of the way in time and he missed, but then he twirled and ran for the exit that was still open.

The two Crispies were just standing there, unsure of how to handle the situation. I took off after Ishmael, ignoring the burning pain in my hip. I could feel pieces of shattered bone grating together as I ran back outside. Ishmael was hurtling down the trail, ignoring obstacles. I limped after him, knowing I'd never catch up. Suddenly I thought of the guards we'd left behind. What of them? I yelled something unintelligible to try drawing their attention.

Ishmael looked back over his shoulder at me. The bastard was grinning about something. I paused to take a shot at him but he moved just in time and I missed. Damn it, I'd never hit him again, not with him using his perceptive sense.

Ishmael looked back over his shoulder at me but then he wasn't there! I shook my head, wondering how he'd disappeared so fast then I remembered my unbuttoned blouse that day. Shit! How could I fight him when he was close enough to tamper with my short-term memory? But I couldn't let the likes of him loose on humanity.

I gathered my courage and ran toward where I'd seen him last, hurrying as fast as I could. My vision blurred with the almost overwhelming pain in my hip and I stumbled. That probably saved my life because a bullet zinged by overhead as I was on my way down. I rolled and came up firing before I even knew where he was. Anything to keep his mind occupied.

I guess I managed it just long enough because the guards heard the shooting and came running. I couldn't see them, but I heard them crashing through the brush as they came toward me.

"Watch out!" I yelled, not wanting them to run into Ishmael.

I had one more look at him. He stopped running and stood for a moment, indecisive. He looked backward at me and his face was twisted up into a cruel mask. I aimed my gun at him.

He looked backward at me and his face was twisted into a cruel mask. Then I was on the ground and blood was coming from a hole in my side. Shit! He was doing it again. I fired at him and missed.

I was on the ground and blood was coming from a hole in my side.

Shots rang out. I looked up in time to see Ishmael exchange fire with someone down the trail, probably a guard, then he turned and ran back toward me. I tried to lift my little automatic but it was too heavy. I didn't have the strength to bring it to bear on him.

"Goddamn bitch!" he cursed and aimed his pistol at my head and pulled the trigger. It clicked on empty. He cursed again and ducked as a bullet sang by and impacted on a tree. He changed magazines with a dexterity I could only admire while I waited for death. I tried one more time to lift my gun. It rose slowly.

He grinned then his arm fell to his waist as a shot rang out. He stared stupidly down at the hole in his chest. I couldn't lift my arm but I had just enough strength to flex my wrist upward and fire one more time. It wasn't enough to kill him, not with his perceptive senses helping him evade.

He lifted his gaze from his chest. Then his head disappeared and the rest of his body slumped to the ground with blood pumping from his neck. A disintegrator! The Crispies had chosen sides.

That was my last coherent thought for a long while.

ഇൻൻ

We learned later that he had been snooping back at the Enclave and found out where the Crispies were hiding. He went there and misled the two Crispies, using his perceptive sense to prevent them from knowing how many lies he told. He wanted to get them to change into human form and the three of them gradually accumulate enough money and power to run the world and then build another spaceship. Or something along those lines. I never learned exactly what. Maybe by that time he was so far gone he didn't know himself. I doubt seriously just the three of them could have succeeded anyway.

I guess it's a good thing Sira had changed my body so much. My wounds were much worse than I'd thought. I would probably have died on the mountain without the quick healing talents Sira had given my body as well as help from the two Crispies there. As it was, I was gently tranquilized by the Crispies so I wouldn't feel any pain while I was trundled down the mountain to where our guards were waiting.

Except half of them were dead. Before entering the hideout, Ishmael had killed them by altering each of their short-term memories in turn, then cutting their throats, so silently and quickly neither the other guards nor the two Crispies inside the mountain had noticed. That was how he'd been able to get past them and confront us. If he'd bothered to kill all of them he might have gotten away but the three he bypassed held him up just long enough when he tried to run away that the Crispies had time to decide. The son of a bitch had deserved to die. If he had lived and it had been up to me I'd probably have executed him myself.

General Shelton hadn't been hurt that much. He was wearing armor and only had the breath knocked out of him. I guess Ishmael hadn't bothered to use his perceptive sense to notice it. Or maybe he'd been using it to confuse the other two Crispies and keep them out of it.

When Shelton recovered from the impact that had knocked him down he was able to talk again. He told the Crispies that Ishmael's behavior was partly our fault. I know it must have taken a hell of a lot of restraint for him to say that after seeing the bodies of the soldiers. I think General

Shelton's last act, blaming Ishmael's behavior on us for not being more perceptive, no pun intended, was inducement for them to see how different we were from Ishmael and to come with us, bringing their survival gear from their lifeboat with them.

"I got my ass chewed out good by both the President and Chairman of the Joint Chiefs for leading that mission myself instead of sending a subordinate along," General Shelton said later. He was seated by my hospital bed in the Enclave infirmary, smiling at me like an insurance agent seeing a patient with a big policy on her life come back from the dead. In short, he was happy.

"Results count, don't they?"

"Fortunately. The Crispies were impressed that I'd come along rather than send someone of lower rank."

"Then they did come here?" I was just getting caught up on all the news. I'd been unconscious for the last two days while my body healed.

My attending physician was a nice man named Dr. William Harrison Honeywell that I'd only just consciously met about an hour before. I learned later he was an Army major, and he worked right alongside the Crispies to get me patched back together, the one stitching, the others… well, I guess "sealing" is as good a term to use as any. Good man, that, because fuzzy, lime-green BEMs evidently don't faze him a bit. I got to know him… er, intimately, the way a doctor/patient relationship goes, in the ensuing days.

"Oh, yes!" Shelton nodded emphatically. "They're here, and happy, by all indications. And they're very impressed with the way Sira has turned out despite her initial difficulties. They were wondering if you could be their mentor when they decide to change."

"No! I want to go on the ship!" I struggled to sit up and noticed for the first time my wrists were restrained. "Get those damn things off me!" I said, jerking with my arms.

He laughed and began unbuckling the padded straps. "They wanted to make sure you didn't move around on 'em while they worked on you. I guess the nurses forgot to take them off."

"Did you hear me, sir? I don't want to stay here. I want to go on the ship."

"That's what I told the Crispies you'd say. However, they will accept your recommendation for mentors if you won't stay for them."

"Sorry, sir. I've dreamed all my life about going into space. I'm scared if I put it off something will happen and I won't get to go at all."

He nodded sadly. "Yeah. That's how I'm feeling. I'm not going to be allowed to go exploring for a while yet, damn it. Anyway, we need you on the ship because of your knowledge and I have to stay here."

"Penalty for doing a good job running this place, sir."

"Carol runs it as much as I do these days. Be that as it may, I just wanted to stop by and see you for a few minutes and thank you for a job well done. You're going to receive a medal, by the way, but of course it can't be publicly awarded."

"No biggie. I don't deserve one anyway."

We talked for a few more minutes before he said he had to get back to work. I was left lying in bed, going back over the mission and wondering if there was anything I could have done to make it come out better. The next day when the medal was pinned to the breast of my gown, General Shelton saw my expression and took the time to have some encouraging words with me.

"Mai, every soldier who's ever been in combat and lost friends always wonders the same thing as you. Could I have saved them? Did I do something wrong that led to their deaths? And it's even worse for commanders, like me. I'm the one who has those boys' deaths to live with. I had my mind on the new Crispies and never considered Ishmael might have been involved, even after seeing that room set up for humans. I should have known then. And not to scare you, but you're going exploring and something like that will happen again. God knows what we'll meet out there. The Crispies have told us some of the things they ran into but with their perceptive senses they were able to avoid situations that would get us killed."

"I guess so. Thank you, sir."

"No thanks needed. You did fine. I wish I was going with you." His eyes looked off into the distance for a moment and then he was gone.

ଔଓଓଔ

Sira was there to help when I took my first shaky steps a couple of days later. I wouldn't have been walking near that soon with a normal body. The high-powered bullet had shattered my hip and the other had torn me up inside, but other than some residual soreness I felt okay. Not a hundred percent but ready to leave the infirmary and get back to work.

The *Galactic* was going to be leaving before long and there was still a lot to do.

"It would be great if you could come along, too, Sira," I told her.

"I'd love to, but you know as well as I do it's not possible now. What I have to count on is one of our ships finding the home planet. In that case, not only could I go home if I liked but a lot of Crispies could come here!"

"Would you go home if you could?"

"Maybe for a while, to help others who wanted to convert to human form, but I think I could do more useful work right here on Earth. The planet is not in good condition, as I'm sure you're aware, neither environmentally nor politically."

"Once space travel becomes routine I think some problems will be solved," I said defensively. "That's if we find good planets to colonize. Even if we don't, we can begin moving heavy industry off Earth."

"Oh there's bound to be lots of them, Cherry! We found one Earth-like planet just on our voyage before it went wrong and previous voyages had found several as well."

"Did you colonize any of them?" The answer popped into my mind before she said anything. The Crispies in their original form weren't that interested in colonizing and only minimally interested in exploring. They were very nearly a static culture insofar as the urge to go other places went. They were neither territorial nor warlike, which when you think about it are two of the big reasons for exploration. Just think back to when the Americas were discovered if you want some historical perspective.

Sira saw from my expression she needn't bother answering. She did have something to say, though; she hadn't come by just to visit.

"Mai, I think one of my compatriots is ready to convert to human but she's a little scared after what happened to Lau and Ishmael. Have you come up with any acceptable mentors yet?"

I had been thinking about it and I knew she was really serious by her use of my real name rather than calling me Cherry. "Have you met Robert and Martha E. Lee?" I asked.

"I've met them, but don't really know them well."

"Jeri thought highly of them. They were trapped in the place where Ishmael was being held captive and risked their lives to help him stay alive. I've gotten to know them pretty well. They're good people. I think if you and I took a week or so to work with them and show them what they have to do and what they have to look for during the conversion—the danger points so to speak—then I could leave them in your hands. With you helping them and doing only one conversion at a time the three of you would make great mentors."

"Good. I was scared the whole load would fall on me, and I don't think I've cured all the ills that befell me from too fast a conversion yet."

"You're doing great, Sira. I can tell the difference, for sure. You don't look or act nearly as unsure of yourself any more, nor as unhappy, either." I raised my brows.

She smiled sweetly. "You know me too well. John is a really nice guy. No problems there. But you're right. I am doing fine and I feel much better as a person now. When do you leave, by the way?"

"Soon is all I know. It can't be much longer, though. Have you noticed how many people went missing while I was off playing soldier? They were all slated for the ship so I suspect they're already living in it, getting the systems they have to work with checked out and the ship stocked and so on."

"Yes, I've noticed. Or rather now that you mention it, I have. I'll miss you."

"I'll miss you, too, Sira. And thank you again for what you did for me. It almost certainly saved my life during that encounter with Ishmael."

"Oh, poo! The Crispies would have saved you."

"Maybe. But remember, they were still making up their minds. Oh well, that's over and done with. How's your work coming now that you switched jobs?"

"Wonderful. In another six months I think I'll be able to call myself a geneticist; then I can really begin working on methods of helping humans enhance their bodies without our help. That's one of the things I believe accounts for a lot of strife in human affairs. The short lifespans and susceptibility to illness."

"I agree." In fact, I couldn't have agreed more. I just hoped the public wouldn't find out about the few of us who had already been changed. The first thing we'd hear would be favoritism, cronyism and all the other epithets they could throw at us. And that would just be the preliminaries. After that they'd get physical.

CHAPTER EIGHTEEN

I BEGAN GETTING ANTSY after I was told to pack my bags. Each person was allowed 30 kilos of personal luggage. That sounded like a lot, but suppose the ship was gone for two years? It's not much, then. In fact, it's hardly anything at all. I tried to pick for the long term. Fortunately, we weren't like the old pioneers in one aspect. By storing them digitally we could take as many books and movies as we liked; we'd have entertainment for as long as the ship supplied power and the computers worked. So far as that goes, readers that had a solar power adjunct would last practically forever.

Clothes were something else. Exploratory gear was furnished, which meant anything we'd wear on another planet outside the confines of the ship, and that meant two sets of chameleon fatigues each. We were told we could also wear them in the ship if we liked but frankly, they don't do much for a girl's figure, so I doubted I would. Other than cammies we had to pick and choose. I selected a couple of dressy outfits and the rest in lightweight jeans and pullovers, blouses, slacks, undies and a couple of jackets. And good shoes, a couple of pairs. Slippers, both bath and dress.

My personal weapons. The ship's arsenal would furnish those for us if necessary, but if we had a preference we had to bring our own, complete with ammo. I packed my big automatic with plenty of cartridges and very reluctantly put my small pistol into storage. Then I thought about it again. I removed a few trinkets I could get along without and replaced them with the .40 caliber pistol, two clips and a box of ammo. The little gun had saved my life twice, whereas I'd never used the .45 outside of a firing range.

I didn't plan on bringing any food for myself like some people did, so that left room for a few cosmetics. Very few. I had no idea if there'd even be an eligible man on board. I certainly hadn't had any luck where I was, but a little planning to go along with some wishful thinking wouldn't hurt a thing. When I was finished I still had a bit of mass allowance, and filled it with a liter of Jack Daniels Black Label. Indulgent? Yeah, but I couldn't think of anything else to take.

The two new Crispies were a godsend. General Shelton very reluctantly allowed one of them to go along; I later heard he had to get permission all the way up his chain of command to the President. We really did need one, though. Suppose we never found the first ship but did find the Cresperian home planet? We'd have to have an interpreter and go-between. And guess what? It wanted to convert to a human male and wanted me as his mentor! It gave me goosebumps, remembering how Ishmael came out and having heard the stories about Lau, the Crispy who'd been in China and converted to a human male, then went completely around the bend.

Well, at least I knew now what had gone wrong but we still hadn't had a successful transition from Crispy to human male, not unless one of them in the U.K. or India or the one still in the hands of the Islamic Confederation had managed it.

I talked with the Crispy—he was already a male, not that it made much difference with them—and we decided to wait until we were on the way and start the conversion then. That decision had to be bucked way on up the chain of command. Suppose something went wrong during his conversion? We'd be one hell of a long way from help! Regardless, we really needed a Crispy aboard and my research showed plainly that the transition from Crispy to human needed to go slow, so that did it.

Gordon seemed pretty likable. That was the name he picked for himself. Gordon Stuart. I asked him why that particular name and it turned out that he'd run across an old song by Gordon Lightfoot, a folk singer I'd never heard of. Whatever rings his bell, I decided. Then I gave it another thought. The name did seem to fit him somehow, even though he still was in his original Crispy form. I think it was his voice. It was a nice resonant baritone. Even coming from something you'd run from if you weren't aware of what it was, speaking to him almost made you forget about it.

ꟙ

About that time I got called in to the infirmary. Seems it was time for my flight physical. A mixed blessing, that. I got to be poked and prodded in every conceivable way, and every orifice examined; but then I got to go into space if it all checked out. And I knew it would. Sira had already verified that.

I undressed and put on the lovely disposable paper gown just before the nurse and Dr. Honeywell came in. "Well, hi there," he said. "How are you doing?"

"Pretty well, all things considering," I decided. "No after-effects."

"That's good." Honeywell smiled. "Gotta love the Crispies. They're a real godsend." He grew solemn. "I don't think I could have saved you without them, or a miracle, otherwise."

I winced. "That bad, huh?"

"Yep." He and the nurse eased me back onto the exam table and commenced poking and prodding.

"I hope you don't have too many more of these exams to do," I noted, shooting for small talk as areas that I normally didn't expose to strangers got poked and prodded. "It's getting kind of close, isn't it?"

"Yes, but you're my last physical," Honeywell observed, jotting notes on his Blackberry. "We saved you for last because of your injuries. We wanted to give you plenty of time to heal first. The general made it clear that flunking your pre-flight physical wasn't an option, or you might turn the infirmary into Pamplona during the Running of the Bulls." He grinned as he leaned back over me to use his stethoscope, considerately warming it in the palms of his hands first.

"Thank you," I said gratefully, for both the thoughtfulness of the scheduling and the comfort of a warm stethoscope. Just then something swung out of the neckline of his scrubs, and he tucked it back inside, but not before I'd had a chance to see that it was a gold cross pendant. That caught me by surprise.

"Pretty necklace," I said. It was, but okay, I admit it, I was fishing. It wasn't too often that I saw people in his profession, or at his level, displaying a symbol of religious belief. He was, after all, a highly experienced surgeon and internist, having seen the insides of more MASH units than the television show. That might be an exaggeration, but not by much, from what the general had told me.

"Thanks," he answered casually. "Means a lot to me."

"Somebody special give it to you?"

"No. I bought it myself. It just... means a lot to me."

That was telling. But interestingly enough, that was all he said. And just because the man was now poking instruments around between my legs didn't mean we knew each other well enough for me to press further.

And likely, I considered, we never would, because who knew when we'd
see each other after this?

"When was the last time you had a period?" he asked then.

"Um… 'bout two, two and a half weeks ago," I said. He let me sit up,
and I glanced at the calendar on the wall. "Yeah. It'll be right at two weeks
in two days."

"Okay, good. Where do you want the implant? We recommend upper
arm or belly, but it's your call."

"Implant?"

"Contraceptive. You're going to be gone potentially a long time," Honeywell explained, "and we can't have babies popping off aboard ship.
And the implants last a year, and take up a lot less space in stowage than
months and months' worth of birth control pills. Then there's the added
benefit of no periods while the implant lasts."

"Ah," I said, grasping the idea. Not having a period for a year sure
wouldn't bother me, either! "Good plan. I dunno. How big is the damn
thing, and which site hurts less?"

Honeywell grinned, holding up the sterile package containing the tiny
implant. "In that case, I'd recommend belly."

"Go for it."

Moments later I had the little prosthetic injected just under my skin,
right below my navel. And thanks to a bit of cold spray, I'd barely felt a
thing. "How long does it take to kick in?"

"Stay on your Pill until you run out of the current month," Honeywell cautioned. "By then it'll be dispensing the correct amount. Don't be
surprised if you spot a bit, or have some slight nausea in the meantime,
though. You'll be getting hormones from both systems. If you have any
problems be sure and report them. A small percentage of women can't
tolerate this implant and it's still relatively new."

"Right." I nodded comprehension. "Better that than wups. I doubt the
nurseries of starships are very big."

"Exactly."

∞

Three days later I was told I'd be leaving the next day. And I was
almost ten pounds over my 30-kilogram limit. I'd reconsidered after the
whisky and began adding other odds and ends until I was overweight.
Damn, damn, damn! What to leave behind? I spent two hours agonizing

over choices and wondered whether other passengers and crew were having the same difficulties.

I heard a tap at my door and spoke for it to open. Maddie stuck her head in.

"Hi Maddie. Come on in." I had a sudden idea. Maybe she had some spare space. Wouldn't hurt to ask.

"Just for a moment," she said stepping on inside. "I see you're packing. Got any room to spare?"

I laughed. "I was just going to ask you!"

"So much for that. No one has extra room. Mass, I mean." Her expression drooped. "Well, there go my dress shoes and a gown."

We talked a few minutes; then she left on another errand, probably to ask someone else. I was actually surprised to see her still around. I would have thought she'd already be aboard, being an astrogator, navigator or whatever the hell they finally decided to call her. I hoped that meant our route was already all mapped out. It better be, I thought, or we're all in trouble!

Gordon had already left on a special, well-guarded carrier. I wouldn't see him again until we were in space. It was beginning to be lonely around the old homestead. I decided to use up some of the whisky but right at the last moment I got the word that we could add another five kilos. I repacked then weighed everything again and was right at the limit, including the whisky, so I didn't get to have a going-away drink in my room after all.

I felt certain I wouldn't sleep that night and I was right. I tossed and tumbled until finally I took a tranquilizer, a leftover from my recovery period. I shook the bottle and noted with satisfaction that it was still almost full. I had used very few of them. I poured the rest down the sink. No room for personal medicines. If you were on drugs they had better be something you could do without or were stocked in the ship because it was going to be a long way back to a pharmacy.

ಬಿಂಬ

Along with Maddie and a few others, I was put on a mini-bus that took me to the shabby-looking airport and thence to the spaceport.

"Gordon was asking a lot of questions about you," Maddie said to me after we were underway.

"When did you see him?"

"Oh, I've been at the launch site for a while now, getting my commission straightened out and all. This was just a trip back to pack."

"Commission?" That was news to me.

"Uh-huh. Reinstated with a bump in rank for my good looks and pleasing personality."

I laughed but didn't ask anything more about that. I figured I'd find out later. It was Gordon's questions that interested me. I did ask about them.

Maddie said, "Oh, he's mostly interested in what you're like when you're not working. The books you read, shows you watch, things like that."

"Getting ready for the switch, is he?"

"Oh, yes. I think Sira was regaling him about the joys of sex before you told her to slow down."

"Good. It's better to take things like that slow. Very slow. He's going to have enough surprises hit him in the face when the hormones start circulating. Remember when you were a teenager?"

Maddie laughed and covered her face. "Oh, God, don't remind me! The poor fellow!"

"Uh-huh," I said, and meant it. I remembered my own teenage years. I mused for a moment then continued. "You know, Jeri really did hit the jackpot. When she was a Crispy she fell in with Kyle and they were more or less alone, at first. He turned out to be perfect for her. He was a well-read and even-tempered man with enough scientific knowledge to help explain a lot of our contrary traits and the idiotic parts of our society. And he was single but had been married; a good marriage, so she said. And they went at it slow. All the things pointed out by my research that are either necessary or highly recommended for a successful conversion."

"Right. And you have a lot of the same traits as Kyle."

Finally it dawned on me what she had been getting at. Some days I'm brighter than others. "Um. You think he's already looking at me as a potential... um, girlfriend?"

"Uh-huh. Or more. Of course he can't have human sexual feelings yet but he likes you already."

I stayed silent for a while. Being a mentor might turn out to have some side benefits—or handicaps, depending on how he developed. I decided I needed to think and closed my eyes. The image of Technical Sergeant Juan Melandez's strong brown face and hard muscular body kept intruding on my thoughts. I found myself wishing he were going.

CHAPTER NINETEEN

I DON'T KNOW WHAT I was expecting from the starship. I guess I was still visualizing rocket propulsion and I should have known better. You don't go plying the stars using rockets!

What I saw looked something like four cans of soup turned on their sides. At one end the cans appeared to be squashed toward the center. They were attached snugly to each other with heavy bracing. The other ends had the same squished look but it had more protruding aerials and weird looking apparatus extending from it. The whole thing was cradled on short fat landing legs. At first I thought it wasn't very large but then I saw the tiny figures walking around beside it and the size came into perspective. It was *huge!* And I should have been expecting that, too. If you're going on a trip that might last two years—although it wasn't planned for that—it would pretty well have to be sizable to support the scientists, crew and military aboard. And it was.

What surprised me most was seeing it inside its hangar, which was my first sight of it. Spaceships always took off in the open, didn't they? Yes, and this one would too, as I found out. It was built inside a covering to conceal what it was, and to keep its size and appearance hidden from satellites.

"Impressive, huh?" a voice said as we stood and stretched after getting off the jet that had taken us to the spaceport. I didn't know exactly where we were; from the terrain I'd seen as we descended, I guessed New Mexico or west Texas. The terrain was similar at any rate. Sometimes I think secrecy is carried to ridiculous extremes but perhaps not in this case.

I nodded, even though the question hadn't been directed at me. It was indeed impressive. And the most remarkable thing about it was the propulsion system. Again I was fooled. I was used to thinking of spaceships as mostly massive fuel tanks and cramped living quarters. This one was just the opposite. Most of what I was seeing from the outside was either living area or storage space. What I took to be the unreality impellers and artificial gravity apparatus took up less than a tenth of the mass. Fuel tanks and maneuvering jets for moving short distances after leaving Earth took only another tenth. I learned those last facts later. At the time I wouldn't have known an impeller from an incinerator.

ೞಅ೦೮ಃ

We walked to the ship after being taken close to it in a cart, with it growing more and more massive as we neared. Considering the speed with which it had been constructed, I figured something that large had to have started with the four "soup cans" taken from off-the-shelf cylinders originally meant for something else. Airliner bodies, maybe. Railroad tank cars, but probably not; those would have been too small. Perhaps storage tanks from a refinery. Or I suppose it could have been built from scratch on site, given the incentives and plenty of money.

A floating golf cart with our luggage aboard trundled around to the other side, presumably to a loading bay of some sort. An airlock with both doors propped open on one cylinder, and a small loading ramp extended from another, provided our entrance into what would be our home for a long time to come.

"Follow me, folks. Don't lag or you can get lost in here." A short female corporal just inside the airlock grinned at us, flashing white teeth in a tanned face. She had on the same type of chameleon uniform I'd seen on Captain Jenson when I first reported to SFREC. "Don't worry about your luggage. It'll catch up to us pretty quick."

The interior of the ship seemed even larger once we were inside, especially considering we were in just one of the four subdivisions of the ship. We were led through hallways and passages and past larger rooms, some open, some not. People came and went as we walked, seemingly in a hurry and obviously intent on last minute errands or duties. It didn't take long to get me lost. I'm the type of person who needs a map to find my way across a street.

Before long we entered what was clearly passenger country. Fewer uniforms were evident and the narrow hallways had doors that opened or closed into recesses. The entrances, or hatches in navy parlance, were lined to provide airtight seals. Most doors came with names attached, some single, some couples. The military people I saw were all dressed alike, in the silvery camouflage with sleeves rolled up.

"This is your stateroom, Ms. Trung," the little corporal said. "Please look at the schedule of events and the diagram of the ship as soon as possible. Both are available from the ship's computer monitor in your room. Next chow—meals for civilians—is at 1600 hours and there's a general orientation at 1800 hours, That's four o'clock and six o'clock for civilians, but get used to the military method of keeping time. You'll be briefed on it tonight. There's a FAQ section displayed on your monitor that also explains it. Read them; it'll save you lots of time and maybe some grief. Your luggage will be along shortly." She glanced past me and said, "In fact, here it comes now."

Sure enough, a little cart came along hovering a few inches above the floor, or deck as the navy called it, and I saw my two suitcases. I was very glad they were lightweight, since their mass was included in the personal goods limit. I thanked Corporal Smithson, then closed the door behind me and began sorting out the bulk of my worldly possessions, all 35 kilos of them, not counting the clothes I was wearing.

I felt a little guilty because of my .40 S&W automatic in the side pocket of my windbreaker. Once I learned that the clothing we weighed in with wasn't included in the baggage allowance, I'd decided to carry it and take my chances of it being confiscated. Not surprisingly, we had to go through a detector before entering the ship and my weapon was spotted, of course. That resulted in a brief phone call, a smile and a request to turn it in to the armory before liftoff.

The stateroom was about like what you'd find on a cruise ship, minus a porthole. One room contained all the furniture, including the bed, and all of it was bolted to the floor. There was a bathroom with a shower, sink and toilet, and that was it. It looked kind of spare until I started going through the FAQ and discovered some seats that let down from the wall—bulkhead—as well as a few cabinets I hadn't known were there. The main room could also be partitioned with folding wall dividers. I should have gone through the questions before unpacking and storing my possessions. After finding the cabinets I had to take the time to rearrange things. It was then that it struck me: the ship was designed as if it would be gravitized to something like we were used to. I thought about it and decided it must be an adjunct of the propulsion system, or possibly a whole separate system that provided gravity. Whatever; it seemed I wasn't going to be allowed to experience weightlessness after all, one of the experiences I'd been looking forward to. Kitty mess and other bad words.

ஐ‍ௐ

The evening meal was sandwiches and tea or water. The cooks were busy stowing their pantry. Not that we'd get many cooked meals, I'd heard. The military MREs were going to be fairly standard fare and I expected they would get to be very old by the time we returned.

Orientation was in a big auditorium kind of room, but with a low ceiling and seats attached to the deck. I won't mention that again. Just take it for granted that everything movable was locked into place—or should have been. Gravity or no, weightlessness had to be allowed for.

I moved down the narrow aisle between two rows and found a seat. A moment later I felt the presence of someone beside me and turned to see. Tech. Sgt. Juan Melandez looked much handsomer smiling than he had while glowering at us as an instructor. Except he was no longer a sergeant. Brand new CW2 insignia were attached to his cammies. He'd skipped the basic warrant officer rating of WO1, signifying that his CW2 was a presidential commission. It also signified that someone thought very highly of him.

"Hi!" he said with a grin. "We have to stop meeting like this."

"Hello." I felt my face turning red as I remembered what I'd been thinking just before being shanghaied into the mission to the newly discovered Crispy hideout. "And congratulations. I see you've been promoted."

If he noted the blush he made no sign of it. "Thanks. Reward for keeping all my ducks in a row, I guess. Y' know, I wondered what in hell you people were up to when I was dragooned into that quick training course, but never in my wildest dreams did I think you were going somewhere on a spaceship."

"Not just a spaceship, Mister Melandez. A starship."

"Yeah. Starship. And you're not in training now. I'm Juan to my friends unless I'm on duty."

"Okay. I'm Mai. Or Cherry, but not many call me that."

"Why not? It's a pretty name."

"Not a clue, Juan, but call me Cherry if you like." I smiled while thinking I'd given him the name only my closest friends called me by and started to wonder why but, really, I knew. He looked better than ever. Then what he'd said hit me. "Are you just now finding out where we're going?"

He nodded and smiled ruefully. "Yeah, I'm a last minute addition. One of the original crew came down with the heebie-jeebies two days ago and someone pulled my name out of the hat and asked if I wanted to go on a special mission. I didn't have to be asked twice. Anything to get out of a training slot, but I sure never figured I was going on a starship!"

"It's the same way I felt at first. Well, I'm glad to see you aboard. I'll feel safer now."

"Thanks. I think."

I was still wondering how to answer that remark when a man in a black and silver dress uniform I'd never seen before joined several others on the stage. They all wore similar attire. He had a strong face with a hawk nose and high cheekbones and stood several inches taller than the others.

"Who's that?" I asked, as if Juan would know since he'd just joined us.

He did know. "That must be the dress uniform for the Space Force since I was given one just like it, and since I haven't seen anyone but the few up there wearing it so far, I suspect one of them is our captain. "

Sure enough, the last man who'd joined the others on the stage took the podium with three confident strides while the other six sat down, two women and four men. "Good afternoon," he began. "I'm Colonel Jules Becker, captain of our ship. It was christened yesterday and shall henceforth be known as the *USSS Galactic*. In case you aren't aware, this is the second in a line of starships being built. The first one has already left, the *USSS Zeng Wu*. It was named to honor the memory of two very special men whose sacrifice in part made this trip possible.

"Our primary mission is to contact the *Zeng Wu*, if at all possible, before it locates the Cresperian planet. All of you should by now know about the Cresperians. They are members of an intelligent species, some of whom were marooned on Earth. To that end we shall proceed directly to the last star system we know is on *Zeng Wu's* itinerary. If we arrive too late to catch them, we will then proceed to try locating the Cresperian home planet alone.

"Once in this ship you are subject to military discipline. This means orders from me or my officers and NCOs will be obeyed with alacrity. The only appeal is to my superiors on Earth, upon our return. I cannot emphasize this enough. We are on a dangerous mission. We have no idea what we may encounter. Strict discipline is our only recourse when the going gets tough. That doesn't mean the military is going to be hanging over the shoulders of scientists and other personnel on board and monitoring their every move, but it does mean that any disputes are ultimately my responsibility to resolve.

"It also means that you are responsible for reading and abiding by the ship regulations posted on your computer. So be nice. Do your best to get along with your crewmates. This may be a long voyage and it is very important that we meld ourselves into a smooth working and smooth sailing ship.

"Now I'd like to introduce you to my officers."

One by one they stepped forward and he gave their names, rank and duties.

My surgeon, Dr. Honeywell, was presented as the ship's Chief Medical Officer. That made me feel good. Anybody that could patch up what Ish had made of my insides while working right alongside Crispies in their natural form was exactly what we might need in a head physician. Hopefully not, I thought, but I also knew Murphy tended to go along on any space flight. Better to have Honeywell and not need him than vice versa.

Madeline Graham was introduced as our chief astrogator, so I guessed that title was official now. She was wearing the silver leaves of a naval commander or an army lt. colonel. Wow! I hadn't realized how high-ranking she was. Then I remembered she'd just been promoted for this trip. Whatever, I made a mental note to use her military title unless we were alone.

I hadn't slept well the previous night and it had been a long flight. The meal had also made me sleepy. Probably Captain Becker realized this held true for many of the crew because he cut his orientation speech mercifully short with a final statement.

"Now I'm going to turn the meeting over to Commander Edward Prescott, our executive officer. He and Commander Graham are going to be describing the ship, its function and design and how we intend to operate while on the voyage. Good Day."

"Attention!"

All the military and most of the civilians stood as the captain departed. I suspected the ones who didn't get out of their chairs were in line for a very pointed lecture on ship's etiquette before the day was done.

CHAPTER TWENTY

ONCE CAPTAIN BECKER WAS GONE, Maddie and Commander Prescott took over. It was mostly Maddie who did the talking, while Prescott stood silently beside her. The chest full of ribbons said all about him that needed saying just then, assuming you could read them.

Maddie got right to it. "I believe the first thing I should make clear is that our ship is organized along naval rather than army lines. For you in the military, that's probably already clear just from the ranks of the principal officers such as myself. Even so, I do want to mention one very important aspect of this subject. Captain Becker is always, repeat, *always* referred to as Captain Becker, never Colonel Becker. This may not seem important to civilians but it is. While we are in space, Captain Becker is our ultimate authority. What he says goes. He may ask for debate on occasion, but once he's made a decision, that's it. You do things the way he orders them done. Same for when he gives an order. You obey it. Period. No matter whether you disagree with the order or not, you obey it *right then*. The only persons he has to answer to are his superiors on Earth, if and when we return."

She held up her hand to discourage the few people who were practically bursting with questions, then went on. "And speaking of return, first we have to leave." That got a few chuckles. "Departure, or perhaps I should say launch, will be at 0800 tomorrow morning. That's eight o'clock in civilian time. And while we're on that subject, so long as we're aboard ship, we go by military time. A day is equal to 24 hours, so for example, three o'clock in the afternoon will now be 15 hundred hours and so on."

I looked around as she spoke and saw heads nodding but was willing to bet some of them weren't getting it. And that wasn't the worst of it. She had problems explaining why some of the landing force officers had ranks that were equivalent to the ship's officers but different, even though they were both listed as Space Force. She finally got smart and told us to think of the Security detachment as marines and the majority of the rest of the crew as navy. That did it, except for the confusion of having an army colonel as captain. I suppose that was because the army was the first to take control of any Crispies and was instrumental in getting the Space Force going. They'd subsequently been rewarded with command of this ship. However, it was run along navy lines simply because of the navy's vast experience in operating ships on extended duty. I found out there's a definite art to controlling that many people in an enclosed space over a period of time. It's not a job that I'd ever want.

Someone asked a question, and while Maddie was answering it, I whispered one of my own to Juan. "Why are you here? I don't see any of the other troops from the camp."

"I was a late addition, remember? I was told to report here, just in case I needed some of the briefing."

"Do you?"

"Sure. When you're going someplace you haven't been before, you can't know enough."

He had a point. We knew where we were headed, but hadn't a clue what we'd find there. Hopefully, we *wouldn't* find a satellite placed in orbit around a planet belonging to the star of our first stop. No satellite meant the *Zeng Wu* hadn't reached it and would be along directly. All we'd have to do then was wait until she showed up. If she did.

"Will we be in zero gravity on the ship?" someone asked.

"*In* the ship," Maddie corrected. "No, other than for short periods while obtaining navigation data. The unreality drive also encapsulates and carries with it a pseudogravitational force corresponding to that set into the impeller and drive before launch."

Damn, I thought. That clinched it. I'd heard that sex in freefall could be quite stimulating if you managed to avoid space sickness during the activity. Unfortunately, rumor had it there was about a 50-50 chance of tossing your cookies. Still, I was willing to chance it. Given the right partner, of course, and assuming he and I were in proximity when the time came.

A bell rang, marking the end of the brief. I glanced at my watch and saw that it was seven o'clock. Nineteen hundred hours, rather. Almost immediately on its heels, Captain Becker made an announcement over the ship's com.

"Attention. As of 1900 hours today, the ship has gone on internal power for a final check and will be closed to further interaction with the outside world. Launch time remains at 0800 hours tomorrow morning."

It was repeated, then Maddie had a final word. "Tours of the ship will begin at 2000 hours from the central dining room for those who wish it. Please be aware that you are responsible for knowing the general layout of the ship and where your battle and lifeboat stations are located, so I suggest you take one of the tours. They'll be done in small groups in order to avoid cluttering any one station with too many bodies."

Juan walked me back to my stateroom, then headed off to somewhere else. I took the time to go over the diagrams of the ship once again, then decided I'd better take the tour.

It was both interesting and informative. Impellers and drives were located at both ends of where the "tin cans" narrowed and were attached together. Smaller, emergency impellers were secured in each of the four larger sections. The unique design of the ship had it split into four sections and each was stocked with food and other goods as well as some personnel. That meant that any of the four sections could be jettisoned in an emergency, and make its own way home, although it would take significantly longer. Or the captain might decide to detach a section and have it put down on a habitable planet while leaving the rest of the ship in orbit. I doubted that would happen, because it would take a lot of effort to separate a section and reattach it, but it was doable. Someone had put a lot of thought into both the ship and the possible dangers we were headed towards.

Besides an area for quarters on each deck, I traced the ship diagram in three dimensions through electronics labs, biology labs complete with live animals and the accompanying smells, a spare communications mode, the chief engineer's domain and section engineering spaces, arms rooms, computer rooms, physics and chemistry labs, and the handful of other scientific specialties they could squeeze in. The tour didn't take us through all of them, but I have to mention one.

"…and this is the office and working area of Mai Li Trung, Chief Science Officer," the Petty Officer leading the tour said. "All civilian science departments report to her. She will…"

Huh? Chief Science Officer? That was news to me. Nothing like letting a person know in advance, I thought.

The rest of the group moved on but I decided to stop and see what in the hell was going on. I didn't want to be an administrator; I wanted to do my own research. Not to mention that I was going to be busy mentoring Gordon. However, the nameplate on the door didn't leave much room for argument. It listed my name and right beneath, CHIEF SCIENTIST.

I turned the latch and slid the door aside. An idle thought made me wonder whether naval terms like hatch for the square entrance I stepped through would take over, or if it would simply be called a doorway. There was a desk just inside and sitting at the desk, turned half away from me, was a female Chief Petty Officer. When she heard the sound of the door sliding on its tracks she swiveled in her chair. She took one look at me and stood up.

"Good evening, ma'am. I'm CPO Dianne Meadows, your administrative assistant."

Obviously, she'd seen a picture of me.

"Nice to meet you, Chief. When did all this occur?"

"Ma'am?"

"Me being appointed Chief Science Officer. I wasn't aware of it until a few minutes ago."

"Really?" She seemed amazed. "I've been busy setting up files and getting your working quarters organized for the last two weeks."

"Hmm." Someone playing a joke on me, obviously. Gene? No, so far as I knew, he wasn't slated for the trip. I put it out of my mind for the time being.

"Would you like to see?" Chief Meadows asked. The smiling, expectant expression on her otherwise rather plain face made her look almost pretty and told me plainly that she wanted to show off what she'd done.

"Sure. Lead the way."

The floor space was minimal. A small office was separated from the genetics lab by a partition. The lab held the usual replicators and splicers along with light, electron and tunneling microscopes, centrifuges and a number of other instruments necessary to the research, and closed cabinets and coolers that held supplies. It wasn't impressive to look at, but I dealt with small bits of biological material that didn't require a lot of space. Chief Meadows pointed out the three computers in the office.

"This one is for your personal use. Mine is netted with it and we'll share, but if there's anything you need to keep confidential there's a separate hard drive you can access and password protect. The one over there is tied in with all the others in this part of the ship, Section A, as well as with the main ship's computer. There's the monitor and keyboard for it, and the whole ship can access it." She pointed.

"Sounds like a good compartmented setup," I said.

"Yes ma'am, but only if necessary. Otherwise, the whole ship is tied together. Oh, and as one of the crew chiefs, you have automatic access to Command Control, up to and including the Flight Deck, although you'll have to go through a procedure for that area. But it's assumed that, if something comes up, you may need immediate access to the Officer On Deck."

"Wow. Hot shit. Thanks, Chief. Good job. Um, I believe I should probably try to catch up with the tour now." I nodded to her and left.

It was too late. I couldn't find them and didn't want to ask. I returned to my stateroom and accessed the FAQs.

I'd been on a cruise ship once. The *Galactic* wasn't arranged like a sea-going vessel but there were many similarities. I was amazed at how much cubic space could be put to use. The designers of the ship had done a fine job, as far as I could tell, especially considering how little time they'd had.

The most interesting part of it to me was the main control room. I brought up some holographic images and found it was at the front part, behind the mashed noses of the cylinders and in turn protected by two steel-reinforced hatches which opened out into an area with a number of small portholes. The room had a half-dozen comfortable-looking chairs with computerized workstations at each. One in particular was intriguing: a weapons station. I hadn't known *Galactic* was armed with anything other than light infantry weapons. I asked the computer about it and got a recording and text description.

It looked as if we could fight a battle in space from the weapons console, but that was a little misleading. Part of it was simply communications to and from the ship to a landing party, for instance. However, we did have the capacity for launching several missiles from space and there were two cannons that fired explosive shells as well as a laser cannon powered by the core of the unreality drive. The big weapons wouldn't work while under thrust but were mean mofus otherwise. Our offensive power was limited, though, compared to what we might find out there. Hopefully, we wouldn't run into armed or hostile ships in space on our journey. And the security troops were pretty well fixed with their own weaponry. A single soldier today can put out almost as much firepower individually as a tank used to.

So much for that, although I had no doubt eventually we'd see starships armed to the teeth on exploratory missions like ours. I had heard that a whole array of exotic weaponry was in the R&D stage, being adapted from Crispy technology.

On a sudden impulse I called and invited Juan to watch the launch the next morning with me via the ship's monitor in my room.

"Golly, Cherry, I'd really like to but I'm on duty right then. We've already started standing watches. Not that us warrior types will be doing anything notable at the time, but this is kind of a thrown together unit. We're going to be doing a lot of virtual training while en route. Can I take a rain check?"

"Sure. Talk to you later."

So much for that. I spent the next couple of hours before bedtime going over some of Jeri's notes one more time. Once underway, Gordon's conversion to human would begin. I couldn't help but wonder what Juan would think of me working so closely with another man, supposing he and I got something going. That was my last thought before I dozed off with the reader still in my lap.

℘℘℘

Passengers, or rather everyone but the crew actually involved in running the ship were advised—translate: ordered—to remain in their staterooms, cabins or bunks during launch. I hadn't met my neighbors yet, so I sat in my easy chair with a cup of coffee and waited out the countdown. At the moment right before launch, the screen showed an expanse of desert. Prior to that all I'd been able to see were the metal walls of the construction building; but as launch hour neared, a faint rumbling shook the ship and the walls began sliding past—or appeared to. It was actually the ship being moved outside. The launch had been precisely timed so that no observation or spy satellites from other countries could zero in on us when it occurred.

I suppose I was still expecting some kind of giant rumble of rockets along with an increasing force of gravity pressing on me as we lifted, and this was despite seeing the ship and knowing it wasn't propelled by rockets. A lifetime of conditioning, watching giant rockets blasting off, is hard to shake. Instead, a sudden feeling of vertigo and nausea swept over me. I had to lean forward and lay my head on my forearms in order to keep from falling out of my chair.

There was a queer sense of wanting to crawl out of my skin that went on and on as if I were suffering from withdrawal from an addictive drug. Just when I thought I could stand it no longer, it passed, leaving me weak and light-headed. The first step was somewhat akin to diving head first into a vortex but once that was over it was hard to tell I was even in a spaceship.

As soon as I was able to look at my monitor again, the desert vista was gone. It was replaced by the sight of a rapidly receding Earth and the appearance of utterly black space filled with the bright unwinking pinprick of stars. Talk about fast, we were really zooming away from Earth, and at that, we were barely getting started. Once past the last of the atmosphere and the final remnants of the Van Allen belt, there was a jerking sensation I felt throughout my body. Then that nauseating, inside-out sensation washed over me with a renewed vigor that made my head swim. That was the unreality impellers shifting into high gear.

The stars blurred into a roiling whiteness that was unpleasant to watch. I had to turn away from it, but a moment later it was replaced by an image of Captain Becker, speaking in the command voice that seemed to come naturally to him.

"Good morning. I'm happy to announce that all ship systems are functioning normally. We are now leaving our solar system and are on our way to a star system formerly designated by a number. It has been named in honor of one of our fallen comrades, Captain Alex Swavely, who died to save one of our Cresperian friends from a very unpleasant captivity. The star and the habitable planet we believe is orbiting it will now be referred to as the Swavely system and the planet as Swavely.

"Swavely is the last star system on the *Zeng Wu* itinerary before it was to begin a search for the Cresperian solar system. As most of you know, we are hoping to arrive there before they do, so that we may exchange some crucial data concerning Cresperian psychology. Whether we beat them there or they have been there and departed will determine our actions from that point on.

"You are now free to leave your quarters, duty permitting, and wander about. The control rooms, engine rooms, arsenals and several other areas are off limits to unauthorized personnel. If you aren't certain whether you are authorized, you probably aren't. Please note that this information is part of your initial briefing and is filed in all networked computers for your perusal. Thank you."

His image disappeared.

We were in space, en route to the stars. The stars!

I hugged myself gleefully and grinned wildly, all alone in my stateroom, still hardly able to believe it.

CHAPTER TWENTY-ONE

THE MILITARY CONTINGENT who crewed the ship stood regular watches. The marines spent their time with virtual training, equipment maintenance and the study of basic astronomy and xenobiology as taught by Jeri when she had time to spare. The civilians on board were mostly scientists like me and we had no set hours. I suppose as Chief Science Officer I could have established a routine, but you don't treat creative people that way, not if you expect to see their best efforts. Besides, I'm no martinet. I decided right from the start to leave them to their own devices. If they needed me they should know where to find my office. If not, they weren't bright enough to be on the ship in the first place. As for myself, I was ready to get to work.

I had several surprises that first morning in space.

I met Gordon, our sole Crispy, on the way to my office. It shouldn't have been a surprise but it was. At the enclave he had been pretty well secluded. I doubted that some people had even known he was there. Evidently he was going to be allowed to roam freely on the ship despite still looking like something that had crawled out from under a bed on a stormy night. Almost seven feet tall with a pyramidal head that scraped the overhead deck and no neck. Four two-jointed arms terminating in six limber fingers and a sleek olive green pelt. I wondered briefly if he was considered handsome on his homeworld, or if that was even something they thought about.

"Good morning, Gordon," I said amiably, meeting the gaze of his orange bifurcated eyes. I wondered idly if that was a designed shape or one given Crispies by evolution. Probably designed, I thought. Evolution doesn't necessarily produce the best solution; only workable ones.

"Hello, Mai. Are we both going to the same destination?"

"If you're going to my office, we are."

"I am. I would like to begin the first steps of my conversion as soon as possible."

"Well, come along, but we may not get started quite as soon as you like. I have to get oriented first. I only learned yesterday that I'd been appointed Chief Science Officer."

"Should I then return to my stateroom?"

I stopped in the passageway for a moment to think. Other people passed by, most trying hard not to stare at Gordon.

"You may as well come to my office," I told him. "We should at least have time to map out a plan for you. First thing, though, is to see if Chief Meadows knows how to make good coffee."

"She does make coffee but I am no judge of its worth since I don't consume it yet."

"You've met her already?"

"Oh yes. She's very nice."

Hmm. Nothing like being the last to know anything.

ဆဌ

"Good morning, Ma'am. You have someone waiting in your office."

"Thanks, Chief. You and Gordon have met, I'm told. Is the coffee ready?"

"Coming right up," she said with a smile.

I walked on into my office. Gene Smith, the man who had recruited me, was sitting in my chair with his feet propped up on my desk, drinking a cup of coffee. He set it down and grinned cheerfully at me. He wasn't the least bit discomfited at being caught like that.

"Hello, Mai. Fancy meeting you here."

"The recruiting business must be slowing down." I tried to avoid showing how surprised I was at him being aboard the ship. "What are you doing here?"

"I thought we hadn't been seeing enough of each other so I decided to come along on this little jaunt."

I didn't know quite how to take that. All I said was, "Mind if I have my chair back?"

"Why not? It's yours." He stood up. "Hi, Gordon. I was going to stop by your stateroom but I heard you were on the way here."

Gordon said nothing, obviously waiting for me to make the next move. And they had obviously already met. I sighed. The man was irrepressible, but a genius at getting things done. He'd probably be an asset to the crew.

"Don't mind him, Gordon," I said. "Smith probably isn't even his real name. However, if past experience is a guide he can be helpful when you need something or there's a bottleneck in your way."

"Just one of my many talents." Gene came from behind my desk and began searching the bulkheads with his eyes. He moved to one of them and flipped a chair down.

"How about one for Gordon?" I sat down at my desk.

"They're a little small for him, aren't they?"

"Yes," Gordon said. "I'll stand. Or do you have business with me?"

Chief Meadows came in with two more cups of coffee.

"Thanks," I said. I sipped gratefully at my own but Gordon set his politely aside. Jeri and Sira had both developed a liking for it but only after becoming human. After Dianne had retreated back to her little alcove, I added, "What are you after, Gene?"

"I wanted to talk to Gordon, but it can wait until you're finished with him for the day. Actually, I came by to invite you to have a drink with me after duty hours."

Jesus Christ! First Juan and now Gene, the last man I'd have thought about going out with, insofar as you could go much of anywhere aboard the ship. But eligible men were liable to be scarce and Juan was sort of slow getting off the mark, supposing he had any intentions to begin with. I tilted my head and peered at him. Hell, why not? He wasn't bad. In fact, he might be fun.

"All right. I'll call you when I'm finished for the day."

"Good deal. Thanks." He emptied his cup. "Catch you later, Gordon." He smiled cheerfully and was gone, flipping a two fingered salute on the way out.

"Humans are a curious species," Gordon said, not for the first time.

"You don't know the half of it. Listen, are you sure you're comfortable standing? We might be spending a lot of time together here in the future. Before you've fully assumed human shape, I mean."

"I can stand it for a long while," he said with a chuckle. He knew how to make a pun already. "If not, I'll just ask Gene to supply me with something along my line."

I could see he was trying to develop a sense of humor. Good. I liked cheerful men. I hoped it would carry over when he converted.

"Miss Trung, a gentleman to see you."

What in hell was this? A tandem shipboard convention? And Dianne had used Miss instead of Ms., just the way I liked to be addressed. She must have boned up on me already.

"Send him in," I said. "Sorry, Gordon. I'm beginning to think this might not be the best place for us to work together."

As if to reinforce that statement my monitor flashed twice in large red font. *HEADS UP! HIGH BRASS!* And my next big surprise of the day walked in.

"Hello, Mai," General Shelton said as he entered with a cup of coffee in hand. He waved casually to Gordon as if he had been expecting the Crispy to be in my office. Knowing the general, he probably had.

"Uh… what are you doing here… sir?" I said stupidly.

"Same thing as Gene. Going for a joyride." He smiled and took the seat Gene had vacated.

"But… but… what's SFREC going to do without you?"

"Oh crap, Mai, Carol has been running the place since two weeks after she arrived. I probably won't even be missed. Anyway, our friend here told the powers that be he wanted me along so here I am. It was sure as hell a tight squeeze, though. I damn near missed the boat before President Morrison gave in, but Gordon can be awfully persuasive when he sets his mind to it."

I glanced over at the Crispy. Their faces are hard to read since so much conversation among them utilizes their perceptiveness. They don't usually have much of a sense of humor either, not in the Crispy form. Humor has a lot to do with emotion which in turn depends to an extent upon hormonal influences, which are modified by environment and cultural effects and other genes coding for related proteins and a zillion other factors.

"I did indeed insist on having General Shelton along, Mai. He has been dealing with us almost from the start. This is not to belittle your own expertise but I've also found his understanding of us to be very astute. Jeri also recommended him highly, as she did you indirectly."

"If you say so. How about Gene? How did he manage to hitch a ride?"

Shelton shrugged disparagingly. "Gene finagled his way on board somehow but I haven't a clue how he did it. He's been here for several weeks."

"Did Esmeralda come with you?" That was his wife. I'd met her several times. She was a gem.

"No, she thinks it best to let me ply my trade by myself. We got used to being separated early on in my career but it's been a while now. Probably be good for us. Absence makes the heart and all that malarkey."

"Are you going to replace Captain Becker?"

"Oh, no! I'm just along for the ride so far as the ship goes. I'll be more of a diplomat than anything else, supposing we find Cresperia or other aliens we want to deal with. That's my primary assignment. Otherwise I'm on call for anyone who thinks an old mud-pounding spook might have something to offer them. I'm probably going to be bored stiff."

"Um." I couldn't imagine a man like him being bored. Only dumbasses think idleness is fun. And three-stars are intimidating even to civilians. I suspected he'd have more influence on the ship than he was letting on. "Well, what can I do for you this morning, sir? Anything special?"

"No, I just wanted to stop by and say hello and let you know I'm on board."

That was a diplomatic way of telling me to contact him if Gordon had any problems with his conversion to human. However, something wasn't computing. There had to be more to it than that.

"I don't suppose you being here has anything to do with..." I saw the warning look in his eyes. My voice trailed off like it was being muted with a rheostat but it was already too late.

General Shelton stood. He glanced in Gordon's direction then back at me. "You may as well go ahead and say it."

"Problems with India or China? Or both?"

He sat back down.

"Just keep it quiet. And Gordon, that goes for you as well. Don't repeat this to anyone. Understand?"

I nodded. "Yes, sir. Understood." Gordon gave him the Crispy equivalent of assent, a small bow.

"I saw you'd guessed. Yes, we've confirmed that both China and India have Crispies working for them. I don't know how advanced their research is, but we figure if they don't have FTL already, it won't be long. We don't know about the IC but they don't have scientists of our caliber, so they probably aren't nearly as advanced as the rest of us."

"Did you ask for permission to share my research with them in case any of them should contact the Crispy home planet before we do?"

"Politicians!" He practically spat the word. "Yes, damn it, and the stupid asses were still dithering over whether to do it or not when I left SFREC."

"Seems like a no-brainer to me. If by chance anyone else finds Cresperia before we do and they don't have the results of my research to guide them it could turn into a disaster."

"I agree," Gordon said. "If one of us has converted to male but doesn't understand what's gone wrong, as in the cases of Ishmael or Lau, and then tell the whole planet how wonderful it is to become a human, it could completely disrupt our society. Why will your leaders not share Mai's research? What possible reason could they have for not doing so? There's certainly no military value to be gained by concealing it, is there?"

General Shelton was slow in answering. By the time he did I already knew what he was going to say.

"Gordon, some aspects of our species are not very admirable. In this case I believe a few of the politicians who are advisors to the president are underhanded immoral bastards. They probably think letting the Crispies go crazy in the countries that are competing for power and influence with us would be a good idea. They're thinking the psychotic Crispies will damage those countries somehow. I'm sure I don't have to tell you what a stupid idea that is, having unstable Crispies with perceptive powers at large."

"If what I've learned of Ishmael and Lau are any indication, they are terribly wrong. Ishmael was trying to convince us that we should attempt to subvert and control the leaders of the United States. It's even possible he could have eventually succeeded had you not intervened. We had little to guide our actions other than the internet, and it is not a very reliable source, even if you are as familiar with it as humans are."

"The Crispies who convert to male too quickly and without adequate mentoring don't actually go crazy in the classical sense," I said. "They simply become very self-centered, selfish and hungry for power. Those attributes are tied into the sex drive as well, which really complicates matters. That's what my research is telling me. And with their perceptive sense they can wield influence beyond simple numbers. Having power and authority also sets up a positive feedback condition even in humans. In Crispies who have converted to human it's magnified by a large factor, or so I believe. There's a lot of truth in the old adage, 'Power corrupts; absolute power corrupts absolutely.'"

I told Gordon how Ishmael had tried to seduce me. And how he had succeeded with other women back at the enclave by aborting their short-term memories, as well as how I had been able to resist him only by knowing of that talent and suspecting him of using it on me.

"It was tantamount to rape, Gordon. That's an extremely serious crime."

"I know. I can't describe in English what my people would think of such a horrible misuse of the perceptive ability. Suffice to say I'm unable to comprehend how it could be possible for one of us, although obviously it is when in human form."

"What's done is done," General Shelton said. "I just hope our leaders come to their senses and release Mai's research to the nations with Crispies. I wouldn't bet a lot of money on it, though."

CHAPTER TWENTY-TWO

AFTER CONSIDERING a number of factors, Gordon and I decided his conversion would work best if most of it was done in his own stateroom. He had a special chair and bed there designed to his specifications as well as one for human proportions. We decided to get started the next morning. That would give me a chance to review all my data one more time. Once I got into it, I discovered another change in my body. My memory had always been good, but now it was exceptional. Not eidetic, but not far from it. And I found I could read and assimilate data much quicker than before, although nothing near Crispy speed.

Sira had obviously made those changes in my body while she did the physical revamping that gave me an indefinite life span and a powerful, illness-proof body. Since very few people knew about it, I made a mental note to ask General Shelton to warn me if he saw any personality changes as a result of the enhancement. For instance, beginning to believe I was superior to other people simply because I now had a body that worked at its highest potential. It wasn't a one-to-one comparison but I sure as hell didn't want to go the way of Ishmael or Lau!

༄༅

I spotted Gene waiting for me in the officers' lounge, and for once he looked a little serious. I started toward the dispenser but he waggled his hand and held up a glass, indicating he'd already gotten something for me. I changed directions and headed toward him.

"Hi, Mai. Drag up a chair."

I sat down and tried to slide my seat forward. It wouldn't move, of course. Even though we had artificial gravity, every object of any size was bolted in place.

He snickered.

"Very funny. If that's not whisky you have there, I'm leaving."

"You were one of my favorite research subjects. I wouldn't forget that."

"Oh? Who were the others?"

"Have you met John Smackers?"

"Unfortunately, yes."

"Ouch!" He pretended to wipe blood from his face.

"There must have been a reason for recruiting him, but it sure couldn't have been his pleasing personality."

"Right, but he's a blithering genius. He's forgotten more about quantum physics than most specialists in the field will ever learn."

"That's still no excuse for being an asshole."

"Juvenile delinquent might be more like it, except he's in his twenties. When he was confirmed as Captain, *El Jefe* wanted the best quantum physicist in America so I found him."

"Don't let Captain Becker catch you calling him *El Jefe* or you're liable to get tossed out the nearest airlock. He didn't strike me as a man who'll put up with much nonsense."

"Point taken. Maybe he'll take a hand and rein in our young genius. So, when do you and Gordon begin his conversion to human?"

"Tomorrow, first thing."

"Um. I suppose that'll keep you pretty busy?"

"Most likely. I've read over Jeri's notes a number of times and I believe she and Kyle accidentally hit on the optimal method of converting from Crispy to human."

"How so?"

"Mmm. Language immersion is a good analogy. Are you familiar with the concept?"

"Uh-huh. It's how I learned to speak Español. Total immersion in the language and culture. Six weeks of that and I was rattling it off like I'd been born in South America."

"Right. That's how we'll do it with Gordon. I'll be with him practically all the time and my assistant will have to run the science section, not that there's much to do until we hit a planet. Too bad we won't have the internet. Crispies don't sleep and it would help for him to have access to all the good and bad both, while I'm with him to help guide him and keep his learning objective."

"We do have the internet." Gene grinned lazily and waited for my reply, certain it would be more than a mundane reaction.

"What?! How? Are you kidding me, Gene Smith!?"

"That's been my main job once I was able to turn the recruiting over to others."

"But... but..." Damn the man! He had me sputtering like a baby blowing spit.

"Don't have a fit right here in front of everyone, Cherry. It's bad for your image. And we don't exactly have the net but it comes close. Once the ship was half built it was loaded with stacks of petabyte hard drives that were stuffed to the gills with billions of pages of the internet. It doesn't include everything by any means but we've had a veritable legion of programmers and operators downloading as much of the net as we could grab to the drives. We even collected a good random sampling of the porn sites and the weirdoes and asswipes and every other website belonging to nut cases you can think of."

"Why so much useless… no, I take it back. Hardly anything is totally useless. I do hope you concentrated on scientific data first, though."

"Of course, but after that, what we were wanted was a good representative sample of human knowledge, just in case."

"In case we get stranded somewhere?"

"Exactly. Want another drink?"

"You bet. After that revelation, I need another."

He tried sliding his chair back, and I got to snicker at him this time when it stayed immobile. He slid out sideways and went to fetch more whisky for us.

I had another question for him when he returned.

"Gene, I'd always heard navy ships were alcohol-free. How come we aren't?"

"We aren't navy."

"We're not?"

"Space Force, remember?"

"Yeah, but it's about the same. So how come, huh?"

"It was left up to Captain Becker. He came down on the side of sanity. It's going to be a long voyage, six months minimum but probably longer." He sipped his drink appreciatively, then continued. "That's not to say he'll allow a bunch of drunkenness. For instance, these portions are only two thirds of what's normally a shot and you get cut off after no more than a half dozen. That's all in your FAQ, by the way." He raised a brow.

"Guess I better read the rest of it before I get thrown in the brig for breaking some reg or another," I responded while trying not to look like a schoolgirl who hadn't done her homework.

"Wouldn't hurt," he said seriously. "We do have a brig, y' know."

We were chatting casually over our third drink when I admitted to myself there was more to Gene than just the able recruiter or the can-do fixer-upper a lot of people went to with problems. He was knowledge-able in history and politics and sociology and psychology among other subjects. He was, in fact, a generalist, as he told me.

"I found out soon enough in school I wasn't cut out for the subjects with decimal points and squiggly equations, so I majored in General Stud-ies. There's too goddamn many specialists as is. Take our young friend Smackers. He's brilliant so long as you confine him to quantum mechanics and its applications, but for most other things he can't pour piss out of a boot without getting it on his head."

A mental image of the boy spilling urine all over himself from a leaky boot make me guffaw just as a group of officers entered the lounge. They were top heavy with gold and silver leaves on the lapels of their cammy uniforms. I caught a couple of glances that held mild reproof from them and ducked my head while I stifled the laughter that was still trying to bubble up from inside me.

"See the light colonel, the brunette with her hair in a bob?" Gene mo-tioned toward the group when I finally got myself under control.

"Uh-huh." The woman he pointed out had the face and figure of a model, one of the type becoming popular that weren't thin as a rail and looked as if they were mad at the world. She wore her dark hair shoulder length and was *very* well built. I caught Gene admiring her from the cor-ner of my eye as I turned away.

"That's Major Loraine Wong. She has a doctorate in physics and an-other in engineering."

"What's her duty?"

"Chief Engineer, what else?"

Ask a dumb question. However, she hadn't been there for Becker's introductions or the orientation so I hadn't seen her before. It was a fairly unusual combination for a woman, but certainly not unheard of. I was sure she'd manage. Our ship's captain hadn't struck me as one who would brook incompetence in his personnel.

Major Wong emanated a confident bearing to go with the face and body of the model. She had dark silky black hair to go with her other assets. I wondered how she felt with her doctorate in physics as well as engineering but now being described as a simple engineer. She'd probably take it in stride was my guess.

"Who's the man sitting next to her? The one who looks like he wres-tles grizzly bears for a living?"

"That's Lt. Colonel James Jones. He's the CO of the security contingent on board as well as commander of the landing force."

Landing force? I guessed that had to do with when we touched down on a planet. Lt. Col. Jones' broad shoulders filled out his uniform nicely. He was short, sturdy and well muscled. I'd have bet his bronzed face had seen more than a little action, too. I hadn't met him yet, either, and found myself wondering if he was married.

I finished the dregs of my whisky and wondered how long it would last. I was sure there'd always be alcohol from the recycling system but I seriously doubted the labeled stuff would be around after the first few weeks.

"Another?" Gene asked.

"I've had enough for tonight, I think. I need to do a little more review before starting with Gordon tomorrow."

"I'll walk you back."

We passed Juan on the way out. I nodded and smiled at him. He returned it, but didn't look all that happy seeing me with Gene. *Get a move on*, I thought.

The central passageway was busy with crew going both ways. It was mostly officers, but there were a few enlisted sailors or petty officers, and the lot was spotted with civilians like me. My quarters were down a set of stairs, ladder in navy speak, and on one of the narrow side passages.

At my hatchway I surprised myself. I leaned into Gene and gave him a nice little non-sisterly kiss and didn't really give a damn who might be watching.

"G'night, Gene. It was nice talking to you."

"We'll do it again," he said confidently.

I suspected he might be right, especially if Juan didn't make a move soon. I went to bed thinking I might decide to do it myself. On the other hand, I had a crazy dream with Gene in it. The mind works in funny ways.

CHAPTER TWENTY-THREE

I INTERRUPTED A SEAMAN in the process of wiring a doorbell to Gordon's entrance. It seems as if in the hurry to get the ship commissioned the designers had forgotten all about how to let someone inside a compartment know you'd like to come in. It took a hard knock to get the sound through, as I'd found out. The whole ship was like that. Bigger than the first one but thrown together even more rapidly. Supplies, tools and materials were stuffed to the gunwales with plans to sort it all out once in space.

"I'm just finishing up, ma'am. Would you like to test it?"

"Thanks, uh, SM3 Chaglow?"

"Right. Seaman Ernest Chaglow, Engineering." He had dark hair and a thick mustache. "Call me Chag if you like. Most folks do."

"Will do, Chag. I'm Mai Trung, Science Officer."

"Um." He glanced at his clipboard. "Yup. Ms. Trung. Chief Science Officer. I'll be getting to your hatchway sometime today. Say, is this BEM really gonna change to a human?"

"Sure is, Chag, but you won't see much of him for a while. It takes time."

"Yes'm." He finished the wiring and capped the device with a magnetic cover. "There y' go. All done. Ready to test."

"Thanks, Chag."

"No biggie." He flipped me a salute of sorts and went on to the next stateroom on his list, not waiting to see if it worked. I liked that kind of confidence. I hoped all the crew shared it.

I rang the bell. It worked.

ॐ

"Come on in, Mai," Gordon said as he opened the door. He already had the coffee going for me, and the odor of the brew made from freshly ground beans brought a smile to my face.

"Thanks. I sure hope we don't run out of coffee on this trip."

"The navy can't operate without coffee. Or so a machinist's mate told me not long ago."

"Good, because I can't either!"

He laughed with me as he poured then handed me the cup, knowing I take my coffee the right way, without anything to dilute the fragrance and taste. Why ruin good coffee with cream or sugar?

"Ready to get started?" I asked. I sat down in one of the chairs he'd already pulled down from its niche in the wall.

"I've already begun the first stages of the physical changes. They're all internal so it's not obvious to you yet."

"Just remember, Gordon—don't get in a hurry."

"I won't. This is just an internal organization, so to speak."

"Good. Before we do anything else let's get our terminology straight. Okay?"

"Fine. It is even necessary since so much of what we do in a conversion is very nearly instinctive."

"Even to a different species?" The Crispies changed sex as naturally as a cat has kittens but it seemed to me that changing to another species should be somewhat different.

"Yes. All of us assume the form of some of our more intelligent animals at one time or another. It lets us perceive the world from a different viewpoint."

"All right, but explain it to me as best you can."

I sipped at my coffee and let him talk.

"Suppose I review what we learned from Kyle and Jeri's experience, since that's an outcome we'd like to emulate?"

I nodded.

"Jeri first got a gestalt of the human genome from Kyle then added to it by using her perceptive sense while analyzing other humans, and human females in particular. Kyle was under somewhat of a misapprehension when he spoke of Jeri being a blank slate, with her genome not having been influenced by environment. It's possible to create an organism in that form but it wouldn't function well, if at all. She used him as a general template and added and changed it after observing human females and other males. In other words, the human genome she created was one which functioned just as if it had been influenced by the environment and all that entails, with some genes turned on or off or functioning only in congruence with others, and so on.

"Furthermore, once the human genome was functional, but before letting it take over the body, she modified it according to her own experiences over a lifetime. And then over a period of weeks, she modified the expression of her genes even more as she and Kyle lived and worked together, and she learned more of the world. I can't tell you in words exactly how all that works, but in essence the first part sets the gene changes in motion and then it cascades to envelop the whole body at a controlled rate. Some of it is moderated by MicroRNA where it's needed.

"Of course that doesn't tell you how any of it works at the molecular level, but just so we know we're talking about the same thing, let's start with the human gene. One definition of a gene is a sequence of base pairs, ATGC. Adenine, thymine, guanine, and cytosine, respectively, make up the nucleotide bases of DNA. Each gene's code combines the four chemicals in various ways to spell out three-letter words, so to speak, that specify which amino acid is needed at every step in making a protein the gene codes for. But a single ATGC sequence can code for multiple proteins and some of these can be blocked or speeded up by MicroRNA.

"Some sections of the codes are switches that turn other sections on or off. Some have to be activated by environmental factors in order to work. Some are active only during periods of development, and others are active and inactive throughout a person's life. And interactions among and between genes affect others, along with environmental influences and hormones. There are also some other factors that you haven't discovered yet and consequently we have no words for. There are trillions upon trillions of permutations, and that's not even counting what you call the 'nonsense' portion of the genome."

He made quotation marks in the air to emphasize the word "nonsense," then continued. "I can perceive how it functions but we don't have the terminology to describe most of the way I see it. I can tell you that the so-called nonsense portion of the genome isn't really nonsense, though. Parts of it is code for microproteins that have specific functions, although most of them aren't germane to this discussion."

"Whew!" I blew out a lungful of air. "I'd love to have had you lecture in some of my postdoc classes. Let's leave it for now though, and get to specific actions. Have you been accessing the internet volumes from the main drives?"

"Only skimming so far. I was waiting on you, but I did set up some categories and organization so that the data I survey won't be quite as random as it was for Jeri."

"Good. We'll pretty well follow the same process she and Kyle did. I'm going to be with you about 16 hours a day most days and available at night if you need me. If I understand it right, you won't need to sleep at all for the first week or so."

"Correct. When we're not talking I'll be reading. And may I remind you that I read *very* fast."

"Right." Don't I wish I could do that! "I know you've talked to various people already and gained a pretty good understanding of what a contrary species we humans are?"

"Yes, Mai. You're very strange to a Crispy but... the human species is much more... dynamic, shall we say, than Cresperians."

"If you say so."

And so it began.

౭౦ౚ

The big difference between Gordon and me and Kyle and Jeri is that I was forewarned and prepared, while those two had been thrown together willy-nilly with no preparation at all. A second factor was that they were almost constantly in danger, or at least under the threat of it, the whole time. It had pretty obviously drawn them close together as the conversion proceeded, and culminated with them falling in love once Jeri became fully human.

I certainly wasn't planning on that. Falling in love with him, I mean. Nor was I planning on introducing him to sex personally. I had no intentions at all along those lines. Not at first.

I suppose I could write a really long book about what took place over the next four weeks and maybe I will someday, like Jeri had intended to do before being rushed into space. All she had time to do was dictate a lot of notes for those who'd follow. I'll just hit the high spots. Besides, most of what I did was talk with Gordon whenever he ran across subjects or things he didn't understand clearly or thought were crazy. Some of them were. We certainly have enough craziness in our own species to confuse ourselves, much less an alien.

One thing we discussed a lot was religions and all their perturbations.

"We have mathematical proof that there is no creator," Gordon remarked during one trying day while he was attempting to sort out how we could possibly believe and practice so much contradictory and impossible nonsense as our religions encompass. I had no real answer for him other than the one Kyle had used to good effect.

"Gordon, there seems to be something inherent in our genome, our very nature, that impels a high percentage of humans to believe in something greater than themselves. And as senseless as it sounds, most religions personify their gods in human forms. I personally believe it began as a survival trait while we were just becoming self-aware. We had to have some explanation for the world about us; death, birth and aging, tornados and lightning and earthquakes, drought and abundance.

"Our caveman ancestors would have gone mad and been unable to survive if they hadn't invented gods to explain the natural world. And you're well aware of how, at our level of understanding, we haven't yet been able to rid ourselves of the genes, or the genes that code for proteins that contribute to the wiring in our brains, that let us believe such stuff. It still has survival value, you see. Even today in many parts of the world if you don't follow the acceptable religious practices you won't live long, or if you do, you won't thrive because you'll be discriminated against."

"I see. And children will be tormented if their parents don't believe like the majority. I can see that the practices aren't universal, though. You, for instance. You don't believe in a God, do you?"

I shrugged. "I neither believe nor disbelieve. There's no proof either way so far as I can see. I most certainly don't think religions as they're practiced have anything to do with the real world. They are all fabrications and perpetuated by human inertness and the power of the majority. As has been said, the majority is always sane. I don't believe it, but there's some truth to the statement."

"Uh... that would indicate that you don't personally become involved in trying to dissuade your associates from their beliefs?"

"Correct. It's damn near impossible to win a political or a religious argument. It takes the slow roiling of history to eliminate the truly contra-survival practices, but we're slowly getting there. I think. It's damn frustrating sometimes, though."

"I can see how it would be for a person of your or Kyle's nature. You believe the scientific method should guide mankind's actions."

"Yes, although not completely. But Gordon, don't expect humans to act that way. Don't even expect scientists to be rational. And, to really get personal, don't expect *me* to be rational in all things. If you begin to believe I am, you'll be disappointed. I'm as subject to rationalization as the next person, even though I try to avoid it."

There was a long silence while he integrated our conversation with his prior knowledge. Then he smiled with his mouth that was not yet quite human. Had I not grown used to the gradual changes toward his human form by then, it would have been nauseating. That was one big reason we kept the conversion confined to his stateroom.

CHAPTER TWENTY-FOUR

THERE CAME THE DAY when I could look at Gordon and not see a sign of the alien form he'd once worn. He looked just as human as the next person. No, let me rephrase that. He looked like a tall, well-built and handsome human male with dark wavy hair, and skin the color of a mid-summer tan. He was also forming a personality as pleasing as his body with the help of my gentle guidance. He was soft spoken with a deep voice that resonated well and was as congenial as a boy scout on Sunday, but with a bit of occasional mild stubbornness that differed enough from his other traits to be sort of attractive. He had a wry sense of humor and was fun to talk to. And of course he was more knowledgeable than just about any other man in existence. In short, he turned into a dreamboat of a man. So why wasn't I attracted to him sexually?

Well, I guess I was, in a way. It wasn't just a sense of duty that made me decide to introduce him to sex myself, rather than take a chance on him getting off on the wrong foot from being hurt by some woman because of his inexperience. After he became fully human we kidded around a bit and kissed some and one day I took him to bed, more in the sense of a graduation ceremony than anything else. Or possibly I was just horny.

He was tentative at first but proved to be a quick learner and eager to please. The first time was pleasant enough but failed to produce an orgasm on my part. It was over too soon. After he'd recovered a bit we lay side by side while he expounded enthusiastically and at length over what a wonderful thing sex was. Finally I gently put my hand over his mouth.

"Gordon, dear, there's such a thing as being too analytical. Now let's try it again, slower, and if you can, use your perceptive sense or whatever else it takes to make it last a while."

"Of course. I'll try." He was aware that I hadn't climaxed but had mistakenly attributed it to the fact that we weren't in love or really even very close in a sexual way.

"Good. And Gordon... try not to think of just yourself."

He was silent for a moment, considering that, then said, "I'm sorry," very contritely.

"You don't have to be sorry, but just remember it takes two to really make it work right." I moved into his arms again and he immediately tried to enter me.

"Oops, not just yet!" I said and laughed. He was like a puppy, so eager to please it was funny. "Don't ever get in a hurry unless the woman encourages you. You'll never go wrong by taking the time for a bit of foreplay even if you've already made love once."

I had already discussed a woman's erogenous zones with him and now I showed him in person. Of course he'd read more about the mechanics of sex than just about any man on Earth or off it, but it's like flying; you have to do it a lot to get really good at it. However, he accepted advice willingly and adeptly. I had no complaint the second time, once we got there. It went on and on, and I felt the sense of impending release singing in my body. Then it was there and I screamed loud enough to wake the neighbors. It's a good thing the rooms are built to be airtight and strong enough to handle vacuum or I would probably have been too embarrassed to show my face the next day.

"And this," I told him later on as I slid down the bed, "is something you don't generally ask a woman for unless you're getting along really well. Of course, some may initiate it without asking, but as a rule, you don't ask." I proceeded to show him what I meant.

He gasped, then managed to ask, "Why?"

But as my mouth was a little busy, I couldn't answer him just then, although I did later as best as I was able. I don't think either of us slept that whole night. It was quite an experience. I hadn't been with a virgin since my first boyfriend and I learned together.

Unfortunately, as enjoyable as the teaching was, I still had Juan on my mind. Not that I'd tell him about this night, though. If there was a spark there with Gordon, it wasn't lighting anything yet. Or maybe it was, but if so, I could see it was going to be a while before it burst into flame. In the meantime, I told him he had graduated and could get out into the world, so to speak.

After I was caught up at the office and had a bit of time to spare, I called Juan to see what he was up to. There definitely was a sexual overtone to my wish for his company.

"Hi, Mai. Still tutoring our Crispy?"

"A bit, but he's mostly on his own now. You'll see him out and about."

"So you won't be working with him any more?"

"Oh, no. We'll still be seeing each other a lot but I've given him the goal now of getting out on his own and mixing with other people and just reporting back to me. You'll probably be working with him yourself eventually because right now he's on a tour of the ship, spending a few days in each section and getting to know everyone. I want him to mix as much as possible with all types of humans because he's going to be our chief liaison with the Crispies if we find them."

"Oh. Okay with me. What... I mean, would you like to, uh, maybe meet me in the lounge one evening for a drink?"

Yes, I'd love to, but I didn't say that. Instead I said, "How about this evening? Are you free then?" Well, maybe it was the same, just in different words.

"Uh-huh. Seven okay?"

"Sure. See you then."

Sometimes I think women are crazy. Here I had this All-American male—from another planet, granted—who I was sure would love nothing better than to take me to bed on a regular basis. But what was I doing? I was panting like a hungry puppy after Juan, an army sergeant with probably a limited education and not much life experience away from the military. Which shows how silly preconceptions can be.

ಬಂಛ

I took a shower and changed from my working costume of jeans and a pullover to casual slacks and blouse and dabbed on a bit of my limited supply of perfume before heading toward the lounge.

Juan was already there but had waited on me before getting anything to drink. Courteous. His face brightened when he saw me and I gave him a big smile that I didn't have to force. I was really glad to see him again, sexual feelings aside. We had connected on some level right from the first and that was what was dictating my feelings. The psychologists say we like even features in the opposite sex and I suppose there's some truth to it, but there's more to attraction than that. With Juan it had been his no-nonsense attitude and competency as much as his looks that had first impressed me.

He stood up and held out his hand as I neared. I took it, practically feeling the electricity between us.

"Hi!" I said, and without even thinking about it, leaned forward and pecked him on the mouth.

He grinned. "Hi, Mai. You look good."

"Thanks, but call me Cherry. What are we drinking?"

"Do you like whisky?"

A man after my own heart. "Uh-huh, but does the ship still have any?"

"A very limited amount, I've heard. But I brought one bottle of Jack Daniels Black Label along. I thought this might be a good time to crack it open. Mix or water?"

"Just lots of ice."

"Be right back."

He rose and fetched glasses and ice, then returned and poured whisky over our ice cubes and replaced the bottle in a little handbag he carried. When he saw my eyes following the bottle he smiled.

"If I set it on the table we'd draw lots of curious looks once the crowd gets here. And since I'm a generous soul, I'd probably give it all away once people saw it and started asking."

I laughed and we talked a few moments, then I commented on his scar. He was wearing jeans and a long-sleeved shirt with the sleeves rolled up almost to his elbows. The scar began near his wrist and wrapped around his arm and ran up beneath his shirt sleeve. I reached over and ran my finger along it.

He glanced down, then back up to meet my gaze.

"What happened there?" I asked softly.

"Got too close to a knife once."

"Where was that?"

"Uh, a place. Sorry."

"Can't talk about it?" Me and my big mouth.

"No. In fact, I regret that there's a lot of my life I can't talk about. Penalty for being in SOCOM."

"Special Forces Command, I take it?"

"Uh-huh."

"What led you there?"

"Hormones and stupidity, probably." He shrugged negligently.

That got a chuckle out of me. "Did you go in right after high school?"

"No, I had a degree in physics but I decided to play soldier and save enough money to go on to graduate school."

See what I meant about preconceptions?

"Have you got enough money to go back to school yet?"

"Oh sure. The army pays pretty well for enlistments and most places I've been there wasn't a lot to spend money on."

"Then you'll be getting out when we come back, huh?"

"No, I'm going to stay in the army. I found out I liked being a soldier." And see what I mean about silly assumptions?

I was curious. "It seems like with a degree and your experience you could probably get a commission. Any reason why not?"

"Umm. I've been thinking about it. In fact, I've been asked by higher ups. I was still thinking during that break with the training command but hadn't made up my mind. I was already on a fast track for Warrant Officer and wasn't really sure I wanted a commission. It sort of limits you in some ways. Can't go around tearing up bars, and have to learn to dance, and what all. Can't be getting into fights."

"Do you fight a lot?"

"Nah, rarely if ever. But I couldn't if I wanted to, see?"

I got it. He was gently pulling my leg.

We talked a bit more. He asked if I'd ever been married and I did the same for him.

"I was engaged. She couldn't stand the constant deployments. No, that's not right. What bugged her was that I wouldn't talk about them."

"Women like to be involved with a man's life if they're going to marry him."

"I suppose. Anyway, that's what happened. What's your story?"

We had another drink while I made dishonest excuses about still being single. Even if he was smarter and more knowledgeable than I had assumed, I still wasn't going to give him any hints about my I.Q. We bantered back and forth like men and women will on first dates, then when he reached for the bottle again I saw some eyes turned our way.

"People are watching the bottle. Why don't we take it back to my place and have another?" I said without stopping to think about it.

"Okay."

As we rounded the last corner I saw Gene just turning away from my door. He glanced at us and took note of the way my hand was entwined with Juan's by that time. He merely smiled and nodded as he passed, but I could tell he was disappointed.

Bringing the bottle to the room was just an excuse, of course. It was more than another drink I wanted, but we had one nevertheless. A little later I leaned my head on his shoulder momentarily while laughing at something he'd said and that led to us turning and facing each other. His big brown eyes were enough to get lost in but I didn't look at them very long. He put his arm around me and drew me to him. Our lips met, softly at first then more eagerly.

Juan was nice. He didn't grab for my breast right off like a lot of men do but took his time, stroking my back and moving his hands over the curve of my hip and to my back again. We grew closer and eventually he did begin caressing my breasts but by then I was ready to move to the bedroom. I leaned back and he saw the desire in my eyes. He stood up, bringing me with him by my grasp on his arm. I could feel the corded muscles beneath my fingers and it sent a thrill through me.

There were no more words right then, or if there were, I don't remember them. We walked the few steps to the bedroom, kissed one more time, then got undressed. I threw back the covers and practically wrestled him onto the bed. Seconds later I was in his arms and his hands and lips were moving over my body, caressing me with the kind of gentle firmness I loved. I embraced him tightly and urged him over me then guided him inside. A little gasp escaped me as we connected and his weight settled on me. I locked my legs around him and gripped his back as he moved inside me. It took very little time until he had me screaming with pleasure. God, it was so good to feel that release again. A little too good, maybe. I heard him cry out and realized I'd forgotten how strong I was.

While I still had my arms and legs around him and after I had settled down enough to be able to talk again, I moved my hands over his back and buttocks. I could feel the little ridges where my fingers had dug into his skin and where I'd grabbed him so hard.

"I'm sorry," I said. "I forgot I was..." And then I stopped, having forgotten I hadn't intended to tell anyone what Sira had done for me.

"It's all right. I know."

I smoothed a path of circles on his back and ran my bare foot up and down his calf. "What do you know, Juan? I haven't told anyone."

He laughed and kissed me gently. His face was shadowed in the dimmed lights. "I'm not a dummy. Remember, I had you in the training course. I noticed how easily you accomplished tasks that should have been much harder. Besides that, I'd heard rumors of how much stronger than normal one of our Special Forces guys was. I was already primed to see the unusual."

"Um. Did I hurt you?"

"'S okay. It hurt so good. But don't you know it's the man who's supposed to ask that?"

I bit him on the neck, but gently.

"Seriously, Cherry, it's all right. I'd be interested to see just exactly how strong you are sometime but not now. Am I getting heavy?"

"No, but let me up for a minute."

I kissed him and went to the bathroom and tossed a hand towel out to him while I took care of myself inside. I came back out and snuggled up to him. It was so good to be in bed with a man I really liked again. It had been a long time.

I guess it might have been a while for Juan, too. He didn't leave until an hour or two before first bells. We made love three more times that night and I lost my last assumptions about rude, crude soldiers during the process. Casanova could take lessons from that boy!

CHAPTER TWENTY-FIVE

SHIPBOARD LIFE was a curious blend of military and civilian. We were all under military discipline, of course, and that entailed all the little courtesies and formality the captain enforced. He wasn't harsh about it, though. As long as the civilian crew observed the necessary restrictions of shipboard life they were pretty well free to do as they pleased. The military was much more structured, with specific times for duty and non-duty, and regulations governed almost every aspect of their lives even though it wasn't usually apparent. I understood it because I had been in the military, but others didn't and that occasionally caused some friction, but not enough to matter.

I continued seeing Juan, much to Gene's aggravation. I suppose he might have thought those few kisses I exchanged with him meant more than they did. One day he joined me for a few minutes in the dining room at lunch after I'd already sat down.

"Hi Gene," I greeted him. "You've been kind of scarce lately."

"Not really. I think it's you that's been tied up and not noticed I was around."

"Maybe." I felt my cheeks tingle from a blush although I don't know why. I had nothing to be ashamed of. "So how goes it with you? Still solving problems?"

"Uh-huh. In fact one of them has to do with our Crispy. Gordon."

"Oh?"

"Uh-huh. There's a certain young lady who's not pulling her weight in the ship right now because of him."

"What's her problem?" I could guess but I wanted him to tell me.

"She's heart-broken."

"I can't help you there, Gene. She's gonna have to deal with it."

"Okay, but when's the last time you talked to Gordon?"

I felt the tingling return and begin creeping down my neck. I tried to think... "Uh, about four or five days, I think."

"And before then?"

"What is this, an inquisition?" I was beginning to figure out his purpose and it aggravated me.

"No, Mai," he said gently. "It's just that you're the person more than anyone else on the ship who's responsible for Gordon. Shouldn't you be spending just a little more time with him?"

My anger died as quickly as it had begun. Gene was right. I had been so wrapped up with Juan I had been neglecting my duty.

"Um, I suppose you're right, Gene, damn you. I'll talk to Gordon."

"Fine. Remember, while chances are we won't find the Cresperian planet, there's always the possibility, and it wouldn't hurt to have Gordon happy if we do."

"Thanks."

He nodded and stood up, then walked off leaving me sitting at the table alone and wondering if Captain Becker had sent Gene to chide me in his worldly, inimitable manner. If so, he'd done a good job. I got back to business.

That didn't mean I quit seeing Juan. If he hadn't had a platoon to take care of we would have moved in together. Once we hooked up I hated to see him have to get up and leave my bed before the night was done but there wasn't much to do about it.

I did talk to Gordon about his love life, or rather brought it up in the course of another conversation so he wouldn't think I was intrusive.

He grinned like a teenager. "My fellow Crispies are missing out on the best part of life, Mai. I couldn't judge before experiencing it, but sex is something that's completely outside the bounds of Cresperian under-standing. My fellows have no idea of what they've been deprived of."

"They aren't your fellows, Gordon. You're human, now. By choice."

He frowned. "You're right, of course. I am human, with all that entails, but along with it, I'm a Cresperian by birth and I still retain my percep-tive sense." He stared into space for a moment as if musing. "I wonder what it would be like to have a Crispy who's converted to human to share this with, merging our perceptive senses as our bodies merged. I believe it would be an even more intense experience."

"Really? And just how much more intense could it get?"

"I'm sorry. Without the perceptive sense you can't understand. It would be…" He stopped, nonplussed. "Hmm. Perhaps you're right. I don't know how it could get much better."

I nodded. "Crispies can't understand our type of sexual experience un-less they become human. Perhaps it might be even more intense shared by two converts, but let's leave that for now." I paused, then let him have it. "Gordon, you need to be... considerate of your partners."

"Just so. Mai, I'm sorry about Midge. I didn't intend for her to become so involved."

"That's what I wanted to talk to you about, Gordon. If you're not looking for a permanent partner right now, it would be best to let a woman know in advance."

"Yes, I see that now. Trust me, I'll be careful in the future."

And he was. He didn't lack for sexual partners if only for the novelty, but nothing like that ever came up again. Nothing I heard about, anyway, so I didn't ask.

There were other issues that did come to my attention, though. Fortunately, even if he did look like a very young man he didn't think like one. He didn't see things in black and white like a human youth would have. He had a long lifetime of Crispy experience to guide him and he retained all those memories. On the other hand, he tended to be impatient and vexed when someone offered an opinion that was at odds with what he believed. And since he had a wealth of knowledge to draw on, and with his blinding reading speed and eidetic memory, he was almost always right. I had to call him to my office one day to remonstrate with him after an argument with one of the ship's officers.

"Gordon, you're going to have to realize that you can't go around getting angry simply because you disagree with someone, nor can you convert everyone to your way of thinking. It's neither possible nor even desirable."

"But Mai, *astrology?* How can any sensible person—"

He looked pained when I held up a hand to stop his outburst.

"Yes, I agree. Astrology is ridiculous on the face of it but some people like to believe it has merits, regardless. You have to allow humans their foibles. It's not like she's starving her children or abusing animals or knocking down old ladies on the street. Astrology, as you should know, actually contributed to science way back in our history by instilling an interest in astronomy. And it's harmless. Besides, history will take care of it in the long run. So leave it be, okay?"

He thought for a moment, then gradually his expression changed. Finally he laughed.

"All right, Mai. I'm sorry. Hormones."

And then I laughed. "Uh-huh. Your body is that of a male barely out of his teens. So go think about sex and leave that poor woman to her charts and signs. And damn it, Gordon, you of all people should know how to watch for the influence of genes that code the proteins that coordinate brain wiring with hormonal influences. So *watch*. Please?"

"I shall. You're a doll, Mai. One day I'm going to have to figure out how to thank you properly for all you've done." He winked and I grinned at him. He really had turned into a good human. It made me wonder if perhaps I should have participated physically in his sexual education more than that one time and see what happened. I thought I probably would have, had it not been for Juan getting in the way. I hoped he would find someone permanent soon.

"No thanks are necessary, Gordon. You're doing fine and I'm glad. But now that you're here, tell me what else you're up to."

"Oh, this and that." He leaned back in his chair and crossed his hands over his stomach. "I haven't decided yet on a profession, so mostly I've just been wandering through the ship and meeting people."

"That's good, so long as they're not real busy."

"I'm being careful about that. Y' know, Maddie is an interesting person. I've been talking to her a lot. Once we get back, I may go into astronomy."

I started to say, "if we get back," then decided not to. Why be a pessimist? Instead I reminded him of why he was on the ship in the first place.

"Gordon, I don't want to discourage you, but if we find Cresperia, you're going to be awfully busy for a long time."

"Umm. You're right about that. Maddie says she thinks there's a chance. We've got better data than the folks on the first ship, and she thinks eventually we'll find it. Maybe not on this trip but one day."

"That's great, Gordon. But how will you feel about it?"

He shrugged. "I'll stay human, Mai. You should know that. But it would be nice to see the home planet again. I haven't said much about it before, since chances seemed so slim of ever going home… but if we do make it, you and everyone else may as well prepare for trouble."

"What!" I leaned forward, scrutinizing his face, and saw that he was serious.

"Uh-huh. Jeri didn't say much about it, but if me or any other Crispy begins advocating conversion to human on a large scale the older, more conservative Crispies may well begin discouraging it. Forcibly."

"You're serious, aren't you?"

"Yes," he said solemnly.

"Have you spoken to the captain about it?"

"I haven't seen the point, not unless we find Cresperia."

"Gordon, I think we'd better let him know. It's never good to sail under wrong assumptions."

Chapter Twenty-Six

As THE TIME WOUND DOWN before our projected arrival at the Swavely system I noticed a change in Juan. He seemed less talkative and kind of withdrawn. He'd never been big on casual conversation like a lot of men are, thinking they have to talk or you'll believe they're missing one of their balls or something like that. But now he was *really* quiet. One night after we'd made love and I was all snuggled up next to him with my head on his shoulder, I finally asked him about it.

"I'm not sure, sweetheart," he finally said after I'd begun to decide he either hadn't heard me or wasn't going to answer. "It's... I don't like to talk about it, and it's probably nothing."

"You're worried about something." I ran my fingers through the thatch of hair in the center of his chest, then over the rise of his pectoral muscles. His heart was beating faster than normal, when it should have had time to return to the resting state.

"I don't know why I should be, but... I've got a strange feeling about our stop here."

"Like what? Something bad?"

He sighed. "Yeah, Cherry, something bad. But hell, it's probably just a case of the heebie-jeebies like you always feel right before combat."

"You think we'll get into a fight there? That's foolish, Juan. We don't even know yet whether the planet's inhabited or not." We did know there was a planet of the right size and distance from the primary to support life. That was about all.

"I know. Hey, I'm sorry. I shouldn't spoil our time together."

He turned and kissed me and began caressing my breast. His hand was calloused but he had such a gentle touch that they didn't feel rough. Instead, the way he smoothed his hand over and around and then lowered his lips to my nipple made me shiver. A wave of anticipatory pleasure coursed through my body and made me forget all about anything else for a while.

It was only later that night, after I was there by myself that I remembered how he'd said "our time together" as if it was a limited thing, not meant to last.

ುಃಃ

Three days later we arrived in orbit around the planet Swavely. There were only a few portholes on the *Galactic* and by the time I got a turn to look we'd been there for hours. The planet looked much like Earth did from space, all green and blue and brown. I couldn't make out much detail about the continents other than to see that they weren't the same shape as Earth's. Naturally.

I knew *Zeng Wu* was supposed to have left a satellite in orbit around each of the planets they orbited, so it was no surprise when the captain reported that we'd made contact with it. I thought that meant their ship had probably gone on from Swavely and was now searching for Cresperia in earnest. However, no one heard a thing from the captain for hours and hours after that.

I was in my office having a cup of coffee with Nancy Silveras, another civilian scientist, a biologist and now a rather limited xenobiologist, what with only Crispies to study. That would change as soon as we set foot on the planet. Then she would become a full-fledged xenobiologist.

"I can hardly wait," she enthused. "A whole different biology and ecology from Earth! I could spend a lifetime here and not even make a start on all the things there'll be to discover." She was bubbling over about the prospective landing, making her look so young and happy you hardly noticed the crow's feet around her eyes or the strands of grey in her hair.

"Same here," I agreed. "I suspect the genetics will be different, just as the Crispies are. They weren't much of a challenge, though, because Jeri explained it all before we had much of a chance for research."

"This will be different, I'll bet. I wonder if there's any intelligent life here?"

"I suspect the captain would make an announcement if Maddie noticed any."

"She wouldn't have to notice," Nancy told me. "Captain Becker is probably querying the satellite for all the data the *Zeng Wu* left us."

It turned out that she was right. But the data from the satellite wasn't good news at all, because *Zeng Wu* was still on the planet. It had landed and never taken off again.

৪০০৪

I learned what was going on when Captain Becker called a department head meeting. As Chief Science Officer I was there and I suppose I may as well mention now that a couple of other scientists on board had their noses a little out of joint because of me being named to the position at my young age. Looking not much older than a teenager because of what Sira had done for me didn't help matters.

Smackers was the worst. That young jackass wasn't but two years older than me and he thought he should have had the spot simply because he understood more of the theory of the ship's unreality drive than anyone else on board. Hell, he probably thought he should be captain!

Captain Jules Becker always looked as if it would cause him physical pain to smile, but now he was really grim. He was sitting at the head of the conference table staring straight ahead, looking at no one in particular, and appeared mad enough to be able to floss his teeth with barbed wire. Not good, I found myself thinking. Not good at all.

Once everyone was present, he led off and wasted very few words.

"Gentlemen, ladies, thank you for coming. I have some extremely bad news. Our sister ship, the USSS Zeng Wu, is down on the planet. It has not been damaged too badly and is still quite capable of leaving. However, the planet is inhabited by inimical aliens."

He paused and looked around the table to make sure we all understood, then continued.

"Here is a brief rundown on the present situation. At first it appeared as if Swavely was inhabited by intelligent beings with a low population and fairly advanced technology but as yet incapable of space flight. The ship landed near one of the settlements and began contact procedures with the beings according to our diplomatic protocol. I'll show some footage later, but for now, suffice to say that at first they pretended to be friendly.

"Eventually many of the crew disembarked and were away from the ship doing studies and learning the language. Then the aliens let slip that they were merely a colony of a large interstellar empire. At that point they turned on the crew of the Zeng Wu and attempted to capture the ship. There were heavy casualties but they did not succeed. However, they did manage to take some captives. There is a standoff at present.

"I'm sorry to report that Captain Bronson died during the hostilities and General Haley has taken command. He is not allowing the ship to lift off while some of the crew is still alive and in their hands. The aliens threatened to kill the captives if he did not surrender but General Haley warned them that he would destroy the planet if they hurt anyone. He can't, of course, but they don't know that. What he is afraid of is that one of their warships will arrive on a visit and he will *have* to leave the captives in order to prevent the destruction of his ship.

"That's where the situation stands at present. I shall now open this meeting to discussion but before we begin let me note that I agree completely with General Haley. We will not leave while humans are in custody of those creatures. Therefore the discussion should center on rescue operations."

Colonel Jones, the marine commander, spoke first. "Is there any reason why the aliens haven't simply bombed the ship?"

"General Haley believes they do not want to harm the ship but do want very much to capture it. He thinks they believe our technology might be ahead of them is the reason. So far they haven't used any heavy weaponry and again, he thinks it's for fear of harming the ship."

Jones nodded. "Good so far. Do we know where the hostages are being held?"

"Yes. We know that much. Commander Graham's also made satellite images of the the area."

He nodded to Major Eleanora Wisteria, the communications officer and chief electronicist. She brought up the images and waited to explain any points that needed clarifying.

Commander Prescott, our XO, began pointing out various sites. "Here's the city. Infrared images lead us to believe some of it is underground. Here you can see the ship and over here is where General Haley says the captives are being held. They have moved heavily armed aliens into positions here, here and here. That's in addition to the fact that almost all of them carry some type of hand weapon on their persons."

"What kind of weapons?" Jones asked without moving his gaze from the images. He was studying them as intently as an undergraduate studied class notes the night before finals.

"Laser or possibly a type of energy weapon but better than anything we've got. I suspect their space ships might also be armed with them, same as ours but as a corollary, they're probably also more powerful."

"How many casualties?"

"Almost half of the crew. And half of the remainder are prisoners," Becker said stoically.

Jones winced. So did I, for that matter. I couldn't help but wonder whether Kyle and Jeri had survived. I just couldn't picture two such *alive* people as them no longer existing. Which didn't mean a thing. The universe doesn't operate on wishes.

"I suppose we have no idea when the next alien ship is due?" Graham asked.

"Not a clue. I've put the computer to analyzing everything we know, but it's doubtful it will be much help. What I want is for each of you to take a copy of the recordings Bronson got before he died and go back to your people and study the complete layout down there. Get them to thinking in terms of a rescue mission. You may share this data with anyone since I'll be making an announcement shortly. We'll meet again in three hours. If you come up with anything really important beforehand, pass it on to Colonel Jones. He'll be responsible for the final plan."

"Sir, do they know we're up here in orbit?"

"We haven't spotted a satellite so I don't know, but it makes no difference. We're going to try for a rescue." He got up and left as abruptly as the President ducking a mob of reporters.

I didn't say so but was willing to bet one reason General Haley refused to leave the captives was that he expected our ship to be along eventually. So long as it was a stalemate, he could afford to wait.

I was also willing to bet that by now, they were getting awfully damned impatient.

Chapter Twenty-Seven

No one I talked to had a lot of military background, which figured since I was the head of the civilian science department. That made it a fairly small group. I could have wished it was short one more person. Smackers pretended he was Napoleon reincarnated but it quickly became apparent that he had no more idea of tactics and strategy than a blind pregnant Muslim suicide bomber. His idea of a rescue mission was to land beside the other ship and start shooting.

"John, the crew of *Zeng Wu* would already have rescued everyone and leveled that alien community to the ground if shooting off a bunch of ammunition was all it took. I think the captain is looking for at least a modicum of a strategy that doesn't put all of us in the same position as the captives."

"Goddamn bug-eyed monsters. Why don't we start bombing their cities, then?"

"First, because we don't have any bombs. And second, according to Captain Bronson's report, they have threatened to kill all the captives if he lifts off. And last because they only have one large city. The rest of the population is spread out. Anyone else?"

Smackers got up and left in a huff. I didn't try to call him back. Good riddance.

The one married couple in my science department was Eugene and Margie Preconder. Her doctorate was in quantum physics and Eugene was the microbiochemist of the family. He and I worked together a lot.

"I take it we're looking for a diversion of some sort?" he asked. He had short brown hair and wore glasses. I had never asked why.

"That would be my thinking," I said. "I was in the military but not with the sharp end of the stick, so my experience in tactics is limited. I'm open to any kind of idea and so is Captain Becker. That's why we're meeting here." I might add right here that my respect for Colonel Jones went up by a magnitude when he solicited opinions from everyone instead of simply devising his own plan and carrying it out.

"Where would be the best place to land the ship, I wonder?" Eugene asked. "Do we have some elevation markers?"

"Let's see." I fiddled with the graphics, then had to go back to the first survey to finally get the numbers. They were fairly rough. No one had been thinking about a fight at the time. Despite that, it was apparent there was only one high spot that wasn't already encumbered with buildings of some sort.

"That looks suspicious," I said.

"How about infrared?" Margie asked.

I pulled up the survey and sure enough, there was a pretty good heat source buried under that little hill.

"I'll bet a shot of Mai's whisky that there's something under there I wouldn't want us to get in front of," Eugene said grimly.

"How'd you know I still have whisky? Never mind, no bet. Might be a good place to land the ship, though. Or maybe not. I'd think if it was a laser cannon emplacement we might set right on top of it where they could open the hatch and blow the ship to bits."

"Maybe not. Blowback. That close, unless they could step down the power, it'd kill them as well. And besides, seems like they would have used it already if they could."

"Good point. I'll pass that one on. Now those..." I pointed to a close up of one of the BEMs. It wasn't really bug-eyed and neither was it a monster. It resembled a duck-billed platypus with tentacles as much as anything else. If you replaced the bill with a toothed beak and added a double-tail that provided support when it stood upright and balance when it was running. "...Those things are as tall or taller than a man when standing upright. Notice how the tentacles all end in little graspers for fine work. It's actually a pretty good design except for their meanness."

"It might not be mean by its lights," Margie said. Ordinarily she kept her short red hair in order but at the moment it was in disarray from her running her fingers through it.

"Point. But it is by ours. General Haley says they deliberately tricked them and did their damnedest to capture the ship. When that failed they began threatening to kill the hostages. Fortunately this is their equivalent of a frontier world so they apparently don't have any really heavy weapons on the planet."

"Right," Eugene said. "And I take it our job is to figure out how to grab the hostages and get both ships back into space before one of their interstellar ships arrive."

I nodded. "Right you are. Other groups are thinking about this as well, and the marines in particular. The captain just wants as much input as possible before he makes a decision. Any other observa-tions? Anyone?"

"There doesn't seem to be that many of them in the immediate area," Margie said. "Does that mean anything?" She ran her fingers through her hair again.

"Probably just means there's more somewhere else," I said, chuckling. "I can't imagine those few defeating the marines that were there, although I guess surprise helped. In fact, I suspect that's why the *Zeng Wu* hasn't been able to mount a rescue. Not enough fighters left."

"Would the Captain accept civilian help in the rescue operation? I can shoot," Nancy Silveras asked. She was another of my scientists. She had touches of gray in her dark hair but looked rather young. I guess she hadn't brought hair coloring along but I'd never asked.

"We've all had the training, so I don't see why not. In fact, it may be necessary to use every person on board. I'll pass that one on, too."

I made a note of it to go with the other factors and the discussion continued.

I wasn't under any illusions that the subjects my group discussed were going to lead to a grand battle plan. Becker just wanted to make damn certain the professionals didn't miss anything, and he was calling on all the help he had—and there were lots of brilliant people in our crew. I let the discussion go on until nothing new was being said, then stopped it and dismissed everyone. I can't see the point of talking when you're no longer contributing anything useful.

I checked my watch. An hour until Captain Becker wanted to see us again. I went back to my stateroom and rummaged around until I found my little .40. I tucked it into the side pocket of a windbreaker where it would be handy, made myself a quick snack and rested for a few minutes.

What Juan had said that one night about using our time together came back to mind, and I began thinking about it. Had he intuited something days in advance? It almost seemed that way, now that we knew the planet was inhabited by warlike aliens. I tried to make my mind quiet down and not get in a panic over something that hadn't happened yet and probably never would. I had to think though, that this must be something like what military spouses went through all the time when their other half was away at war or on the way to a war and it made me appreciate how little ruckus most of them made.

ೞೞಚಚ

At the next meeting Captain Becker listened to everyone else, asked some astute questions, and then let Colonel Jones speak. He didn't look happy, and I knew why a few moments later. He must have already had a plan drawn up in his mind and simply incorporated a few other tidbits of information from us that he or his staff hadn't thought of; it still wasn't enough.

"Captain, I think it may be possible to rescue our comrades, but it's not going to be easy, and it's going to take just about everyone aboard ship who can handle a weapon."

Uh-oh, I thought. Not good.

Captain Becker nodded to him. "Proceed."

"All right, sir, here's what I and my staff have come up with. I know we can't use the ship directly but we have the two exploration vehicles. I want to commit both of them from atmosphere." He held up his hand to stifle objections before they got started. "And no one needs to tell me they weren't designed to be launched that way, but I believe they must be for us to have a chance. I don't have that many troops, just a rump company of less than a hundred men divided into three short platoons and a head-quarters staff. The aliens must be observing their surroundings, so we'll deorbit on the other side of the planet and come in at a very sharp angle. They may or may not have caught on to the satellite in orbit but we have to assume they have. I doubt they will have broken our encryption yet, though.

"What I propose is to launch both exploration tenders with a fire team of marines in each with half our heavy weapons. They'll come in low and set up here and here." He used a laser pointer to touch the screen at points beyond the edge of what he said were formations of enemy troops on three sides of the ship. "Captain Becker will set the ship down on this slope here after we've neutralized what we believe to be a laser emplace-ment in this little hill." He pointed both out and waited each time to be sure we had the areas fixed in our memories. "From where the ship lands, one of our laser cannons can be pointed at a low enough angle to engage reinforcements as well as whatever else is hidden inside that hill.

"Immediately upon landing, the captain will drop the loading ramps which will be concealed by the rest of the ship from observation by the aliens. Half of the rest of my troops will deploy at that time, swing around to the left and right and engage the enemy in a crossfire while the other half makes a dash toward the structure where the captives are being held. Now…" He paused to sweep the room with his gaze, eyeing each of us briefly.

"…Now if you've been counting, you'll realize I've run out of marines. That's where the rest of the crew comes in. They're going to have to participate and help provide some cover while the rescue party makes a fighting withdrawal to the ship, but not to our ship. They'll head to the *Zeng Wu*, which will drop its loading ramp at the appropriate time. We're hoping they won't be expecting them to head that way and the captives will be able to get aboard before the aliens have time to react. In the meantime, our people will be laying down a covering fire, as I said. They're civilians, I know, but they won't have to expose themselves for too long, I hope. Their purpose is to let the rescue party reach the *Zeng Wu* and then they're to immediately withdraw back into the ship so it can get the hell out of there."

He grinned mirthlessly. "I wish to hell there was some way to run through this exercise before committing ourselves, but there's not. I will have very loud noise signals at the appropriate times to tell everyone what stage of the battle we're in but I certainly don't expect that to solve everything. For you non-military people here, there's one primary rule of combat and I want you to keep it in mind. Pass it on to your people, too. 'No battle plan survives first contact with the enemy,' so be prepared to improvise if necessary." He stopped talking again and scanned the group. "Questions?"

There were, of course, but Captain Becker was getting antsy. When Maddie called from her office to tell him she was observing some suspicious movement he cut the discussion short and set deployment for one hour later.

I knew some big brains back on Earth were going to second-guess the captain over risking his ship, but they weren't here. We were. And I doubt he would have done it if the odds hadn't been good. Not necessarily for freeing the hostages, but for keeping the ship from major harm. It was armored well enough that hand lasers couldn't hurt it much, and he didn't intend to land until the emplacement under that hill had been taken out. I would have done the same thing myself.

CHAPTER TWENTY-EIGHT

THE ONE PERSON CAPTAIN BECKER refused to risk was Gordon. It didn't set well with him, not with him being so young in body and with all that testosterone running rampant through his system, but Becker was adamant. We *had* to have a Crispy with us if we ever found the Cresperian planet, so he had to stay inside. Becker did ask him if he could get anything useful from the aliens with his perceptive sense. I overheard that bit of conversation.

"No, Captain. It is much too far away. And since I've never had anything to do with the ship or its crew, there's not even any entanglement."

"Oh, well." The colonel shrugged. "I was hoping for some help there but if you can't, you can't. Once we're down, though, if you find out anything useful let me or one of the officers know right away. I'll tie you in to the command circuit. Not having any idea of what the aliens intend is gonna make it a bit harder but it's still doable. I need to talk to the platoon leaders right quick and get the troops loaded up now, though. Thanks, Gordon."

I hoped that would at least make Gordon think he was helping.

With General Shelton not being in the line of command, he volunteered to lead a small group to help suppress the concentration of aliens we'd spotted moving in. That meant drawing a few marines from each of the other groups and selecting a half dozen civilians with prior military experience to fill them out. His face was grim as he left to get his people together, but his eyes were bright. It had probably been a long time since he'd led a squad-sized group.

We left orbit immediately after that conversation. Even as we were descending we all had to begin moving toward where we'd be exiting, the Shelton group to the big loading ramp and the rest of us to the small people ramp and the two airlocks. Only that part of the crew absolutely necessary to operate the ship was going to be left aboard.

I felt the ship give a quick shudder twice in succession, indicating the explorers had been launched. No way to tell if they were successful until we grounded, but the time passed so quickly for me that it seemed to happen almost immediately.

Becker had thought the best way for the civilians to fight was under the command of the individual department heads, which meant all of my scientists were with me, including, unfortunately, Smackers, whom I'd just as soon have left behind. He kept yammering about how we were going to stomp hell out of the BEMs until I finally told him to shut up or he'd stay in the ship.

ಬಿ೦೧

I could hear the loud stutter of machine-gun fire the minute the second airlock door opened, and I led my people outside. We were second in line behind a contingent of yeomen and technicians from operations and analysis. Some of them were already shooting at something.

"Take cover and hold your fire!" I yelled. We were supposed to be shooting toward each narrow flank of the rescue team, but only *after* they had the captives and were on the way back; and at that, we had a miscellany of weapons that made us look like the proverbial people's militia.

Off in the distance I could see marines and aliens mixing it up, way too far for accurate fire. Smackers began shooting anyway, trying to pick off aliens with a sporting rifle. I ducked low and ran over to him and popped him on the top of his head. "Hold your fire, goddamn it, until we have some targets! You're going to kill some of our own people shooting like that," I shouted into his face. "If I see you fire that rifle one more time before I tell you to, I'm going to shoot you myself!"

He rose halfway to his feet, face red as a beet, and attempted to slap me. I blocked the move, caught his wrist, and squeezed until he yelped with pain.

"Listen to me, you goddamn fool! You'll hit one of our people from this distance. Now hold on!"

Sulking and seething, he lowered himself back to the ground. I got back into position and tried to see what was going on.

The marines on the right flank seemed to be doing fine. They had machine-guns hammering away, mixed with small arms fire, but none of it was panicky. It was timed and professional, just as I'd seen on the training course in basic. But on the left, something was happening that hadn't been planned for.

A big vehicle with corrugated tires rolled into view spitting laser beams. In the distance, I saw marines die while their bullets bounced off its armor. It swept a path through that squad and began moving up the streets toward the right flank. The marines left behind flung bullets at it futilely. The vehicle drove behind an intervening building; then, just as it came into sight again, our laser cannon opened up. Its wheels caught on fire; then the thing began smoking. Abruptly it erupted in a ball of thunderous flame.

Way back behind all this action the two explorer vehicles had landed and their crews were pouring all the fire they were capable of into what I figured must be reinforcements moving up. I couldn't see what was happening for sure, though.

Commander Graham had gone as far as the people ramp but remained at the entrance, observing the battle from a higher vantage point than I had. I wished there was some way of communicating with her and finding out about the captives but there wasn't. Only the marines and a couple of others had access to the general net – an oversight I was sure would be corrected later, but that did no good at the moment. Instead, she left her post and ran at a crouch to the foot of the ramp where we were.

"Mai! Take Smackers, Henry and the other of your people who have rifles and go reinforce the left flank. They've been mauled and need some help. If you go to them down that side street—" ...she pointed to the one she meant "—then you can add some firepower from a different direction. Maybe it'll throw the bastards off long enough to get the captives to their ship. They've been freed, but it's slow going and they're under a lot of pressure." She ducked as a laser beam scorched the air near her head.

"Got it."

I yelled out the names of the people I wanted and began leading them off, but suddenly I had the feeling I was missing someone. I turned around. Smackers was hanging back.

"Get your ass up here, Smackers! Those people need help!"

Reluctantly he joined our group but I wondered if I'd done the right thing. It might have been best to leave him behind, the way he was acting. His gaze was dancing wildly back and forth as if looking for a safe place to run to. I motioned for him to come on and turned away. If he followed, fine. If not, I didn't have time to worry about him.

We ran and dodged just as fast as I could chivvy them along. Most of the group had never been in the military. All of them had used guns before or they wouldn't have been out there, but none of them had ever thought they'd be involved in a battle. Hell, *I'd* never thought I'd be involved in one. This might not have been a war but it would do until a real one came along.

I lost Henry along the way. I don't know why he stood up like that, maybe hoping for a clear shot, but whatever his reason, he caught a laser beam to the face that didn't kill him immediately. He ran blindly into the open, screaming about his eyes and died when another beam sliced across his abdomen, spilling his guts into the street. I heard someone vomit but there wasn't time to see who it was.

"Get some fire going, people! Now!" I yelled and set an example by raising up briefly and emptying half a clip from my rifle in the direction of the nearest Snappers. Before I ducked back down I saw several of them fall, spurting orange blood. What was left of the marines and the rest of my people joined in and gradually began suppressing the laser fire.

In the meantime, the captives had somehow been freed just as Maddie had told us, although I hadn't able to see that part of the action. What I did see was a gang of men and women erupt from the center of the battle area and begin running toward the ships. At the same time, the marines must have been ordered to give as much covering fire as they possibly could: it picked up considerably, drowning out all other noises. Exploding grenades added to the din, as well as the roar of flames shooting from some of the openings and roofs of the alien homes or offices or whatever the hell they were. We had failed to take them into account. Several of us began firing back at the snipers.

Eugene dropped his weapon when a laser beam hit him in the upper arm. He fell to the ground screaming and trying to beat out the flames with his other hand. I couldn't do anything for him at the moment because the former captives were coming closer and they needed all the help they could get: they were unarmed and completely helpless.

I caught a glimpse of one of our tenders as it rose from the planet. Why, I don't know. A heavy laser beam sought it out and finally caught it, burning directly into the canopy. It fell back to the ground in a trail of smoke and crashed. It hadn't been too high; maybe some of the crew had made it out alive.

As the people from the *Zeng Wu* got closer we had to watch what we were doing to avoid hitting them. I cautioned everyone and told Smackers twice. He seemed to be off in la-la land so I don't know if he heard me or not. His face was white and he was moving his bowed head back and forth like a duck looking for bread in the water. I saw that his rifle had ejected its clip and he was making no effort to insert another. Shit. For all his braggadocio he was useless when it came to the crunch. I decided to let him be for the moment.

The marines were running through their ammunition at a furious rate, but that was just what we needed right then. And our laser cannon finally found the big one that had gotten our exploration vehicle and a fire team of marines with it. Its pulsing beam burned into the bunker for several seconds – and then it must have hit something flammable. The bunker blew up in a thunderous explosion; beams of wood, and fragments of metal and Snapper bodies were hurled through the air. Once it was disabled, the rest of the marines began slowly closing in on the ships, killing anything that got in their way.

One group of the captives got ahead of their guide marines and came our way instead of toward the *Zeng Wu*. "Careful!" I yelled. "Don't hit our own people!" Our fire slacked off and I thought they were all going to make it but just at the last moment a laser beam cut the legs from under two of them, both women. They were naked from the waist up. It didn't look as if their legs had been amputated, but both fell and couldn't get up. Hamstrung, maybe.

It took only a second to make the decision. Fortunately, General Shelton had seen what was happening and committed the civilian reserve.

"Margie, Smackers, Brenner, and you, let's go!" I yelled. "We can drag them back!"

I got up and so did two of the others.

Smackers began crying and shaking his head worse than before. "No, no! They'll kill us."

"Get your cowardly ass up and come help or I'll kill you myself, you sorry son of a bitch."

"I'll go," one of the technicians said, looking disgustedly at Smackers, who was beginning to curl up into a fetal ball.

"Okay, but move! Leave your rifles here. The rest of you, cover us."

In the meantime others were passing us and running on into the ship. They were panting and sweat was streaking their dirty faces and chests and arms as it ran down their bodies. For some reason the aliens had taken all of their upper garments, men and women alike.

My three other crewmembers and I ran out into the open and dropped beside the two wounded women. We began dragging them back toward the ship. It was an effort, and they couldn't help much. Besides being exhausted, they had thought they were being left behind and were on the verge of complete hysteria. And just then the remnants of the marines from the left flank came running up.

Juan was among them. He grinned at me though a face so dirty and smeared with blood I hardly recognized him. I breathed a sigh of relief to see him alive—but it lasted only a second. Two laser beams converged on him at the same time and cut him in two.

CHAPTER TWENTY-NINE

WE GOT THE REST OF THE ONES who had been held by the Snappers aboard not long afterwards. I moved mechanically, trying to blot Juan's awful last moment from my memory while we moved on back into the ship, making room for the marines who were still coming in. There weren't as many as had gone out and some of the wounded were being helped by others, but the mission had been successful. As soon as the last marine was aboard, we took off.

Thirty-two captives had been freed for the loss of one of our exploratory vessels and twenty dead marines as well as a number of civilians. Some might think it wasn't a good trade, but goddammit, those fucking miserable Snappers needed to learn not to mess with humans. That was what the other crew began calling them, Snappers, after the partial resemblance of their heads to the duck-billed platypus but with the bill turned into a toothed beak. That, and the sound the beak made when it clacked together. We didn't know if it was a language or not.

I never saw Smackers again. I don't know whether he was killed or simply lay where he had been curled up and was taken captive. I couldn't make myself care and I doubt if anyone else missed him either.

After everyone was aboard, the two ships left the planet and headed out of the system. Once we were well away from the planet, they met so that we could compare notes in person and distribute the remaining crews more equitably. And most of all, decide on what to do next.

೮೦೦೪

After we were in space I stayed in my stateroom for the next 24 hours, refusing to speak to anyone. It was hard to make myself believe that Juan was gone. It had happened so quickly, so nightmarishly, and right when I thought he was safe, that it didn't seem quite real. And of course there was no question of recovering bodies, not with plenty of aliens still available to fight. Also, both captains wanted to get out of the system as soon as possible so as not to get caught by an alien ship arriving on what was clearly a colony world of the Snapper empire.

At noon the second day after the battle on Swavely there came a knock on my door, sounding faintly through the tight seal. I guess I hadn't heard the bell. I was sitting in my chair and staring at a framed picture of

Juan he had given me a couple of weeks before the fight. He was smiling gently like I had seen him do on all the occasions after we'd made love. I had asked him about it once and he told me he was smiling because he enjoyed making love to me more than any woman he'd ever been with. A tear left the corner of my eye and trickled down my cheek. *Shit! Why? Why him?*

The knock came again, more forcibly this time. I sighed and got up and went to the door. I opened it and there were Kyle and Jeri. I stepped back, more in surprise than invitation to enter, but they both came in.

"We heard," Jeri said, her voice soft with compassion.

I stared at her for a moment then the next thing I knew she was hugging me and I was bawling my heart out, wetting her shoulders with my tears.

She let me cry for a few minutes, then moved me over to the couch and made me sit down. She and Kyle unfolded seats from the wall and sat with me.

I rubbed my eyes and started to get up and fetch a hand towel but Kyle held out his handkerchief and I took it instead.

"Thanks." I sniffed again, wiped my eyes dry and blew my nose. "I don't know what came over me. I don't usually break down like that."

I didn't, really. And I hadn't loved Juan, not with that deep abiding passion of someone who means the universe to you, but I had been extremely fond of him and it was certainly moving toward that kind of love before he died.

"Sometimes crying is good for you," Kyle said. He gazed off into what would have been a far distance if we weren't in a confined room. I thought he was probably remembering some lost comrade from one of the wars he'd been in. Somehow that made it easier for me to accept the fact that Juan was gone.

"I guess so. I'm glad to see you two made it out of the ruckus. I thought about you."

"That's nice to know," Jeri said gratefully. "I'm just sorry I couldn't gauge the Snappers' intentions and been able to prevent it, but their thought processes are too weird. Strange, because they have brains and metabolisms somewhat akin to ours."

"That's in the past, sweetheart," Kyle said. "Mai, if you think you're up to it, Gordon could probably use a little consoling. He's feeling kind of down right now because he wasn't allowed to participate in the rescue."

"He shouldn't feel that way," I said. "He's too important to risk in a gun battle. Laser battle, I should say."

"Some of both," Jeri said, "but he still thinks he should have done something more. Even after I told him I had been in the same position as him, it didn't help."

"Where were you?"

She smiled wryly. "With General Haley. He was making damn certain I didn't go out on my own."

"Maybe you should get the general to talk to him."

She rubbed her chin. "Might help. I hadn't thought of that, but it's you Gordon respects more than anyone else in the ship. Besides, General Haley's kind of busy right now. Listen, we didn't come here solely to commiserate, although that was certainly one of the reasons. The other is to tell you that there's a general meeting of the officers from both ships this evening at seven here in the *Galactic*. We have to decide where to go from here."

"And I'm invited?"

"Your presence is requested, along with Gordon," Kyle said. "Go see him and drag him to the meeting, forcibly if you have to. We need him there. We need both of you there. It's going to be in the big conference room."

I took a deep breath and let it out. "All right, I'll talk to him. In the meantime I'll offer you some Jack Daniels Black Label if you'll stay for a while and tell me what you've been doing since leaving Earth."

Kyle checked his watch. Jeri didn't need to. All the Crispies have a built-in time sense and retain it even after converting to human.

"Okay," he said. "I can't resist a shot or two of Blackjack. We can stay for a while."

༄ঙ৪

The *Zeng Wu* had had six definite and another dozen possible star systems on their itinerary while on the way to Swavely, after which they were to begin searching for Cresperia. The six definite systems were those where new compound telescopes on Earth had spotted what they believed to be Earth-like planets. The others were possibilities. They hadn't discovered any other intelligent species, but had found two planets where it appeared that humans could survive and live, if not very comfortably. And one that was pretty nice.

"Of course we can't be certain until humans have lived on them for a while," Kyle said. "It might turn out that there are long term consequences, like a lack of vital trace elements in the soil or conversely, too much of certain substances. However, we left a satellite at each one, claiming it for the United States and England."

I smiled for the first time since Juan died. "The diplomats are going to say you've been naughty. Space should be for everyone, not just some nations."

"Too bad for the diplomats. We're the ones who took the chances; we get to claim the prizes. And one of those planets really appears to be a prize. If Jeri and I decide to colonize one day we might go there."

"How about the others?"

"Hmm. Some danger. Jeri would say a lot of danger." Kyle looked at his wife and winked. She smiled back at him.

"Like what?"

"The fauna is big, fast and smart. We lost several marines by underestimating a couple of the things. And the climates aren't that great. But all in all we thought we'd done a good job up until Swavely. Damn it, I still feel rotten about letting those devils get the jump on us."

"They seemed so friendly, though," Jeri said.

"Yeah. We're still trying to decide whether it was that particular gang or if it's a species trait. Jeri believes it's the nature of their species to take every advantage they possibly can by any means they can."

"Do you know that for sure, Jeri? No, that's not right. What I meant is *why* do you think that?"

Rubbing your chin looks stupid on some women but with Jeri it's an attractive trait. She did it again.

"Cherry, it's kind of hard to explain. Sometimes I get what the psychologists call hunches but it's more than that. I think what I'm doing is assimilating a whole ream of data and putting it together subconsciously. Eventually I believe I'll learn to use this... talent, if that's what it is, more productively but for now, let's just say I'd bet a whole bundle of whatever you'd like to name that I'm right. Which means that one of our ships *must* return to Earth and give warning. Now that the Snappers know we're roaming around in interstellar space, they're going to come looking for us. Especially after what we did to one of their outposts."

"Captain Bronson didn't allow our astronomers out of the ship, other than right near it, so that there was never a chance they could be captured," Kyle said. "Unfortunately, they dragged some information about Earth's location out of one of our crew. Not the exact coordinates, mind you, but they got enough data to enable them to find us eventually if they look hard enough."

While we talked I had gotten out the bottle of Jack Daniels, still half full, and made drinks for all of us. I needed it but had been wary of drinking alone, fearing I'd give in to self-pity and over-indulge. Now I sipped the hundred proof whisky gratefully. It was diluted only by some ice cubes and I got on the outside of the first drink quickly enough to make my head buzz. It was soothing. I should have had one the day before.

Jeri raised her brow as I nodded. She poured one more round and returned the bottle to its cupboard.

I followed her motions. She winked at me. "It wouldn't do to show up at the meeting on wobbly legs, would it?"

"Umm. Guess not. So what you all are saying is, one ship has to go back home to warn Earth."

"Yup. That's a definite," Kyle said. "What we need to decide now is who goes back and who goes looking for the Crispies."

CHAPTER THIRTY

KYLE AND JERI STAYED long enough to finish the second drink before leaving me to myself. I think they decided silently that I was back on track and I'm sure they had other calls to make. Jeri was helping to heal some of the wounded with her perceptive sense.

"Thanks for coming by," I said when they got up to leave. "I hope you come along on the hunt."

"Then you're thinking of staying with the *Galactic?*"

I blinked. "There's no question of going back until I have to, whether on the *Galactic* or the *Zeng Wu*. The job's not done yet despite our losses. I'm... not ashamed of grieving for Juan, but I shouldn't have let it affect my duty." Then I had a thought. "You're going to come too, aren't you?"

"Oh yes, if we're allowed to," Kyle said. From the expression on his face I wouldn't want to be the one who told him he couldn't. It was set in stone.

"We'll go," Jeri said, her countenance matching her husband's.

"Great!" I said, and meant it. I really did like them. If there was such a thing as a "perfect couple," those two fit the description. One day I hoped to be part of a marriage like that.

They left a few minutes later and I headed for the shower. I needed one. Mentally, if nothing else.

ಐೞ

Captain Becker and General Haley, or Captain Haley I should say now, were meeting together privately while I was talking with Kyle and Jeri; or maybe while I was showering and washing away some grief. I put Juan into a special place in my mind where I could go back and remember him later when it wasn't so painful, and got back to work.

The two captains made a number of decisions before the general meeting that weren't subject to argument. The first and most important was the resolution to send *Zeng Wu* back to Earth as soon as the crews were sorted out. The second pronouncement was to ask for volunteers to go back with the ship and if there were enough to fill all the necessary positions, then all the rest who desired could go on with *Galactic* in the search for the Cresperian planet.

One problem wasn't quite that simple. Which Crispies should go and which stay? Or should they all go? That impacted me even before the meeting because after I had freshened up I went looking for Gordon.

I found him just where I thought he would be, in his stateroom.

"Hello, Cherry. Come on in," he said with a notable lack of enthusiasm.

"Hi, Gordon. Why the long face?"

"You know why."

"You forgot to pack spare underwear?"

He tried to hold it back but finally he chuckled. Not loudly, but it was a start.

"You know why. I wasn't allowed to fight. I feel like a fool."

I cocked my head and raised a brow. "Have you suddenly become invulnerable?"

"More so than those poor marines who died. Damn it, I could have helped!"

"And you might have been killed, too. And suppose Kyle and Jeri hadn't made it? What would we have done then?"

He sighed. "Oh hell, Cherry. I know all the intellectual arguments. Yes, I shouldn't have been risked, but it still doesn't make me feel any better. Sometimes the best solution isn't as good as it looks on the face of it. How can I face my brethren on Cresperia when they know I—"

I held up my hands to stop him. "It's not your brethren you're worried about. It's the other men on the ship, isn't it? You don't feel as manly as them, do you?"

He held it back for a minute while he thought. Finally he spoke. "Yes. If I'm being honest with myself, then that's what's bothering me. Damn it to hell Cherry, even the women—"

"Now hold it right there, buster. Don't let your hormones run away with you. That kind of attitude might have been valid 50 years ago but all it does right now is make you look small."

He got up and walked around the room, back and forth, back and forth, while I waited.

Finally I broke the silence. "You do realize Jeri wasn't allowed to risk her life either, don't you?"

He stopped pacing and stood facing me. I felt sorry for him, especially when I realized I'd probably have felt something akin to shame in his position, too. I went to him and put my arms around him. "Hush. It's okay.

You're a good man, Gordon. Your time will come. Want me to tell you when?"

"I wish you would." He sighed.

"How many other Crispies are there back on Earth?"

He thought. "Several."

"And where are they?"

"One in America. Two in England." He stopped talking and began thinking.

I finished it for him. "And at least one in the Islamic Confederation, and at least one each in India and China. Perhaps a couple more in South America. What's the chances of smuggling them out of Iran or China without some help from a Crispy?"

"Very little."

I waited for it sink in.

"I'll have to help if I go back. Sira couldn't do it with the IC, not being a woman."

"Correct. That is your chance for derring-do if you insist on being a hero. Personally, I think you'd be better off staying safe and trying to advance our technology, but some of the higher-ups on Earth are going to want to grab your brethren, sure as shooting."

"You really think so?'

"I do, if for no other reason than we can't afford to have them in the hands of nations who are enemies of America. Now let's take another subject. You think eventually we're going to find your home planet, don't you?"

"You know me too well. I haven't said so in so many words because I didn't want to disappoint if it turns out I'm wrong, but yes, after putting all the data together that was milked out of me and Sira and the others after the *Zeng Wu* left, I think it's a good possibility. If not on this voyage, then the next."

"And I'm sure you expect everything to go smoothly when we do contact them?"

A slow grin spread over his face, then abruptly disappeared as he got the point. His hazel eyes widened.

"No chance of that. We're a conservative society. It took roughly forever before we began exploring space and it's only the young Crispies who are interested. The corollary is that once they learn what it's like to become human there's going to be a giant schism in our society."

"That's not all, Gordon."

He thought for a moment. "It may even lead to war or something akin to it. Oh shit, Cherry. The aliens! What if they find Cresperia before we do? They'd be helpless! We don't have any warships at all!"

"None?"

"Not a single one. Oh, the exploration ships, what few we have, are lightly armed, but they're designed for defense while down on a planet. Besides, it's likely none would be there when the Snappers arrive. They stay out a long time and what worlds they find with life are thoroughly explored before moving on."

I thought about that. It made sense for a species like his. They were effectively immortal and their society changed very slowly. Between us and the *Zeng Wu*, I thought we'd probably already explored almost as many worlds as they would have. And now if humans found them, they'd not only have to deal with us but with the threat of a hostile species as well.

"How do you think the Crispies would take the idea of an interstellar war?"

"Badly. And with humans trying to convert them… oh shit, Cherry, it's going to be bad news any way I think of it."

"And that's not all, Gordon. Suppose India or China has built a ship and gets to Cresperia before we do and talks some of them into converting to human males? Without knowing the consequences of the Y chromosome, most of the conversions would probably go bad. Just think of people like Ishmael loose on your world."

"That would be bad, bad news."

"Right. Hell, Gordon, just look at how upset you are at not getting in on the fighting, and then think of Ishmael in your position. I don't think Jeri has thought this out as much as I have, especially if she hasn't read my notes yet. She's so enamored with Kyle and being human she thinks every one of you will feel the same way. It's not going to happen like that, though."

"No. Even though you took your time and mentored me during my conversion, I see now how much worse I could have come out. I have a lot to thank you for."

"You don't need to thank me so long as you see now why we couldn't risk you in a fight. Situations like this are just part and parcel of being human, Gordon. Honorable men and women are always being presented with dilemmas where they have to choose a course of action they may not like. The good ones choose correctly. The others indulge in actions they know in their heart are wrong because they're scared other people will think badly of them. It's a self-image sort of thing. Most truly great men never worry about their images; they just do what they think is right."

"Which doesn't mean they're always right, though?"

"Correct. No one is right 100% of the time."

"Crap. You should have been a psychologist."

"No. I'm just your friend, Gordon."

It took some more talk and hand holding, but by the time of the Captain's meeting he was quite reasonable. I kissed him before he left, sort of a mix between sisterly and girly. Despite our one previous night together, I certainly wasn't ready for anything else just yet.

Chapter Thirty-One

SAM HALEY AGREED to take the *Zeng Wu* back to Earth while the *Galactic* began hunting for Cresperia. Kyle and Jeri asked for permission to go along, which made me happy. Watching them together, I found myself again hoping that someday I'd find a man I could love in the way Jeri loved Kyle. So far it hadn't happened. Juan had been extra, extra nice, but that final spark had never ignited a sense of true undying love. Maybe there just hadn't been enough time. Or maybe it wasn't meant to be. I supposed I'd never know.

Before the ships parted company, they meshed the com units and a ceremony was held to honor the dead. No bodies had been recovered, but two rescued marines and a civilian scientist had died afterward from wounds. We were far enough out so that the bodies would never fall back to the planet. They might orbit the sun, or perhaps not.

Since the other ship had lost the most people, General—Captain—Sam Haley conducted the ceremony. His olive brown face was solemn beneath his curly black and gray hair.

"…And let us never forget. These brave souls died so that the rest of us might live. May they rest in peace."

And then he gravely read off the name of each of the fallen, as taps played softly in the background, over and over. Tears were running down my face well before it ended. I remembered Juan and all the others I had known, some well and others hardly at all and some I'd never met. In my soul I thanked them, thanked them from the bottom of my heart. They died doing their duty. Even Smackers, as much as he'd been able.

෴

After the ceremony I returned to my office. It wasn't long before Jeri came to visit. By the time she was seated and Chief Meadows brought fresh coffee, she was practically in tears.

"What's wrong, Jeri?" God, if she had something to cry about we were all in trouble.

"It's what I did. Or didn't do, I should say. I finished reading your notes just before the service. All the tears I shed weren't just for those who died on Swavely. I was upset over the damage I caused."

"You? What did you do?" I had no idea what she was talking about.

"You know. The Y factor."

"But Jeri, you aren't responsible for that."

"I should have deduced that a Crispy converting to a male would react differently than one taking a female form. Do you realize how many deaths I've caused?"

I thought rapidly for a moment while trying to decide how to answer her. Finally I said, "Jeri, right now Captain Becker and General—damn, I'll remember eventually—*Captain* Haley are probably sitting in their cabins agonizing over all the men they lost. Going back over their decisions and thinking exactly the same thing you are. How they 'should have' anticipated this and that, and how many men and women were killed because they didn't. You acted in light of what you knew at the time, and that's all anyone can do."

She looked at me with tears glimmering in her lashes. "Have you ever had anyone killed because of a bad decision?"

I nodded, remembering that poor fool Smackers. "I led one young man into combat when I knew ahead of time he was unstable. I should have had him pulled from the mission, but I didn't. And because I didn't, he lost his life and probably one or two others were killed because he froze up at a critical time and couldn't fire his weapon."

"Oh. I'm sorry. I didn't know."

"Neither does anyone else. It's my mistake and I'll have to live with it for the rest of my life. You couldn't have known what was going to happen with Ishmael. I worked with him, too, and so did our psychologists. None of us saw it coming."

"But..."

"Oh, hush, Jeri. You're probably the smartest woman on the ship, so start acting like it."

She gripped her coffee cup with both hands. I saw the skin tighten over her knuckles and turn white. It's a wonder she didn't crush the cup and spill hot coffee all over her lap. Finally she sighed and relaxed. The frown lines on her face disappeared and she managed a little laugh.

"Know what, Cherry?"

"What?"

"I think *you're* the smartest woman on the ship."

She was wrong, but I didn't say anything. We sat for a while in a companionable silence until she'd finished her coffee, then she got up to go.

"Thanks, Cherry. You're a good friend."

"So are you. How's Kyle managing?"

"He's in our quarters by himself. That's how he grieves. I know he's seen a lot of combat and this was just another episode, but he's suffering from it. He knew a lot of the marines. When we didn't have much else to do he worked with them, teaching special ops techniques he'd learned from experience, rather than the book." She glanced at her watch. "I think he's been alone long enough by now, though. I'd better go check on him. If he has a fault, it's taking things he can't help too hard."

"Don't we all," I sighed.

考

Once we began the hunt for the Crispy home planet, consumables became the critical factor. The one good thing about Swavely was that we were able to eat some of their food, and Captain Bronson had stocked up on some before the shit hit the fan. Still, the Master Chief Petty Officer who ran the materials section calculated we had no more than six weeks left before we had to start for home. We'd return with cupboards bare or so he said, but if I knew anything about CPOs we probably had a two-week margin over the official figure. None of this was announced, in order to prevent the crew from looking toward home rather than ahead, but it was soon fairly common knowledge.

We entered three systems in succession that were essentially worthless to humans. All of them had life-bearing planets, but one thing or another was wrong with them for our purposes, either an atmosphere that was toxic over the long term, or flora and fauna that made nightmares look like kindergarten stories. Then on the fourth one we hit the jackpot, a twin of Earth or close to it, that wasn't already occupied. So close that Captain Becker decided we must take the time to land and find out if it was as good as it looked. If so, we had another whole, pristine planet that could be opened to human settlement.

Of course there'd be the nut cases back home who'd argue that we ought to leave it as is and never so much as tread on a blade of grass, if it had grass, that is. The sort of Luddites who'd have us back in caves if they got their way. They'd much prefer us to be at the bottom of the food chain than the top, and don't ask me why. I don't know and I doubt they do either.

At the very least, the captain knew we all needed to get out and stretch our legs a bit before resuming the hunt for Cresperia, and that planet looked like a damn good place to do it.

The ship landed on a rise that sloped down to a river below, with a series of low, brush-covered hills rolling off into the distance above us. To the left the river curved away and disappeared into a forest of bright growth that looked somewhat like mesquite but was much taller and greener. There were more hills the other way that eventually rose in height until they turned into a mountain range. It was a beautiful vista.

ஐ௧ௐ

I was one of the first ones off the ship after a squad of marines debarked in containment suits and formed a perimeter. I really should have let one of the others do it, but rank hath its privileges.

On any planet where we landed there had to be a quick *in vitro* lab analysis to see if the local bugs were attracted to our cellular type. What that meant was getting samples of soil, flora and fauna and mixing them with various types of living human cells and observing them both macroscopically and microscopically.

I was able to declare the place safe three days later. The little microbes and microscopic life wanted nothing to do with us, it appeared. That had been the case on every planet visited so far, even when the amino acids and proteins were mostly the same type as ours.

Captain Becker allowed half the crew at a time to come out and the scientists were put to work in their various specialties, measuring and observing. I began helping Eugene with some specimens, not that he really needed much help but I wanted to stay outside for a while and enjoy the fresh air and sunshine while I had a chance. When Gene debarked I spotted him and stood up and waved. He started toward me and I left the outdoor lab to join him.

He was armed with an automatic pistol strapped to his waist and was wearing his usual cheerful grin.

"Hello, Gene."

"Hi, Cherry. Nice day, huh?

"Yep. Want to take a walk?"

"Sure. Where's the nearest lover's lane? Or is it too soon?"

"One day I'm going to see you when you're not so flippant. Or maybe just take you up on one of your proposals." I had to admit his attitude did a lot to help ease the pain of Juan's death. He had been serious and properly sympathetic as soon as he'd heard about it, but was soon back to his old self, perhaps knowing that I, as well as everyone else who had lost friends or lovers, needed to get back to normal as soon as possible.

"Good. Surprise me."

"Maybe I will." I couldn't help returning his grin. His infectious personality tended to rub off on everyone he was around—except maybe General Shelton and Captain Becker. "There's no lovers lane here, though. We're confined to the immediate area."

"Then let's just walk." He clasped my hand and we wandered around for a while, watching others of the crew out for the same reason as we were. It was very relaxing.

We stopped back by the lab after making a circuit of the camp. Eugene was absorbed with some microscopic life and didn't have much to say. His arm had healed and he had full function.

I spotted Kyle and Jeri and pointed to them. We left the work to Eugene and went to join them. They were armed, as was just about everyone else. The place was probably safe from disease but there were still some pretty big, mean-looking critters wandering around. There was a reason the marines kept a perimeter manned at all times.

"Nice place, huh?" Kyle said. He took a deep breath of the fresh air and smiled like a little boy just out of school for the summer. He and Jeri appeared to be their old selves, happy and cheerful. They were holding hands and smiling as if they hadn't a care in the world.

"You bet," I said, "but I keep expecting to see a monster coming over the hill. This place is too nice to be real." I squeezed Gene's hand.

He laughed. "No monsters. Just good-looking space girls."

I stuck out my tongue. He grinned at me.

"I talked with Gordon this morning," Jeri said. "We compared notes on my conversion and his and Ishmael's. I have to agree with you now. There's no way I could have predicted what happened to Ishmael. I don't think you would have caught it either if you hadn't had Lau's example to go on."

"I freely admit it. The way he turned out made me curious and sent me searching for a cause. Do you feel better now?"

"Yes, and I'm ashamed of the way I acted."

"Don't be. As far as I'm concerned anyone who's willing to take responsibility for their actions rates high in my book."

"I'll second that," Kyle said. "Would that more people did."

The four of us stood together and looked out over the rolling hills that faded into a forest in the far distance. The day was illuminated by a full blue sky. It had rained the previous day and it all looked fresh and clean.

It was a peaceful moment, one I thought I would call up at odd times when I wanted something nice to remember.

The only thing missing was another man the caliber of Kyle. I started to make some silly remark on the subject but decided not to, not while I had my fingers entwined with Gene's. I was feeling good again, and the others looked so satisfied with life right then, and the day was so perfect, that I didn't want to take a chance on spoiling it.

I didn't have to. The Snappers did it for us.

CHAPTER THIRTY-TWO

THERE WAS NEVER A QUESTION in my mind. They were after the ship, and casualties be damned on either side. Two sleek metallic aircars came zooming toward us from over the hills, traveling so close to the brush-covered terrain that we didn't see them until they were right on top of us. They came to a stop only about 50 yards from the ship. A ramp fell open on both sides of the vehicles and spilled dozens of laser-armed Snappers onto the ground. They weren't the least bit interested in prisoners. Only the fact that most of us were armed gave us any kind of chance.

"Drop!" Kyle shouted, the first person to react.

I did, even before I saw the vehicles come to a halt. As the Snappers charged out of the vehicles on their stubby legs, the four of us were already firing. The popping of our pistols sounded tame, however, compared to the heavy rifles manned by the marines who came to bear on them a few seconds later, mixed with laser beams from both sides. The marines remembered the Snappers with extreme prejudice. The machine guns cut a swath through the first group of aliens but the second wave quickly became tangled up with those of us outside enjoying the air and they couldn't fire on us.

The damned little beasts knew what they were doing. Some of them went for the machine guns as soon as the weapons dropped their troops. A heavy laser beam moved over one of them and burned the marines and the gun to cinders and molten metal.

"Get that laser!" Kyle yelled.

Easier said than done. At the moment we were up to our ears in alien alligators. It was total mayhem. Frankly, if I'd had time to think, to register the whole thing coherently, I'd have probably emulated a certain bastard of a quantum physicist no longer with us, and curled into a fetal ball. The stench of burning flesh and fresh blood and gushing entrails spilling their waste, the bright scarlet sprays of blood mingled with the sounds of popping small arms fire, the roar of the machine guns, loud hums coming from the lasers, the shouting of orders and the screams of the wounded and dying. Added to it was the cacophonous, loud clicking of the Snapper's beaks that was almost as deafening as the machine gun fire. We still hadn't been able to decide if it was from anger or some sort

of communication, but there was no time to observe now. It was hell
on... well, not Earth. Hell wherever it was that we were.

About then some of the Snappers started disappearing, and holes started appearing in the ground where they'd been standing. They screamed
just before they died, horrible high-pitched sounds that cut off abruptly
as they vanished. Some part of my brain registered the fact that somebody, Jeri I assumed, had begun using a Crispy disintegrator. She evidently widened the beam as she got closer to them because entire packs
of Snappers started obliterating, and the holes in the ground got bigger.
Still, it felt like there was a googol of Snappers, I'd swear. They were like
Hydra heads: for every one we killed, two more seemed to spring up.

I shot one Snapper that had just burned one of Eugene's lower legs off;
the poor man simply had to learn to get out of the way faster, I thought
inanely. The alien shrieked and slumped to the ground only to be replaced by another. I shot it in the head, then saw an opening and began
firing toward the aircar. My bullets bounced off the canopy as if it were
made of steel. It was no match for heavy .50 caliber machine-gun slugs,
though. The remaining marine gunner punched holes through it and shattered the material but the laser continued to fire.

I saw Kyle running toward it while Gene stood and pumped bullets at
it with his rifle, not even bothering to take cover. Kyle ducked and rolled
as a Snapper tried to shoot him with a hand laser. He kicked it hard in
the head, apparently breaking whatever it had for a neck, and ran on. He
jumped up on the body of the car but I had no time to see what else he
did. A laser beam seared the air as it sizzled past my head, almost hot
enough to set my hair on fire. I killed the alien that missed me then got
bumped by another that was running toward the ship. It didn't make it
there, though, because Gene gunned it down while I was busy with two
more.

Someone inside our ship saw what they were after and closed the airlock. The small people ramp that had been dropped for easy access began
rising with a Snapper hanging on the edge of it for a moment before dropping to its death on the point of a biology tech's dissecting knife.

I was already on my second magazine when I saw the heavy laser from
the second vehicle moving my way. I was on my knees and rolled to my
feet and out of the way just in time. It burned a path in the ground right
next to me and moved on, seeking someone else or maybe the ship. I was
too busy to look that way. But someone had to do something about the

thing. So far it had only been used on personnel, but I knew it could burn through the ship's side in seconds if it was turned that way. It made me wonder why they hadn't used it to disable the ship to begin with.

Jeri had the same thought as I did. We both began running towards the laser's source while Kyle was dealing with the other one. Dead marines lay around – they in their emplacements had been the Snappers' first target, and very few of the Marines outside the ship were still alive. I jumped over two of their burned bodies on my way to the alien vehicle.

Jeri made it there first, but I was right behind her, getting close enough just in time to slither in under the beam at the point where it couldn't depress enough to hurt me. I needn't have bothered. The canopy above me and part of the alien car just disappeared. Jeri had maneuvered herself into position to effectively target her disintegrator on it. The bottom half of its occupants were still in place, leaking a thin ruddy orange fluid through severed alien entrails. The stench was horrible.

I turned back around but by then it was almost over. The airlock opened again and another squad of marines came charging out.

"Inside, everyone inside!" one of the sergeants cried above the noise of his rifle as he fired three shots together, then three more.

I looked around and saw Kyle running back toward the ship, assisted by Gordon. I didn't know when Gordon had come outside; he'd been under orders to stay inside until Jeri came in. But he had his own arm around Kyle's waist and Kyle's left arm gingerly over his shoulder. Kyle was pale and missing part of that left arm. Jeri grabbed hold of his right one and hurried him into the ship over his protests; Kyle wanted to help with the mopping up.

As soon as Jeri had Kyle, Gordon let go and rapidly began helping to hoist what wounded there were inside the airlock with that immense strength Crispies have.

I had no desire to do anything. I was nauseated and weak. All I wanted was to get inside and away from the sight of the charred bodies of friends and marines, men and women who had died so far from home.

&)(&

Again there was no question of recovering bodies. Captain Becker decided to get the hell away from there before the spaceship that had obviously been home for the Snapper aircars arrived. We had no idea of where it was or how it was armed, but almost certainly it would have lasers. That seemed to be their primary weaponry.

There was no real way of being sure but those aliens we met on Swavely's planet must have either had a starship in the system and deliberately concealed it for fear of it being destroyed, or one had entered the system right as we were leaving and somehow followed us. Or it might have remained hidden, intending to follow us if their attack failed. Or hell, maybe our unreality drive was leaving a trail of some kind and we didn't realize it.

I preferred the last theory; at the Captain's department heads meeting a few hours later, I said so.

"Both our satellite and the ship's system have picked up emissions of the same sort the Snappers used for communication between their settlements on Swavely," he replied. "That means there's a ship *somewhere.*"

We were already hightailing it out of the system as fast as we could go anyway, so there was little else we could do at that point. Jeri, Kyle, and Gordon headed straight for sickbay. I was headed for my quarters until a general announcement summoned me to sickbay, too.

Shit, I thought. What do they want me there for? Then I realized that they were probably inundated with injured, and as a geneticist I had enough background to at least make a decent orderly.

I went.

I wished I hadn't.

ೞೞ

It wasn't pretty at all. Doctor Honeywell and his chief surgeon, Dr. James Frederick Kingston, or "JFK" for short, as well as one other physician I hadn't had occasion to encounter, were up to their elbows in blood and guts, literally. As soon as he saw the mess, Kyle insisted that his arm be bandaged and Jeri and Gordon concentrate on helping those who were in more dire straits.

I scrubbed up and donned a clean lab coat, then did what I was told, as our three nurses triaged the patients. Between carrying trays of surgical equipment and locating bandages, I heard one of the nurses call, "Dr. Honeywell!" in a tone that... well, that made all of us stop and look up.

Honeywell handed over to his assistant to close the patient being operated on, and headed for the triage nurse. He looked down at the soldier on the stretcher and blanched. "Jeri, Gordon, I need you," he said immediately.

I managed to pass close enough to see what was going on, and then struggled to keep from heaving up my guts: One of the marines was lying there with half of his own guts missing, but he was still alive and conscious. Oh, God, I thought, and it was, even for me, nearly a prayer.

Jeri and Gordon, followed by a newly-bandaged Kyle, moved to Honeywell's side, as did JFK as soon as he could finish with his current patient, and they all looked at each other, trying to hide their horror. Honeywell and JFK looked questioningly at Jeri and Gordon. Both Crispies shook their heads, and I understood: they had to have time, as well as something to work with, in order to perform healings. This soldier, Murphy by the name on his uniform, wasn't going to last long enough for that.

Murphy saw their expressions and knew what it meant. He grabbed Honeywell's hand. "It's okay, Doc," he managed to grate out. "I've seen you in the chapel, too. You and I know where I'm goin'. I'm not afraid of death. It's... the dying... it hurts, and I..." Fear filled his eyes. "Don't let me lose it, not right at the end. Help me cross over in peace."

Honeywell and JFK exchanged looks. "That, we can do, Murphy," he said softly. "That, we can do."

JFK glanced up and saw me. He pointed at the nearest nurse. "Give that stuff to her," he said urgently, "and go get a morphine pack."

I shoved my surgical kit into the arms of the indicated nurse and sprinted for the supply cabinets. In seconds, and with the assistance of another nurse, I was back with the morphine. By then, Gordon and Jeri were using their perceptive abilities to help anesthetize the dying soldier. I handed the drug kit to JFK, who opened it and carefully injected a substantial dose into Murphy. Honeywell was bent over Murphy, holding his hand and murmuring what was evidently a quick prayer with him. Then their eyes met in understanding; doctor and patient squeezed hands lightly, and Honeywell was gone, off to work on a patient he had a chance of saving.

I started to go, but JFK turned. "Stay here, Doctor Trung, if you don't mind," he murmured. "I'm going to see this boy through, the nurses are needed elsewhere, and I may need someone to fetch something. I hope you don't mind. It... won't take long."

I nodded mutely and stood behind him, out of the way. Once the morphine took effect and added to what Gordon and Jeri were already doing, Murphy seemed to relax, fear fading away. "Thank God," he whispered softly, with a slight smile. "I can handle this."

"Good," Jeri murmured in reply. "Forgive us for being unable to do more."

"It's okay," Murphy told her acceptingly. "Comes everybody's time, sooner or later. Some of us are sooner," he gestured weakly at his missing guts, "and some come later." He looked at Kyle and the Crispies.

"True," Kyle agreed quietly.

We were all silent for a moment, contemplating that thought. No one knew I was like Kyle now except a very few. I knew that, unless I got shot or otherwise hacked up, I was one of those "laters." But Murphy didn't have the luxury. His time was now.

Suddenly his eyes lit up. "It's here!" he said, excitement and recognition showing through the death glaze that was starting to descend on his face.

It was the last thing he said. After a moment, JFK gently closed his eyes and pulled the sheet over his face. He turned and looked for his next patient.

I would have done the same, except for the expressions on two of my favorite Crispies' faces. Jeri and Gordon were staring at each other in a kind of shock.

"What's wrong?" Kyle asked in concern, putting his good hand on his wife's arm.

"Gordon… did you feel it, too?" Jeri asked in an awed whisper.

"Yes," he responded in a similar tone. "At least… I think I did…"

"Feel what?" Kyle wondered.

Gordon shook his head. "His life force… it didn't fade, at least not like usual," he explained, confused.

"It… sort of… left," Jeri finished, puzzled. "Into the quantum foam. At least that's what it seemed like. That's just… peculiar. Or is it? Can it be explained by quantum mechanics? Or unreality physics? Can it… can it be explained at all?"

We all stared at each other. Judging by their expressions, I had to wonder if our converted Crispies might have discovered something humans had been agonizing over for ages.

ജ⊙ഗ

Once the rush was over, Jeri and Gordon worked on Kyle some, beginning to get the missing part of his arm regenerating. Eugene's leg was already beginning to heal. Both men were certainly in stable condition, thank God.

That's when the call came in.

"All section chiefs to the control room. Repeat, all section chiefs report to the control room immediately."

"Surprise," Kyle muttered.

"No rest for the weary," Honeywell said quietly. He checked to make sure he could be spared, captain's orders or no, and then we all headed for Control.

ॐ൏

We met in the control room so that the captain would be right there in case of emergencies or unanticipated repercussions from the fight on the planet.

"First of all," Captain Becker began, "I want to thank a certain Crispy for disobeying initial orders and making a tactical decision in an emergency situation. Gordon, it is my considered opinion that your entrance into the fight kept it from being a total debacle."

"Thank you, sir," Gordon said quietly. "I sensed what was going on a few seconds before the call to general quarters sounded. You might say I got a head start."

"You did excellently, and I, for one, thank you," Becker noted.

"It seemed... right," Gordon shrugged, evidently slightly embarrassed.

"You've definitely proven yourself, I'd say, as well as Dr. Trung's theories about mentoring the transition process. Speaking of the good doctor: I have it to understand she believes we're being traced. What makes you think we've been leaving a trail, Ms. Trung?" Captain Becker said, turning his attention to me. He had his hands twined together on the conference table but they weren't making any nervous movements. It's just the way he liked to sit at meetings.

"Please, Captain Becker. I hate that term. Call me Mai or, if you insist on being formal, it's Miss Trung." I always had to remind him.

He nodded and I continued, still not knowing how he was going to address me next time. "Sir, it's just too much of a coincidence for another spaceship to show up in this system the same time as us and to be the same kind of aliens as the last contact *and* to attack us both times while we were grounded. If it is just chance, then this area of space ought to be swarming with their ships."

"Do you have anything else to base your conjecture on?

"No, sir, other than that I don't believe in coincidences, not of this kind. And we saw no signs of occupation before we landed."

"Comments?"

"I have to agree," Jeri said. Both the Crispies were present at the captain's request, just as I was. I suppose he was looking for opinions from his top scientists.

Before she could say anything else we were interrupted. While Captain Becker handled that, she closed her eyes and went back to concentrating on growing a new arm for Kyle. Jeri had insisted on bringing him along so she could be close to him and keep the healing process going.

"Com."

"Go, Com."

"Sir, we've picked up a tail."

"How close?"

"Just on the verge of our capabilities, sir, but they're maintaining a bit more than our speed. At first they were flicking in and out of contact, but it's constant now. At the present rate, we'll be inside the diffusion range of a heavy laser cannon in four to six hours."

"Major Wong?"

"That's an extrapolation, Captain," the chief engineer said, leaning forward in her seat to speak. "We have no factual data on how powerful their laser cannons will be if that's what they use in space. Nor do we have any idea of what other weaponry they might have. However, if the projections are correct, then that's what we have. And it is all we have to work with at present." She eased back upright and waited.

"Comments?" No one had more to say on that subject. "Then let's discuss intentions. Does anyone care to venture an opinion?"

"Perhaps they believe they can chase us home. Back to our home system, I should say," Commander Prescott ventured. His voice was muted from having to talk around a bandage on his face. "They may think we're already headed there."

"That may be, but they're crazy if they think that. Wait, I take that back," Maddie said. "Twice now they've attempted to take our ship. Perhaps they were after astronomical data, and when that failed, they decided to try a pursuit."

"Possible," Prescott said.

"Recommendations?" Becker scanned the circle of the control room.

"Try to outrun them," Commander Prescott advised.

The rest of us agreed and Captain Becker nodded.

"XO, I want all available speed, same bearing. Let's see what kind of legs they have."

"Aye, aye, sir."

"And let's drop a torp and see what happens."

Aye, sir." He commed Captain Larry Morrison, the weapons officer. He was an MIT graduate with a doctorate in physics and had worked for DARPA —Defense Advanced Research Projects Agency—before being pulled for duty with The Group. His long brown hair and chubby face made him look like a college kid. He looked up from his alcove across the way, nodded and began preparations with CPO Perkins to launch a missile at the alien ship.

Becker didn't ask any of us who normally had no duty there to leave the control room, so I stayed. Probably he wanted us around to help interpret anything the Snappers did that the control room personnel couldn't figure out.

After a while I began to wish I had left. The tension began mounting as our speed increased, and I began anticipating that horrible creepy-crawly sensation when the unreality drive kicks in to FTL speed.

But before that happened, I got to see our torpedo blossom into a red blotch on our screen and then fade to nothingness before it was close enough to do any damage. It seemed they had very good defenses.

I was sitting back in one corner out of the way with Kyle and Jeri beside me. Presently Jeri pointed to a power gauge. It was blinking yellow. The captain ignored it so I tried to do the same. I watched the monitor avidly. The Snapper ship had first been sighted when it was right at the edge of the screen. During the conference it had crept away from the edge as it gained on us. Now, with the *Galactic* going all out at its maximum speed of about 2 light years per hour—that's 12 trillion miles an hour for the uninitiated—the Snapper ship began to lose ground. The foremost perimeter of the screen seemed to creep up on it as it fell behind.

The power gauge began blinking from yellow to red. A few minutes later it settled into the red and stayed there.

"Redline, Captain," Prescott warned, as was his duty, even though the captain was staring directly at the gauge.

"Maintain speed," he said grimly. He clearly intended to get away from the alien or destroy his ship trying.

I found myself hoping a big safety margin had been built into the unreality drive. Eventually the gauge blinked back to yellow as if the ship was thinking for itself and decided it wasn't in danger. Then the ship jerked as it left the real universe and I became very ill.

Hours passed while we all sat there, relieved only by occasional cups of coffee or quick runs to the bathroom. Finally I had to take a break from the tension, and as if asking for permission to leave had given a signal, the captain dismissed half the control room personnel with orders to report back in four hours.

&OCß

The next day the captain commed and asked me to report to his cabin. When I arrived I found Jeri there as well.

"Just so you both know, I will have your com screens modified to have a direct punch-up link to the control room permanently so Prescott or Maddie or myself can consult you immediately. No sense in your having to run halfway across the ship to come to the control room each time I'm there. Should've been done from the first, but we weren't fully thinking battle mode then." He paused. "You can probably tell, we're running fast."

"Yes, sir," Jeri noted, and I nodded. "Any signs?"

"Hard to tell," Becker sighed. "You know how it works."

"Yes, sir," Jeri nodded. I didn't, but I didn't plan to admit it to the captain. I'd ask Jeri as soon as we left his cabin, though.

"That's all I had," Becker said. "I figured my two top scientists needed to have direct access to Control without having to run over the entire damned ship. The orders are already in the works. Expect it in your cabins by later today. Offices, a day or two more."

"Good," I agreed. "Anything else we can do, sir?"

"Keep your eyes and ears open, and your brains in gear. Try to figure out if they really are trailing us, and if so, how. Dismissed."

We nodded and left.

&OCß

Once outside the closed door, I turned to Jeri. "Why can't we tell they're following?"

"Oh," she said. "That's right; you wouldn't know. That's physics, not genetics. Well, we're not in normal space, we're in... 'unreality.' How much physics and mathematics did you have?"

"Enough to get by for the genetics."

"Okay, then you know about real numbers and imaginary numbers," she said, and I nodded. "And you know that imaginary numbers sometimes come into play in physics, for instance when solving for the kinematics of a harmonic oscillator, like a pendulum or a spring." I nodded again, and she continued. "But normally, you discard the imaginary components. But we discovered that there's actually a facet of physics that utilizes those 'imaginary' solutions, and we used it to build the unreality drive. So that's why our sensors don't work like they do in normal space."

"Are you saying we're running blind?"

"No," Jeri grinned, "more like with Coke-bottle glasses."

We both laughed.

ಬಿಂ

Jeri and I met up about once a day to discuss the possibility of our propulsion system leaving a trail, but Jeri wasn't an expert on the prop, and I knew a hell of a lot less. We didn't get very far.

Within about two days, however, the captain's promised com links to our office and cabin screens had all been installed. I checked up on the external schematic once and it looked pretty much the same as the last time I'd seen it in the control room. Neither the captain nor his XO contacted me for several days, despite the new links. I guess they figured if we had anything to say, we'd call.

About five days after the link was installed, I checked on the external schematic again. The alien icon was missing, of course. Like Jeri said, our instruments didn't work while out of the universe as we know it. Captain Becker had kept the speed just as it was, though. If the Snapper ship was the same one that had somehow followed us before, he wanted us to get as far ahead of it as possible before coming out of unreality and entering the normal universe again. On the tenth day after the fight, the power gauge went back to red and stayed there, then began blinking rapidly, telling us the ship couldn't take the strain much longer.

I heard all that from one or another of the crew but I was present at the end. Becker had ordered Jeri and me to the control room.

Captain Becker's face was streaked with the dried residue of old sweat and marks his hands had made as he wiped his face. He had hardly left the control room the whole long time of the chase, as if he didn't trust his ship to hang together under the stress without his presence.

Finally, when the red light began blinking frantically and Prescott's hands were shaking where he was clutching his knees, the captain gave the order.

"Bring the drive down to normal."

"Aye, sir. Normal it is," Prescott said, relief evident in his voice.

Once we were back to a sensible speed, Captain Becker dropped the ship out of unreality in order to see if the Snapper ship had followed us.

That creepy-crawly sensation of entering or leaving unreality was worse than ever when it came down after that horrific red-line speed run. I felt my gorge rise. Maddie did vomit. Even Jeri looked sick, what I could see of her through my blurred vision.

When coming out of superluminal unreality a ship will always wind up at the nearest gravity well, no matter how far away. We entered a star system of a white dwarf sun about 48 light years from the site of the second clash with the Snappers.

When they didn't appear after we'd waited two days, we again entered unreality—this time at our normal cruising speed, just under a light year per hour—and went on with the search for Cresperia. It was even more urgent that we find them now. We needed to warn them and we needed their technology to build better weapons in case the Snappers found *us*.

And three weeks later and almost 360 light years away from our last stop, we came out of unreality near a G type star. Again that creepy-crawly, nausea-inducing sensation enveloped everyone in the control room except Jeri, including the captain. I was there by request in my capacity as chief science officer for each new system we entered. Major James Henry, the operations officer, was present as well. It was the first time I met him. We all watched the screen as Maddie searched the "life zone" where earthlike planets might be found. We were lucky and came out near the ecliptic and near the orbit of a planet that was on the same side of the sun as us, offset by only about 30 degrees.

"It looks like a good one from here," Maddie said a little later. She outlined it in the battle tank in relation to another two planets she'd spotted.

"Com."

"Captain. Go," Becker said as he looked toward one of his screens.

"Sir, we have emissions indicative of high technology," Major Eleanora Wisteria, the electronics officer said, so calmly that her Swedish accent was barely detectable. I could see her in the little alcove she worked from. She had a big grin on her plump, pretty face.

That was when I heard Jeri make a noise, saying something in the Crispy language. Her hyperacute hearing must have tapped into one of the low level com bands Eleanora was playing with.

"Captain!"

"What is it, Jeri?" He caught the excited tone in her voice but you'd never know it from his face.

"Sir... sir, we have arrived at Cresperia. This is my home system."

CHAPTER THIRTY-THREE

WHAT WE WERE GETTING was leakage from normal communication to and from satellites or some of the moons of the Jovian planet in the system. Jeri had told us that the Crispies had long ago moved most of their industry into space, farther back in time than they had records for. They don't dwell nearly as much on history as humans do, we had been told.

Jeri stayed in the control room while we headed for the main planet. At the speed we were traveling inside the system we were about six hours away.

Four hours later we got the first bad news.

"Com."

"Captain. Go."

"Sir, I just picked up something from orbit that sounds more like an Earth language than what the Crispies use."

"Jeri?"

She listened for a moment, being the best linguist in the ship by far. "Sir, I believe what we're hearing is the Hindi language. It appears that India beat us here."

Shit. What a stupid damn mess! Now what were we supposed to do?

"Continue present course," Captain Becker decided. "Maddie, unless told otherwise, place the ship in a stable orbit, say about 300 klicks. Eleanora, continue monitoring and record. Play any more Hindi for Jeri to listen to."

"Aye, aye, sir," they both answered.

"And Jeri, you may begin trying for official contact with the Cresperian government."

"It's not really a government as you know it on Earth, sir."

"Whatever. Make contact with whoever can make decisions."

Jeri looked troubled, but brought up the contact protocol prepared by the American diplomatic service. She examined the first bit of text and videos the State Department had prepared for her and shook her head.

"Sir, if I may, I'd like to... paraphrase the protocols. The ones who recorded this were under a good many misconceptions. I'm sorry I wasn't consulted."

Becker smiled wryly. "I am, too. Go ahead, Jeri. I should have shown the protocols to you before now but... things happened. Do it however you think best."

Good for him. He had enough sense not to stick to actions dictated from Earth by people who knew nothing of Cresperians.

She began broadcasting but spoke for only a few minutes. "I'll really have to do this in person and merge my perceptive sense with some of the elders before it will mean a lot to them. That depends on how long the Indian ship has been here, of course. They may have already set up a dialog, but this will possibly get us started."

Becker nodded, obviously considering the implications of the Indian ship. I sure didn't have a clue what we'd do about it.

Before Jeri had an answer, the second piece of bad news reared its ugly head.

"Com."

"Captain. Go. Never mind, I see it. Damn them to hell and back!"

Startled, I glanced up from the notes I'd been reading. The captain *never* used profanity in the control room. At the edge of the battle tank the Snapper icon became visible again. They had followed us despite all we could do. Now what?

I began running all the possible permutations of the situation through my mind. We could wind up with two factions of Crispies at odds with each other and one of them feeling the same way about us. The Crispies might decide that converting to humans wasn't in their best interests and throw us and the Indians both off the planet. The Indians may have bad-mouthed us all over the planet and we wouldn't even get permission to land. The aliens might invade and conquer Cresperia while their slow-motion society was still debating what to do. The aliens might follow us home and invade Earth. They might invade both systems at the same time. The Crispies on Earth might try gaining enough power to tell us what to do. Earth nations might start fighting each other over Crispies instead of cooperating in fighting aliens. And on and on.

It wasn't just a mess. It was the biggest FUBAR in history, maybe the biggest the human race had ever faced, and most of them didn't even know it yet. It made me glad I wasn't in Captain Becker's shoes.

శుర్దా

Just as we were entering orbit, Jeri made contact with one of the faction of Crispies who had initiated space exploration. She talked for almost an hour. She remained calm but I could see the strain on her face from some sort of problem. So could everyone else, including the captain. He kept one eye on her and the other on the battle tank. So did the other officers and I. After emerging from unreality, the Snapper ship had slowed, but was still gradually creeping nearer, toward the Cresperian home planet.

Commander Prescott arrived in the control room to stand his watch. The captain acknowledged him but stayed.

"We're in orbit, Captain," Maddie announced.

"Thank you. Now go take a break. I'll let you know if we need you. XO, take the helm." He did so.

Maddie signed out and left. She needed to get away for awhile. She had been in the control room far longer than I had.

Jeri was still talking, but apparently following other events at the same time. She smiled at me, then looked at the battle tank, over to the captain and back to the screen in front of her where a Crispy had appeared. They had somehow altered their communications, probably when the Indian ship arrived, so that we could receive voice and picture, not that any of us could follow their conversation. I had learned a little of it but it is complicated and many of their sounds can't be pronounced by ordinary humans.

"The alien ship is still slowing, sir," Eleanora announced even though the captain had to be aware of it from the battle screen. "They have not attempted any form of communication I can register. I've also picked up what I think is the Indian ship. It's just now moving behind the planet."

"Thank you," he said, nodding to her.

"Captain, there is a situation with the Indians—" Jeri was cut off by Prescott.

"Separation! Sir, the Snapper ship has detached a smaller one. It is moving toward us now."

"Thank you. XO, call battle stations. Jeri, you were saying?" He was as stolid as a rock and his voice never wavered while three different situations were demanding his attention and the call to arms was clanging in his ears.

"I said there's a situation that's not good with the Indians. According to the information I've received so far, the Hindu religion has possibly undergone a huge revival-like rejuvenation on Earth. At any rate, the crew of this ship believes utterly in it and claims they have an avatar of one of their gods with them."

"Is this important right now?"

"Yes, but it can wait until we see what the aliens are up to. The nasty aliens, I should say. The Snappers. I'm trying to make the old friends I contacted believe in the danger from them, but I'm having a hard time of it. They have seen what happened to at least the one Crispy on the Indian ship and are being very… hard to convince that there is another side to the conversion, a positive side."

She went back to her conversation. I would have given a lot to be able to follow it in real time but the most she could do was stop every now and then and interpret a bit of it for us. In the meantime, other things were happening.

"Two of the Crispy ships are moving toward the main Snapper ship now," Eleanora announced.

"Those are unmanned freighters," Jeri said. "I asked my friends to relay the information that only unmanned ships should approach the Snapper at first. They still don't believe me when I tell them the Snappers are not to be trusted, but they are doing that much. If the Snappers follow their usual pattern, they will attack those ships."

The nasty little bastards were smarter than we took them for. They ignored the freighters as if they knew they were harmless. They passed them and came on toward us, still not making any attempt at contact, either with us or the Cresperians, at least so far as we knew from our instruments, or Jeri knew from her conversations with the surface.

"XO, weapons free. If the Snapper ship continues on this course, take it out."

"Aye, aye, sir." Prescott hovered over the techs who were handling the missile launch console and the laser cannon. Both of them were alert and ready to fire.

"That won't help you with the Crispies, sir," Jeri said hurriedly. "We— they, I mean, their society doesn't care much for violence."

"I can't help who it annoys, Jeri. If that Snapper ship continues on its present course, I'm going to fire on it and I'll fire on the little one, too."

"The Indian ship is coming back into view, sir," Eleanora said.

All kinds of good news. It had been on the other side of the planet for the last hour or so.

"Keep an eye on it. Jeri, anything more from the surface?"

"Yes, sir. They ask that you not fire on the new visitors and that you either land the ship or send down a tender with representatives. Personally, I wouldn't let those Snappers get much closer, sir. Firing on them won't hurt our chances with the Crispies much more than the Indians already have. And I would also keep an eye on the Indian ship, sir. They are not our friends."

He nodded to her and stared at the battle tank.

Maddie came back to the control room, responding to the call to general quarters. Her hair was tousled as if she had just jumped out of bed, which she probably had. Larry Morrison was right behind her.

Becker glanced at them and moved aside. "Maddie, give us a vector that will place us behind the Indians relative to the Snapper mother ship. Larry, take over from the XO and reset the laser cannon for anti-missile fire."

I couldn't figure out what he was doing at first. Then I got it and grinned. He was trying to maneuver so that the *Indians* were in the first line of fire of the Snapper auxiliary ship, supposing that was its intentions.

"I've seen clusterfucks before but this is ridiculous," I heard him mutter. I know he said it. I was the closest person to him and the only one in the control room that didn't have an immediate duty to perform.

He saw by the look on my face that I must have overheard him. The tiniest of smiles flickered across his face and then he was all business again.

The Snapper auxiliary was now almost at rest relative to us, but going much faster in order to keep us in view as we orbited. The Indian ship began to break orbit, seeing what Captain Becker had done. The Snapper fired at it with a laser cannon, hitting it near the center, where the power core resided if it was anything like our little prototype ship had been. It had that same general shape, rather than looking like the *Galactic* or the *Zeng Wu*, as if they had taken—or stolen?—our original design and multiplied it by a factor of 20 or more. Chances were they hadn't had access to ultra-miniaturization of electronics like we did, I figured. How in the world they'd managed to get this far without being a rich superpower nation either didn't bear thinking about, or was some kind of real tribute to human ingenuity. Or maybe both.

A spot on the Indian icon flared and died. The laser apparently did little damage, indicating the ship was well armored. I wondered if that was deliberate, or merely the result of cruder, heavy-duty manufacturing. The Indians poured on the power, then fired off a missile at the small auxiliary ship.

The same thing happened to their missile as the one we had shot at the big Snapper ship long ago. It disappeared well short of its target. For some reason, I suddenly wondered if it was the same ship or a different one. And that led me to wonder if the second time we'd been attacked was from the first ship as well. Perhaps we'd inadvertently stumbled onto the edge of the Snapper Empire. I put the idea away for the moment.

"Damn, even those little buggers can do it," Prescott muttered when the missile disappeared without a trace, just as when we'd fired on the Snapper mother ship.

Or *a* Snapper ship. I was still wondering.

But the Snapper auxiliary slowed after the missile shot. None of us had any idea why—it certainly hadn't hurt it, at least that we could tell. The Indians took advantage of its slowness and fired a laser cannon next. It punched far enough into the little ship for atmosphere to begin streaming. That got its attention! It turned tail and tried to run. Another beam from the Indian cannon hit it and it exploded in a cloud of debris.

"That was a heavy one, Captain. I don't think our laser is that powerful," Larry said from the weapons alcove.

"Which says something about their intent, I suppose," the captain decided grimly.

The main Snapper spaceship began retreating but the Indians didn't follow. I tensed, expecting them to come after us, but they simply returned to orbit just as they had been.

The Snapper ship retreated until it was barely within detection range. There it hung, just as if it knew what our limits were. When neither it nor the Indians had made an aggressive move after another 15 minutes, I relaxed.

"It looks to me as if they were testing us and the Indian ship both," Loraine said. She blew at a tress of hair that had gotten loose; then, when that didn't work, brushed it back.

"I agree," Becker said, then turned his head. "Jeri? Tell us about the Indians now that the action has slowed a bit."

CHAPTER THIRTY-FOUR

JERI RAISED A HAND to indicate she was still conversing with the surface. She continued talking for a moment, then sighed.

"Is everything okay?" the captain asked.

"For the time being it is as well as can be, considering. Now about the Indians." She paused for a moment as if gathering her thoughts. "How much do you know about the Hindu religion, Captain?"

"Very little, I'm afraid," he said. "How about the rest of you?"

At the moment there were four other officers, Jeri, and myself in the control room. Those officers were Maddie, Larry, Eleanora and Loraine. All of us shook our heads negatively. I knew others were connected to Jeri's lecture and revelations through their coms, and none of them spoke either.

"All right," Jeri said. "I'll give you a very brief summary, then speculate a bit." No one questioned that she should be the one to explain. With an extremely fast reading speed and an eidetic memory – and fluency in Hindu – she certainly knew more on the subject than anyone else in the room.

I noticed that even while listening to her, Captain Becker's eyes never strayed far from the battle tank.

"The Hindi believe in a multitude of gods but for our purposes here—and back on Earth, as well, I think—we'll just concentrate on one: Vishnu, the Preserver. However, their religion says that Vishnu has ten incarnations, or 'avatars,' the tenth of which has never appeared. That one would be Kalki, the mighty warrior, who will come to rid the world of the oppression of its unrighteous rulers. With me so far?"

We all nodded and she continued.

"Well, here's what I gather has happened. One of our lifeboats landed in a relatively unpopulated area of India. It came down lightly and two Crispies were able to save all their survival equipment. You know what that entails; a disintegrator and invisibility mechanism among other effects. Eventually, after learning the local language and customs while still in hiding, they both decided to convert to human males. Afterward, without mentoring and with a very fast conversion, the Y factor came into play. You can guess the conversion went wrong, I'm sure, after our experiences with Ishmael and Lau. In their case they decided to pass themselves off as gods. To this end they made more changes in their bodies until they were both eight feet tall but perfectly proportional men. They then declared themselves to some gullible rural inhabitants, claiming to be Vishnu the preserver, and Vishnu's tenth avatar, Kalki the warrior, returned to Earth to set things right. They went further, picking two normal women and using their perceptive senses and ability to manipulate genomes to make them outsize as well. They called both these women Lakshmi, their goddess consorts, responsible for wealth and prosperity.

"They then began converting Indians to the belief that they were indeed gods, and apparently found fertile ground. With what they could do themselves, along with their survival gear, it appeared that they could perform miracles. Their great size contributed to captivating—or cowing—their followers, and they gained converts rapidly.

"I suspect that back on Earth, the one who stayed behind as Vishnu has pretty well taken over India, but that is only speculation on my part. The one calling himself Kalki and his consort came with the ship in order to find more Crispies to take back to Earth to help them rule India. I believe their ultimate objective is to rule not only India but all of Earth."

"Surely the Crispies don't believe they are real gods, do they?" Captain Becker questioned skeptically.

"Of course not, sir. However, it's possible the Indian Crispies might believe it of *themselves* by now. Remember the Y factor and remember how mad Lau was at the last."

"Yes, I've heard. Go on, please." His expression showed he was paying intense attention to what she was saying. So was I.

"Kalki, his Lakshmi consort, and a number of Indians have gone to the surface in one of their tenders. I think they may have convinced a few Crispies to convert to human. I don't know what gender, if this has indeed happened, nor whether they have accepted the religion as well. Now bear in mind that all this information is being filtered through my friends, and that we have no means from here to converse using our perceptive sense in tandem, so I could be missing many, and perhaps vitally important, nuances."

Becker rubbed his chin when she paused. "What do your friends want us to do? And remember, we're representatives of our country. You must emphasize that we are not responsible for what the Indians have done, nor for anything they might have said about us, nor for any other country on Earth, other than perhaps England."

"Captain Becker, Cresperia doesn't have a government anything like the ones you're used to or that the diplomats who framed the protocols know of. You might say it is a government by consensus where other Crispies necessarily follow that consensus, and in any case, it's not much of a government at all. Oh, the elders are listened to more respectfully than younger ones but even they don't form policy as such."

"Sounds sort of like anarchy," Loraine said. "I mean, true political anarchy, not just chaos."

She shrugged. "Yes, you could think of it that way, too. I've been speaking to several old friends who were instrumental in getting interstellar exploration started, and through them, to some of the elders."

"And what do the elders think?" Becker asked.

"Of us or the Indians?"

"Either. Both."

"From what I can gather, they are not impressed. Again, bear in mind that the elders don't necessarily agree among themselves, either. Adding to that, I've informed them through my friends of what happens when Crispies convert to human too quickly, especially to human males, and that without mentors, neither gender conversion works very well. I've asked them to watch for that with the Indians. I'm not sure how well that message is playing, since the Indians will of course deny it and probably have. But having mathematical proof for the lack of a directing intelligence in our universe, you can understand what they think of religion and by extension, what they probably think of the Indians, since the group on the surface are apparently eaten up with their religion. I believe they really think some of their gods have come to Earth so I suppose we have to grant them their sincerity. However, another aspect of Crispies is... oh, call it passivism for lack of a better word. They don't like taking hurried action, most especially violent action, so no consensus has been reached." She sighed. "I'm sorry. I'm probably explaining this badly. I could do better if I were on the surface and could interact with the other Crispies by using our perceptive senses. As I've mentioned."

I'm pretty sure that was a broad hint.

"So what are your recommendations?" That tiny smile I'd observed once before flitted across his face.

"I believe we should do as a few of the elders suggest. That is, land so they can observe us in person."

"Will they protect our ship from both the Snappers and the Indians if we land?"

"I doubt it, sir, since they don't know anything about the Snappers other than what I've told them, and after being exposed to the Indians, they have no real reason to believe me. However, if I could speak to some of them in person and with our perceptive senses, they might be more amenable. I must remind you again, though: at the time I left Cresperia, there were no armed ships anywhere in the system."

Becker shook his head, obviously not quite able to comprehend a whole solar system operating on the Crispies' principles.

"Very well. We'll remain in orbit and send our tender down. Jeri, you'll be in charge of the mission. I'll let you select your crew with the exception of the XO or astrogator."

"Yes, sir. When shall we depart?"

He shrugged. "Whenever you're ready. Consult with the pilot on your landing site."

ಬಿಂ

Jeri picked me, Gene, Kyle, Margie Preconder for a physicist and Eleanora for an electronicist among other scientists. I could see she was taking people who could learn the most while on the surface. If anyone learned anything, that is. Captain Becker told her to take a squad of marines. She tried to veto the idea.

"It wouldn't be productive to send armed men, sir. Crispies are generally non-violent."

"I realize that, but the Indians *aren't* non-violent and they have people down there, including Kalki, their 'warrior god,' if you heard right. If you're going anywhere near where they are, I insist."

"Yes, sir. I'll take them since I was planning on going to the same area where they have allowed the Indians to set up housekeeping. However, armed men won't produce an encouraging picture to the Cresperians."

"Suppose I send them with sidearms only? Would that be acceptable?"

Jeri considered for a moment, then shrugged. "I suppose that would be all right. They have already learned that we're a violent species from the Indians, so marines can't do much more harm."

"Having them with you would make me feel better."

Hell, it would make *me* feel better having marines along. I'd had two occasions to see them fight. And I intended to bring along my little pistol, the one that had saved my life a time or two. The Crispies would spot it but perhaps the Indians wouldn't.

Gordon and Jeri had a long conference before we left. I don't know what they talked about, but I don't believe Gordon was all that upset at not being allowed to go down this trip, since Captain Becker wouldn't risk both Crispy humans at once. Even when Gordon argued politely that he had been the only one aboard before Jeri joined us wasn't enough to sway him. Gordon took it gracefully and told those of us going to have a safe trip. He'd proven his worth in a crunch during the second battle with the Snappers and his male ego problem had just about disappeared. I gave him a slight smile, subtly displaying my pride in his behavior. He met my eyes, the corner of his mouth quirked a little, and he nodded just a bit.

We debarked in the tender only a couple of hours after the decision was made. I didn't know if the others realized it, but if it turned out that the Snapper ship which was still jinking around in the system decided to go after the *Galactic*, we might be left behind. I had figured that out from the moment the captain excluded the XO and especially Maddie, our astrogator. Besides that, I believe he and General Haley must have thoroughly discussed Jeri while the two ships were together, because he was giving her broad power to make decisions. I thought he would do that only if he trusted her implicitly.

I don't know to this day why she included me in the crew, since the genetic problems had already been pretty well solved and Jeri could discuss the manifestations better than I could. I don't know why she selected Gene, either, but he was grinning happily as he took his seat in the tender beside me.

∞⃝

Jeri and the pilot conferred up front for a few minutes and then we were off, separating from the ship with barely a bump.

"You've been making yourself scarce again," Gene offered once we began decelerating. With the unreality drive, there was no problem with breaking orbit almost immediately. There was a vector toward our destination, of course, but Jeri and the pilot had already figured the shortest, most comfortable way there.

"It's our good captain who's been keeping me busy, Gene. I'm glad you're coming along with us, if that will help your disposition."

"Touché." He grinned, licked his fingertip, and made a mark in the air. "One for you. D' you know, no one has even told me what our agenda is down there. Hell, I don't even know why I'm here."

I tapped his knee playfully. "Would you believe I don't either?"

"You don't?"

"No, but I trust Jeri. She must have some use for us other than to hold her hand, because Kyle has that well in hand, no pun intended."

"Doesn't he, though? I don't know what the man has, but I wish I had some of it."

"You manage okay, Gene."

"And how should I take that?" He wriggled his brows. The man was irrepressible.

"However you like, but please keep whatever you think bottled up until we get back to the ship." I said that because I felt a little heart thump tugging inside me when I'd seen him enter the tender, the same kind I always have when I see a man I really like. However, I didn't want to think about things like that again until we were on the way home. Time enough to sort out my feelings then.

"As you like."

"You did fine in the last battle, you know. Hell, you did better than fine. You're on for this, whatever happens."

"Thanks. I was trying to keep some special people from biting it. Pretty planet, isn't it?"

"What we can see of it is," I agreed, trying hard to drive away that little tug.

But the feeling stayed with me all the way down.

Cresperia had smaller polar caps than Earth and more land area, or so it seemed from orbit. As we came lower I began looking for cities and didn't find them. We passed over almost half a continent and all I ever saw were small towns with tall spires in the center and a few two- or three-story buildings surrounding them. Occasionally we passed over what must be crop land or in some cases regularly spaced large growth that had to be their equivalent of orchards of some kind.

The land was beautiful and looked as if it could support a thousand times its apparent population. Occasionally we passed over an aircar, but saw few roads. I suspected if they had them they would be underground, then suddenly remembered Jeri telling me exactly that at some time in the past.

The little spaceport looked new. I don't know how to explain but it had a rawness not obvious in the other places we passed over before landing. It crossed my mind that perhaps they'd built it especially for the Indians and now us. Hell, maybe even for the Snappers! God, what a revolting thought!

We landed on the opposite side of the field from where the Indian shuttle was parked. It was bigger than ours, just like their starship was bigger—and differently shaped.

"Keep your seats for a moment," Jeri said, loud enough for us all to hear.

She walked down the aisle between the two rows of seats and to one of the side airlocks and waited until the pressure equalized. It opened and she departed. A few minutes later she stuck her head back inside.

"You can all come out now. Bring your gear. They have a place ready for us to stay."

As we filed out I wondered what the Crispies would think of us. There were the marines, all dressed alike in their unpowered cammies. There were the two officers, Eleanora and Major James Henry, our semanticist, both dressed in space navy uniforms, and General Shelton in army dress blues who was both a diplomat and ultimately responsible for any decisions that became a matter of fight/no fight. And me and the other civilians in a motley of civilian clothes or cammies, as we chose. Gene and I were both being sensible and wearing jeans and shirts and windbreakers. I had a pair of slacks and blouse along that were sort of dressy, and suspected Gene did also, but I was carrying a set of cammies, too. The other civilians wore more dressy outfits that were already becoming wrinkled and mussed. Then finally the crew of the tender, wearing the enlisted version of navy work uniforms, other than the pilot, who wore a flight suit. How's that for variety?

CHAPTER THIRTY-FIVE

THERE WERE TWO CRISPIES outside. Jeri was conversing freely with them as they began walking, but of course none of us understood more than a word here and there. They stayed beside Jeri while we ambled along behind. They led us to a row of three interconnected domed buildings and on inside one of the end structures. The domes also had a newly fabricated feel when I looked at them, but the interior of ours was… homey? Yes, that's the word. It looked more like the lobby of a fairly decent hotel than what you'd expect on an alien planet. That area was right past the entrance. All around the circumference of the great room were half-open doorways leading to rooms that I could see were furnished for humans. About 30 degrees to our left was a big hallway that I presumed led to the center building. There was no need to check in; the lobby was simply a common area. Jeri and her friends stopped in the middle of it.

"You can spread out here and find a room," Jeri said. "Make yourselves comfortable. There's food and drink in each room that's compatible for us. One of the crew will be along in a minute or two with the big coffeepot. Sorry, but there are no alcoholic beverages."

We all trundled off to find a room and then, like strangers anywhere, we sought our own kind. Gene and I roomed next to each other without discussing it. Within a half hour everyone was back in the lobby, either seated or standing around talking. Jeri was gone, as were the Crispies.

Gene spotted me as I joined the throng and came over. He was grinning, naturally.

"Not quite what we were expecting, is it?" he said.

"Not really." I sat down and patted a place beside me on the couch. He took it.

"I wonder what happens next?" he said as he crossed his legs and leaned back comfortably, looking around as if he expected a Crispy delegation to walk in at any moment.

"Jeri will let us know, I'm sure. Hey, I wonder if any of the Crispies here know how to speak English?"

"Hmm. Good question. We'll have a hard time getting much done if we all have to go through Jeri for translations. By the way, did you try the com in your room?"

"Com?"

He shook his head sadly. "Com. You know, something you communicate with?"

"I didn't know there was one."

"I suspect there'll be one in every room, all tied in to the ship. I tried mine but it told me it wasn't ready yet. I imagine they're fixing up some sort of relay system so we can talk even when the ship is on the other side of the planet."

"That would be nice," I said, then noticed Gene was looking past me. I turned and saw Jeri returning from the center dome where she'd gone with the Crispies. Now there were a half dozen with her. She made several stops and each time one of our scientists or officers or crew was paired with a Crispy. Finally she got to us but by then all the Crispies had been taken except one. She introduced it.

"Mai, Gene, this is Fsrssddtst, but call him Fred. He is a male Crispy. He is interested in talking to you both about life on Earth and what he could expect if he decided to convert to human."

Wow! "To male or female?" I asked.

"He's not certain yet and he may very well decide against it in the end. I'll be talking to him as often as I can but otherwise I'll leave him in your hands. And he does speak English, by the way."

He did, too, but in a rather limited fashion. I invited him to come to my room while Gene and I had coffee.

"Please feel free to bring any food or drink you like with you, Fred," I told our Crispy while Gene and I drew cups from the big coffeemaker the crew had set up.

"Thanks hyou," he said. "Please to corrects my proper English untils I learns it all." The Crispies Jeri brought to us all had learned English from a couple of the Indian crew who spoke it and had provided texts to read.

So we helped, and by the second day Fred was speaking very well indeed. They can make a wider variety of sounds and speak among themselves in both higher and lower frequencies than we can hear, and have practically eidetic memories when they bestir themselves. I learned that later, though. For the time being Fred wanted to talk, and by that I mean either Gene or I was speaking almost continually, answering his questions. I quickly figured out that they were almost all designed to help him learn the language. It was only several days later I learned the texts had all been derogatory toward any country other than India and in particular toward the United States. But then, once he was well-versed in English, he brought up other subjects of interest. You can't say I didn't invite it.

"What else would you like to talk about?" I asked on the morning of the second day. We were still meeting in my room and that morning I was still on my first cup of coffee.

"Sex and violence," he said without missing a beat.

⅋γ

I sputtered into my coffee. Gene thought it was hilarious, of course. But then, when he finished laughing and tried to explain to Fred *why* he had laughed, he became a little more serious.

"Those are the two biggest forces driving human affairs, and you might say one is derived from the other," he said.

"Which one?" Fred asked.

"Either. Our sex drives are what initiates violence, although it isn't always apparent."

"Do you really think so, Gene?" I know I was frowning but I was also thinking furiously.

"No, Cherry. It's not that cut and dried. However, there is a lot of truth in the statement. Our self-images are derived in large part from our unconscious sexual self-image. And when our self-images, which are tied into our history, upbringing, social environment, and so on are threatened, violence is often the answer. Not consciously, though. You do know the old adage about rationalism, don't you?"

"'Man is not a rational animal; he is a rationalizing animal.'"

"True, but it goes even deeper. Our brain works to pick out explanations and experiences that give us a shot of dopamine, which makes us feel good, and these are words or actions which agree with our previously formed concepts. It's self-reinforcing, too. Perhaps even addictive. How often do you hear of anyone who's changed their basic political or religious philosophy from an argument? Or hell, for that matter, even a friendly debate?"

He had me there. I could tell him how many, right off. Exactly none.

Fred followed our conversation with great interest but eventually he wanted to talk more about sex. Crispies had sex, naturally, but it wasn't anywhere close to the pleasure-inducing phenomenon that human sex is. For them it is much more tied up with basic reproduction. Whether naturally or artificially part of their genes, they don't know. They are very poor historians. Anyway, Fred was insatiably curious about sex, its techniques, its hows and whys and whens and everything else imaginable. He also told us that other Crispies were doing the same as he was, seeking information in order to decide whether or not to convert. I saw this in action by noticing other Crispies hanging out with our fellows like Fred was with us.

Fortunately Jeri dropped by during one of the earliest discussions and contributed a key ingredient. Fred was asking, or rather trying to find out how to compare the pleasures of sex with anything he was familiar with. They did experience pleasure, he said, but apparently their emotions were not nearly as intense as ours.

"I can give you one answer," she said. "I converted to human and I would never go back. Sex is one of the reasons. I don't want to ever give it up, at least so long as it's with Kyle." She said something else in Cresperian while getting the look on her face that told me she was also utilizing her perceptive sense. I assumed she was repeating the English in a more emphatic way in their own language. "And that goes for other experiences as well," she said in English. "Many of them are also intensely pleasure-producing although not necessarily done for fun."

"So human emotions are that... strongly satisfying?"

"It is impossible to explain how much, even in our own language, especially for sex. It simply has to be experienced to be believed. It would be good in and of itself, but when it is with a person you love and who loves you, there is nothing else in the world better."

And that, naturally, brought the discussion around to love and what *it* was. All three of us took turns trying to explain, but I'm not certain we made much progress. Nevertheless, Fred the Crispy thought he would like to become human, at least for a while, in order to explore its nuances. We left it at that after cautioning him on how it should be approached should he decide in favor.

I was certainly having an interesting time, even if I wasn't learning all that much xenobiology. Like the Crispies with sex, I couldn't understand their perceptive sense, but it was one of my favorite subjects of conversation with Fred, trying to get a handle on it.

I guess all the nice talk was too good to last. The damned Indians spoiled it, but even before that, the Snappers began causing trouble again.

ഇന്റ

Each night before going to bed and every so-often during the day, we went back to our rooms to catch up on the overall situation. The

third night Gene and I were having a drink together in his room. It was
something alcoholic the Crispies concocted for us by copying from a bit
of contraband volunteered by the boatswain chief. It didn't taste exactly
like whisky but it wasn't bad and it *was* alcoholic. I felt myself relaxing
under its influence while we caught the latest summarized download
from the com.

"Why, those nasty little bastards!" Gene exclaimed when we heard
that the Snapper ship, contrary to its previous actions, had begun preying
on the Crispy freighters that plied the industrial lanes from the Jovian-
type planet's moons and a thick asteroid belt where most of the Crispy
manufactured goods were produced. "They're trying to create a damned
blockade!"

"Maybe it will help us," I said.

"How so?"

"I hope it will give the Crispies a notion of how vile they are and impel
them into producing some weapons we can use. Somehow I doubt the
Snappers intend to let us leave this system peacefully, although I'd be
willing to bet they let us go in the end."

Gene opened his mouth, then closed it. "Why do you say that?"

"Because I think they could have wiped our ship out had they wanted
to. I believe they intend to scare us, then when we skedaddle for home,
follow us."

"How could they do that?"

"How should I know? There must be some method though, if the
Snapper ship here is the same one as before. Twice."

"You may have something there. I guess getting weapons
from the Crispies would depend on how long it takes them to
get riled up about the Snappers attacking their freighters, huh?"
"If they do. From what I understand a good many of those freighters are
not manned."

"Still..."

"And the Crispies aren't violent. Maybe they would rather surrender
than fight." I didn't believe that, but I supposed it was possible.

Gene looked properly skeptical.

"Just thinking," I said.

"Me, too, but I've been wondering what the Indians are up to rather
than the Snappers."

I pointed to the com. He shut up, listened, and watched.

The summary showed the Indian starship had left orbit and gone out to challenge the Snapper ship. It wasted a couple of missiles with no result and no reprisal, then a second recording showed them trying to get in close for a laser shot. Instead they were on the receiving end of an energy beam. Curiously, it simply touched them for a moment and died but the Indian ship backed off in a hurry. The next recording showed the Indians returning to orbit and the Snapper ship again moving around but no longer attacking the freighters.

"Looks to me like the Snappers pulled their shot," Gene said. "And the Indians knew it and got the hell away."

"Same here. I think they could have done more damage had they kept on."

Listen to us, I thought. Analyzing tactics and strategy of one completely alien ship and another with humans aboard whose worldview was almost as foreign.

He sipped at his drink and frowned. "Maybe they're scared. They haven't tried to butt heads with our ship, either."

"Maybe, but I don't think so." I thought of the hand-to-hand fighting and how viciously the Snappers pressed ground attacks or stood and fought in defense.

"No, I really don't think they're scared, either," Gene said, "but... maybe wanting to be sure they get back home with their information? Two different intelligent species discovered, with one of them practically defenseless?"

"Could be they think there's three. The Indian ship doesn't really look much like ours for all that it's powered the same. I suspect it's because of the different national resources involved in the construction. I still favor the Snappers trailing us home, though. We have an interstellar ship here. The Crispies don't."

He nodded. "Could be. Think we ought to pass our suspicions on to Jeri?"

"Couldn't hurt. I'll send our thoughts over to her. Anything else before I do?"

He rubbed his chin studiously. "Maybe. The Indian big shot is supposed to be a mighty warrior and a god. Is he on the ship or down here? And if he is here, what's his reaction?"

"Maybe he's not quite so warrior-like as he thought he was after hearing what we told the Crispies about the Snappers."

He laughed. "Could be."

I punched up the com, had a brief conversation with Jeri, then turned back to Gene just in time for him to hold up my empty glass.

"Another drink?"

I nodded. We were in the middle of it when Jeri came visiting after listening to our suppositions.

"Hi Jeri," Gene said. "Care for some of this ersatz whisky we're drinking?"

"I believe I will, thanks. And thanks to both of you for your speculations. I passed it all on up to Captain Becker. He believes, and I concur, that the Snappers intend to try following us home, just as they followed us here. I really, really wish we knew how they did it."

And that made me remember an earlier thought, one I'd had briefly then lost in the press of our business with the Crispies.

"Jeri, do we know for certain all three of our encounters with Snapper ships are from the *same* ship? And for that matter, how can we be sure the Snapper ship here is really that? A Snapper ship, I mean. We've certainly not seen any of its crew this time and we've never received any kind of communication from them on any of the encounters. Maybe the one here is yet another species?"

She nodded as if she had been thinking the same thing. "For that matter, General Haley said he'd never had any ship-to-ship commerce with them. However, I'd say this ship here not being Snappers would be pushing coincidence to the breaking point, especially since it looks the same. On your other supposition... well, we just don't know."

"I've had another thought," I said. I crossed my legs and drank more of my whisky. It wasn't really that bad, considering. When they were both watching me I continued. "Suppose the Snappers have a large empire. Could it be that the Crispies are just outside the edge of it and that we've stumbled into its boundaries in our previous encounters? We know both were apparently colony worlds."

"Captain Becker has already considered that. I think you're right. At the least we've encountered the edge of their explorations. However, it doesn't solve the problem of whether they followed us or whether this is a different ship, does it?"

"No," I admitted. "So what do we do?"

Sitting on the bed, she smoothed her hand down the seam of her jeans. "That's going to be up to Captain Becker and I don't think he can make a decision yet. You see, tomorrow some of the Crispy elders who were involved in setting up this little spaceport and these reception buildings want us and the Indians to see if we can come to some kind of agreement that we can both live with. We're to meet in the morning in the central dome. I personally have my doubts about this but if we don't try, our position will become rather shaky.

"Somehow, though, we have to try to make them believe in the threat of the Snappers and at the same time understand the dangers of converting to human form too fast like the Indians have done. The faction interested in exploring will be observing, as will many who think Crispies would do better sticking close to home and having nothing to do with any of us. Some friends of the Crispy who became Kalki, and some of my friends will also be there. Captain Becker has instructed me to play it by ear and do the best I can for humanity and the United States."

Uh-oh, I thought; I've got a baaaad feeling about this.

Chapter Thirty-Six

After Jeri left, Gene and I decided to have another drink.

"I suppose Jeri has told everyone else, or will be doing so," Gene said as he mixed them.

"I should hope so," I responded absentmindedly. I was already running various scenarios through my mind, trying to think of some way to influence the impending event.

"Relax, Cherry. There's not much we can do until the wingding tomorrow happens. In the meantime let's try to relax."

I took a deep breath and then another and let them out slowly. He was right. I knew that, but still… oh the hell with it, I told myself. Do like he says. Relax.

So I did. I leaned back on the little couch we were sitting on and willed my muscles to loosen up. By the time we had talked a bit more and had some more of that flavored ethanol, I began feeling the tension leaving my body.

"You're better now, I think," Gene said.

"Uh-huh. When you can't do anything about a situation, there's no point in beating your brains out. If there's anything either of us can do, it will be tomorrow. I guess I've been trying to shoulder the world's burdens. Stupid of me, huh?"

"No. It's one of the things I like about you."

"Really?"

"Yup. Really." He grinned.

I caught the twinkle in his eyes and sat my drink on the end table.

Gene is much smarter than most people give him credit for. He caught the signal immediately and slid his arm around my shoulder then gave a very gentle little tug.

I came willingly and tilted my head back so he could kiss me. He was very good at it. And I was as ready as I had been for a long while, what I had said earlier to him notwithstanding. I fumbled for the little bulb on the side of the table and pressed it. The lights dimmed but didn't go out.

"That's as close to candlelight as we're going to get," he said.

"Umm. Shut up and kiss me again."

A few minutes later we were undressed and on the bed. I was so help-lessly aroused that I momentarily forgot how strong I was. Maybe his well-built body caused me to think subconsciously that he was the same. Whatever. He let out a little yelp.

"Sorry," I murmured and pulled him over me.

He was good at that, too.

Very good.

ಬಉಗ

Fortunately, some of the changes Sira had made in my body tempered the effects of alcohol. I woke up at three o'clock and was momentarily disoriented. Then it all came back to me.

Mai, you are a *bad* girl, I thought as I sat up, intending to tiptoe on out and get back to my own room.

"No need to rush. It's early." Gene's voice was husky with sleep. Or perhaps desire.

A *very* bad girl, I thought as I lay back down. But hell, why not? I liked Gene. I had no idea if it would go beyond that, but for the moment I didn't care. I was light years from home and his presence was comforting. I was very relaxed and a little while later became even more so.

I made it to my room in time for a quick shower before breakfast.

ಬಉಗ

The central dome was larger than the ones on each side of it. Had the Crispies planned it that way? No, they hadn't even known we were coming. Or had they? Maybe one of the Indians let slip that other Crisp-ies had survived the breakup of their ship and might possibly be on the way. Either way, there was plenty of room and plenty of seating in the amphitheater-style dome. Each row of seats was higher than the one in front and the seats circled three-quarters of the perimeter against the wall. The central area took most of the space but it was just a floor, no stage or anything like that.

Gene had tapped on my door by prearrangement. I felt just a wee bit awkward with him at first and noticed he wasn't quite as sure of himself as he had been the night before. It passed as we walked together to the dome. There were already plenty of people there from both sides, al-though it looked as if the Indians outnumbered us. Well, we knew that already.

I spotted Jeri down in the center of the huge room where the floor was bare of seats. I nudged Gene.

"Uh-huh. That's Kyle with her, too. I wonder what his position in this affair is?"

"I suspect Jeri just wants him close for whatever we're going to accomplish, if anything." I broke off and stared. "Oh, shit! Would you look at that!"

A bizarre giant of a man entered from the Indian side passage and proceeded toward the center space where Jeri and Kyle were waiting. He must have been nearly eight feet tall. All he wore was a white cloth covering his groin and thighs—called a lungi, I remembered from Jeri's briefing on Hindu culture. Probably chosen to show off his massive chest and superb musculature. He was barefooted. His hair was shoulder length and black.

His face resembled the classic Indian features but he had a strong chin and glittering black eyes that roamed constantly as he strode confidently toward Jeri and Kyle. I felt his gaze on me for a moment and felt a surge of adrenalin. Fight or flight? Clearly that was what my body was preparing for. I told it to be quiet and his gaze passed on to others. He stopped about 20 feet from where Jeri and Kyle stood waiting.

"Impressive, huh?" Gene said.

"Physically, at least," I agreed.

We found seats together as the last few people from both sides trickled in. As they did, I saw that Jeri was whispering something to Kyle with her lips very close to his ear. She plainly wanted no one other than him to hear her. His head was tilted to the side and he was listening intently and nodding his understanding of whatever she was saying. There were only a few Crispies present. I didn't know what their presence meant. No one had said they would be there, but then no one had said they wouldn't, either. Observers? Referees? Elders? No way of knowing since I still couldn't tell one Crispy from another. They all looked alike to me, except for some differences in fur color, although Jeri had told me there were as many distinguishing characteristics among them as among humans.

Jeri looked like a midget beside the giant Indian. He stood with his mouth set in firm lines as he scanned the room. He then crossed his arms across his chest and spoke. Somehow the acoustics were fixed so that everyone could hear what was said from that middle space.

"I am Kalki, Tenth Avatar of Vishnu the Preserver," he announced in a firm, deep bass voice that rumbled like a giant cat pleased with himself and purring to show it.

"You are a freak of a human who was once a Cresperian," Jeri retorted just as strongly. "Your mind is deranged from converting too fast and without a human mentor. You should revert to your Cresperian form and seek the elders for mergent therapy."

Kalki's black eyes glittered with scorn. "I was once Cresperian but no more. I am become as a god. And you are no longer Cresperian, but it is you who should seek therapy for associating with such mongrels as the English and Americans have become. Their day is done. Their star is falling. The power of Vishnu and Kalki will cleanse the Earth of their taint with the assistance of our worshippers and such Cresperians as recognize reality," he paused, and somehow I detected menace for those Cresperians who didn't, "and then our Lakshmis will bring peace and prosperity."

"You are mad." Jeri shook her head in annoyance. "You are mad and your arrogance is not going to be allowed to prevail."

I heard her say the words, but I wondered what on earth she intended to back them up with. There were more of them than us, the Crispies were as near pacifists as mattered and that big hulk looked strong enough to wipe up the floor with us all by himself. At least he didn't have four arms like most of their gods.

"Allowed. *Allowed!*" Kalki burst into laughter that roared and crashed around the room. "And who is to stop me, little lover of stupid Americans? Yes, I have learned of your alliance with the one beside you. What is he compared to Vishnu or to *me*, Kalki The Warrior? Best for you to come to our side and take your place on Earth as one of the elite. You could become Lakshmi, a state others of our followers have attained." He nodded his massive head toward the group of Indians.

While I had been following his and Jeri's debate, the person he referred to had come in and all the Indians had risen to their feet. She was standing with their followers. Worshippers. It was very easy to spot her. She was seven feet tall, at least, but was proportioned as normally as he was. One of her breasts was covered by the white toga-like garment she wore, the other bare. I thought her boobs were too big and hips too wide but I suppose that could be the woman part of me assessing another. Had it not been for those little flaws she would have been beautiful despite her size.

"I agree with my wife. You are mad, Kalki," Kyle said with a calm forcefulness I could only admire, considering how close he was standing to that giant.

I recognized his voice and turned my gaze from Lakshmi back to the center of the room as he continued.

"You are mad and must be suppressed. Neither the Cresperians nor the people of Earth deserve such as you, nor do they want to follow your deranged philosophy."

Kalki stared at Kyle with those unnerving, glittering obsidian eyes. Jeri made a motion toward Kyle as if holding him back. Well, that's what it looked like. But surely he's not thinking of fighting that man-mountain, I told myself. I could only imagine the results, because Kyle wasn't all that big. The disparity in size made it look as if Kalki could wad him up in his hands and toss him into a trash basket.

"Ah, you think you are a warrior, do you, little man? Do you really believe the likes of you could defeat me, Kalki The Warrior? It is laughable. You are the one who is insane."

"Not at all," Kyle said pleasantly as he removed his jacket and began unbuttoning his shirt. "I see that the only way to convince you and your followers that you are unfit to show Cresperians the human way is to beat you to a pulp. If that doesn't do it, I'll have to kill you." He tossed the garments to Jeri. "Are you ready?"

"You? Kill me?" Kalki roared with laughter. "Come, then, little man! Come to your death!" He threw his head back and laughed again. No, he roared and ranted and bleated with mirth at the very thought that Kyle might defeat him. Or maybe he was laughing at the thought of killing Kyle and then turning his wrath onto Jeri and the rest of us.

"Ah, shit," Gene muttered. "I like him, but what can he possibly do against that giant?"

"Especially without a slingshot," I said inanely.

"Try not to kill him, sweetheart," Jeri said, loudly enough for everyone to hear.

The instant that Kalki bowed his body forward, still laughing and holding his stomach, Kyle charged.

I didn't believe it was happening. I was horrified. What was worse, Jeri quickly moved out of range, all the way back to the front seats with Gene and me, giving them room.

The sound of the first blow Kyle struck was like a maul hitting a side of beef or the bursting of a melon dropped from a height. It would have felled an ordinary man and knocked him unconscious. Kalki barely moved. His laughter stopped abruptly, though, and he straightened up. He reached out as if to grab Kyle and crush him but his hands met empty air and another loud wet smack of a hard, calloused hand meeting unprotected flesh reverberated around the room.

Kalki grunted and swung a fist. It hit nothing. By then Kyle's body was a blur of motion, and the sound of hands and feet, knees and elbows striking tissue so swift and hard it sounded like loud drums playing, a tune of violence so fast and furious I couldn't follow it. Kalki staggered and moved this way and that but Kyle was all over him, behind him, in front and to the side, bent low one moment and feet lashing out the next. He was constantly moving, whirling, striking and moving again, giving Kalki no chance to set himself or even think. It was awesome, like a man armed with only a revolver going up against a machine-gunner—and winning.

Blood spattered and flowed, and it all belonged to the giant Indian. His face was a red pulp, the black eyes swelling closed, and even his chest and back were split in places from the rain of blows Kyle had poured on him. And while he pummeled Kalki's head and chest, he struck what was the beginning of the end: a heel kick to the side of Kalki's knee. The sound was grisly. Even that giant couldn't stand with every tendon in his knee snapped. One leg folded the wrong way and the purported god staggered.

Yet he was so solidly built that somehow he still remained upright. He spat blood from broken teeth and mangled lips and went into a defensive position, arms covering his head and upper body. It made no difference. Kyle kept moving, kept striking from different angles. Every blow drew a grunt of pain from Kalki. I could tell the giant was about done by the sluggishness of his moves, by the way he seemed to no longer know where he was or what was happening.

I was so intent on the battle that I didn't know when Jeri grabbed my arm. She moved against me and I suddenly realized she was clutching me above the elbow and leaning heavily on my shoulder in order to keep herself upright. Her eyes were closed and she had a look of awful concentration on her face, as if some force was beating against her mind. While I was staring at her and wondering what on earth had happened to her, I saw Kyle deliver the coup de grace from the corner of my eye: a powerful heel kick to the side of the giant's remaining knee.

Kalki simply toppled. He fell on his side and tried to prop himself up, but Kyle was having no part of it. His foot struck Kalki's chin. His massive head snapped back. Kyle whirled and his other foot lashed out, hitting him squarely on his neck, just to the side of his Adam's apple. It must have shattered his trachea. It would have killed an ordinary man and I had no doubt that was what Kyle intended. Somehow Kalki kept breathing, but not for long. His massive body was now undefended, in perfect position for a truly killing blow. I think Kyle might have delivered it; but before he could, Jeri shouted at him.

"Kyle, watch out!"

Her voice stopped him. He looked back just in time. He must have felt like a cowboy who had fallen off his horse in the middle of a stampede, for a Lakshmi was running toward him, and that had caused the other Indians to follow. She stopped suddenly as if she had momentarily forgotten what she was doing, but the other Indians came on. She recovered and followed. Kyle felled the first two or three, then went down under the swarm.

Our marines were already moving to counteract the Indians, and Jeri, Gene and I followed in their wake, along with the rest of our group. Soon the center of the domed room became a mob scene with men and women striking blows, falling, getting up, shooting and being shot.

Jeri was shouting, "Try not to kill them!" to the marines and then immediately countermanded herself.

"Mai! The man in the blue shirt! Kill him!"

My gun was already in my hand. I'd drawn it the moment I saw the mass exodus of the Indians from one side of the room toward where Kyle and Kalki had been fighting. Or rather where Kalki had been getting his ass pounded into the floor; the giant hadn't gotten in a single blow.

I didn't question Jeri's order. The only reason I hesitated was so I could sort him out from the others and not kill someone else, because our people were intermingled with theirs and for a moment I couldn't see who she meant. Then his head raised up from where Kyle was lying on the floor and he was separated from the others for a second.

I took my shot and fired. Something had already told me he was a Crispy who'd converted to human. His stance, or the inflection in Jeri's voice, and the fact that he was pointed out to me as obviously more dangerous than the others, all went into it. That was why I didn't aim for the body. A Crispy human could have kept going with a chest wound. His head was a much smaller target, but I didn't hesitate. His right eye blinked out and the back of his head exploded in a spray of blood and tissue, bone and brains.

Killing that convert didn't change much. The fight went on in a tangle of intermingled bodies.

"Don't kill them!" Jeri shouted as she saw an opening and ran toward Kyle's prostrate form. Amazingly, her voice rose over the mêlée, clearly understandable, but shots kept ringing out and screams and shouts mingled with the gunfire. Some of the Indians were armed, too. I ran after Jeri, and Gene was right beside me carrying a little automatic pistol. We threaded our way through the throng toward where Kyle and Kalki were lying.

The opening where I'd seen Jeri kneeling beside Kyle closed and they disappeared from sight. The whole great room was in an uproar. I doubt that very many people understood what was going on. The impetus was to protect and succor our own people and if any Indians got in the way, too bad. I'm sure the Indians must have felt the same way, or perhaps worse. After all, their god had been defeated. Perhaps he was dead. He was as unmoving as Kyle. Maybe that hampered the Indians. I tried to simply fight my way toward Jeri and Kyle and let the marines take care of everything else, but I kept my pistol ready.

Unfortunately, there were too few marines for them to do it all, especially with Jeri's admonition not to kill hampering them. It left room for one more converted Crispy to get close to Jeri. He came wading through the mass of bodies like a boat moving through rough water. People stopped whatever mayhem they were committing as he neared, just as they had for the Lakshmi earlier. I had lost sight of her after shooting the converted Crispy threatening Kyle and Jeri and then lost her again as I tried to keep my mind unhampered, knowing the new one was up to no good, and knowing what he was doing from past experience, but it didn't work. He was befuddling whoever got in his way by messing with their short-term memory, including mine.

The next thing I knew Jeri was falling and Gene was shouting.

"No!" he screamed and a shot rang out almost in my ear. It stunned me and took away my hearing, making me even more befuddled than

I was from the loss of a tiny slice of my life, a few moments' worth of memory.

A huge body fell against me, taking us both to the floor with me on the bottom lying in a puddle of warm liquid that I dimly realized must be blood. When a seven-foot-tall woman lands on you there isn't much room for doubt about gravity being a force of nature. I was stunned into immobility while the fighting swirled around me. Amazingly, I still had my gun in my hand but even if I'd had the sense to use it right then, I didn't have a target. The Lakshmi was so large she was practically smothering me; her body mass prevented me from seeing what was going on around me. I struggled to get out from under her, using my enhanced muscles to shove her away.

When I could see again I was on the floor beside Gene and Jeri, both lying very still. Kyle was just sitting up and crawling over to Jeri. We were surrounded by what was left of the squad of marines. Beyond them bodies lay helter skelter, most of them Indians. Crispies were streaming into the dome.

Jeri blinked her eyes. Kyle gave a sigh of relief and knelt beside her. Her arms rose up and pulled his face down for a kiss. Afterward, she struggled to her feet with Kyle's support. I had thought they were both dead but they seemed to be relatively unharmed. Gene wasn't. He had been practically decapitated by a long, sharp curvy-bladed knife that was still impaled in his neck and if that hadn't been enough, he had also been shot in the head. Even Crispies couldn't help him. I looked bleakly at Jeri.

"I'm sorry, Cherry. He took that knife in order to keep it from you. She came at us wielding it and a gun, too. Yours isn't the only life Gene saved, but it was you he was thinking about."

I stared down at his body and let the tears flow unchecked. My God, he must have loved me. I shuddered at the thought of that knife blade entering his neck and practically slicing his head off. I found myself thinking through the tears that I was glad I'd given him that one night together. I would have felt worse than awful if I hadn't. Not after he died for me.

CHAPTER THIRTY-SEVEN

FOR A WHILE we didn't know what was going to happen. There had been more violence done in that dome in 15 minutes than the whole of Cresperia had seen in centuries. I knew it wasn't our fault but that didn't necessarily mean anything. It was almost certainly *not* what we, or the Crispies of any faction, had expected. It certainly wasn't what our group had wanted. I doubted the Indians thought it would get to the stage of fighting. They had probably thought Kalki would just awe us all into submission.

The Crispies quickly began clearing the bodies out of the central dome with manipulator carts. Jeri told us not to worry, that they were being preserved until the various factions decided our fate.

"Our fate?" Kyle questioned. He finished buttoning his shirt back up and slipped into his jacket.

"Bad choice of words," Jeri reassured him. "No one is going to hurt us, but there are a number of different factions discussing the situation with some elders of various persuasions. We need to wait here."

We retreated from the bloody area to the seats. I made no suggestions at all but simply followed along. My mind was still numb over Gene's death. I just couldn't picture that energetic, congenial grin being gone forever.

Someone brought coffee. I accepted a cup and sipped at it. The aroma told me before I tasted. It was heavily laced with something akin to brandy. I drank more of it and felt some of the numbness leaving my body. I blessed whoever thought of it. It gave me the energy to recuperate somewhat and take part in the discussion that followed.

While we were waiting for the Crispies to decide what they were going to do, Jeri and Kyle related their part in the fracas. Mostly it squared with what I remembered, but there were lots of questions. I asked a lot of them, simply to keep my mind off Gene.

"What were you whispering to Kyle so urgently about right before he challenged Kalki?" I asked Jeri.

"Oh, that. Kalki apparently never saw the need to enhance his musculature since he was so large. I noticed it right away and told Kyle I thought he could take him if it came to a fight, and that I could keep Kalki from using his perceptive sense if he tried. I really wasn't expecting it to come down to a brawl, though."

"I was," Kyle said. "I've met his kind before. He came into the dome prepared to dominate us and nothing would have prevented it except our complete surrender. I just decided to get it over with, since it was going to happen whether we liked it or not." He shrugged like a little boy caught stealing cookies that would have been given to him anyway. "Jeri had already told me he was only proportionately strong for his size, and I was pretty sure he wasn't the type to have practiced any of the martial arts, like I have since way back when. And Jeri was going to keep his perceptive sense reined in."

"You were that certain he would want to fight rather than compromise?"

"Absolutely, although it wasn't much of a fight."

"I agree now," Jeri said. "I should have trusted Kyle when he whispered to me that Kalki wanted to demonstrate his superiority." She leaned into him and he put an arm around her.

"I guess that's why Jeri grabbed my arm, then. She must've been blocking Kalki. But what happened when you got buried under all the Indians?" I asked Kyle. "I thought for sure they had killed you."

He chuckled but there was little mirth to it. "Once upon a time I saved my own life by playing dead. It was a long time ago, but I remembered how well it worked. All I had to do was lie there with my mouth gaping open and my tongue hanging out. They pummeled me a bit but didn't hurt me much—until someone conked me with a piece of firewood. That was about the same time Kalki recovered enough to know he was lying next to me."

"Firewood?"

"I think it was someone's skull meeting yours, dear," Jeri said. "Or... maybe it *was* ersatz firewood, torn from some furniture. Anyway, it put you out for a minute while I was beating my way to you. Then I suddenly knew you were fighting for your life again."

"Yeah," he said. "Jeri was still tying up Kalki's perceptive sense but I was groggy. He tried to choke me to death and damn near succeeded. That's when I had to kill him."

"How? It sounds like he had the advantage."

"It's strange. Despite the beating I gave him, he *still* didn't realize how much Jeri had enhanced my body. He couldn't crush my trachea as he intended to, but it was a very near thing. I couldn't get my breath. That's when I used the last of my strength to poke my finger into one of his eyes and then the other."

"You killed him by poking him in the eye? Come on, Kyle." He had to be kidding me.

"Well, I sort of kept poking. Y' know?" He extended his finger straight out to demonstrate. "Right through the eye socket and into his brain."

I tried to visualize it. "And that killed him?"

"I wiggled it. Back and forth and up and down. I scrambled his brains until he let loose of my throat then I finished the job by crushing *his* trachea."

I shuddered. "God, Kyle, that's... gory!"

"Yup, sure was. He deserved it, though. Even then, I might have stopped, but Jeri was real close and she suddenly fell. I couldn't waste any more time on him. So I gooshed him, but good."

"So then what happened to you?" I said to Jeri. "I saw you fall but didn't know what did it."

"Oh, I was so mad at myself. I misjudged Kalki, or the Crispy who became Kalki, and how thoroughly he had convinced some of the Crispies of the benefits of converting to human. I also never thought any of his converts would try to kill me while the elders were observing. Even after the fighting started, the elders knew *I* didn't want any killing, because they heard me say so. And finally, since he and his partner already had more than enough Lakshmi to satisfy their sexual desires, I was sure they would discourage any Crispy from converting to female. I was wrong and I almost died because of it. One Crispy had converted to human female and had subsequently had sex with one of Kalki's followers. That convinced her Kalki was right. Then when she thought her lover was dying, she went a little berserk. Uh, berserk-ER. She tried to kill me with a powerful surge of lethal perception. There were two things that saved me: one, that I already had my own perceptive sense at such a high level from fending Kalki off of Kyle, and two, I was furiously angry that Gene was dying and I couldn't help. Crispies, even Crispies in their new human form, aren't used to anger. She wasn't expecting it and it delayed her a second or two. Nevertheless, I was knocked cold."

Christ! I'd thought I had been in on most of the action, but it turned out I'd missed some of the most important byplay.

"So what kept the Crispy from killing you once you were unconscious?"

"Why, you did, Cherry!"

"I did? How?"

She stared at me as if I was crazy, and I was beginning to think I might be. I sure didn't remember any female Crispy. *Oh!* Memory loss from a Crispy. That had to be it. But...

Jeri smiled and shook her head. "You were stunned when Gene killed the only other male Crispy and then was killed himself by the Lakshmi wielding that knife. You shot the Lakshmi first and then the female Crispy, both in the head. At the last moment the Crispy tried to prevent it by taking your short-term memory. She succeeded, obviously, but not soon enough. Your finger was already pulling the trigger."

"But... how did I know she was a Crispy? I know I don't go around killing women just for fun!"

"Of course not, Cherry. But give that fine mind of yours some credit. She obviously wasn't from our ship, and she was near me when I fell. She also hadn't been human long and you subconsciously noticed the difference. You put two and two together and did exactly what you should have. Gene saved your life... but you saved mine."

I had to sit down. Everything that had happened surged into my mind at once. I didn't say another word until I had finished the "brandy" and coffee. It helped me sort out all the pieces and put them together in proper order. While I was doing that, Jeri had gone to report the events to Captain Becker.

Kyle sat down beside me. I looked at him almost as if he were a stranger. He smiled gently at me.

"What's funny?" I asked belligerently. No one should be smiling. Not now. Not after that massacre.

"Nothing at all, Mai. I was just paying tribute to a warrior."

"You were? Who?"

"Why, you, of course. You've proven it over and over on this trip. If you weren't such a great geneticist I'd say you missed your calling."

"I think I need another drink," I said weakly.

ഇൻ

A little later we were told we could go back to our own dome. I went straight to my room and sprawled out face down on the bed. I cried for what seemed like an endless time, but finally the tears stopped. I got up and took a shower and changed clothes. It made me feel much better in an odd sort of way. I toweled my hair as dry as I could, then went back out into the lobby. From the looks of them, everyone else had damp hair, too. I couldn't blame them for wanting to wash off after the blood bath we'd been through.

There was fresh coffee. I drew a cup but didn't add anything to it. Just coffee. I sat with some of the young marines for a while. I told them how much we all appreciated the way they had protected the civilians.

"From what I saw and heard, I think you did a bit yourself, ma'am," a corporal told me respectfully. Others nodded.

"Third time," I said. The remark came out of the blue. "Third time what?" the corporal asked, confused. I looked at his name tag. It read Miller.

"That this little Smith and Wesson has saved my life," I said, patting the side pocket of my windbreaker.

"May I see?"

I ejected the cartridge, removed the clip and handed it over.

He examined it with a professional interest. "Nice."

"Mai?"

I looked around. It was Jeri.

"Come on. The tender is going back up and Captain Becker wants to see some of us in person."

I retrieved my weapon and stood. "Nice talking to you, fellows," I said and waved goodbye.

౸౦ఴ

An hour later we were on the way to the *Galactic*. It made me realize I had forgotten all about what our friends the Snappers might have been up to, but I didn't ask about them. I didn't want to know. What I wanted to know was what the Crispies had decided. Since I was sitting with Kyle and Jeri, it was easy to find out.

"Some factions of the Crispies aren't very happy with us, but the majority are prepared to work with us," Jeri told me.

"In what way?"

She sighed. "It's not easy to explain. Whenever I've had time I've talked to friends I had here before I left on our spaceship. They are intrigued at the change in my... not attitudes but..."

"Point of view?" Kyle offered.

"Something like that, but more." She looked pensive for a moment, almost guilty. I was just getting ready to ask her what was bothering her when she let it out.

"I can tell you something now that I couldn't earlier. Do you remember those three Crispies who were present for the, uh, meeting?"

"Some meeting!" Kyle interjected.

"Yes, dear. Anyway, those three were not only elders, but three of the most powerfully perceptive Crispies on the planet. They had learned both Indian and enough English to get along in it beforehand. You know how quickly we pick up languages. Anyway, they were observers but were also… merged… with many more Crispies who were, in turn, following the proceedings through them. Our audience was much bigger than you knew. The only other person I told was Kyle."

I stared at him. "And you attacked Kalki when you knew those supermen were observing every little emotion and intention?"

"It didn't go that deep, Cherry. We can't read minds any more than you can. Even when removing short-term memory we don't know what the person was truly thinking. It's just a process. No… oh, never mind that. Kyle knew he was being watched but he also knew they were watching Kalki even more. Kalki didn't realize it, but he hadn't made a very good impression on most Crispies, or he would have had more than just those three converts. Anyway, Kyle wasn't taking orders, even from me. He just did what he felt was the right thing—and they could sense that. On the other hand, they could sense that all Kalki wanted was power.

"While they can't feel deep emotion, they can sense how it works for me, like how much I love Kyle, for example, or how deeply troubled I was at what the Indians were doing here. They've also been speaking with Gordon through one of the gizmos they put together and wired into our com. Between him and me, we've about convinced them that being human is something very good indeed, if gone about in the right way. And Cherry, I told them how you figured that out. You've got a fan club here."

"What!?"

She laughed merrily. "Uh-huh. Not really, of course but there are quite a number of Crispies who would readily convert to human so long as you were in charge of the proceedings."

"Hmm. I don't know how to take that." I really didn't. And I didn't know how it was going to affect me yet, either.

"Just take it as it comes. Captain Becker will have more to say after we arrive."

"I'll bet!"

I spent the rest of the trip to orbit wondering exactly how the events on the planet were going to turn out. I also tried to imagine what kind of impression we'd made on those three old Crispies with the super percep- tive sense. God, what they must have been thinking! And how on earth did they stand to perceive all that violence when they weren't used to such? I was ready to barf, and I'd already experienced two battles with the Snappers.

And come to think of it, Jeri still hadn't said what they wanted from us, if anything. Or whether they would cooperate in some things we wanted, like preparing a defense against the Snappers or giving us the means to either outrun them or destroy them so we could warn Earth.

Shucks, I still didn't know what they intended to do with the Indians, either. Or the Chinese, if they showed up. I didn't give the Islamic Con- federation much chance of building an interstellar ship even if they did still have their one Crispy.

CHAPTER THIRTY-EIGHT

DIANNE FOUND ME almost as soon as I cleared the tender bay.

"Miss Trung, the captain wants to see you in his cabin in one hour. I have some coffee waiting on you in your stateroom and made sure you had clean clothes ready."

"Dianne, you are a wonder. That's not even in your job description, but thanks. Thanks a lot, and I mean it."

She smiled prettily. "Your image reflects on me."

"Sure it does. I'll tell you about our trip when I get a chance."

"Please!"

I laughed ruefully and hurried off. Now what? Becker surely must already know everything important that had happened, so what could he want me for? Were the Snappers acting up again? No, or I would have seen signs of general quarters. I shrugged and went on about my business.

Dianne had laid out a trim pair of red slacks and a white blouse. They were fine. What really needed attention was my hair! Evidently one of the Indian Amazons must've gotten a handful of it at some point, and it was a wreck, broken and torn. My scalp felt bruised, too. I spent most of my hour trying to get my locks back into some semblance of repair.

When I reported to the captain's cabin there were others present, but not many. XO Edward Prescott was one. Jeri was there, but not Kyle. Gordon was sitting in a relaxed attitude, looking happy for some reason. A couple of others.

Becker stood when I entered the room. He reached across the conference table to shake my hand.

"Thanks for coming, Mai. We'll get to business in a moment. For now, would you like a drink? Coffee?" He raised his brows invitingly.

"Both, sir. About one third brandy if you have it and two thirds coffee."

In a minute there was a big mug in front of me, steaming faintly. It was topped by whipped cream. The aroma was magical. Jamesons, maybe? The captain had good taste. I wasted no time sampling it and it tasted as good as it smelled. I made a note to myself not to drink too much of it because there was a miasma in the air, as if I was being offered a last indulgence before being made to walk the plank. The café royale was so good that it might have been worth it, though.

"Now then." Becker crossed his legs and leaned back comfortably in his chair. "The Snapper ship has retreated to the edge of our ability to monitor it. We don't know what that means other than they aren't a concern to us right now. That gives us time to relax and enjoy a congenial drink while we discuss other subjects of importance.

"I've been told that some Cresperians are interested in converting to human *and* going back to Earth with us. That alone would constitute a successful mission for the *Galactic*. However, our time is limited. Our primary mission was to find Cresperia. We've done that, but now we've unintentionally been given another mission, that of warning Earth of inhospitable aliens."

He stopped to make sure we were all following him. I was, so far, but still didn't know what he was leading up to. Seeing that no one intended to comment, he went on.

"I'm hoping the Cresperians will agree to retrofit our ship with better weapons before we leave if they can. I'm not counting on it, though. They didn't seem too interested when Jeri approached them."

"They still might, Captain. I think it depends on what else the Snapper ship does." Jeri tried to look hopeful.

He nodded. "Yes. Well, we'll see. I said that some Crispies wanted to convert to human and go home with us. Alternatively, I'm told one faction of them would like some humans to stay here and help others in converting to human. They would provide very reasonable living conditions for what would certainly be a long stay."

He paused to sip at his drink, which gave me a moment to consider what he'd said. I began to get the idea about the time he resumed speaking.

"They insisted that one of our human Crispies stay as well, so that they can be certain the conversions go smoothly. Gordon Stuart has very kindly volunteered to fill that position. However, I also want someone down there who is familiar with the intricacies of Crispies converting to humans, particularly to human males."

He was looking directly at me. Curiously, so was Gordon, who was sitting next to him. I met Gordon's gaze first. He was relaxed and his smile was clearly meant for me. All at once I knew what he wanted, not only now but in the future. Had he been pining away for me all this time? I didn't think so—hadn't thought so, anyway—but I could see the desire in his damnably gorgeous bedroom eyes now. They seemed to see right through me. While no one else was looking at him, he winked at me. I almost burst out laughing, and might have, had the situation not been so serious. Instead I turned to Captain Becker.

"I assume that's me you're talking about, sir."

"Yes. It is you. I don't want to order you to stay here, but it would certainly be for a good cause. You could repair some of the damage the Indians did, and at the same time, begin forming Crispy humans who would share our world view."

I could understand that. It was important. But... "How long are you thinking of, Captain?"

He shrugged. "At least until General Haley gets his ship back to Earth and another ship comes this way. I passed on to him the direction we intended to go and we didn't deviate too much from it even while trying to outrun the Snappers. I'm sure the government will send more heavily-armed ships in view of what he ran into. I'll be taking the *Galactic* directly home, of course. That way, another mission can get back here sooner."

There was one little factor he wasn't saying anything about. Sure, General Haley had probably gotten the *Zeng Wu* back safely, but there was no guarantee. Another Snapper ship could have followed him, for all we knew. So far as I was concerned, it was a sure bet that they'd want to find our home world. I was pretty sure they could have wiped out either ship if they'd wanted to, but they chose to let them go. Also, there was no guarantee he would get the *Galactic* home safely, either, better weapons or not.

So what it came down to was that if I stayed I might be marooned for a long, long time. I glanced at Gordon again. He seemed to be musing now and wasn't aware of my look unless he was using his perceptive sense. *Maybe* marooned, I told myself. No, be honest. Not maybe. If I stayed, *probably* marooned. At the very least I would be looking at a long stay on Cresperia.

"What about the Indians, sir?" I said. It was a sudden thought.

"They're gone. Home to Earth, presumably, with the remainder of their crew. And much humbled, I believe."

"Tail between their legs, you mean," Prescott muttered under his breath with no little satisfaction. The corners of Becker's mouth quirked briefly.

"I need to think about this, captain. How long before I must make a decision?" I asked, thoughts whirling almost as badly as my emotions.

"There's still lots to talk to the Cresperians about," Jeri said. "There's also going to be a couple of more shuttle trips to get everything down that needs to stay with the colony here."

"Who else besides me and Gordon?"

"Eugene and Margie Preconder have volunteered. Some of our few remaining marines will be staying; a couple of officers. A physician."

I figured he deliberately didn't tell me who each person was so that it would seem more casual; there was, I decided, some probability that a few had been ordered, rather than volunteered. I hoped not, and knowing the captain, he wouldn't have done it unless he'd had to, to ensure an appropriate number of defenders.

I nodded silently, then added, "I... give me a bit of time to think."

"She's been through a lot, Captain," Jeri said quietly. "I'd hate to think how I'd feel if I'd lost Kyle, and she's lost two men she cared about lately."

"I know," Becker said softly. "I hate to be asking. And that's one reason for her drink. I thought she could use it about now."

"Thank you, sir," I said gratefully. "So how long do I have to decide?"

"Take a couple of days. It'll be that long, at least, before we have everything set up. Longer, if the Crispies outfit us with a bit of offensive and defensive gear. Is that enough?"

"Yes, sir, I think so."

"Good. Dismissed."

છબ્ઝ

As I headed back to my quarters, Gordon fell into step beside me. "Are you okay?" he asked gently.

"To be honest, I dunno, Gordon," I answered heavily. "I will be, though."

"I know. You always are."

That got a wan smile out of me. "You're biased."

"Mmm... yes and no."

I snorted.

When we arrived at my quarters, he followed me in. "Gordon," I began, turning toward him, "I'm really not in the mood…"

"I know," he replied, "but I'm here on orders."

"Orders?"

"Jeri's and Dr. Honeywell's. They know—we know—how upset you are. I'm here to just be with you." He led me to the armchair and sat me down in it, then knelt before me. "Mai, we do need to talk, though."

I nodded, suspecting some of what was coming. He still managed to surprise me, though.

"The reason they asked me to stay with you for now is because they know how I feel… or at least, Jeri does," Gordon corrected himself. "I love you, Mai. As much as Jeri loves Kyle. I didn't really know it until I'd been human for awhile, but the night you… showed me what lovemaking could be, I… I was certain." He paused and swallowed. "It's been hard. I knew you weren't interested, and I tried to move on, like you wanted. But no one else was like you. No one else touched me… here," he put his fingertip on his breastbone, "like you do.

"I'm not trying to pressure you into anything, Cherry," he continued, an earnest expression on his handsome face. "I just want you to know that I'm staying on Cresperia. If you choose to stay, I'll be overjoyed, and I swear I will try to court you as properly as possible, given Cresperia isn't Earth. But if you choose to go, I won't chase you, or try to convince you differently. I'll stay here; but more than likely, I won't form a permanent attachment with a woman, or at least not for a very long time, even by Crispy terms."

Coming from a Crispy human, that said volumes. I didn't know what to think, and I certainly didn't know how to feel. Tears welled in my eyes.

"Hush, hush," he murmured soothingly, rising and pulling me to my feet. "I wanted you to know that, so you'd understand that there's someone here who loves you, looking after you."

And with that, he turned and sat in the armchair, then pulled me down into his lap and wrapped his arms around me. I went willingly.

"Now," he said softly, "have you cried for Juan and Gene yet?"

"Some," I admitted, sniffling.

"Not enough," he declared, putting his hand on my head and easing it to his chest. "Let it out, Cherry. Let it out, love."

How he had turned the tables and gotten to be the counselor, I'll never really understand. But in that moment all I knew was that I was safe in the strong, gentle arms of someone who loved me. I turned my face into his chest and cried for a long, long time.

ॐ⌘ॐ

Gordon stayed the rest of the evening, seeing to it that we both ate properly without having to go to the ship's mess, and that I had a quiet, early evening. He was a good companion, thoughtful and considerate and understanding. I didn't protest when he put me to bed, but I was surprised when he didn't leave. He rummaged in a storage closet and extracted a spare pillow and a blanket, then moved nearby. I sat up in bed.

"Gordon, what are you doing?"

"Following orders."

"What do you mean?"

"I'm supposed to watch you overnight. Jeri didn't want you having nightmares and waking up alone. And neither do I." He plopped the pillow into the armchair and sat.

"You... you're going to sleep in the chair?!"

"Yes."

"That's going to be damned uncomfortable."

"I told you, Cherry. I'm not going to pressure you."

And with that, he settled down to sleep.

ॐ⌘ॐ

The next morning after breakfast, Gordon led me to Jeri and Kyle's quarters and left me there with a gentle hug.

"Hi," Kyle greeted me cheerfully. "You're off duty, pending your decision, so don't even think about going to your office today."

"So... what am I doing here?" I wondered.

"Spending time with grateful friends," Jeri smiled. "Friends that have been there and listen well if you need to talk. Or can talk about other things if you'd rather. Or just be silent, or play card games, or whatever you need right now."

I nodded, not quite trusting myself to speak yet. After a few moments of swallowing a very large knot that had formed in my throat, I finally managed, "I don't think I'm ready to... to talk, yet."

"Then we do something else," Kyle decreed. "Movie, cards, general scientific shop talk, old Playboys, charades?"

"Hell, Kyle," Jeri muttered, "what a list." Kyle's eyes twinkled mischievously.

That managed to get a snicker out of me. "It's too early for a movie," I decided. "How about a game of cards?"

"Name your poison," Kyle declared, going to the wall and opening one of the hidden cabinets. "Poker, bridge, spades, rook; hell, Jeri even brought along Old Maid."

That got more than a snicker, which was, judging by his smirk, exactly what he'd intended. "Poker and some whisky—no, it's too early for that, too. Just poker."

We played poker, mostly Texas Hold 'Em, until lunchtime, but we didn't play for anything except fun. At lunchtime, Gordon stopped by, and Jeri invited him to join us for the meal. He shot a quick, querying glance at me, then relaxed, and I realized his perceptive sense had told him he was welcome.

We headed for ship's mess together, a companionable foursome. No, a companionable double date, I suppose I should say. Because that's how it felt.

We got a table for four and sat down to eat. By and large, everyone else left us alone, although a few of the soldier types came by and patted each of us on the shoulder, a silent, comrades-in-arms acknowledgement. Of ability, and of grief shared. I accepted it as it was offered, and handled it okay, I suppose.

After lunch the four of us went back to Jeri's and Kyle's quarters. By that time it was tacitly accepted that Gordon would stay; even though I hadn't made up my mind, it was good knowing he was there and that he cared. We made some small talk initially, then Jeri turned to Gordon.

"I'm glad you're here, Gordon," she said. "I've been wanting to talk to you... about..."

"Yes," Gordon agreed. "Me, too. The sickbay experience, with the dying marine."

"Exactly. I wanted to... I dunno, compare notes, try to understand. Kyle and I have done a lot of discussion, but since he didn't feel it, I wanted to talk to you, too."

"I think that is an excellent plan, Jeri," Gordon agreed immediately. "But... where to start?"

"How about by explaining what you... sensed... to Kyle and me?" I suggested. "I've always found that teaching is the best way to understanding. If you grasp a concept well enough to explain it to someone else, you *have* to understand it pretty well."

Jeri and Gordon nodded thoughtfully. "Very well," Gordon said. "It seems reasonable. First of all, you know that our mathematicians have constructed a proof that there is no Supreme Being. And likely no afterlife."

Kyle and I both nodded.

"Yet," Jeri pointed out, "as a mathematician myself, I have begun to realize there may be more than the one way to interpret that proof."

More nods.

"So imagine my agitation," Jeri continued, "when, instead of the simple diffusion of... of, essence, into the quantum foam that I expected, that I'd always encountered before, that young marine just..."

"Left," Gordon said blankly, finishing for her. "Not a dissipation, not a dispersal, not even an abrupt vanishing into nothingness."

Jeri nodded. "He left," she elaborated, "just... left. Without fear."

"Maybe he willed it," I suggested. "Even the human mind is powerful enough for some amazing things."

"Maybe," Jeri agreed. "I know that a few Crispies believe that, when we die, we go into another existence in the quantum foam, but I've never experienced it. The only other time I've ever experienced anything remotely like it was when Swavely died. He didn't exactly dissipate, either, but it wasn't... he didn't... he didn't *leave*," she finally finished, somewhat lamely. "He went, more or less all at once, sort of like what we're talking about now. Not as, as 'firmly,' though. Swavely and Murphy both went into the quantum foam, but..." She hesitated.

"Go on, Jeri," Gordon urged.

"No, you explain, Gordon," Jeri said, obviously uncomfortable. "I want to see if you and I perceived it the same way. I didn't notice anything after Swavely died, but, but I might have been too upset to 'see' it. Or maybe it just didn't happen. I don't know. I'm totally confused."

Gordon nodded. "It's like Murphy's soul went *through* it, or beyond it, or, or something," he ended, at a loss for words. "Like there's something past the foam, or the foam isn't All, like we'd thought."

Kyle considered that for a bit. "Maybe it's not. After all, there's always a new discovery just over the metaphorical horizon. Newtonian physics was fine until Einstein came along, and then there was relativity, which explained everything until quantum mechanics came along. Now there's unreality physics. Stands to reason there's something more to discover. I wouldn't go so far as calling it a soul in the classical sense just yet, though."

"Are you saying...?" Jeri queried.

"I'm saying that we only know what we know," Kyle pointed out reasonably. "I never said that there *wasn't* Something, or Someone, Else out there. I just said I hadn't seen any proof of it, personally. If I start seeing proof, well... that's different."

"There's more," Gordon stated hesitantly. "When Murphy's essence... left," he stated, "it... I don't know what it was. The quantum foam... it... reacted."

"What?!" Kyle and I both exclaimed in unison.

Gordon nodded. "I'm not sure if Jeri noticed this. And I'm not certain, myself, but... it was like it, I don't know quite how to describe it," he said unhappily, obviously confused and conflicted. "Churned? Boiled? Swirled? Not violently, but..." He shrugged. "If I were to personify it in order to classify the reaction, I'd say it welcomed him. But personifying the foam is... well, it makes about as much sense as saying interstellar space thinks."

Jeri stared at him. "It reacted? Like a response? Gordon, are you sure?"

Gordon shook his head. "No, like I said, I'm not sure," he murmured. "I'm not sure of anything, at this point."

We all pondered that for a moment. Suddenly a memory popped out of my mouth. "His last words were, 'It's here!' And the look on his face... was like he saw, and recognized, whatever 'it' was."

"Yes," Gordon nodded. "And his emotional response, and that statement, coincided within nanoseconds of the...event... in the quantum foam."

Kyle shrugged. "Maybe you were right, baby, when you postulated that we all go into the foam," he told Jeri. "It might explain certain situations where probabilities are skewed from the theoretical. Or certain paranormal events for that matter. I've had a couple of weird things happen that can't be put down to coincidence."

"Or maybe there's more to it than the foam," Jeri pondered. "Oh, *I* don't know," she said then, throwing up her hands in aggravation. "There isn't enough data for me to interpret. Gordon?"

Gordon shook his head. "I agree; insufficient data. Vastly insufficient. I do know I should like to look into it a bit further, now. Especially after this incident. Perhaps humans and Cresperians together can discover something that either alone could not."

"I'm up for that, I think," I decided. "If I stay on Cresperia, maybe we can do some research on the subject, and even come up with some viable experiments."

Gordon's eyes lit up. "An excellent plan, Cherry. I would like that."

"And it would give you something to do in addition to mentoring Crispy conversions to human," Jeri offered.

"True," I agreed. "Assuming," I added with a wry, one-sided smile, "we can do it without killing anybody else."

"Then may I suggest we adjourn the discussion for now, before we start having to shovel out horse manure, and go for some lighter entertainment?" Kyle said, cutting his eyes meaningfully at me. I pretended not to notice.

Jeri and Gordon tried to hide their guilty starts. "Works for me, sweetheart," Jeri said in a smooth segue.

"I was watching an old science fiction movie the other night," Gordon offered up, "and found it incredibly funny, especially in our current historical context. It had a person in a furry bipedal animal suit, saving that the head had been replaced with a crude space helmet. I couldn't help but wonder what the filmmakers would have made of us, Jeri, in our original Crispy form."

The room burst into laughter. "I know that one," I snickered. "A baddie, but goodie."

"Shall I fetch it to watch?" Gordon grinned.

"Oh, please do," Kyle guffawed.

Gordon was out the door and back with the movie in short order, while Jeri made popcorn. Laughing uproariously, we all watched the movie, then a second, before it was time for dinner. We headed for the mess again, with results identical to lunch, then broke up for the evening. Kyle and Jeri headed back to their quarters, and Gordon turned away toward his. I grabbed his hand before he could leave.

"Gordon, would you come with me? Just for a little while? I, I need to know something."

He turned toward me, an eyebrow cocked. I had no illusions that I was hiding much from his perceptive sense, but that was okay. I simply didn't want to discuss the matter in public.

He walked beside me to my quarters, and I let us in. Once the door was closed, I turned to him. "I need to know something before I decide anything," I explained. "It's not exactly about you. It's about myself. But I need your help."

Gordon nodded. "It's your move, Cherry."

He stood very still as I slid my hand up his chest, around his neck, and into his soft, wavy hair. I tilted his head down as I leaned up. Our lips met, and he let his part. I kissed him deeply, and after only a few moments he began responding in kind. My other arm slid around his neck, and his arms gently enveloped me, holding me close while still allowing me room—to escape, I suppose.

But I didn't want to escape. I'd learned what I wanted to know: the spark *was* there, and as we kissed, it ignited into flame. I pressed close, wanting more, and his arms tightened in response. After awhile he picked me up and carried me to the armchair, sitting down with me in his lap. There, we continued to kiss and caress and cuddle for over an hour.

Finally I got up and caught his hand, tugging him into my bedroom. I reached for his shirt and unfastened it, throwing it to one side, then began caressing his chest. He had already been breathing heavily, and now a pant escaped him.

"Cherry, are you sure about this?" he asked softly.

"Yeah, I'm sure."

Our undressing was half utilitarian and half striptease. By the time we both got in bed, he was obviously more than ready, and I realized he'd done a little tinkering in the regions below the waist: he'd enhanced his assets. Not unreasonably so, but wow, did he look good.

But instead of pulling me to him, or rolling on top of me, he bent over me. Delicate yet hungry kisses contacted my bare skin and trailed across my body. Flame became bonfire as I caressed him in return.

Finally I playfully pushed him on his back and crawled onto him. He grinned up at me, those beautiful hazel bedroom eyes coming into play again. It suddenly dawned on me that with Gordon, I didn't have to worry about my increased strength. I could turn loose and let go. And I did.

But to my surprise, he was the one who held out. And held out. And held out. The hormonally-teenage Crispy human had matured into a man, regardless of what his chronological age may have been. By my fourth climax, he had me groaning. On my fifth, I was screaming. And he was still going strong. The hell with bonfire; this was wildfire, and I was reveling in it. By number six, I screamed out instinctively. "Gordon! I love you!" I heard his gasp, realized what my subconscious had said, and knew I meant every word. So did he. And dammit, it was his turn!

Somewhere in the course of things, he'd gotten back on top. So I flipped us over and went at him. In seconds he was panting, then gasping, moving with me as desire built between us to the flashpoint.

He arched and fairly roared my name, and even without a perceptive sense, I felt him finally lose control. I let go at the same time, and baritone and alto voices joined in a harmony as perfect as their owners' bodies'.

ಬಾರ

There was no question of him staying the night. We cuddled after that, content in each other's arms. "This is... a dream, Cherry," he whispered, almost disbelieving. "I wanted... but I never really thought..."

I shrugged, then grinned. "One more thing you gotta learn about us humans, Gordon. Sometimes we miss what's right under our noses."

"You still need to grieve and recover," he pointed out.

"Yeah," I said, sobering immediately as Juan's and Gene's faces flashed into my mind. "But just like you converted to human better with someone beside you to help, I'll heal emotionally a lot better if you're beside me."

"Then that's where I'll stay," he declared. "I assume you've made up your mind?"

"Yep. I'm staying. I'll tell the captain... in the morning."

"Good," he said with a devilish grin, rolling back on top of me.

Chapter Thirty-Nine

THE NEXT MORNING there was a general call of officers and crew chiefs. At the meeting, I announced my decision to stay on Cresperia to Captain Becker and his officers, Gordon beside me. Jeri and Kyle were there, too. They all nodded, pleased, then JFK stepped forward from his place beside Doc Honeywell.

"I'll be staying, too," he noted. "We figured you might need some medical support, and frankly, I find it an interesting challenge."

"One of the nurses has volunteered, as well," Honeywell added. "You'll have a small, but effective, sickbay although I doubt it will be used much with Crispies around."

"Sounds good, anyway," I decided. "Who's in charge of the place?"

"Before we discuss that, we should probably fill the two of you in on what happened during your sleep shift," Becker noted with a grim face, and my heart sank.

"That doesn't sound good," Gordon said with some trepidation.

"It's not," Jeri said, and the anger in her voice was evident. "The Snappers got impatient. They attacked one of our cities."

Gordon and I both gasped. "Which one?" he asked anxiously.

"Xxtrflm," Jeri responded. "Evidently they have sensors that can detect underground population centers."

"How bad?" Gordon groaned, and I remembered something he'd said about friends there.

"Not bad," Kyle grinned wolfishly. "Jeri's friends listened to her and convinced the elders it was better to be safe than sorry. So they constructed some force screens, similar to what your starships use, around the main cities. And it wasn't the big ship that attacked, it was another of the smaller scouts."

"So Xxtrflm wasn't harmed?" Gordon asked, face lightening.

"Not a bit," Jeri smiled. "The Snappers, on the other hand..."

"Let's just say that a force screen wasn't the only thing they adapted," Prescott said in satisfaction. "Those disintegrator beams of yours don't have much range. But they scale up really *nicely*."

I decorously refrained from punching a fist into the air.

"Gordon, our friends have agreed that the *Galactic* needs force shielding and at least one disintegrator cannon, too," Jeri noted. "They're constructing them right now."

"So, in answer to your question, Mai," Becker resumed, "there will be three colony leaders. A triumvirate, of sorts. Major Bennett, the ranking marine who's volunteered, will head up the military. Gordon will lead the Crispies, human or indigenous. And you will head up the civilian Earth humans."

"Shit," popped out of my mouth before I thought. I hadn't expected that. "Er, sorry, sir."

This time a grin did appear on Becker's face, and damn but it looked good. His face didn't show any signs of breaking, after all. In fact, he was downright handsome with that smile. "You've performed in an exemplary fashion. Both as a scientist and a warrior. I think you're up to it, and so is Gordon."

"Thank you, sir," Gordon said, and I'll be damned if he didn't execute a perfect salute.

Grin broadening, Becker returned it with respect.

৪০০৪

It took two more weeks to properly outfit the *Galactic* and get all the necessary supplies for the colony offloaded to planet. During that time, the Snapper ship faded from our scanners completely, and we had hopes the Crispies had driven them off. Certainly the unmanned freighters now plied their lanes unmolested.

And Gordon and I only grew closer. It wasn't long before I realized that Gordon and I were developing what Jeri and Kyle had, and we were both happy and content in that. I didn't know if Crispies had anything like a marriage ceremony, and strongly suspected they didn't, but that was okay. We knew who and what we were to each other. After the first week, we moved planetside to the colony, only needing one housing unit.

"Everything's almost ready, Cherry," Gordon told me enthusiastically as the date for the *Galactic's* departure drew near. "We have enough prepackaged food to last until we can… gene-gineer… enough food that Crispies and humans can both eat, and we've got defensive and offensive weapons ready. And so does the *Galactic.*"

"I know," I agreed. "But I still have a feeling… it may be a long time before we see our friends from the *Galactic*, Gordon."

"Yes," he said, sobering. "But we'll manage, Cherry. We have each other."

"We do, Gordon," I said, kissing his cheek. "We do."

ဆာငၢ

We had a ceremony the evening before they left orbit. The big amphi-theater where Kyle had beaten the Indian "god" had been totally gutted and refitted to eliminate all reminders of the fight, and now the audito-rium on board ship was visible on a big viewscreen there. Captain Becker declared the Cresperian faction that favored interstellar exploration to be allies of Great Britain and the United States of America of Earth, Sol sys-tem. The Crispy elders, while declining to become involved in anything except minimal defense, at least agreed to stay neutral. Gordon thinks they will come around eventually. It just takes a long time for the older ones to do things. They did thank us for the enlightenment of intelligent interspecies contact and cooperation, and acknowledged gain on both sides. That was more than he and Jeri expected so I have great hopes.

Then it was time for the goodbyes. That was hard. None of us knew when, or even if, we'd be seeing each other again. There were a few tears shed, and I'm not ashamed to admit I was one of 'em doing the shed-ding.

But not because I wanted to go back to Earth, only because I'd miss my friends. I had what I truly needed. And all of that was in one package standing right beside me. And his name—the one I could readily pro-nounce, anyway—was Gordon Stuart.

When the com link finally ended, we all went outside and looked up, watching as the bright star in the night sky began to move. Gradually it shrank and dimmed. We knew as soon as the *Galactic* had gone into unreality drive, because the star just disappeared. A collective sigh went through the colonists, and our faces turned back to Cresperia.

Gordon caught my arm in a gentle grasp, and drew me along as he moved through the crowd. "Cherry, come here. There's someone impor-tant I want you to meet."

I followed him through the crowd until we reached a group of three indigenous Cresperians, bright green fur and all. I wondered if these were Crispies interested in becoming human.

"Cherry," Gordon announced proudly, "these are my parents. You can call them George, Emily, and Casey. Mmrd, Ddrd, and Iird, this is my Earth mate, Mai Li Trung."

Three sets of bifurcated eyes lit up, and three slits of mouths formed into something that I'd come to recognize as Crispy approval. I smiled back, warmth filling me as I met my husband's parents for the first time. "Hi," I said happily. "I'm pleased to meet you. You have a wonderful son…"

"Please excuses the Englishes, we is learning," the Crispy called George said. "But we is pleased is meeting you, too. Is… brave…?" He glanced at Gordon, who nodded affirmation of the word choice. "Is brave hyuman, is you. Is we proud havink you in famiry."

I couldn't help myself. I opened my arms and did my best to envelop them in a group hug. Having more arms than I did, they were a lot better at it, of course. "I'm proud to be in the family, too," I told them.

It wasn't like having Earth in-laws, of course. I learned that many Crispies together form perceptive groups to nurture their young since they have so few of them. But what the hell. Maybe his parents would eventually convert to human. Then we really would be a family.

- End -

ABOUT THE AUTHORS

Darrell Bain is the author of more than three dozen books, in many genres, running the gamut from humor to mystery and science fiction to humorous non-fiction. For the last several years he has concentrated on humor and science fiction, both short fiction and suspense/thrillers.

Darrell served thirteen years in the military as a medic and his two years in Vietnam formed the basis for his first published novel, *Medics Wild*. Darrell has been writing off and on all his life but really got serious about it only after the advent of computers. He purchased his first one in 1989 and has been writing furiously ever since.

While Darrell was working as a lab manager at a hospital in Texas, he met his wife Betty. He trapped her under a mistletoe sprig and they were married a year later. Darrell and Betty owned and operated a Christmas tree farm in East Texas for many years. It became the subject and back-drop for some of his humorous stories and books.

Visit Darrell's web site: http://www.darrellbain.com

Stephanie Osborn is a former payload flight controller, a veteran of over twenty years of working in the civilian space program, as well as various military space defense programs. She has worked on numerous Space Shuttle flights and the International Space Station, and counts the training of astronauts on her resumé. One of the astronauts she trained includes Kalpana Chawla, who died in the Columbia disaster.

She holds graduate and undergraduate degrees in four sciences: Astronomy, Physics, Chemistry, and Mathematics, and she is "fluent" in several more, including Geology and Anatomy. She obtained her various degrees from Austin Peay State University in Clarksville, TN and Vanderbilt University in Nashville, TN.

Stephanie is currently retired from space work. She now happily "passes it forward," tutoring math and science to students in the Huntsville area, elementary through college, while writing science fiction mysteries based on her knowledge, experience, and travels.

Stephanie's web site: http://www.stephanie-osborn.com

Don't miss any of these highly
entertaining SF/F books

➤ Alien Infection
(1-933353-72-4, $16.95 US)

➤ Burnout
(1-60619-200-0, $19.95 US)

➤ Human by Choice
(1-60619-047-4 $16.95 US)

➤ Savage Survival
(1-933353-66-X, $29.95 US)

➤ Shadow Worlds
(1-933353-79-1, $16.95 US)

➤ Strange Valley
(1-931201-23-4, $15.50 US)

➤ The Focus Factor
(1-931201-96-X, $18.95 US)

➤ The Melanin Apocalypse
(1-933353-70-8, $16.95 US)

Twilight Times Books
Kingsport, Tennessee

Order Form

If not available from your local bookstore or favorite online bookstore, send this coupon and a check or money order for the retail price plus $3.50 s&h to Twilight Times Books, Dept. LS1209 POB 3340 Kingsport TN 37664. Delivery may take up to two weeks.

Name: _____

Address: _____

_____

Email: _____

I have enclosed a check or money order in the amount of

$_____

for _____ .

If you enjoyed this book, please post a review
at your favorite online bookstore.

Twilight Times Books
P O Box 3340
Kingsport, TN 37664
Phone/Fax: 423-323-0183
www.twilighttimesbooks.com/

Breinigsville, PA USA
30 December 2010
252459BV00001B/4/P